PENGUIN BOOKS

THE AUTOGRAPH MAN

'A witty account of celebrity obsession' Peter Bradshaw, Books of the Year, *New Statesman*

'A sly sideways slide around the nature of celebrity' Laurence Norfolk, Books of the Year, *The Times Literary Supplement*

'A fine novel – funny, briskly paced, thoughtful and never boring' Tim Lott, Books of the Year, *Evening Standard*

'Smith writes with dazzling gaiety; you don't just read the novel, you bask in it' Sarah Sands, Books of the Year, *Daily Telegraph*

'A terrific advance even on her excellent *White Teeth*, a brilliant comedy with a tantalising throb of mystic philosophy underneath' Philip Hensher, Books of the Year, *Spectator*

'Confirms Smith as one of Britain's brightest young talents' *Sunday Mirror*

'Savvy, witty, exuberant' *Daily News*

'Succinct observations that convey the zing of a punch line and the sobering weight of truth' *Washington Post*

'Tracing her hero's odyssey, Smith scatters marvellous sentences and sharp insights on nearly every page' *Los Angeles Times*

'Intellectually agile . . . ecstatic inventiveness' *Time*

'Brims with a confidence and intelligence that leave many other established British scribblers in the dust' *Face*

Dig: I'm Jewish. Count Basie's Jewish. Ray Charles is Jewish. Eddie Cantor's goyish. B'nai B'rith is goyish; Hadassah, Jewish.

If you live in New York or any other big city, you are Jewish. It doesn't even matter if you're Catholic; if you live in New York, you're Jewish. If you live in Butte, Montana, you're going to be goyish even if you're Jewish.

Kool-Aid is goyish. Evaporated milk is goyish even if the Jews invented it. Chocolate is Jewish and fudge is goyish. Fruit salad is Jewish. Lime Jell-O is goyish. Lime soda is *very* goyish.

All Drake's Cakes are goyish. Pumpernickel is Jewish and, as you know, white bread is very goyish. Instant potatoes, goyish. Black-cherry soda's very Jewish, macaroons are *very* Jewish.

Negroes are all Jews, Italians are all Jews. Irishmen who have rejected their religion are Jews. Mouths are very Jewish. And bosoms. Baton-twirling is goyish.

Underwear is definitely goyish. Balls are goyish. Titties are Jewish.

Celebrate is a goyish word. Observe is a Jewish word. Mr and Mrs Walsh are *celebrating* Christmas with Major Thomas Moreland, USAF (ret.), while Mr and Mrs Bromberg *observed* Hannukah with Goldie and Arthur Schindler from Kiamesha, New York.

– Lenny Bruce

The Autograph Man

ZADIE SMITH

PENGUIN BOOKS

PENGUIN BOOKS

Published by the Penguin Group
Penguin Books Ltd, 80 Strand, London WC2R ORL, England
Penguin Putnam Inc., 375 Hudson Street, New York, New York 10014, USA
Penguin Books Australia Ltd, 250 Camberwell Road,
Camberwell, Victoria 3124, Australia
Penguin Books Canada Ltd, 10 Alcorn Avenue, Toronto, Ontario, Canada M4V 3B2
Penguin Books India (P) Ltd, 11 Community Centre,
Panchsheel Park, New Delhi – 110 017, India
Penguin Books (NZ) Ltd, Cnr Rosedale and Airborne Roads,
Albany, Auckland, New Zealand
Penguin Books (South Africa) (Pty) Ltd, 24 Sturdee Avenue,
Rosebank 2196, South Africa

Penguin Books Ltd, Registered Offices: 80 Strand, London WC2R ORL, England

www.penguin.com

First published by Hamish Hamilton 2002
Published in Penguin Books 2003
019

The Acknowledgements on p. 420 constitute an extension of this copyright page.
Every effort has been made to trace copyright holders, and if there is an unintentional
omission we would be pleased to insert the appropriate acknowledgement in any
subsequent edition

The author would particularly like to acknowledge the importance of Leon Wieseltier's
wise and poetic memoir, *Kaddish*

Set in Trump Medieval
Printed in England by Clays Ltd, St Ives plc

www.greenpenguin.co.uk

To my amazing brothers Ben and Luke,
And for my friend Adam Andrusier, who knows funny
from funny

Naturally things cannot in reality fit together the way the evidence does in my letter; life is more than a Chinese puzzle.

– Franz Kafka, *Letter to His Father*

I would always make believe that Clark Gable was my father.

– Marilyn Monroe

ACKNOWLEDGEMENTS

My gratitude goes, as ever, to Yvonne Bailey-Smith and Harvey Smith for their peerless support and patience. Thank you to Adam Andrusier and Rachel Miller for the kind of facts that can't be found in libraries, and to my valued first readers: Michal Shavit, Toby Litt, Adam (again), Tamara Barnett-Herrin, Nick Laird and Paul Hilder. Thank you to Jessica Frazier and Lee Klein, both of whom have the ability to make philosophy an everyday affair. Thank you to Alex Adamson for making everything easier.

I made use of two writers' retreats and thank both institutions and the remarkable women who run them: Drew Heinz at Hawthornden and Beatrice Monti at Santa Maddelena. I am indebted to Georgia Garrett, Simon Prosser and Ann Godoff, who make books happen and keep me sane.

PROLOGUE

Zohar
The Wrestling Match

He has the ability to imagine himself a minor incident in the lives
of others. It is not an abstract thing. Alex-Li Tandem would not
know quite what you meant by 'abstract' – he is twelve. He simply
knows that if he imagines swimming in the sea, well, while most
children will think immediately of the cinematic shark below
them, Alex, in his mind, is with the lifeguard. He can see himself
as that smudge on the horizon, his head mistaken for a bobbing
buoy, his wild arms hidden by the roll of the surf. He can see the
lifeguard, a bronzed and languid American, standing on the sand
with his arms folded, deciding there's nothing out there. Alex sees
the lifeguard wander off down the beach in search of those half-bare
German girls from yesterday and a cold drink. The lifeguard buys
a Coke from a passing vendor. The shark severs Alex's right calf
from his body. The lifeguard sidles up to Tanya, the pretty one.
The shark drags Alex in a bloody semicircle through the water. The
lifeguard speaks kindly to her ugly friend with the flat chest, hoping
for brownie points. Some vertebrae snap. *Did you see that? A seal!*
says Tanya, mistaking Alex's desperate hand for the turn of a glossy
flipper. And then he's gone. Is it a bird? Is it a plane? Is it a seal?

No, it's me, drowning. This is how things go for Alex-Li. He deals in a shorthand of experience. The TV version. He is one of this generation who watch themselves.

YHWH

Just now, he is in his father's car, on a day trip. Overhead flies a plane, so low it looks as if it might worry the corrugated roofs of an industrial estate to the left. They are on a minor A-road, in congestion, near an airport. To his right sits his father, Li-Jin, who is also his best-friend. From the back seats two boys flick an elastic band at his head for no reason. Now he leans forward out of their reach and puts his fleshy arm out of the passenger window – can he really be seen from up there? Hello! The anorexic February trees stretch towards him on either side. In return he offers an open hand to let the wind shuttle through his fingers. He catches a slick leaf round his thumb like a bandage. Ug ug. Ugg*arama*. They are going to see a wrestling match. This is unusual. Alex is not a very social fellow. His spare time is spent either in front of the TV or accompanying his father to his surgery. He is perfectly content to skulk around the reception area speculating on who has what while Dr Tandem does whatever he does in the small room with the white door. Alex will take with him a book of crossword puzzles or a comic and is always left alone, which is the way he likes it. Foot-fungus, angina, the plague: he assigns these diseases willy-nilly to the simply bronchial or menopausal as they slump in the child-sized plastic chairs. No one ever notices him. He's just a boy, watching. It is like a TV show. Only in the past year he has become conspicuous. He has grown and filled, he's now soft-bellied, woman-hipped and sallow. His new glasses magnify the crescents of his eyes – does he look more Chinese? His boyhood is falling away. People have started to fuss with him. Constantly he is being grabbed by the shoulder and asked idiotic questions by the elderly. If you are twelve, suddenly everyone has an opinion about you and the open air, and you and a good football game, and you versus the sporty, red-cheeked boys of some godforsaken distant era. The consensus is that he should get out more. Alex has sensed that some kind of day trip, if not this particular day trip, was inevitable.

A conversation between his parents, which he was not privy to, occurred three nights earlier, as Alex slept in a next-door room, at the very edge of his bed, dreaming of cliffs and water. His mother, Sarah, sleepily lifted herself up on one elbow, waited for the drone of a plane to pass them by and then said, 'Li, you know, maybe on Saturday we could just do something different with Al, instead of, you know, this silly *moping* around *you* all the time – I mean, not that . . .'

And this fading sentence concealed an old antagonism between them, for there has not always been enough space for Sarah in this adoring duo of father and son. Now that he is twelve, his mother would like to see Alex, as she puts it, 'Going up to the world, going *into* it, and, you know, sort of *engaging it*, getting that vital interplay . . .'

Li-Jin opens his eyes and groans. What is it she's reading these days that makes her speak to him like a self-help book in the middle of the night? His head hurts. It's 2 a.m. By now he should be stamping down the corridor in his underwear, yelling, heading for the guest bedroom. That used to be the routine. But he doesn't have time for all that any more. Marital rows, street riots, bar-room brawls – these seem to him now to be the great luxuries of modern

3

life. You need time for that stuff, for the fighting, for the making up. Although he has told no one, Li-Jin has lost this luxury. He can't risk the escalation. He simply doesn't have the *time*. And he has been surprised to discover that when you subtract the rows what you are left with is love, a huge amount of it, leaking out of you. Now he plumps a pillow and moves closer to his wife, signifying agreement. It is a sort of gift. But wait, there's *more*: he kisses her fingertips and puts his throbbing head in her hands.

YHWH

So just now a plane is flying overhead and Alex-Li is imagining what he looks like from 10,000 feet. He is on his way to watch a wrestling match with his father and two acquaintances, Mark Rubinfine and Adam Jacobs. Rubinfine (fifteen), called Rubinfine by everybody, including his mother, is the son of Li-Jin's accountant, Rubinfine. He is a tall and cunning kid, with a beauty spot on his cheek and that permanent look about him that suggests it would take more than a man excreting gold to impress him. Li-Jin is not sure whether he likes him, exactly. But when the idea of going to the wrestling was mooted at a dinner party Rubinfine was there with his father and so here he is now. The other one, Adam (thirteen), is a nice boy with a bit of a weight problem, which may or may not be the root cause of his niceness. He is black as peat, with curled hair tight on his scalp, and eyes so dark the pupil and iris have merged. Though these three boys have known each other for years, they do not go to the same school, and they are not the best of friends. Their connection is heder, which they all attend in a local community centre, funded by the synagogue. Li-Jin was rather worried that this day trip might appear somewhat manufactured, but they seem fine, there's lots of talking. But what are they talking *about*? References to programmes he's never watched, songs he's never heard, films that came and went without him noticing. It is as if there is some high-pitched frequency in the everyday life of his son which Li-Jin is tuned into only once a year, at Christmas, when he is told to go and buy the bright plastic merchandise which accompanies these mysterious entertainments.

'No, but if you listen,' Alex pleads, thumping the glove box, 'I'm actually talking about the "Coming Home" episode when Kellas found out about his, you know, his wotsitcalled, his *bionic* features.'

'But that's not the "Coming Home" episode,' says Adam. 'That's a completely different episode, with the bionic thingy.'

'Don't thump the glove box,' says Li-Jin.

'Once again,' says Rubinfine with a sigh, digging at the wax in his ears with a crooked finger, 'you are all talking out of the wrong ugging hole.'

The heated, artificial air steams up the windows. Li-Jin turns on the radio and is rewarded by white noise, soundtrack to his headache. With a fingertip, Alex begins to trace triangles in the condensation of a window. Adam's chubby, exposed thighs stick to the plastic seats. Rubinfine is getting those random erections that are oddly insistent even though they have no cause, nowhere to go. He shifts slightly and rearranges.

YHWH

There's an exodus going on, out of living rooms and into the world: fathers and their boys are on the move. Alex has spotted other cars with boys in them, pressing their laminated posters for the match (big, red, with gold lettering, like bibles) up against the windows.

Sometimes Rubinfine will mime a choking hold and the boy in the next car will pretend to be strangled. All of this is unprecedented. There is not a thing that will move them from their Saturday morning TV usually, not a bloody thing. Forget it. TV would have to pull itself from its socket and request that Adam and Rubinfine and Alex follow it now, NOW, YOU LITTLE UGGING FREAKS (it would have to insult them), NOW I NEED YOU NOW, YOU GAYLORDS, and then waddle out into the open air on its awkward wooden legs. Of course, this is what has actually happened. They are being drawn towards the Royal Albert Hall by one huge man from the TV. His name is Big Daddy and right now he is the most famous wrestler in Britain. He is like a god. He is fat and pink and from the North and totally *sans* glamour. He is about fifty, white haired, and he wears a red Babygro. It turns out his real name is Shirley. Somehow even knowing this cannot diminish him. Everybody likes him, and it is exactly this, this *everybody*, that is important to Li-Jin. He doesn't want Alex 'standing out from the crowd'. He knows that soon the boy's life will become difficult and hopes conformity might be his saviour. And so he wants him to be ready, normal. He wants him to be part of this *everybody*. But you can't plan for every eventuality. For example, his son is probably the only boy on his way to see Big Daddy versus Giant Haystacks whose father is trying to convince him not to attend his own bar mitzvah.

Li-Jin is saying, *You are quite sure that you <u>want</u> to do it?*

Alex-Li is saying, *Da-aaad!*

In the back seat Rubinfine is testing the term 'man-breasts' on Adam's developing fat-person sensitivities, and in the front seat Li-Jin is trying to influence Alex-Li in this certain way he promised Sarah he would never do.

'*Alex*. I'm asking you a question.'

'I know. I said yes, didn't I? Well, then. *Yes*. I s'pose.'

'But are you sure you *want* to?' says Li-Jin uselessly. 'Or could it be more that your mother wants it?'

Alex makes the International Gesture for vomiting.

'Well, is it?'

'You *know* it's Mum that wants it. So obviously that's partly it, isn't it?'

'But you want it too.'

'I s'pose. *God*, Dad, shut up about it, *please*.'

Rubinfine makes the International Gesture for masturbation. Alex gives one last loud pluck to the catch on the glove compartment, and then switches his attention to opening and shutting the ashtray. They stop at a traffic light. Li-Jin turns to look his son in the face, licks his own thumb and wipes a smear of something from the boy's cheek.

'Come on, stop that now. Look. Are you? That is not too tedious a question, is it? I'm only wondering whether you intend to wear the boxes. Name of, again?'

'Tefillin. You just strap them. On your head, you know. And a bit on your arms.'

Li-Jin feels desolate. He dips the clutch. He is allergic to the idea of those straps. Too violent and strange a lurch from the normal, peaceful, almost *imperceptible* Judaism he married into. What *is* this stuff? Was this in the small print? And how tight will they be, these straps?

'Good. Boxes. Like Rubinfine did.'

'*God*, Dad. Does it matter? I just do it. And then it's done.'

'The record,' says Adam, 'for holding your breath under water belongs to "Big" Tony Kikaroo of Nuku'alofa, Tonga, who held his

7

breath for 19 minutes and 12 seconds in the pea-green water of the bay.'

'What's all this about me?' says Rubinfine.

At a junction they stop talking all at once, and the silence sticks for a while, as if someone spat it at the windscreen and they're watching it slide down. Mountjoy is slowly going by, with its squat suburban palaces and pruned trees. This is where they live, and this traffic is testament to the fact that on a Saturday, at the first opportunity, anyone who lives in Mountjoy is looking for a way out. They are exercising their rights as home-owners. They have not forgotten that ambitious young man with the thin moustache and acrylic tie who led them through their future property talking of reduced flight schedules and dado rails and original features and promising that fantastic – perfectly fictional, as it turned out – thirty-minute car journey to the City. Nobody makes any fuss. Anyone who expected anything different of Mountjoy, who possessed any illusions about the one-way system of Mountjoy, well, such a person would not live in Mountjoy. The people of Mountjoy have based their lives on the principle of compromise, and each night they quietly embrace the earplugs and migraines and stress-related muscular discomfort they receive in exchange for cheap houses sitting directly in the flight path of an international airport. This is not the Promised Land. This is an affordable, fifties built, central heating/locking as standard, schools included, commuter village on the northernmost tip of the city of London. It suits Li-Jin because parking is not a problem and his surgery has always been here. Also, he knows everyone. There is a considerable Jewish presence and this pleases Sarah. It suits Alex-Li because anywhere would. Adam, the only black kid for miles – *possibly the only black*

Jew in the ugging world – he hates it, he just hates it so – just – really – *viscerally* and if he looked up the word he'd say yes, that's where I hate it, I hate it in my internal organs, in my bowels. And as far as Rubinfine is concerned, if Mountjoy were a person he would rip off its head, piss in its eyeballs and shit down its throat.

YHWH

Interesting fact: Rubinfine's father, Rubinfine, wants Rubinfine to grow up to become a rabbi. Every time Rubinfine tells Li-Jin about this, his dearest wish for young Rubinfine, Li-Jin has no idea what to do with his face. The first time Rubinfine mentioned it, they were eating spaghetti Bolognese during a lunch meeting to discuss how Li-Jin might rejig his expenses and he was caught so unawares he had to repair to the restaurant bathroom to pull the noodles out of his nose.

YHWH

Rubinfine: 'Ug ug ug. Bloody hell, I'm hot. Mate, could you not turn that heating off? Are we there yet? Are we there yet? Are-wethereyetarewethereyetarewethereyet?'

Doing the impression of a kid in an American movie who's tired of a car journey. I'm not going to kill him, thinks Li-Jin. His head is hurting.

'I am not going to kill you,' he says, eyeing Rubinfine in the rear mirror.

Rubinfine sucks in his cheeks like a fish. 'Hmm. Now, let's see. Oh, yes. Er, as if you could in, er, *40 million years.*'

A fairly accurate assessment of the situation, Li-Jin being around 5'6" at a push, and Rubinfine being a lumbering giant freak of a child.

'You were smaller once,' says Li-Jin.

'Yeah?'

'Oh, yes. Unless my memory plays tricks. Not nicer, mind you – just smaller.'

'The record,' says Adam, 'for a man being buried alive belongs to Rodrigues Jesus Monti of Tampa, Florida, who spent 46 days buried in the Arizona desert breathing through a very long straw-type device.'

'Where'd you *see* all this, exactly?' demands Rubinfine furiously. 'What *channel*? What'd it *look* like?'

'Not on telly at all. In a book. Of records. I read it.'

'Well, shut *up*, then.'

Taking one hand off the wheel, Li-Jin grips an inch of the skin by his temple and starts to rub it between thumb and forefinger. He used to tell his patients that it is helpful to imagine the centre of your pain as a ball of plasticine or clay and that by kneading it thus you can narrow it down to a thread and then break it off completely. This was a lie.

'Mercy!' shrieks Rubinfine. 'Me and Ads first. Alex plays the winner.'

Rubinfine and Adam lock their fingers together. It's some kind of a game. They want Li-Jin to count to three. But Li-Jin is elsewhere, deep in his own headache. He looks at two waving six-year-olds in an adjacent car, smudgy through the rain-streaked glass, like a sentimental watercolour. He tries to remember when all the children seemed small and unsure. But no, even at six years old Rubinfine was the same suburban tyrant, though with different tactics. Back then it was all screams and snot and hunger-strikes. Rubinfine was the kind of child who would set fire to his own clothing just to see the look on his mother's face. Adam, if Li-Jin is remembering correctly, has changed utterly. When he was six, he was American. More than this, he had no parents. He was like something out of a book. They all turned up in Li-Jin's surgery one winter: a blue-black grandfather, one Isaac Jacobs, Adam and Adam's little sister . . . name? Anyway, she was the reason. An almond-eyed girl with a bad heart in need of the United Kingdom's free medical assistance. All of them black Harlem Jews, claiming the tribe of Judah. Dressed like Ethiopian kings! The adults of Mountjoy took their time accepting the idea of Isaac Jacobs. For Adam it was different. Adam was instantly lord of the playground. Li-Jin smiled at the memory of Alex coming home one day speaking of a 'boy from the films', as if Adam had stepped off the screen into the suburbs, one of those beings of the cinema who never die. But for Adam, it couldn't last. His accent melted, his body grew. Seven years later and Adam Jacobs is still being punished for ever turning up in a suburb, acting like he was made of magic.

Esther – the girl was called Esther. With hair plaited like a puzzle. They fitted her with a pacemaker.

And now Rubinfine, bored with waiting for permission, has bent back Adam's hands. Adam is howling, but Rubinfine is unforgiving.

'The word is *mercy*,' says Rubinfine coolly, releasing Adam, who weeps and blows on his knuckles. 'That's *all* you had to say.'

'We're stopping here,' says Li-Jin, pulling up suddenly, outside a pharmacy. 'Any complaints?'

'You smell?' says Rubinfine.

YHWH

When Alex was eleven, when Li-Jin first began to experience his headaches, a Chinese doctor in Soho diagnosed it as the influence of Alex-Li's obstructing his father's *qi*. This doctor told Li-Jin he loved his son too much, like the widower whose child is the last remnant of his wife. Li-Jin was loving Alex in a feminine way instead of a masculine. His *mu qi* (maternal air) was excessive, blocking his *qi-men* (air gates). This had caused the disturbance. *Nonsense.* Li-Jin rebuked himself for ever succumbing to the superstitions of his Beijing childhood; he never went to see this man or any other Chinese doctor again. Air gates? Everybody in Mountjoy had a headache. Plane noise, pollution, stress. The unholy trinity of Mountjoy life. It was vanity, surely, to assume that he had been singled out for something special, for the rare tumour, the under-researched virus. Vanity! Why would it be anything more? For a year after the encounter this clever doctor told himself it was nothing, he behaved like any one of his stupid patients. No tests, continuous pain, muddling on. Even though, somewhere in him, he knew. He always knew.

The bell goes ting-a-ling. Ting-a-ling!

'Nice weather for ducks!' says the girl behind the counter. Li-Jin brushes off some raindrops and shakes his perfectly straight black hair that becomes wet so easily. Somehow, just by walking into the chemist's, he has made her laugh. She is a bird-featured girl, with stiff yellow fans of hair, one under the other under the other, as Li-Jin has seen in the cinema (but surely some years ago?). She has a vast burgundy birthmark climbing her throat by way of five tentacles, like the shadow of some man's hand.

'It doesn't rain but it pours!' begins Li-Jin, confidently striding to the till. He parts his legs slightly and lays his small hands on the counter. In the village that crouched at the foot of his English boarding school, Li-Jin learnt all there is to know about this particular conversation and how to have it. Before TV was everywhere, before the catchphrases, one learnt the sayings, the homilies.

'Of course,' he says, preparing to invent an area at the back of his house that does not exist and never could in the current property market, 'my garden will be grateful. There was that cold dry snap last month ...'

But the girl has decided to be indignant. 'Well, I wouldn't mind, but it went and rained all bloody *last* week anyway! I don't know, I really don't ...'

Li-Jin bends and nods, agreeing that he also does not know, no, not about the rain or about the world and what it is coming to, what with one thing and another; smiling and nodding; waiting patiently for the girl to turn matters round to the transaction. She talks too much. But maybe she has stood here for a long time, bony hip pressed against the counter, eye on the door, forgetting and then cruelly remembering her own birthmark – all of this, for several hours, alone. She could die in here. No one would notice until the smell brought them leering over the counter. Ting-a-ling!

Into this stillness comes the bell again, and Alex walks in, clunks across the room and stands just behind his father, his second in any duel.

'Er, how long you gonner be?' he asks urgently, turning from his father and looking with alarm at the burgundy throat-climber.

'A minute.'

'Sixty elephant, fifty-nine elephant, fifty-eight elephant, fifty-seven elephant, fifty-six elephant –'

'*All right*. Five minutes. Why aren't you in the car?'

'I think Adam Jacobs may have emotional problems at home. He says the world record for kissing is nine days and seven hours and is held by Katie and George Brumpton of Madison, Wisconsin. With food breaks. Is that –' he begins, raising his hand to point at the girl's neck, but Li-Jin catches his wrist.

'Day trip,' explains Li-Jin. 'My son, his friends. Very noisy. Boys will be boys. Headache-inducing.'

'I see,' says the girl. 'Now, any particular brand? They do different sorts of things for different pains these days, you know. No point taking something meant for, well, for example, frontal-head pain if you've got . . . you know . . . some other type of pain.'

'Dad,' says Alex, tugging at him, 'there's no *time*.'

Finally, finally, he gives her some money and she hands him a bottle of perfectly ordinary paracetamol, which Li-Jin grabs and begins to struggle with. He is still struggling with it in the street, in the rain, even though nothing in that little bottle can help him and he knows it.

'Oh, come *on* – can't you wait till we're in the car?'

'No, Alex. My head is hurting *now*. Go on into the car, if I am embarrassing.'

'Dad, I *swear* I think Rubinfine might be a – wotsit – a paranoid schizophrenic. I'm worried for our safety in an enclosed vehicle.'

'Alex, *please*. Damn this thing!'

'Fifteen is the age for boys. Fifteen is when it starts. Do you think the girl in the shop had skin cancer?'

'Birthmark, only.'

'Didn't you just want it to grow and take over her whole face?'

They get in the car.

'But his *foot*,' Rubinfine is saying very slowly, as one would speak to a retard, 'which was inside his *shoe*, came down on Big Daddy's *face*. Understand? *On his face. Shoe. Face. Shoe. Face.* Capeech-ay? Speaka da Engleesh? You cannot fake a *shoe* coming down on a *face*.'

Adam, who believes himself to be right, begins the whisper of the defeated that only God hears: '*Well, I still say* . . .'

'*Bloody* child-proof –' says Li-Jin.

Rubinfine, the eldest child in the car, reaches forward, snatches the bottle, and with great disdain and pity uncaps it and hands it back.

YHWH

They sit parked as Li-Jin hunts for a thermos of tea on the floor of the car. Everyone has an argument about fame quantifiables on a scale of one to ten where 10 = Michael Jackson and 1 would be somebody like the black woman painted green with two trunks coming out of the top of her head who played the alien Kolig in the film *Battle for Mars*. OK, so, on this scale, where is the wrestler Giant Haystacks?

'Three,' says Rubinfine.

'Six,' says Li-Jin. This is widely scorned.

'Three and a half,' says Adam.

'Two point one,' says Alex-Li.

'Don't be a royal Ug all your life, Alex.'

'No, look, it makes sense. About ten million people watch *World of Sport* every Saturday. I *think* that's about right. And then there are about 49 million people in Britain. That's 21 per cent. So two point one. And you can only really say that in the first place if you pretend America doesn't exist.'

'Alex-Li Tandem, you have just won the Most Boring Idiot of the Year award. Please come and collect your prize. And then piss off.'

'You know how much he weighs, though, don't you?' says Li-Jin, reaching a hand back to stop Rubinfine delivering his prize punch. 'You do know we have a real match on our hands. You do *understand* how big he is?'

Adam leans forward with that marvellous impression of a frown Li-Jin has noticed in his young patients when he approaches them with a needle. A creased forehead where the lines are not permanent, a sort of magic.

'Giant Haystacks.'

'*Dad*. Don't be rubbish. That's all fixed. Moves may be real or realish but the end is fixed. *Everybody* knows that. Doesn't matter how heavy he is. He still won't win. *Can't* win.'

'Forty-five stone. Forty-five. Four. Tee. Five. Now: observe this money.'

Li-Jin, chortling to himself, pulls three pound notes and a pen from his shirt pocket and places them on the dashboard. 'I am going to write your three names on these three notes. And if Giant Haystacks loses, I will give each of you your note.'

'And what do we have to give you if he wins?' asks Rubinfine.

'You have to promise to be good boys, for ever.'

'Oh, great. Ug, ug.'

'I WANNA LEARN HOW TO FLY!'

'Electric uggaloo.'

Carefully, Li-Jin writes the names on the notes and holds them out very slowly and with great ceremony, like a man who has all the time in the bloody world.

'I'll take mine now, then,' says his son, reaching across for a note. 'BIG DADDY RULES OK!'

The children speak in slogans now. Li-Jin grew up with clichés. The slogans make the clichés look innocent.

'You'll take it *if* and *when* you have won it,' says Li-Jin, with a serious face, covering the money with his palm. 'Albert Hall, here we come.'

Because it is magic, yes, but there are rules.

And now here are some facts. When Queen Victoria first met Albert she wasn't really all that smitten. She was sixteen. He was her cousin. They got on well enough, but it was not what you would call a lightning/fireworks situation. Three years later, however, and suddenly he was right up her street. It was love at second sight. She was Queen by then. It's hard to tell whether that's a significant fact in the story of *How Victoria Fell in Love with Albert the Second Time She Met Him Rather than the First Like Most People Would if They were Intending to Fall in Love Suddenly*. What can be said for sure is that after this second visit Victoria describes Albert in her diary as 'excessively handsome, such beautiful eyes . . . my heart is quite *going*', and then proposes to him, which seems fairly fresh to us with our ideas about the Victorians and how unfresh they were. And then they went and had nine children, which seems rather *more* than fresh. To process the nine children fact you have to, at some point, imagine Victoria as pretty fresh in the bedroom and that takes some doing. But still, the facts are

the facts. Here's another one: after Albert dies, Victoria continues
to have his razor and shaving bowl – filled to the brim with hot
water – brought in every morning to their bedroom as if he were
in a position to remove facial hair. She wears black for forty
years. These days, there is most likely a name for that sort of
thing. Something like: Excessive Grief Syndrome (EGS). But in
the late nineteenth century, with a few exceptions, most people
were still prepared to call it love. 'Ah, how she loved him,' they
say to each other, shaking their heads and buying posies for
tuppence a bag in Covent Garden or somewhere. A lot of things
that are syndromes now had simpler names back then. It was a
simpler time. That's why some people like to call them the good
old days.

More facts. On the magnificent mosaic that wraps itself around the
Albert Hall the following is engraved:

THIS HALL WAS ERECTED FOR THE ADVANCEMENT OF
THE ARTS AND SCIENCES, AND WORKS OF INDUSTRY
OF ALL NATIONS, IN FULFILMENT OF THE INTENTIONS
OF ALBERT, PRINCE CONSORT

He is dead, you see, by the time it opens in 1871, so whether his
intentions are fulfilled is rather a matter for conjecture. Clearly,
Victoria feels that intentions have been fulfilled sufficiently, for
she opens it herself and praises the big red elliptical structure with
its unfortunate echo problem – she visits it regularly throughout
the rest of her life. We can even imagine her touring it alone
sometimes, or maybe with one lady-in-waiting, tracing the increasingly worn red velvet of the seats with her fingertips, ripped through

by EGS, thinking of her dead husband and the fulfilment of his intentions. She feels very certain, Victoria, that she knows at all times precisely what Albert's intentions were or would have been had he ever thought about such and such a thing – she's one of those types of women. She traces his death and her mourning around the country. She leaves a doleful trail of statues and street names, museums and galleries. Albert's intention was ever to become something big in England. Something famous. Not just the awkward moustachioed slightly overweight German who brought us the Christmas tree, but something popular and loved. Victoria sees to it. Every new statue, every new building, causes someone to remark, 'Ah, how she loved him,' while swishing their skirts and patting a little chimney sweep on the head in Whitechapel or wherever. She mourns in public, Victoria, and everybody mourns with her. That's another reason they call it the good old days. Back then, people felt things in unison, like the sudden chorus that leaps from a country church when the choir starts to sing.

Final facts: one could possibly, if one felt like it, date the current pliancy of the phrase 'Arts and Sciences' to the inauguration of Victoria's Albert Hall. Arts and Sciences did at one point mean Painting and Stuff and Petri Dishes and Stuff. It was quite a specific, stiff type of phrase and there wasn't a lot of room in it. The Albert Hall (one could argue, if one had a mind to) helped change that. From the outset, you could go to see pretty peculiar things in that huge elliptical dome with the bad acoustics which caused every whisper in the stalls to be heard. In 1872, for example, you could see some people demonstrating Morse Code [Gladys in Block M, Seat 72, to Mary sitting next to her: Q. *What's he doing, Mary, love?* A. *Tapping something, I should say, dear*]. In 1879 the first public display of electric lighting is given [Mr P. Saunders, Block T, Seat 111, to his nephew, Tom: *Marvellous. Bloody marvellous*]. In 1883 there is an exhibition of bicycles [Claire Royston, Block H, Seat 21: *I can't see the point of that, Elsie, can you?*] and in 1891 the hall is registered as a place of worship. It is agreed that people can pray here now, if they want. And in 1909 they run a marathon.

> *Come on!*
> *He's finished! No legs left on 'im.*
> Go on, my son!
> *Oh, go on, Georgie, go on – for us, Georgie! Go!*
> *Get the boy some water!*

They just keep on running round that stage until the race is done. Now that's an art. And a science. Onwards: rallies by the Suffragettes, the *Titanic* Band Memorial Concert, complete theatrical performance of Coleridge-Taylor's classic saga *Hiawatha*, Ford Motor Show, Yehudi Menuhin (aged thirteen), CLOSED FOR WAR, Churchill television broadcast, Kray Twins boxing, trade fairs, Beatles, Stones, Dylan, Proms, acoustics greatly improved by the installation of fibreglass diffusers – otherwise known as 'mushrooms'. OK, now shout! See? Ech (Oh, Oh, Oh).

Re (Dew Dew Dew) uced.

Substantially. That's nice, isn't it?

Upwards: Muhammad Ali, Sinatra, ice-skating and Liza Minnelli, tennis tournaments, the Bolshoi, the Kirov, displays of Mark Knopfler's guitar skills, and Clapton's, and B. B. King's. Acrobats, contortionists, magicians, politicians. Poets. All kinds of parties. Very entertaining. Albert wanted arts and sciences, and Victoria

delivered them year after year, and when she left this world somebody else delivered them year after year, until they too retired and
passed the job to somebody new. And so it goes. There are many
ways to remember the dead. One of them is to have Tracy Baldock,
a dancer from Scotland who is down on her luck and somewhat too
large, achieve her dream: contemporary dance with a well-
established European troupe, dressed up as a mouse. You can have
Tracy dressed up as a cartoon mouse for Disney's *Holiday on Ice*,
have her skate along the absence where a person used to be. That's
one way. Another is to have poor Mark Knopfler please his audience
by playing 'Money for Nothing' for the God knows how manyieth
time, though he hates to do it, though it's killing him inside – have
Mark sing the words about the TVs and let Albert hear them,
wherever he is.

Li-Jin and his son don't know, as they walk under the arch of
the entrance, jittery with anticipation, that they are about to take
part in the latest episode of a very long wake. But they are both
sharp enough to note the incongruity between these massive
engraved words – ARTS AND SCIENCES – and what they are about
to see. In answer to his son's question: *Well, Alex . . . I suppose it
is an art. Beautiful movement. Graceful violence, this sort of thing.
But also rather scientific – neck holds, trips. You need to time
those things accurately, which is a kind of science, isn't it?*

Rubbish answer. Alex-Li screws up his nose, unsatisfied.

Well? Which is it, then, smarty-pants?

Li-Jin pauses for a moment at the threshold, waiting to hear a
better answer.

Neither. It's TV.

Which, of course, is the better answer.

YHWH

Inside, the hall has the feeling of potential revolution that funfairs and theme parks have: children find themselves in charge, adults discover their own sheer functionality. The fathers have a harassed, dazed look, following their sons like dim pets, carrying what has been passed back or dropped near them. The fathers are silent. The boys are having a 4,000-person conversation. It rings through the tiered seating, circles with the echo and descends with a roar, and Li-Jin's inside it, searching for his seats, with three mismatched boys trailing behind him like a gaudy college scarf.

It is a struggle, but Li-Jin gets his boys seated and settled in the end. He looks down to the stage, at that sad-looking empty square where pure space is under arrest bound by rope three times over. He feels like he has not exhaled in half an hour. He is just about to when the fat man sitting next to him turns and, without any invitation, waves ten quid in his face and barks: 'Fancy a flutter?'

Li-Jin repeats it back to him, uncomprehending. His English is about as perfect as it can be, but some tricks of British idiom ('*And there's me thinking*', '*Unbeknownst to her*', '*Gone to the dogs*') still prove troublesome. The fat man is scornful. 'Oh, come now,' he says, rolling the tenner into a cone and scratching his chin with it. 'Nothing heart-stopping. Simply this: Do. You. Fancy. A. Flutter.' He is so ugly. An alcoholic's nose, broken veined, a superfetation of carbuncles. Below this, a thick and dirty brush of a moustache. And he is persistent.

'A small bet,' he explains. 'You understand . . . to give the thing flavour.'

Li-Jin says no thank you, explaining quickly that he 'has a flutter, as you put it' with his son, and gives a short, inadvertent, unmistakably Chinese bow in his seat, which ordinarily would make his son wince except he's busy, hanging over the barrier with Rubinfine and Adam, spitting on people's heads.

The fat man frowns, unfurls the tenner and forces it into the pocket of his trousers, a difficult manoeuvre given his size.

'Suit yourself.'

Feeling awkward, Li-Jin does exactly that, he suits himself. He turns back to look at the stage. He bites at the nail of his right thumb. He chews the top right off it. What was *that* all about? It's made him nervy for no reason. He looks at the stage. Now that bothers him too. It is very busy with the preparation of nothing. What are all these people *doing*? Why all this fuss? What do you need to do except allow two men to walk on stage, fling off their cloaks, bend their heads low and grasp each other? And yet little blokes in baseball caps run from one end of the stage to the other, shouting instructions. Massive speakers are lifted and then set down again. A white-haired man in a jogging suit walks round and round the ring, tugging at the ropes with a look of absolute concentration. A boy sets a bucket down in a corner and spits in it. Why? After a while Li-Jin's eyes wander involuntarily left. This is a mistake. He is just in time to see his neighbour's massive lips turning a gruesome smile. The lips curl too close to the nose, the moustache is lifted, wide, uneven teeth are revealed – Li-Jin is disgusted and cannot hide it – and now the man thrusts out his hand and says, 'Klein. Herman Klein,' again too loudly, grinning like a gargoyle. Li-Jin reciprocates, politely, but keeps his body language closed, as you do. Trying not to invite conversation. But this Klein is a physical man who violates Li-Jin's space without even trying and, before Li-Jin has a say in the matter, he has lunged forward to give one of those double-handed shakes in which Li-Jin's comparatively small hand is completely swamped, coming out of the exchange pressed and damp. Klein releases him, snorts and rearranges his bulk in the seat, opening his legs and crossing his arms across his belly, satisfied, as if he has won some unspoken competition. Li-Jin cannot remember the last time he was so quickly and thoroughly intimidated by another man.

'So!' says Klein, looking up to the gods where reckless children are craning over the balcony to get a better view, 'have you come from far? We are from Shepperton and now . . . well! Here we are. Well, well, well. Look at all this! And where are you coming from, Mr Tandem?'

Li-Jin can hear an accent – not English, certainly European – he can't tell where from. In his time Klein has come further than Shepperton, that much is certain, just as Li-Jin has come further than Mountjoy, but these conversations require a certain shorthand. Li-Jin describes their journey, which in truth wasn't so very bad once they were free of Mountjoy itself, though he makes it longer and harder in the retelling. He has found that men in England prefer it that way. Traffic, ring roads, pile-ups and the rest. But as he speaks, it becomes clear to Li-Jin that this man Klein will not follow the simple rules that govern such a conversation, *Two Men, Unrelated by Blood, at a Sporting Event in England*, a conversation which, in its etymological roots, is a close cousin of *Two Men, Unrelated by Blood, in a Dress Shop Waiting for Their Wives to Emerge from Changing Rooms*. Just nod; just match anecdote for anecdote. But Klein makes no response. Only when Li-Jin finds his tongue fat and dull in his mouth does Klein abruptly become animated once more.

'Like a good fight, do you, Tandem? Do you? Been before? The thing about wrestling is this: physicality. Don't let any fool tell you different. Brawn. Muscle. Sweat. Titans!'

This last word is rendered so loudly that Li-Jin concurs without meaning to, his head just wobbles assent like a wind chime. Meanwhile the head of this man Klein drops without warning, his big rheumy eyes settle on the buckle of his own belt. Li-Jin wonders whether the man is actually all right in a *medical way*, you know, all right in the *head*. Maybe he should announce his qualifications. But then Klein returns like an animal that burrows for something and comes back with what it wanted.

'For myself, I work in the fancy-goods business. Gifts. Leathers. Bags. Jewellery. Small, fairly priced luxuries for ladies. Now, here is a fact: ladies buy 80 per cent of all the things that are bought on this earth, did you know that? Yes, my friend. They are the engine that drives the cogs to turn and turn. My father was a butcher and never knew where the smart money goes, but let me tell you, Tandem, I know. I have a boutique in Knightsbridge. We get a better class of clientele – people whose name you would know if I told them to you! Famous! But no matter. And this is Klein the younger,' says Klein the elder, and, for the first time since the conversation began, Li-Jin spots a small dangling foot clad in a shiny black shoe, two seats along. Putting his hand behind the tiny boy's back, Klein pushes the child into view, beyond the shadow of his own ripe stomach.

'My son, Joseph. And this, in a nutshell, is why we are here. Little Joseph needs to see Titans. Too many hobbies and not enough physical pursuits. Let these men be an example to him! It is my opinion that Joseph is too much of a little weed.'

Li-Jin opens his mouth to protest but

'Weed! He's a weed! A little weeeeed . . .'

Klein says this in a slimy falsetto, hiding his pupils somewhere in the back of his head, batting his stubby eyelashes and tinkling the air either side of him like a man playing upon two invisible keyboards. Li-Jin is repulsed. He sees Alex, who has just spotted Klein, recoil in his seat. Against his nobler instincts he wishes the man a million miles away from himself and Alex and the boys away from anything he might pollute – not to mention this sad-looking child, Joseph Klein.

'To be great,' says Klein, dropping his hands, 'you need to see greatness. Experience it. Be near it. He who lies down with the dogs gets up with fleas!'

'Yes. Yes, I suppose that's right,' says Li-Jin slowly. He makes a point of looking kindly at the child, who has terror stamped on his delicate, pinched features. A boy like that should be blond by rights, but Joseph is a swarthy little thing, his hair black like an Indian's, his big eyes darker than that. His ears are pointy. Li-Jin smiles firmly at him and lays his hand on his own son's knee.

'Joseph, this is my Alex. And he's here with friends. You boys should probably all sit next to each other. You might find you have things in common.'

The boy looks horrified. Li-Jin tries to retract.

'I mean ... of course, I suppose Alex is quite a bit older than you. And Ru – Mark, certainly will be. Mark, stop that. The spitting. Stop it.'

'HOW OLD?' Klein the elder wants to know. He lunges towards Alex once more, index finger raised in the air, twitching. Alex shrugs and tells Klein that he is twelve, like what's the big deal, but Klein laughs at this, tears squeezing out of the corners of his eyes. He pokes his son a few times in the ribs in what looks to Li-Jin like a painful manner.

'Ha! Twelve! Joseph is *thirteen*! Didn't I tell you he's a weed? Small when he popped out and small to this day. At the time I said to his mother: *I could tear him apart like a fish!* Send him back! Get another one! Ha! You want to know something? He chews his food twenty times a bite, thinking it will build him up. He read it somewhere. Fat bloody chance! Ha Ha! Hey you!'

Klein has spotted an ice-cream seller two rows below and, lifting himself out of his seat, leans forward until the iron-rail barrier that rings their seats is impaling his belly.

'Hey, you down there! Don't you want to know what I want?'

'I collect things,' says Joseph Klein in a tiny voice.

'What's that?' asks Li-Jin, leaning towards him. He is not sure he heard rightly, and now Klein the elder is huffing and puffing in an effort to get out of his seat and push past them all ('Who do they make these seats for? Are they for the munchkin people?'), so as to get to the end of the aisle and down towards the ice cream. Nimbly, Joseph bounces from his own seat into the one his father has just vacated.

'Things, stuff, autographs sometimes,' says Joseph very quickly. It feels like he has a lot to say and no time. 'I collect stuff from things that I like and then I keep them. In albums. I file them. I find it extremely worth while.'

Jesus. Alex smiles openly, but Rubinfine, to his credit, does not turn to Adam open-mouthed, screw his finger into his forehead or repeat the last sentence through a tongue obstruction, although this would be standard procedure as set out in the Code of being Fifteen and he is well within his rights given the scale (*extremely worth while?*) of the offence. Instead he just opens his mouth and closes it again, partly because Li-Jin's look says *no, not today* and besides, even for Rubinfine, there is no sport to be had in stepping on what is truly small and beetle-like.

'That sounds ... *fun*,' says Li-Jin.

'Just anything,' asks Alex, trying his best, 'or . . . ? Sort of *types* of things?'

Li-Jin smiles. Now that's *better*. Normally, if Alex doesn't like the neighbour's boy, because of a squint, maybe, or a lisp, or if he fears the sunburnt, freckled devil who squats opposite him on the tennis court, shifting his weight from foot to foot in that ominous way, well, Li-Jin will not interfere. They have much the same taste in boys, he and Alex. Sports fanatics are no good. Neither of them can find real sympathy for a certain type of fat-faced red-head with running nose and broken skin. They hate show-offs. But sometimes their guts tell them different things, and that's what's happening now. Li-Jin's gut is saying, *yes, we like him*, while Alex's is in two minds, if such a thing can be said of a gut.

'So, er . . .' he says, pouting, pushing his messy fringe back off his face, 'do you just collect programmes from things or something?'

Now Joseph opens his mouth to explain, but first he makes himself neat in his seat, crosses his little legs, straightens his spine. 'Famous things,' he says carefully, giving equal weight to each word. 'That's why I'm here. I like wrestling. I'm a wrestling fan.'

Li-Jin has seen it before. Rich Hong Kong children in uncomfortable suits called up to the edge of the adults' dinner table and asked to explain themselves for the benefit of guests: interests, achievements, hopes for the future. Joseph is like this. There is nothing natural about him.

'One of my collections,' he says, 'is called *European Wrestlers* except now there's Kurutawa so I may have to change the name.'

'OK,' says Li-Jin, 'that's very interesting. Alex, that's interesting, isn't it?'

And, straight after he says this, the five of them sit in silence for too long.

'He started off doing sumo, Kurutawa,' says Adam eventually, to help things along. 'He's Japanese.'

Joseph's face is all gratitude. 'Yes, from Japan! He's been in Yorkshire now for six months and doesn't like the food much. And in the magazine it said *Who would!* You see, because – because – the food tastes awful there, apparently. He doesn't need any more food, though, because he's a *man mountain*. He comes from Tokyo. I've got a signed picture. Of course, if there was more than just him, that would be better. I could have an album and call it *Japanese Wrestlers*. But it's a bit irritating. When it's just him.'

'Who else you bloody got, then?'

This is Rubinfine, who wants a fight these days every day, whether he really wants one or not, because of hormones.

'Well, that depends in what area.'

'Say, what?'

'All right,' says Joseph, 'what.' And then a little sneaky smile. It's not a good joke but it's still a joke and that's a good sign. Alex laughs and that seems to make Joseph relax. He starts to talk.

'I have an English politicians folder, a foreign dignitaries folder – that is my main area – and then Olympians, inventors, TV personalities, weathermen, Nobel Prize winners, writers, lepidopterists, entomologists, movie actors, scientists, assassins and the assassinated, singers – opera and popular – composers –'

Rubinfine puts his hand up: 'Hold on, hold on, did somebody ask for your life story or something?'

Li-Jin slaps Rubinfine's hand down. This is back in the days when you could still hit other people's children.

'OK, OK – which film stars?'

'Cary Grant.'

'Who?'

'And Betty Grable.'

'Who times two?'

Li-Jin tries to weigh in with a brief account of forties American cinema but Rubinfine shouts him down.

'No, no, no – I mean somebody *good*.'

'Mark Hamill?'

And that shuts up Rubinfine.

'That's not really the strongest part of my collection, actors,' begins Joseph cautiously, addressing Li-Jin now. 'So many of them when you write to them just send you back secretarials or imprinted things or Autopen stuff and it's very hard to get in-person items.'

'I see,' says Li-Jin. He has no idea what the boy's talking about. 'That's interesting.'

'YAWN,' says Rubinfine, yawning.

'And also they are not worth as much as you think.'

'You make money?' asks Adam, bug-eyed. If you make money and you're under sixteen, as far as Adam is concerned you approach divinity.

And then the boy says, 'Oh yes . . . Philography's very lucrative.'

Alex: 'Phila who?'

'It's the word for autograph collecting,' says Joseph, and it's clear he isn't saying this to impress. No, he just wants to tell someone. Still, it's hard to forgive him for it and Rubinfine won't, ever. He suggests that everything Joseph has is worth four pee. He goes on to bet him this same four pee that his collection is actually worth *less* than four pee. Which is when Joseph seemingly without malice explains that he has an Albert Einstein worth three thousand pounds.

And that shuts up Rubinfine.

Alex: 'Really? Einstein?'

'My Uncle Tobias met him in America, so it's in-person and it's signed to the lighter portion of the photograph *and* he was kind enough to also write down his super-famous equation next to it, which is where the money is, you see, in the content. But I wouldn't sell it any more than I would sell my own arm.'

'Einstein-Shminestein,' says Rubinfine. 'When's this match going to start? Bored of all this ugging around.'

But Alex wants to know. Why not? Why wouldn't somebody sell something worth three thousand pounds? Like, unless they were crazy?

'Because it's in my most precious folder.'

'And what's that?' asks Li-Jin, because you have to drag everything out of this boy.

'My Judaica.'

'Your what?'

'My folder of Jewish things.'

'We're Jewish!' Adam pipes up in that merry way he will lose in about three years. Exclusive province of childhood: a time when genetic/cultural inheritance feels like this weird but cool thing you just got landed with, like an extra shoe. Hey, check this out, Tom! I'm Eurasian! Whoa, I'm a Maori! Look, no hands!

'Me, I am, and Rubinfine is, and Alex. We go to heder together.'

But Alex doesn't want to be sidetracked. 'And what else is in it? In the Jewish folder.'

'Nothing.'

But he doesn't mean nothing, he means *Here comes my father*, which Alex picks up on immediately, but Li-Jin completely fails to get.

'Come on, Joseph – don't be coy. There must be another thing in there. One autograph can't make a folder, can it?'

'BORING YOU, IS HE?'

Li-Jin stands up to try to get out of Klein's way, and ends up having to stand on the seats with the boys to allow Klein and his belly to get past.

'No, not at all, actually. We were just talking about Joseph's collection – about the Judaica. It's very interesting for me. You see, my son is Jewish.'

Klein licks his ice cream and smiles. Without the slightest trace of pleasantness or good humour. Li-Jin realizes that he has inadvertently given the man some material – of what kind he has no idea – from which he means to fashion a missile to throw at this child.

'Oh, his *Judaica*. Is that correct? Is that what you're working on all night, in the dark, Joseph, ruining your eyes . . . And there was I thinking he was scribbling some nauseating adolescent nonsense in there, dirty stuff, as boys will – but no. How interesting, Joseph. He can't finish his homework, but he has time to assemble his *Judaica*. Well. What is the phrase? Yes: you learn something new every day. Well, well.'

Joseph has folded back into his seat and is invisible beside his father but there is too much noise for the silence between the six of them to be painful. Dramatic music is playing. The precommentary one hears on TV is on loud throughout the hall. In fact there are the two pundits, sitting on a little shelf of their own talking into their mikes, both bald with a few hairs scraped over, down there, down at the very front.

Alex takes a biro from his jeans pocket, lifts his left foot on to his right knee and proceeds to dig at some dark matter that is trapped in the ridges of his trainer sole. But he doesn't take his mind off Joseph. Li-Jin leans forward, casually, his fingers not that he is ill like a human being rather than like a doctor. At first he takes it as a doctor, studying the pictures with another doctor, calmly pointing his finger at the mass; tutting with all the impatience of familiarity as the treatment options are outlined. But a few days later it enters him as a terrible human fact, and leaves by way of a tiny, strained yelp in the night which Sarah mistakes for the cat. He clutches the duvet and presses his knees into the back of hers as if she could keep him here, just by proximity, by means of her own enviable health. In response to the obvious question he tells her *heartburn* and then turns his eyes to the wall and watches the cornered arcs of light from passing traffic climb from the window over the ceiling and then draw in towards them both like a series of embraces. Sarah goes back to sleep. He watches the arcs for about twenty minutes. After that, still agitated, he gets up and pads down the corridor to Alex's room, looks in briefly and then progresses to the kitchen, where he puts two processed chicken slices on a single piece of unbuttered bread, calls it a sandwich and switches on the TV. He stands in the middle of the kitchen half naked (bottom half) and manages three minutes of the BBC test card. The girl. The rag doll. Then he weeps, the sandwich over his mouth to suppress the noise, gulping from his throat like an animal. The death-punch, the infinity-slap, strikes him so hard he falls on to a stool and has to grip the edge of the breakfast bar just to stay upright. He is thirty-six years old.

The next morning he begins to consider his options. As the poor patient, he recalls the words of the good doctor, identical to those that he himself, also a good doctor, has given to other poor patients in his time. But his own insider information means the words come

now with the ugly twist of footnotes, each appendix framed with a
but. He could submit to six months of radiotherapy *but*. He could
undergo an operation to remove the tumour *but*. Li-Jin has read the
case histories. He knows that in the wrestling match between
possibly and *probably* that takes place inside every pineoblastoma,
the *probably* wins nine times out of ten. It is possible, after sitting
dormant for so long, that the tumour will not develop any further.
But Li-Jin is a good enough doctor to know that it will most probably
kill him. *Time bomb. Ticking clock. Russian roulette.* All the
phrases he discourages his own patients from using come back to
him with the full force of a vengeful cliché. But still he finds it
almost impossible to believe. On one occasion he finds himself
rooted to the pavement on a bustling street, awed and dumbstruck,
in the old-fashioned sense. He is going to die and it is not going to
make any sense but it is still going to happen. He is so young! How
can this be?

Years ago Sarah had referred to her only pregnancy as an
unstoppable train, a feeling in one's body that only women can
know. But here it comes, his death, persistent in its forward motion,
chugging on despite the human beings standing on the tracks.
Arriving. Inevitable, inconceivable, so near, so far – is this what
they mean when they talk about its dominion? Li-Jin finds his
death has a dual character: it seems to be everywhere and nowhere
at the same time. He is going to die, and yet when Alex asks him
to lift the wardrobe to recapture a fugitive marble, he does it easily,
without strain. He is going to die, yet when the chairmanship of
the local Neighbourhood Watch comes up for grabs, he wants the
job desperately and campaigns vigorously to get it. Though his
death is always there, waiting for him, he can only feel it sometimes, and then incongruously. Not detecting it during the movies

35

Love Story or *The Champ*, for example, but in the middle of a tea
commercial, in the wild gestures of a ventriloquized chimp. He has
to push Alex off his lap and rush to the laundry room, where he
sobs and breathes in and out of a brown-paper bag until he is calm.
His death is like the soft down on the back of your hand, passing
unnoticed in the firmest of handshakes, though the slightest breeze
makes every damn one of the tiny hairs stand on end.

YHWH

The bell rings! Here we go! And the first thing that happens is that
everyone in attendance realizes that the betting has been pointless.
As a wise guy once said, wrestling isn't a sport, it's a spectacle, and
you can't bet on it any more than you can bet on the outcome of a
performance of *Oedipus Rex*. Of course Big Daddy will win! How
could it be otherwise? Look at him! He wears a red Babygro, he is
ruddy-faced, he is white-haired, he is more *famous*. Not that Giant
Haystacks will lose – he will win too, just by playing his part to its
fullest. The more of a bastard he is, the more the audience loves it.
When he pursues Big Daddy to the ropes in illegal revenge for a
successful hold, when he delivers a forearm smash after the whistle
and behind the referee's back (though in full view of half the
audience), they will jeer him with glee. When he lifts up his arms,
roars and throws back his head like a beast – the International
Gesture for *You stupid fools, did you expect me to play fair?* – the
whole of the Albert Hall rocks and shakes. In every way that he is
vicious and sneaky and underhand, Big Daddy is honest and firm
and suffering unduly. When Big Daddy is helped to his feet by the
referee and shakes his head and puts his arms out towards the front
row imploring them to take note of the outrageous injustice of

having one's head stamped on, Giant Haystacks stalks up to this same front row and shakes his fist at them: *Justice! You talk of Justice! I am simply the mirror of the world and the fact is, the world is mean! People are cruel and death comes to all! You do not like to look at me because I am ugly, but I am the awful TRUTH!* All this in a shaken fist. Every movement is excessive. Big Daddy does not just thump, he *thwacks*, Giant Haystacks does not simply fall to his knees, he *collapses*. This is not boxing and there is no heroism in hiding your suffering. *Look at me! Look how I suffer!* says Giant Haystacks with his upper body. *Can it be that Good will win out despite my Evil power?* Big Daddy trips him and holds him, and the tiny ref in the dapper white suit skips to the scene to begin the count . . . but it is not quite time for the triumph of Good over Evil, not yet. Everybody's paid their four pounds ninety-nine and a half pence, after all.

So they waddle back to their corners, slap their bellies and then slowly begin to circle each other. This is an excursus to the main event, giving the opportunity for the audience to consider them once more as separate lumps of flesh rather than as the one mountain. You notice immediately that though both are obscenely fat, they are fat in different ways. Big Daddy is fat like an inflated ball, with no body hair and no sagging or visible genitals. He is fat like a bouncing, jovial Zeus, skimming the clouds, a circular god. But Giant Haystacks is fat like your average really fat man, covered in raw meat that undulates and shakes and no doubt smells, and he has dark hair and a shaggy beard and is dressed ignobly, in blue dungarees and a red checked shirt, like the madman who lives in the woods at the end of your town. By contrast, B. D.'s Babygro-romper-suit-underwear-combo is somehow *elemental*, like he is so pure and unadorned a man that, if he could, he would fight naked, but in the interests of decency he threw this little number together. Oh, also, it says BIG DADDY on the back in big letters. Giant Haystacks has got none of that.

All of a sudden they run at each other once more and if you have a better phrase than *like thundering elephants* insert it here [   ]. Giant Haystacks wallops Big Daddy across his flank, trips him and then stamps on his face *with his feet, both of them* ('See!' say Rubinfine and Adam to each other at exactly the same time), in response to which Big Daddy waits for the count to reach two, and then 'picks himself up off the floor' (and it's these *fundamental* clichés that wrestling is made for), stands up and shakes his head around like he's just drunk something that made him a bit woozy. As if to say: *Cor, that was a heavy one.*

And of course it's ridiculous, but the thing is, they are not here to express genuine feelings, or to fake them and dress them up *natural* like on TV – they are here to demonstrate *actions*. And all the kids *know* that. Any fool can tell a story – can't they? – but how many can *demonstrate* one, e.g., *This is what a story is, mate, when it's stripped of all its sentiment.* This afternoon these two hulking men are here to demonstrate Justice. The kind Mr Gerry Bowen [Block M, Seat 117] can't get from the courts in compensation for his son's accident; the kind Jake [Block T, Seat 59] won't get from school whether he chooses to squeal on those bastards or not; the kind Finn [Block B, Seat 10] can't seem to get from girls no matter what changes he makes to his wardrobe or record collection or personal hygiene; the kind Li-Jin [Block K, Seat 75] can't get from God.

And then, when sufficient time has elapsed, Justice is served and Big Daddy wins, and it was inevitable, but no one begrudges him

It's chaos. To stay together they have to make a snake behind Klein. Alex and Joseph are at the front, chatting away like old friends; then Adam, clutching to his chest the photograph Joseph gave him; then Rubinfine stepping on the backs of Adam's plimsolls and then Li-Jin. They are pressed in on all sides by hundreds of people at whom Klein is bellowing to get out of his way and Li-Jin is apologizing as he collides with fathers and sons. *Why don't we move a bit slower?* he shouts towards the front of their snake but Klein doesn't hear him and probably wouldn't give up the pace if he did. For a big man he's agile, strong and pushy like a boar and with the same tiny little feet. *Hurry up, slowcoach*, says Alex, and Li-Jin realizes that his headache is so bad he can hardly hear, or that he is hearing in a delayed way, because Alex's voice is sadly out of sync with the movement of his lips, as in the artificially slowed piece of action in a movie when something tragic is about to occur. *Hurry up, Dad!* He's coming, he's coming, Dad's coming as best he can and with a sore head but also an opening out of his chest, because he's a young dad and he's only got one kid and it has just struck him again for the forty millionth time how beautiful that boy is. *I'm coming!* But will they be there soon? How far can it possibly be from Block K to the stage and then behind it? And then just as they seem about to approach there is a huge crowd swell pushing backwards like someone has just shot a gun on the stage. Actually it is the effect of fame – Big Daddy has become visible, appearing at the mouth of one of the stage doors, kingly in his cape, signing autographs. Klein is shouting something ridiculous that Li-Jin cannot work out – probably something like *Personal Friends! Let us through, Personal Friends!* – but whatever it is, it appears to be working, because the six parts of their snake are wriggling towards the star with a little more ease than before. But every time they inch three feet forwards, the gap is filled up again behind Li-Jin, people pressing him, holding on to him to steady themselves, cross-hall traffic barging by.

Klein is the first to get to Him, then Rubinfine by pushing, and then Joseph and Alex – Li-Jin can't see where Adam is – and then the route closes up like the Red Sea in front of him and Li-Jin can get no further. He tells himself not to panic about Adam and concentrates instead on reaching up on tip-toe, and he is in time to see Him ruffle Alex-Li's hair, punch him playfully on the shoulder and take his picture for signing. As soon as the name's across it, Alex whips round, delighted, and jumps up looking for Li-Jin so he can show it to him, and Li-Jin jumps up too and tries to wave, but he is too small to get above a crowd like this and a glimpse of Alex's creased forehead is the last thing Li-Jin sees before his knees crumple beneath him and his head hits the floor. Once on his back, though, his eyes open for a few seconds. He sees the hall squidge, and then squadge. Sounds gloop. The light shrinks. He sees people. Many, many people. Nobody famous, though. No one familiar or friendly. No one to help. No one he knows.

BOOK ONE

Mountjoy

The Kabbalah of Alex-Li Tandem

Take me to the centre of everything.

> – the popular singer Madonna Ciccone to a taxi driver
> upon her arrival in New York City

The unique phenomenon of distance, however close an
object may be.

> – A definition of 'aura' offered by the popular wise guy
> Walter Benjamin

ONE / *Shechinah*

Presence • Alex-Li Tandem was Jewish • A rainbow over Mountjoy •
Hand-print • Superstar • Princess Grace • Marvin is a milk operative •
Alex's feminine goy side • Not talking about the car #1 • Communion
with a snail

I

You're either for me or against me, thought *Alex-Li Tandem,*
referring to the daylight and, more generally, to the day. He
stretched flat and made two fists. He was fully determined to lie
right here until he was given something to work with, something
noble, something *fine.* He saw no purpose in leaving his bed for a
day that was against him from the get-go. He had tried it before –
no good could come from it.

A moment later he was surprised to feel a flush of warm light
dappled over him, filtered through a blind. Non-violent light. This
was encouraging. Compare and contrast with yesterday morning's
light, pettily fascist, cruel as the strip-lighting in a hospital corridor.
Or the morning before yesterday morning, when he had kept his
eyes closed for the duration, afraid of whatever was causing that
ominous red throb beneath the eyelids. Or the morning before *that,*
the Morning of Doom, which no one could have supposed would
continue for seventy-two hours.

Now optimistic Alex grabbed the bauble that must be twisted to
open blinds. His fingers were too sweaty. He shuttled up the bed,

dried his left hand on the wall, gripped and pulled. The rain had come in the night. It looked as if the Flood had passed through Mountjoy, scrubbed it clean. The whole place seemed to have undergone an act of accidental restoration. He could see brickwork, newly red-faced and streaky as after a good weep, balconies with their clean crop of wet white socks, shirts and sheets. Shiny black aerials. Oh, it was fine. Collected water had transformed every gutter, every depression in the pavement, into prism-puddles. There were *rainbows* everywhere.

Alex took a minute to admire the gentle sun that kept its mildness, even as it escaped a grey shelf of cloud. On the horizon a spindly church steeple had been etched by a child over a skyline perfectly blue and flatly coloured in. To the left of that sat the swollen cupola of a mosque, described with more skill. So people were off to see God, then, this morning. All of that was still happening. Alex smiled, weakly. He wished them well.

In his bathroom Alex was almost defeated by the discovery of a sequence of small tragedies. There was an awful smell. Receptacles had been missed. Stuff was not where stuff should be. Stepping over stuff, ignoring stuff, stoic Alex turned to the vanity mirror. He yanked it towards him by its metal neck until its squares became diamonds, parallelograms, one steel line. He had aged, terribly. The catch in his face, the one that held things up, this had been released. But how long was it since he had been a boy? A few days? A year? A decade? And now *this*?

He bared his teeth to the mirror. They were yellow. But, on the plus side, they were there. He opened his Accidental eyes (Rubinfine's term: halfway between Oriental and Occidental) wide as they would go and touched the tip of his nose to the cold glass. What was the damage? His eyes worked. Light didn't hurt. Swallowing felt basic, uncomplicated. He was not shivering. He felt no crippling paranoia or muscular tremors. He seized his penis. He squeezed his cheeks. Present, correct. Everything was still where it appears in the textbooks. And it seemed unlikely that he would throw up, say, in the next four hours, something he had not been able to predict with any certainty for a long time. These were all wonderful, wonderful developments. Breathing heavily, Alex shaved off three days' worth of growth (had it been *three days*?). Finishing up, he found he had cut himself twice and so applied the sad twists of tissue.

Teeth done, Alex remembered the wear-and-tear deposit he had paid his landlord and shuffled back to the bedroom. He needed a cloth, but the kitchen was another country. Instead he took a pillowcase, dipped it in a glass of water and began to scrub at the hand-print on the wall. Maybe it looked like art? Maybe it had a certain presence? He stepped back and looked at it, at the grubby yellow outline. Then he scrubbed some more. It didn't look like art. It looked like someone had died in the room. Alex sat down on the corner of his bed and pressed his thumbs to his eyes to stop two ready tears. A little gasp escaped him. And what's remarkable, he thought, what's really amazing is *this*, is how *tiny* the actual thing was in the first place. This thing that almost destroyed me. Two, no, maybe three days ago he had placed a pill on his tongue, like a tiny communion wafer. He'd left it there for ten seconds, as recommended, before swallowing. He had never done anything like this before. Nothing could have prepared him! Moons rose, suns fell, for days, for nights, all without him noticing!

Legal name: Microdot. Street name: Superstar. For a time it had made itself famous all through his body. And now it was over.

2

Out in the hall Alex met Grace. She was crouched on the second step, looking vengeful. Her tail in the air, her face messy with bird blood. Protruding from her mouth was the greater part of a wing. Alex saw that it was no sparrow either, but a colourful, pinky-blue type of bird, the sort he might have got sentimental over, built a bird-house for, with one of these miniature Welcome Home mats much loved by the widowed of Mountjoy. But he had come too late for all that. When pushed (she had not been fed), Grace became a garden terrorist and made no sentimental distinctions between species of the same genus. A squirrel was as good as a mouse to her, a parakeet equal to a pigeon. Picking her up, Alex forgave her, kissed her on her flat head, tugged her tail and slid her down the banister. In return, she painted a long streak of red, like a design feature, down the length of pine, punctuated by little hillocks of bird guts. And *still* he did not throw up. Ha! Alex was counting this as Personal Triumph of the Morning #3. The second was walking. The first was consciousness.

3

'It sort of hurts, *here*,' said Alex to his milk operative, Marvin, who was on the doorstep. Marvin reached out his dark hand and up went his white cuff. Despite himself Alex thought of Bill Robinson reaching out for the hand of Shirley Temple. It did seem a musical out here today on the chilly street. Bright, awesome.

'Where?'

'Kidney area.'

Marvin felt the area. He had long fingers and he poked deep.

'Careful . . .'

'What am I looking for? A lump?'

'You think it could *create* a lump?'

Marvin shrugged. 'Highly unlikely, Bro. Not in such a short time anyway – but it raaver depends what they put *in* it, you get me?'

Alex pulled his pyjama top back down and frowned. 'I have no idea what they put in it, Marvin. It's not like this stuff is regulated. There was no ingredients list. There was no consumer –'

Marvin waved his hands in Alex's face, dismissing him. He never did sarcasm. He possessed what Alex imagined to be the essential sincerity of urban black males with hard lives.

'Yeah, yeah, *yeah*. Your head isn't itchin' in your skull or nothing?' he asked, stepping back, holding Alex speculatively by the chin. Alex felt depressed. It was clear Marvin's expertise outstripped his own. It is depressing, being out-experted so early in the morning.

'Itching?'

'Then you're fine. It might have been strong, but it sounds pure. Sometimes they've got Floxine in them. Then your head itches in your skull for a bit after.'

'Floxine?'

'Do you want any yogurts, then? Bloody freezing out here,' said Marvin, turning in the direction of his milk truck and employing one hand as a visor against the winter sun. He bounced on the balls of his feet, stepping back, stepping forward. In his left hand, through those long, clever fingers, he passed his small notepad from the first finger to the last and back again, like a playing card. Marvin was bored.

'No, not really.'

'Say again?' said Marvin, in a menacing tone.

Marvin was three months into a government-sponsored job initiative. Before this he had had a brief stint as a parking attendant. Before that he had been a dealer of drugs. At present he was in addiction counselling, the language of which he sometimes spoke on his milk rounds. As soon as Marvin began his deliveries in Mountjoy, a huge leap in demand for expensive yogurts and milk-shakes occurred, a growth that had an exact correlation to public fear of Marvin. Alex too, at first, had ordered a lot of individually wrapped cheese singlets, mousses, pressurized cream cans, etc. But now he wanted to *redraw the boundaries of the relationship*. Now he wanted them both, he and Marvin, to *move towards new criteria*.

'I'm all right for yogurts, actually.'

'Well, bully for you,' said Marvin sourly. He slipped his pad into the pouch at the front of his uniform. He reached forward once more and widened Alex's eyes with his fingers.

'What was this foolishness called, again?'

'I think, a Superstar?'

Marvin clapped his hands together, laughed and shook his head in a move called – if Alex were asked to give it a name – *the Dance of Scoff*.

'And *you're* the intellectual.'

'And I'm the intellectual.'

'And so . . . what?' asked Marvin. 'What was the deal, Tandem? Was joy sown before pain was reaped?'

Alex fiddled with the fly of his pyjama bottoms. From here his penis looked smaller than it had ever looked ever. It was curled in on itself like a mollusc, but where was the hard shell that would protect it? Where its home? Its shield against life!

'Were you . . . like, dancing or chilling or? I know some people,' considered Marvin, 'and they get on a *living-room* trip. The TV sucks them in. They commune with the TV, right? And they take their trip through the channels. *Suburban* style-ee.'

Alex had been in his bed for around three days, that much he had a grip on. In which time he had survived on the bright spangles of Christmas chocolate coins sitting on his night table. He remembered a lucid hour in which he had plumped some pillows behind him, picked up the phone and called a radio talk show during a conversation about early menopause. He remembered the sleep. Deep, padded. But the night before this, the night in question, this was a shut door with its wood warping from some unseen fire, smoke squeezing through. He could not open it. He didn't dare.

'Marvin,' he said finally, 'I have no recollection. On the past week I am drawing a . . .'

Marvin nodded and made the sign for a big empty circle of nothing in the air. Through it Alex could see the embroidered lettering MARVIN KEPPS, MOUNTJOY MILK OPERATIVE and beyond that a tiny blanching gap in his buttons, where the tight corkscrew of his chest hair was suggesting something scary to Alex, some untapped velocity in the coil.

'That will happen,' said Marvin, and placed his hands softly on Alex's shoulders. 'Tandem,' he said, 'let me lay it out for you: in the pros column we have heightened sensory perception, visionary experience and the rest. I don't have to tell *you*. Every note of music, every blade of grass, etc. But here on the cons we have short-term memory *collapse*. Back in the day, they called them Goldfish. For the reason stated above.'

For the second time this morning, Alex felt tears rising. The spectre of *permanent neurological damage*, number four on Alex's Big Five List –

1. Cancer
2. AIDS
3. Poisoned Water System/London Underground Gas Attack
4. Permanent Neurological Damage (in youth, through misadventure)
5. Degenerative brain disease, Alzheimer's, Parkinson's, etc. (in old age)

– grabbed at his gag-reflex, and he swerved towards a bush by the fence. Marvin caught him by the elbow, hugged him to his body and straightened him up.

'None of that, *please*,' said Marvin fondly, massaging his knuckle into the top of Alex's head. 'It's just the problem with those things, and what I've learnt is this: they're meant to be a short-cut to the ultimate . . . thing, the plane, or whatever you want to say it like, yeah? It's meant to be: here's your thirty quid or whatever, take me to higher consciousness, please. And it don't work that way, Bro. You don't get the full benefit. You've got to work your way up that tree, meaning that that is an allegory which is saying: you can't just fly up to the branches. You get me?'

'Right.'

'I know I'm right. So. Mr my-bed-is-my-office. Going out today?'

'Considering it, Marvin.'

'Consider hard.'

'Will do.'

'Will do,' echoed Marvin in the effeminate voice he often used to impersonate Alex. In the past this has made Alex wonder whether he seems effeminate to black men or just to Marvin in particular. A couple of months ago, in Mountjoy Swimming Pool, Alex-Li Tandem did a passable back flip and then, rising out of the water, put the matter to his friend Adam, who took off his nasal clip and said: 'No . . . I don't see that, I don't find you particularly effeminate. You're too bulky, for one. And hairy. And he does that to me too, anyway. And I'm the black guy.'

'Yes,' said Alex happily, kicking some water in the direction of children who had kicked some at him. 'You're *the* black guy.'

'Yes, *I'm* the black guy. No doubt I die halfway through. So. I don't know. I think it's probably more of a class thing.'

Water dribbled out of Adam's nose along with some more viscous material. There should be a law. Alex took an Olympic breath and surged to the gritty, tiled bottom of the pool, performed a rolly-turn thing and kicked off from the side, after which he swam two thirds of the length under water, a personal record. He was a little fat these days, and he smoked. When he returned he got four floats and put them underneath his body in such a way as to enable him to sit upright in the water and bob up and down in a sort of Mer King scenario.

'What do you mean, *class* thing? We're not *posh*.'

Here Adam paused to do some of his weird stretches. These made Alex feel his friend came to the pool with a complex, beneficial, possibly spiritual, certainly undisclosed exercise programme in his mind, while Alex just spent the time pissing around (often literally) examining the incredible potential variance in the curvature of young women's pubic bones. Adam hooked his ankle round the handrail. Near Alex a floating plaster flipped over to reveal a tiny circular concentration of blood. Again, thought Alex, there should be a law. Adam yawned, and seemed to take his arms, turn them backwards and force his hands to pray behind his back. His stretch was impressive and women looked. These days he was the opposite of fat and did not smoke, except for weed. His stomach was a taut drum of rippled jet.

He said: 'No, true, but we're posher than *Marvin*. That's the key fact. But it's subtler than that, though, it's like, the voice Marvin's doing, that's the same voice you do when you're doing your Lenny Bruce goy voice –'

'And? So what are you saying?'

'Well, brainiac, I'm saying that *maybe*, in relation to him and his ex-drug dealer, working-class soulfulness etc., *we're all goys*.'

'And *he's* the Jew?'

'And he's the Jew.'

'That argument is uniquely . . .' said Alex, but couldn't think of the word.

'Yeah . . . but I sort of *like* it for that. You should put it in your book – justifies a whole new subsection.'

After which Adam went alone to the diving tank, while Alex, treading water furiously, internally raged at a repulsive woman in fluorescent costume. Her head was hinged and awful on her fat neck. Her mouth was huge. She was laughing off her son's faecal mishap in the shallow end. There should be law upon law, with commentary.

It was now that Marvin – who had turned his back on Alex to look towards the house opposite – made a sudden little yelp. He rolled back on his heels in the International Gesture for surprise. He thrust one arm out in the air. He looked like Chaplin.

'Mate, isn't that your *car*? Check it! Oh my *gosh*. *Jesus Christ Almighty*.'

Two spaces down from where it was usually parked, Alex could see his vintage MG, Greta, hitched up on the kerb quite desperately, trying to save herself. Her front bumper had been brutally torn from her body and now hung from an iron thread, her door had been punched by a giant. Her front window had been visited by a glass spider.

'*And* the passenger window!' shrieked Marvin, pointing to the passenger window.

Greta's side was scratched from toe to tail, and her canvas roof was sadly pleated and condensed, an exhausted accordion. The whole of the car, in fact, was shorter by half a foot.

'Brer, did *you* do that?'

Alex folded into the door-frame like Lauren Bacall. It was only 8.30 a.m., but already it was time to throw in the white towel. The day had looked good. The day had lied. He felt he could not fight days like this. He believed utterly that there are days in which it is revealed that someone has written a cruel story about you for their own entertainment. He believed, further, that on such days all you can do is follow, dumbly, with your knuckles grazing the ground. In that sense, if in no other, he was a profoundly religious man.

'I can't believe that, Dred! Look at dat!' said Marvin, grinning. Marvin was enjoying himself.

Alex parted his hands, slowly, relinquishing whatever was left. 'What do you want me to say, Marvin?'

Marvin sniffed. 'Don't mistake me, I don't really care, I'm only the milk operative – I was just wondering if you did or did not do that to your own car. Other than that . . .' Marvin grinned some more.

Now Alex let Marvin's face fall out of view, bent his legs and crouched on the doorstep. On its lip, on the doorstep's concrete lip, he met a massive pulsing snail wearing its shell a long way down its back, as a sort of after-thought. Alex peeled it off and held it in the cup of his palm for a moment. Then he launched it towards the grass, but even with that action came the sad thought of more creative possibilities for both him and the snail: the polished dark country of Marvin's shoe, the cool, featureless Lapland of the window-ledge, the barren Arizona of the path that leads down to the road and eventual death.

'Look. Seriously. Are you depressed? I mean, generally?' asked Marvin with genuine curiosity.

'Yes,' said Alex impatiently. 'Yes, I imagine so.'

'You *imagine* so?'

'Marvin, I don't want to talk about this, actually.'

'And you don't know *when* did you do that to your car?'

'Marvin, I have no recollection.'

Marvin said *Ha!* like the first blast of a military horn. He took an elegant hop down two steps and moseyed down the path. The snail found itself somewhere maddeningly familiar, wet and green; a place where bad things, most often revolving blades, might arrive, with no warning, from nowhere. Alex crossed his eyes. Clicked his heels together three times. Closed his door against Mountjoy.

TWO / *Yesod*

Foundation • Famous Phrases #1 • Muhammad Ali was Jewish •
Stress-balls versus funnels • The covenant and the pound notes • Famous
Phrases #2 • God and Garbo • Kitty Alexander's autograph • Joseph
explains the Judaic attitude to transubstantiation

I

Back inside his flat, valiant Alex-Li held up a series of clothing
items at arm's length, and if he could not smell them he put them
on. He took no great care, for the result was always the same,
irrespective of effort. Everything he wore looked as if it had been
flung at him by an irate girlfriend in a hallway; a rag-bag of items
he remembered wearing the night before, mixed with some he
didn't recognize.

With one sock on, he hopped across the room, picked up the
Autograph Association Flip-Calendar on his desk and peered at it.
February 12th. Underneath, a photo of Sandra Dee. She was smiling
and offering up two facts about herself:

> **My real name is Alexandra Zuck!**
> **I began modelling at thirteen!**

Alex ripped through February 16th (Dolores Del Rio) and 17th
(Peter Lawford), settling on the 18th, a Wednesday, as the most
probable date. Archibald Leach was teeing off with his god-like
chin pointed towards the camera, with his perfect golf clothes.

Almost too good to look at. Saying, in speech marks,

Everyone wants to be Cary Grant. Even I want to be Cary Grant.

Underneath this was something in Alex's handwriting:

Auction – 12 p.m. Rock and movie memorabilia.
3 p.m. Vintage Hollywood

So he had business today.

The phone began to ring. Alex, who always felt subtly attacked by the phone if he could not see it, hurried to find his glasses and put them on, remoulding the mad wire arms until they behaved themselves and hooked behind his ears.

'Yes? Yes, hello?'

'Tandem,' said a girl, 'I see you're picking up the phone, *finally*. Good phone voice too. Give the man an Oscar. Oh, and I'm still alive?'

Alex opened his mouth, but the line went dead.

'*Esther?*' said Alex into the void. Quickly, he tried calling her back at each of her numbers. Either by accident or design, all went instantly to the automated message and then the dreadful beep. These beeps still gave Alex stage fright. He seemed the only man left who felt that way about it. He despised the perform- ance aspects. Anyone who is able to leave a successful answering- machine message is a kind of actor. At Esther's home, Alex left some silence. On her mobile he said, 'But no, look, the thing is I've really got to go to work now.' But this was simply thinking aloud.

∗

From the floor of his wardrobe Alex picked up his big leather satchel. He was an Autograph Man. The job fell into three compartments. Collecting. Trading. Verification. The first two, fairly self-explanatory, the third he had sometimes to explain to people at parties. He had been humiliated many times by that ubiquitous good-looking drunk girl who rests against the refrigerator and coolly assesses the validity of your life while people dance wildly in the lounge. She is impressed by the simple career nouns – lawyer, doctor, journalist, even fireman. But *Junior Information Consultant Interfacer, Second Technical Administrator* – jobs like these do nothing for her. Nor do fanciful careers, jumped-up hobbies with aspirations. So try convincing her that you, Alex-Li Tandem, are the man people pay to flick through a selection of ageing paper and give your opinion as to what is real and what forged in their collection. It does not matter to her that this is a skill and an art. It is a skill knowing the difference between the notorious Sydney Greenstreet secretarial (expertly forged by his assistant, Betty) and the curves and loops of the real thing. It is a skill distinguishing the robotic scratch of a Kennedy Autopen from the real presidential signature. Knowing when to lie about these matters, and how much, is an art. But try telling her that. Alex-Li is an Autograph Man. A little like being a munchkin, or a good witch or a flying monkey or a rabbi. Not much, without your belief.

The greatest portion of Alex's work is done from home, but on the occasions when he leaves the house he uses the bag. He puts it on the desk now, opens it and into the many folds and pockets he slips Elizabeth Taylors and Veronica Lakes, Gene Tierneys and James Masons, Rosemary Clooneys and Jules Munshins, back to back, separated by sheaths of plastic. Today, along with the regulars, he fills it with an auction catalogue, some racy photographic items (Bettie Page, Marilyn, Jayne Mansfield, various Playmates – for a private customer he hoped to see at the auction), a folder of private letters from David Ben-Gurion to his tailor, a banana, a difficult Russian novel he had no intention of reading and an autograph magazine he did.

The phone rang.

'Obviously,' said Adam crossly, 'you have no right to mine or anyone else's friendship, really, any more. You've finally disqualified yourself. That's what anti-social behaviour means, Alex, that's the result.'

'Adam? *Adam!*' said Alex. He was delighted to hear from his friend. Hearing Adam's voice sat firmly in the pros column of life.

'No,' said Adam, 'listen. I'm serious. Two facts: she has a broken finger, index. And she also has a strained neck. That's *neck*, Alex. Imagine my reaction. Your girlfriend, yes. But also my sister.'

'Wait: Esther? She didn't say anything.'

'That would be because she's not talking to you. For no good reason, however, I am.'

'That's big of you.'

'Yeah, I think so. *And*, in exchange, these are the things I want. One, you owe me back *The Girl from Peking*. You're now two weeks overdue. You need to *buy your own copy*. Sometimes other people might want to rent it? Two, you need to phone Esther *immediately* and start I don't know what. Grovelling. And three, I want you to go and see a doctor because that was some sort of allergic reaction, Tandem, that wasn't normal. And I'm talking about a *proper* doctor, not some Chinatown con-artist. *Alex*,' sighed Adam, 'you let me down. That evening was meant to be . . . a religious experiment. You turned it into the Tandem roadshow. Not everything in the world has to turn into the Tandem roadshow. You are not the world. There are other people in this film we call life. Alex? Alex?'

'I'm here. Listening.'

'You *scared* me, mate. Joseph said when he went round to yours later you were behaving really weirdly, practically speaking in tongues. Hmm? Alex?'

Alex maintained what he hoped was a dignified silence. He had read about them in novels; this was his first attempt.

'Hello? *Hello?* Do you want to talk about the car?'

Alex's stomach turned over, he began to moan. Adam had paid for half of that car.

'*Ug.* Not really.'

'Good. Me neither.'

'Uu-uug. *Uuug.*'

Adam whistled. 'Oh, Alex. I know, I know. Don't worry, because I still love you. Though I'm alone in that, mate, at the moment. Fan club of one. Come round to the shop later. Promise, yes? You need to get out of the house at this point, I think. Promise? On your note?'

Alex grunted. He resented these promises. Their unbreakability was restrictive. As a rule among them all, his father's notes were to be invoked only with great caution. You had to earn your right to speak of them. Joseph very rarely mentioned them. Rubinfine knew not to refer to them at all.

'Good. We're open all day. Esther won't be in. Which is probably for the best in the current climate. We need to talk seriously about something. You know what date it is today, right?'

The phone went dead. Alex heaved his bag on to his shoulder

and touched, in order, the things he always touched before leaving his bedroom: a small chipped Buddha on his desk, a signed **Muhammad Ali** poster and the old pound note, Blu-Tacked to the top of the door-frame.

2

Reaching the kitchen, he clicked his heels together and bowed to Grace, who was standing on the sideboard, actually standing, on two legs, either stretching or making some last-ditch attempt to evolve. Alex put the kettle on to the boil and got a flask from the cupboard. He untied a little plastic bag of bitter-smelling herbs and Grace retreated, backing herself into a cupboard. Alex emptied the herbs into the flask. He added hot water. It was called *Chia i*, the Tea of Spring, supposedly, but black as all hell. Smelt bad, looked bad. Oh, and hello, tasted bloody awful too. But it was for *widening and dispersing* heaviness in the lungs, according to his Dr Huang of Soho. Alex's lungs felt heavy. Everything felt heavy. He screwed on the cap and put the flask in the pocket of his bag.

Opening the door of his living room, he now remembered quite clearly that under the prolonged influence of a hallucinogen he had swerved his car into a bus-stop while his girlfriend Esther sat in the passenger seat. There were no words for how sorry he was about this. Nor was there anyone to tell. He was not a Catholic. He lived alone. Not for the first time he had the feeling that he lacked sufficient outlets. Instead of his life being shaped like a funnel, through which things passed and maybe refined themselves, it was more like what do you call those things? Stress-balls? Made all out of elastic bands and each day you add another elastic band? Tighter. Bigger. More involved. That's how it was for him. And that's how he imagined the life of a Catholic, anyway. As a sort of funnel. Poor Esther.

He crossed the floor and knelt down before the television. He retrieved *The Girl from Peking* from the video recorder. He put it into its case and felt a soothing pulse of happiness. Prompted by beauty. On the cover were the two beautiful faces of his favourite actress, the musical star Kitty Alexander. In the first picture on the right she was dressed as a Peking girl, her eyes sellotaped into an approximation of his own epicanthic fold, wearing her coolie hat and cheongsam. She was lost on the streets of fifties Broadway. And then, on the left, the same girl but now made-over, dressed as the toast of Hollywood, in a mushroom-shaped ball gown, with the little white gloves, the pink princess slippers, the coil of lustrous black hair peeking over one shoulder. The story of the film, essentially, was the progress from the picture on the right to the picture on the left. You had to read the video case backwards, like Hebrew.

There was a split in the protective plastic. Alex slipped his finger in and felt around, touching first one Kitty and then the other. *Citizen Kane. Battleship Potemkin. Gone with the Wind. La Strada.* It amazed him that so many people, in fact, it would be fair to say, *most people*, were unaware that the 1952 Celebration Pictures musical *The Girl from Peking* starring Jules Munshin as Joey Kay and Kitty Alexander as May-Ling Han was in fact the greatest movie ever made. Carefully, he squeezed her into a fold of his bag.

In the hallway he took his waxy trench coat off the stand and put it on. He felt small in it today. He was twenty-seven years old. He was emotionally undeveloped, he supposed, like most Western kids. He was probably in denial of death. He was certainly suspicious of enlightenment. Above all, he liked to be entertained. He was in the habit of mouthing his own personality traits to himself like this while putting his coat on – he suspected that farm boys and people from the Third World never did this, that they were less self-conscious. He was still *still* slightly thrilled by the idea of receiving post addressed to him and not to his mother. Bending down, he picked up a bundle from the mat and flicked through bills, bills, pizza advert, bank statement, envelopes from America containing movie stars and presidents, a brochure regarding erectile dysfunction, a free package of creamy foundation for an imaginary white woman he wasn't sleeping with.

3

Occasionally he went to Western doctors. They prescribed things to relax him (the ugly neologism of choice was *de-stress*), ranging from fresh air to ball games to little coloured pills. Last year he had visited Poland and walked the placid squares of Cracow dosed up to the eyeballs feeling some sort of communion, holding his breath when the bells rang, keening in cafés over an unbounded loss he couldn't quite name. The pills had a priapic side-effect. Each pair of feminine legs clipping past caused him agony. He had the oddest feeling: a need to impregnate everyone in the country. Walking through a street near Oświęcim he had been confronted by a huge cloud of pollen – at least, he had presumed it pollen and walked straight through it – actually, it was a wasp swarm. Being a young man of Mountjoy, a young man with all the mod cons and every expectation of security, personal and national, he had not been able to conceive that the dark cloud he strode into might be anything dangerous. He had written a poem about all of this, his second poem in twenty-seven years. It was not good. But what might he have been in 1750 in one of these Polish squares wearing boots and a hat and the expectations of the Enlightenment and an impressive gold-buckled belt? What would Rubinfine have been? And Adam? And Joseph? *I saw the best minds of my generation/Accept jobs on the fringes of the entertainment industry.*

The phone rang. The downstairs phone being without cord, Alex picked it up and walked to and fro with it in the hallway for a while, like a new father with a distressed baby, hoping the thing might either make a new noise or fall silent. It did not. On his third fro, he came up against his own front door and stopped. He looked at the door. He turned from it, and tried looking at it again. He drew his fingers along the groove of the unvarnished pine, against it. The phone continued to ring.

4

Autograph collecting, as Alex is not the first to observe, shares much with woman-chasing and God-fearing. A woman who gives up her treasure with too much frequency is not coveted by men. Likewise, a god who makes himself manifest and his laws obvious – such a god is not popular. Likewise a Ginger Rogers is not worth as much as one might imagine. This is because she signed everything she could get her hands on. She was easy. She was whorish. She gave what she had too freely. And now she is common, in the purest meaning of that word. Her value is judged accordingly.

Greta Garbo was not easy. If she put pen to paper at all, Garbo tended to use a pseudonym, Harriet Brown. Garbo would demand that her bank chase up the whereabouts of any cheque she had written that had not been cashed. She wouldn't let her name go, even on a receipt. A Garbo autograph, even a bad one, is still worth about six thousand pounds. Kitty Alexander signed even less than Garbo. Kitty was as awkward and invisible as Jehovah. She was aloof. The public hated her for it. And in time she was forgotten, for the public do not like to be ignored. But Autograph Men are rather more masochistic than the public (the public are primarily sadistic), they *enjoy* contempt. The Autograph Men remembered Kitty, always. These are the same people for whom untimely deaths are good business, along with assassinations, and serial murders, and high-profile failures. Monroe's first husband, the third man on the moon, the Fifth Beatle. They have peculiar tastes. For a long time Kitty Alexander's autograph has been one of the most sought-after scribbles in this peculiar world. Most Autograph Men have given up the hope of ever getting one. Not Alex. Every week since he was fourteen, Alex has sent a letter to Kitty, to an address in Manhattan, her fan-club address. Never once has he received a response. Not once. Only a drawer full of form letters, signed by the fan-club president. And therefore, *therefore*, it takes Alex a long moment, therefore, to remember why, how, *by what means*, a blank postcard with Kitty's autograph clearly written upon it has come to be pinned, like Luther's declaration, to the back of his own front door. Carefully, he unpins it and holds it up to the light. It is exquisite. It is real. Or he is not Alex-Li Tandem. He presses the talk button.

'Alex,' says Joseph in his quiet way, 'listen to me one more time. You did not receive it from God. Nor did you receive it in the post. You forged it, Alex, you were on a very bad trip. Everybody was. Listen to me. It isn't real, it never will be real and things do not become real simply because we want them to be so.'

THREE / *Netsah*

Eternity • Three rabbis • The problem of the bookcase • The world is broken • Alex's secret book • Rebecca's midgets • Rubinfine's goyish tastes • Bette Davis was Jewish

The black trees, vivid against the blue sky, were elms. The crazy boxes, each containing one regretful man, were Ford Mondeos. The birds, for the most part, were magpies. And the tall young man with the oriental look, deliberately slowing his pace down the Mountjoy Road, was none other than Alex-Li Tandem. He realized he was heading directly for three men staring at an open car boot, and he didn't like it. He had not been spotted yet, but soon he would be. One of these men was a rabbi well known to him. Where to hide? From here he could see Adam's video store, Hollywood Alphabet, like an open cave across the street. Closer by, one of these outdoor toilets, fitted with the mechanical doors and the urban myths. But for sanctuary it was too late. There was no escape. Nothing to be done.

'*Alex!*'

'Hullo, Rubinfine.'

'Alex, Alex, *Alex*. What a day, no? What a gift of a day!'

With gloomy clarity, Alex noted that Rubinfine's smile this morning was merely a grimace the other way up. He stood with his right foot crooked up against the *JUSTICE* side of Mountjoy's War

Memorial, a huge stone monolith engraved with four values – *JUSTICE*, *COURAGE*, *HONOUR* and, for some reason, *PATIENCE* – a proud commemoration of Mountjoy's wartime sacrifices, although Mountjoy itself had not been built until 1952. Two other men, unknown to Alex, stood at the corner of *COURAGE* and *PATIENCE*.

'And yet,' said Rubinfine solemnly, 'even on a day such as this, we are presented with a problem.'

He put his hands on his hips in the oddly feminine way he had sometimes and gaped into space. Before him, a parked Citroën, its boot open, gaped back. Quickly, Alex became panicked. Although already outside, he began looking about him in the manner of a man searching for the exit sign.

'Look, Mark,' he said, 'I mean, *Rabbi* Rubinfine – you know what? I actually can't really stop? Heading for the tube. I've got an auction on this morning, you know how it is. Places to go, people to buy. So, if you don't mind, actually, I might just –'

'*Alex-Li*,' said Rubinfine. The beauty spot on his cheek twitched and, with it, his new and unpleasant moustache took a leap to the right. He cupped his hands round Alex's face. He was wearing a salmon-coloured v-neck, paired with some ridged green cords, a long houndstooth coat and a pair of black trainers.

'When a man hurries,' said Rubinfine, trying to sound Talmudic, 'the first things he forgets are his toothbrush and his God.'

This kind of thing drove Alex crazy. In his opinion, Rubinfine was too young to be making up aphorisms. He was only three years older than Alex. He was thirty. Only thirty. You can quote all you like at thirty, but that's where it's got to end.

'Now,' puffed Rubinfine, 'other things being equal, I've some friends here I want you to meet. This is Rabbi Darvick and Rabbi Green. Rabbi Darvick visits us from Brooklyn, New York.

Rabbi Green, you may have met, actually. He's a Mountjoy man. We're attending a rabbinical conference – in Grantam Park? Lasts a week. We're swapping ideas, learning tolerance,' said Rubinfine, grinning at Green, who seemed to barely tolerate him. 'Come and say hello.'

Darvick was small and round and in slacks, indistinguishable from a civilian, an Ultra-Progressive like Rubinfine. Green was Orthodox, much taller and with the corkscrew curls of payes, pale-skinned and flame-haired, wearing a very sharp suit and a tallis.

'Right. Of course. I was being rude. Rabbi Darvick,' said Alex, drawing a hand from his pocket, 'it's nice to meet you. Rabbi Green. I'm not sure . . . have we? We must have, at some point, I suppose . . . Or maybe not?'

Rabbi Darvick made the sound of having had something caught at the back of his throat, having released it and being pleased with the fact. Rabbi Green made a noise of acknowledgement which Alex, a young man without illusions, took for what it was: a grunt.

'Alex-Li,' said Rubinfine, 'we have a problem. Maybe you could help us with?'

Rubinfine tilted his head and smiled.

'What's your hurry? Shift in the cosmos? Is someone selling a Kitty whatshername or something?'

Poor Alex made a fist in his pocket. 'It's Kitty *Alexander*. And no. All right? Just an important auction, and I'm already late.'

'But *Alex-Li* . . .'

Fuming, Alex made a dance to the left, but Rubinfine met him. Alex moved to the right, and there was the rabbi again. Above them two magpies flipped black and blue from one bare tree to another across the street, carrying nothing shiny in their beaks, no gems, no glass, for magpies rarely do. Realizing the battle was lost, Alex grabbed at his flask, uncapped it and took a swig.

'Hmm, that smells *great*,' said Rubinfine, holding Alex by his elbow and ushering him towards the car boot. 'Now. Do you see it?'

It was a mahogany bookcase, grand and in the Georgian style. It was about six inches wider than the boot. It lay on its side on the pavement. This bookcase was not going to fit in the boot, Alex saw that much.

'Rabbi,' he said evenly, 'it's just too big. I mean, it's *too big*.'

Green raised his eyebrows as if this were news. Following a cue of Darvick's, he made a frame of his fingers like a cinematographer and peered at the bookcase. Rubinfine bent down and traced his finger along a shelf.

'I *suppose* we'll have to push it along the back seats . . . maybe even as far as the passenger seat! Or – wait a minute, now wait – what about *your* car?'

Alex pushed both hands deep into the sad wells of his coat pockets. So he had been set up. 'Yes, all right. Well done. Envelope opened. Best Actor awarded.'

He made as if to walk away, but Rubinfine caught him by the wrist.

'Yes, Alex, naturally I heard about Tuesday. And far be it for me to say I told you so, but. Now, what are my two rules? One,' he said, sticking up a thumb, 'mysticism and theosophy of all kinds are to be avoided. Given the old heave-ho. And, two: illegal substances can't help anyone get closer to God. I spend my whole life telling Adam this. I mean, don't I? And now look.'

'Why're you giving *me* the lecture?' asked Alex sulkily. 'Give Adam the lecture. It's *his* thing.'

'I've said it before,' intoned Rubinfine, shaking his head at the floor. 'At best, it's a thirteenth-century fake, Alex, at *best*. The letters, the lights, the *mystic writing*. The Zohar is a pretty good novel, no more no less. It's also eleven hundred years later than they say it is, did you know that? Read your Scholem, my friend. *Yes*. Basically, it's a forgery. It's up there with Shabbatai Zevi, the Lochness, Bigfoot . . .'

During this little speech, a pensive look had come over Green's long face, like the sad mask of Keaton in the silents. He knelt down and placed his hands on the bookshelf. Darvick was agitated, tapping his right foot against the monument, frowning at Rubinfine.

'Rabbi, with all respect etc.,' said Darvick sharply, 'Kabbalah is the centre of the mystery. The point is, surely, that it's only for the truly learned men, for the really big fish.'

'HaShem *needs* us,' Green murmured, 'without us He is incomplete. The world is *broken*. This is the whole of the Kabbalah, Rabbi. This is not to be made light of, or rather,' said Green with a smile at his own sudden pun, 'this is *made out of light*. The Kabbalah is the light hidden *within* the Torah.'

'Woah, woaaah . . . now, stop, everyone,' said jumpy Rubinfine, laughing, trying to pat both rabbis simultaneously. 'Now, everybody calm down. Am I an idiot? Am I? Obviously, I wasn't making myself clear. Try again: what I *meant* was that people shouldn't meddle with what they don't understand. Trust me about this, please, Rabbi. If the world is broken, Alex-Li Tandem is not the man to mend it.' Rubinfine laughed again and encouraged others to laugh.

'Well, one thing's for sure,' said Darvick loudly, 'it's obvious he can't help us.'

Darvick pushed by Alex and stretched over the bookcase, opening his palm to reveal a measuring tape and pulling the ribbon from its cradle.

'He just doesn't look the type to *me*. Looks *schloompy*.'

'He's an *intellectual*,' explained Rubinfine irritably. 'They all look like that.'

'How's Rebecca?' queried Alex in a loud and cordial tone, just for revenge. At the thought of his wife of five years Rubinfine struggled with his face, and, from among several less benign choices, a look reminiscent of Lenin after his second stroke won out.

'Fine, fine. Busy. Arranging a fund-raiser, I believe. Charity. Barn-dance . . .' Rubinfine's voice began to disappear. 'For midgets. Though I'm told they're not called that any more.'

'People of restricted growth,' boomed Darvick with authority.

Rubinfine looked desperate, opened his mouth and then shut it again.

Alex smiled warmly. 'Right. Well, send her my love. Always helping somebody, that's Rebecca.'

Rubinfine tried to restrain it but a noticeable shudder passed over him, the tremor of the target board after a bull's-eye.

'Alex,' he said stiffly, 'I've been meaning to ask . . .'

Rubinfine loved nothing better than to end a sentence before it was actually finished. He thought it appropriately rabbinical. You could ride the awkward silence for as long as you liked with Rubinfine, but he would not speak again until you prompted him.

'About . . . ?'

'That book of yours. The insulting one. Regarding goyishness and what-have-you. I was wondering whether there'd been any recent progress? Or maybe you've come to your senses? Abandoned it?'

Alex swore, very gently, at Rubinfine. Rubinfine gave Alex the

International Gesture for not swearing in front of rabbi-looking rabbis (crossed eyes, flared nostrils). Alex gave Rubinfine the IG for not mentioning his book, *ever* (tongue curled behind lower front teeth, mouth open).

'Fine. Well, another thing: have you any Harrison Ford at the moment? Maybe some Carrie Fisher?'

Alex willed blankness on to his features. Rubinfine motioned to Darvick and Green that the bookcase might be lifted, and now each rabbi took a corner, leaving one corner lurching dangerously, until Rubinfine's long thigh slipped underneath to support it.

'Maybe some later Harrison?' repeated Rubinfine, straightening up, wiping his sweaty forehead with the underside of his wrist. 'From circa *Witness*, maybe. A film still. Just an 8 × 10.'

Alex felt a deep satisfaction at the thought of an 11 × 14 colour photo of Ford in the *Millennium Falcon* boldly signed, coincidentally,

To Mark, keep up the good work,
Harrison Ford

which sat in his briefcase this very day and which he had no intention of selling to Mark Rubinfine even if he gave him twenty thousand pounds and his liver.

'I don't think so . . .' began Alex, rubbing his chin. 'I've got some Marlon Brando, one Brando . . . small, though, 7 × 5. And a bit late in the day. Honestly, he doesn't look his best, but I don't think that overly detracts. I could give it to you for about two hundred and fifty. Or thereabouts.'

Rubinfine shook his head. 'That's not for me. It's really Ford I want. I'm a Ford man, Alex-Li, now, you *know* that.'

Rubinfine's unremittingly goyish taste in autographs was a hard one to get your head round. And it was never just a little bit goyish. It was goyish in the extreme. It was Harrison Ford in a film about the *Amish* type of goyish.

'This is the Autograph Man?' said Rabbi Green.

'This is the Autograph Man,' said Rubinfine.

'You're the Autograph Man?' asked Green.

'For my sins,' said Alex-Li Tandem.

'You collect autographs?' asked Green.

'I'm not a collector,' said Alex-Li, loudly and slowly, 'I'm a trader. It's not really a personal thing. I prefer to think of it as a business.'

Green frowned. The left side of his face hiked up as if some God, fishing for rabbis, had just hooked himself a juicy one.

'You run around after people?' asked Green, wagging a finger. 'You know, with a pen and paper? People deserve a little privacy. Just because people are on the television, this doesn't mean they don't have feelings. You should leave people alone.'

Alex took a long cleansing breath. 'I don't hunt. I don't hunt any more and I don't collect. I collect only in so far as I *trade*. I buy, I sell. Like any other business. I don't wait outside theatres at midnight. That's kids' stuff.'

'Well . . .' said Darvick, going over his front teeth with a muscular-looking tongue, 'if you're so clever . . . have you got *Bette Davis*? You're probably too young to remember Bette but –'

'No,' said Alex firmly, patting his closed case as if to ensure that Bette was absent, 'no . . . I had an early still from *Jezebel* but it went last week.'

Darvick clapped his hands. 'He knows Bette? Now, you see, I *liked* Bette. She had a certain flavour about her. People talk about divas these days, but they don't really know. Well, well. A schloompy guy like this, you wouldn't guess he knows Bette. But he knows Bette.'

Tandem shut his mouth, thrust his free hand into his trouser pocket and felt his own testicles, a familiar action that had saved him from grievous misdemeanour in the past.

'I kind of know everyone,' he answered quietly, admirably. 'This is my card. I'll write my home phone and my name. Look, phone me in a few weeks, Rabbi Darvick. I'll keep an eye out in case any Bette turns up. She's hardly obscure.'

'Bub, I won't be here in a few weeks, this is a flying visit,' said Darvick, reaching over and taking the business card anyway. 'Call that a signature? Alex . . . what? I can't read that.'

'Li Tandem. I thought I wrote it perfe – look, oh, well, it's typed just there, Rabbi, on the other side. Alex-Li Tandem.'

'Alex-Li Tandem? *Tandem Autographs: More Stars than the Solar System.* Huh? What kind of a name is that, anyway? Tandem? You converted?'

'The father, Li-Jin Tandem – *may his memory be a blessing* – was Chinese,' explained Rubinfine, and with so much phoney solemnity Alex wanted to reach over and stab him in the eye with his house keys. 'Tan, originally. Someone thought Tandem sounded better. Odd – clearly doesn't. Mother, Sarah. Lives in the country now. Lovely lady.'

'Is that a fact,' said Darvick, 'Chinese. Is that a fact.'

'Those are the facts, yes,' said Alex-Li. 'Now gentlemen, if you'll excuse me . . .'

'You're excused, you're excused,' said Rabbi Darvick, petulant, bending down and hooking his fingers under the bookcase once again. 'If you're not a help, you're a hindrance!'

'If you're not for us, you're against us!' said Rabbi Green.

'Well,' said Rubinfine, 'maybe you'll stop involving yourself with things beyond your understanding? Maybe. And maybe I will see you on Shabbat. We need to talk seriously, Alex. Maybe we will. Maybe a lot of things. But "maybe" is a word for men, Alex. "Maybe" is for Mountjoy. But in God's mind, no man says "*maybe*".'

'Yeah,' said Alex, 'OK.'

'"*Maybe*",' said Rubinfine. 'This word is not in His vocabulary.'

'Right,' said Alex. 'Got it.'

'And Alex, if you.'

Stress induced Alex-Li Tandem's jaw to lock for a moment and it was some effort to free it.

'If I what, Rabbi?'

'If you get any Ford, remember me.'

FOUR / *Hod*

Splendour • One tube, many people • Goyish mime • She who sees •
Shadows • Jewishness and Goyishness • John Lennon was Jewish • The
night in question • Enduring everyone • The Ballad of Esther Jacobs • The
Tragedy of Alex-Li • The fundamental goyishness of Leonard Cohen

I

By the doors, a very old man who had made a dreadful smell. The
carriage were putting on a brave face, though, for surely he could
not help it. By the NO EATING poster, two schoolboys eating.
Standing at the extreme other end, three women, dressed identi-
cally in bright polyester flecked, supposedly, with colourful paint.
They were telling humourless anecdotes about their weekends.
They were placed at regular intervals along the melancholy arc of
sexual maturity and they knew it. They laughed frenziedly, jiggling
on the hand-straps, demonstrating what *three women having fun*
looks like. They did not like each other, Alex thought.

Sighing, he opened his flask, took a deep swig. The smell made
his eyes water. Rather than ask him to close the flask, a woman-
wearing-Alice-band to his right performed an elaborate goyish
mime; watch-check, realization of missed stop, little gasp, up on
balls of feet; then got out of her seat at the next station and left the
train. Thirty seconds later Alex spotted her in the adjoining carriage
squished between a very fat man and a nun, such a very tidy
example of karma that he found himself considerably moved.

*

The train was stuck overground between stations when Alex's phone rang. Without thinking the thing through properly, he answered it.

'The thing about a delusion,' Joseph was saying rather smugly, 'is if you allow it to continue, it develops, and then it can get *very* serious.'

Alex could picture him, exactly. He had been to Joseph's office, observed him in his booth. Even in that room of five hundred identical booths Joseph's was peculiar for its total absence of personalization. No photographs, no flags, no jokes. Just the neat package of Klein himself, his polished shoes, his compact computer, his hands-free phone. Always the only man in a suit and tie. One of the very few who arrived at his desk by a quarter to nine. Leant forward, both elbows on the desk, his fingers clutching each other in imitation of a church roof. Forehead pressed against the steeple.

'Joe, I'm on a train.'

'Yes. And I'm at work.'

'I'm stuck between stations.'

'Alex, I have to take a call now.'

'Joseph, please don't put me on hold. If you put me on hold I'm going to grow a tumour.'

'We need to talk seriously.'

'Everybody wants to talk seriously to me today.'

'I've got to answer this – you're going to have to listen to some music. I'm sorry about it. I've got a claimant on the other phone. Hold the line, please. Hello, Heller Insurance?'

Joseph had been working for Heller since he left college, a fact that depressed Alex more than it did Joseph. In the world of Heller, as Alex understood it, the principles of Heisenberg were danger-ously ignored: at Heller, certainty reigned. At Heller, effect was always neatly traced back to cause. And someone always had to pay for it. So if a man tripped, for example over a paving stone, or burnt himself with a cup of hot coffee, he was encouraged to phone the number at the end of the advert so that Heller Insurance might sue somebody on a no-win-no-fee basis, the small-type of which agreement involved a fee whatever the outcome. There were no accidents in the minds of Helleric employees. Only malevolent woundings. And, by coincidence, whenever Joseph happened to be speaking of his work, Alex was usually thinking of some way to seriously injure himself.

Tell me he's lazy, tell me he's slow, sang the phone.

Bored, cradling phone between ear and chin, Alex eyed the youngest of the women in polyester, imagining what it might be like to see her in unlikely underwear and awkward positions. Against his will, his mind went along with the singing phone.

Singer: Ava Gardner (1922–90)
Song: 'Can't help lovin' dat man'
Film: *Showboat* (1951)

I was married to Mickey Rooney!
The marriage represented the biggest female-to-male height differential in Hollywood!

As Alex saw it, the only fortunate aspect of Joseph's job at Heller Insurance was the fact that Joseph himself never had to know what it was like to be put on hold by Heller Insurance.

As the song finished and started once more, Alex remembered a sentiment from his favourite (and only) poet. Why let this toad called *work* squat on your life? Joseph should have been an Autograph Man. It was in his nature. He was careful, shrewd. But also passionate, also devoted. The perfect coalescence of collector and trader. When he was a boy Joseph's enthusiasm for the trade was so strong it was viral; Alex had caught it and kept it ever since. At fifteen Alex started to sell seriously, at twenty he had a business. But Joseph, ever under the spell of his father, never had the guts to make his hobby his career. There was cowardice in this, Alex thought, and he blamed it for the strained state of their relations. Alex thought Joseph resented him, and Alex resented Joseph for resenting him. Neither of them spoke of their resentments, real or imagined. And both of them resented that. As a formula for the slow disintegration of friendship, the above is practically mathematical.

'Alex?'

'Still here.'

'What's the music, out of interest? Vivaldi?'

'No. Show tunes. Bad ones. Don't put me on hold again, man. I barely got through the first time.'

'Alex, have you spoken to Adam?'

'This morning. Before I spoke to you. Regarding the car disaster. I drove Esther into a bus-stop.'

'I heard. What did he say?'

'He said he wanted to talk to me, seriously.'

'Yes, he said that he would.'

Alex thought he heard something pointed in this and bristled at the idea of Adam and Joseph speaking together, without him. Rubinfine and Adam, Joseph and Rubinfine – these couplings did not bother him. He knew the measure and the depth of them. But he understood little of Joseph and Adam's relationship, except that it was close, and he dreaded this, vaguely. He knew they shared an interest (Adam's practical, Joseph's theoretical) in mystic Judaism, specifically the Kabbalah. Alex worried that his and Adam's shared interest in marijuana and girls might be the less significant bond.

'Well, Alex, the thing is, he asked me to call again.'

Alex silently chewed the inside of his cheek.

'He's – we're *both* a bit worried about some of the things you were saying, on Tuesday night. Particularly the stuff about the . . .'

Joseph's voice let itself go again in a little expulsion of air, which, from Alex's end, sounded like a kiss in the earpiece. Alex decided to help him out.

'About the Kitty, is that it?'

As he spoke, Alex drew the plastic envelope from his bag and took out the postcard. He felt a genuine rush of blood to the head, as if he were a Catholic touching a reliquary. He tried to regulate his breathing. There she was, there she was. The ink was raised off the coarse paper, like a scab. Kitty, famously, dotted her only *i* with a little lopsided heart. Alex touched it now and loved her for it. He believed she was the first. The first to dot *i*'s thus. He believed, further, that those who create clichés share some splinter of the Creation. *Dog* became a cliché. *Trees* too.

'We-ell,' began Joseph carefully, 'you got a bit out of hand, and that's *fine*, that's nothing to be *ashamed* of – but then, when one wakes up, it's hard sometimes to let go of one's delusions . . . you have to do it softly, I think. It's *OK*, and nobody thinks any *less* of you – we just want to check you're OK. We're just worried about you.'

'Worried I'm going to sell it?' asked Alex in a guarded voice.

The line went quiet.

'Alex?' said Joseph, after a minute. 'But I don't understand.'

'Look, Joe,' snapped Alex, 'I'm not being rude – no, actually, I am being rude, actually – I really don't see what it's got to do with you. You're not even in the business any more, you know? With the best will in the world, why don't you just keep out of it?'

'Wait – sell it? I don't . . . Alex . . . that's academic, isn't it?'

'Academic how?'

'What do you mean, how?'

'I mean *how*?'

Joseph emitted a laugh like his father's, sudden and without gaiety.

'What's funny?' asked Alex coldly.

'OK, well, let's say for the sake of argument,' said Joseph pompously, 'that you tried to sell it, Alex – inside the autograph community. Then how would it be ethical for me not to say something? I mean, I may not be, strictly speaking, *in the business* but I *know* the dealers who would take a risk on something like that, they're *friends* of mine. And knowing what I know, knowing that it's not *real*, I'm not simply going to sit back and become basically a kind of *accessory* to the crime –'

'Joseph *Klein*,' said Alex drily, 'no one's making false accusations against you. No one's coming to take you away. You've done nothing wrong.'

'You're hilarious. Look, *Alex* –'

'No, look, *you* look. I think you're bloody jealous. It's *my* autograph, all right, it was sent to *me* –'

The train chugged back into action. Alex watched the thick coloured electric cords merge from four strands into one rope, hugging the side of the wall as the train slipped briefly into a tunnel. The phone's reception was so clear he could hear the nervous tug of Joseph breathing. Why was he still getting reception? How big were these satellites anyway? Big as planets? Were they carcinogenic? Alex put his head between his knees.

'That's not *true*,' said Joseph very sadly. 'I'm never jealous of you. I'm hurt you'd think that.'

And with Joseph these weren't just words. You could hear the hurt, you could *feel* it. Alex had not yet come across another man so easily affected by the words of others. He'd had plenty of sticks and stones as a boy, Joseph, on account of being small and slender and posh; he'd already done sticks, stones, fists, shifty kicks, flesh wounds and shoves. But it was words that truly got to him. He still flinched at a swear word. Not long ago Alex had seen him on the other side of the high street and shouted his name. Joseph fell over.

'Joseph . . . look,' said Alex with shame, 'I'm sorry. I'm being nasty – I didn't mean to be nasty. I just feel a bit sick, to be honest. I've the worst hangover man has ever known. And I *don't* understand why you're on my case.'

'I don't understand,' said Joseph in a quiet, worried voice, 'what you mean by the word *sent*.'

'I mean *sent*. I have it. It's real. It's in my hands. It was sent to me.'

'Right. And that would be? Post? Heaven?'

'Sent,' said Alex again, with conviction. 'Just *sent*. Look – I'm not saying I can *explain* it –'

'*Bloody* hell. Alex. *Alex*–'

Joseph kept on talking. Alex brought Kitty right up under his nose where he could see her. That exquisite *tt*, achieved with just one lunge of the pen, curling in on itself, carrying on.

'The thing is,' said Joseph, as Alex tuned back in, 'I was *there*. You went into the kitchen and you came back with that autograph. That's what happened. I'm sorry. But that's a fact.'

Through thin, angry eyes, Alex watched the eldest woman in polyester reposition a handbag to obscure the swell of her abdomen. A man across from him sat with his hands cupping his groin. The boys had just finished eating. As the train picked up speed they made a face and put their fingers in their ears. No one travels anywhere any more without imagining, if only for a second, the moment of impact. And if the crucial second were *this* second, thought Alex, every one of these people would be better prepared than me.

'Alex . . . I don't mean to be – but do you know what *date* it is today? That is, next Thursday? Your mum told Adam and Adam told me. Don't you think that might be relevant? Mate, I think you're having a breakdown. Hello, Heller Insurance.'

'What?'

'Hold the line, please.'

Singer: Ann Miller (1919–)
Song: 'Prehistoric Man'
Film: *On the Town* (1949)

I had rickets as a child!

With this space in my brain, thought Alex, I could have learnt Hebrew. I could have been somebody.

The music stopped.

'Why is it,' said Alex, feeling combative, 'that Adam has a mystical experience twice a week and that's just fine, that's dandy, but when *I* do, *finally*, everybody thinks I'm a lunatic?'

There was no reply. Alex assumed the connection dead.

'Are you at all worried, Alex?' came the unheard question, just as Alex brought his thumb to the off button, 'that you might be delusional? That you might be depressed? Alex?'

One of Alex's talents, one of the few left over from his precocious childhood, is knowing exactly how long he's got before he throws up. It is perfect timing, then; conversation ended, bag and flask grabbed, out of the train, across the platform for the Westbound, a lunula of vomit on to the empty tracks and then the arrival of the train taking him to the centre of things. A destination is spelt out in letters made of light.

2

Reaching the surface, Alex snuggled up close to a harassed mother at the ticket barrier so that her ticketed and his unticketed body might pass through together as one. It had never failed him before, this tactic, but here came a hand, heavy on his shoulder, and he was taken to the next level of punishment: a grey-haired woman sat behind a pane of glass. Her left leg was in plaster, resting on a pile of books that in turn was balanced on a stool. Her spectacles hung from a chain. A plastic name tag, printed in a font meant to approximate the natural sweep of a human pen, said *Gladys*.

Alex smiled. 'Can I get one from Mountjoy, please.'

Gladys cupped her ear theatrically, International Gesture for *Come again?*

'You waan what? You goin' Mountjoy?'

'No – no. I just *came* –'

'Bwoy – speak into de ting; me kyan hear you.'

'I said, I just *came* from Mountjoy –'

'So, you want a ticket back dare?'

'No, I – just – the machine at Mount . . . there was a train coming so I just jumped –'

'Oh, I see. You can call me Cassandra, young man, 'cos I see, I see.'

'No, look. Right. No. Let's start again. Wasn't like that, was like this: I just – there was no time to buy . . . so I . . .'

Alex faded. The woman reached for a long piece of home-made something – two pencils bonded with an elastic band – and slipped it down into her cast. Scratched.

'So, what you are sayin' – and feel free to correct me if I am perchance mistaken – is dat you skipped de fare; you jus' skip it like it *nutting* –'

'Wasn't like that –'

'Dareby *ignoring* de executive and legislative decrees of our government –'

'Is this . . . ? I mean – in the wider sense – necess –'

'Not to mention, de *explicit* conditions of travel as set out by de London Underground, available for perusal by anyone *wid eyes*; as well as *violatin'* a communal code of fairness and *right doin's* as implicitly held by your fellow passengers –'

'Yes, ha. Very good. Look, I'm actually running –'

'And last, but *by no means least*, making a nonsense of your own personal conscience wid regard to an *imperative morality* which, if we don't feel it in our bellies, we will find articulated in Exodus. Thou. Shalt. Not. *Steal*.'

Sometimes Alex thought that if you got all the part-time mature students in the world and laid them head to toe around the line of the equator strapped down in some way so they couldn't move, that would be a good thing. Ditto anyone in evening classes.

'Ten pounds, please, young man. Wid de fare on top.'

Alex didn't have ten pounds, so he handed over some plastic, which made the woman suck her teeth, lift her leg off the *The Last Days of Socrates* and go hobbling to the back of her box to get the mechanical swiper thing. She swiped, she passed it through, he signed, he passed it through, she held it up next to his card, he smiled. She looked at him with suspicion.

'Is dis yours?'

'What? Is there something wrong with it?'

She looked at the card again, at the signature, at the card, and then passed it back to him. 'I don't know. Mebbe wid you. You look like you sick or some ting. Like you goin' to fall over.'

'Sorry, Gladys, are you a doctor? Or a prophet? I mean, as well? Or can I go now?'

She scowled. Called for the next person in line. Alex grabbed his flask from the counter. Stalked towards the exit.

Outside, he took a sharp left, intending just to run the length of the street, turn left and walk straight into the auction house. But he had not counted on the sales. On the women. The sun was low enough to spotlight them, they were outlined very precisely. They put Alex in mind of the Chinese shadow puppets of the old Tangshan Theatre. They moved fast and did not blur. So beautiful! In through doors, setting off tinkling bells, back out, doing it again. Handsome, quick, lithe: deer doing the hunting for a change. There was a chasm between this and the manner in which Alex shopped (a sort of blind lunge from store to store, and only for necessities, toilet paper, toothpaste). These women made desire look efficient. There was nothing in this street they wanted enough to induce any loss of poise. They were amazing.

But I am too late already! thought Alex, looking at his watch. His jumper was mohair, his neck was sweating. Still, how could this be resisted? In preparation, he paused in the middle of the street, took off his trench coat, tied it round his waist. He took a tiny pad out of his pocket and pressed it into his palm, ready to take notes. And then Alex began to walk, slowly, among them, splitting them down the centre as they went, as he always did, for his hobby, his research, his book. Goyish. *Jewish*. Goyish. Jewish. Goyish. *Goyish*. Jewish. *Goyish!*

Not them, not as people – there was no fun to be had out of that. Only wars. No, other things. A movement of an arm. A type of shoe. A yawn. A dress. A whistled tune.

It gave him a simple pleasure. Other people wondered why. He chose not to wonder why. All possible psychological, physiological and neurological hypotheses (including the *mixed race people see things double* theory, and the *fatherless children seek out restored symmetry*, and *especially* the *Chinese brains are hardwired for ying and yang dualistic thought*) made him want to staple his eyeballs to a wall. He did it because he did it. He had an unfinished manuscript that maybe someone would publish one day called *Jewishness and Goyishness*, the culmination of his work on the subject. *Jewishness and Goyishness* had once been a fairly academic text by any standards. It had an introduction, it had essays and explanations, footnotes, marginalia (he had imagined it as an appendix, a sequel, if you like, to Max Brod's effort of 1921: *Heidentum, Christentum, Judentum*. He was also indebted to the popular comedian Lenny Bruce). It was split into many different categories, things like:

Foods
Clothes
The nineteenth century
Cars
Body parts
The lyrics of *John Lennon*
Books
Countries
Journeys
Medicines

Each category was then split into Jewish and Goyish things relating to it. In a spasm of superstition early on, he had made the decision to mark the sections of the book with the Tetragrammaton, God's four-letter name:

YHWH

Occasionally, when the section was particularly contentious, he used its more potent Hebrew incarnation:

יהוה

As if the invocation of the holy name would protect his heresy.

He had been young, naive, when he began it. It was a different book now. It was still about Jewishness and Goyishness, but now that was *all* it was about. No essay was more than a page in length. There were no captions to the many illustrations. All stripped away. Just a few footnotes here and there. No commentary. Now he was left with the beautiful core of the thing itself: three hundred pages and counting of what amounted to a two-sided list. Jewish books (often not written by Jews), Goyish books (often not written by Goys), Jewish office items (the stapler, the pen holder), Goyish office items (the paper-clip, the mouse-mat), Jewish trees (sycamore, poplar, beech), Goy trees (oak, sitka, horse chestnut), Jewish smells of the seventeenth century (rose oil, sesame, orange zest), Goy smells of the seventeenth century (sandalwood, walnuts, wet forest floor). And God's unsayable name on every page. Over and over. It was a thing of beauty. He did not let people read it. If ever it came up in conversation, he found himself spoken to as if he were a character in a film. Rubinfine told him he was *wasting his life*. Adam *worried for his sanity*. It was Joseph's opinion that to discuss it at all was to *indulge the dangerous idea* that the thing actually existed. Esther found *the whole thing utterly offensive*.

Well, maybe *Jewishness and Goyishness* wasn't for everyone. But didn't everyone get *everything*? Hadn't they had enough yet? Everything on earth is tailored for this *everyone*. Everyone gets all the TV programmes, as near as dammit all of the cinema, and about 80 per cent of all music. After that come the secondary mediums of painting and those other visual arts that do not move. These are generally just for *someone*, and, although you always hear people moaning that there isn't enough of them, in truth *someone* does all right. Galleries, museums, basements in Berlin, studio flats, journals, bare walls in urban centres – someone gets what they want and deserve, most of the time. But where are the things that *no one* wants? Every now and then Alex would see or hear something that appeared to be for no one, but soon enough turned out to be for someone, and, after a certain amount of advertising revenue had been spent, would explode into the world for everyone.

Who was left to make stuff for no one? Just Alex. Only he. *Jewishness and Goyishness* was for no one. You could call it the beginning of a new art movement if it weren't for the sad fact that no one would recognize a new art movement if it came and kicked them in the face. No one was waiting for *Jewishness and Goyishness*. No one wanted it. And it was not finished yet. When it was finished he would know.

For a while now, his book had been in crisis. It was lopsided. Goyishness, in all its forms, had become his obsession. There was now too much in it concerning aluminium foil, sofa covers, push-pins, bookmarks, orchards. In the book, as in his life, Jewishness was seeping away. Three months earlier he had attempted his greatest audacity: a chapter devoted to the argument that Judaism itself was the most Goyish of monotheisms. He failed spectacularly. He became very depressed. He called his mother, who stopped making things out of clay in Cornwall with Derek (the boyfriend) and returned to London to stay in his flat for a few weeks, to keep an eye. But for Sarah it did not come naturally, this mothering role. That had been Li-Jin's thing. Her gift was friendship, and Alex, for his part, did not know how to lie back and have soup brought and temperatures taken. Their progress together was awkward, somewhat comic, like the days of two crook-backed adults living in a Wendy house. And all without Li-Jin. The terrible, undimmed sadness of it. Every time they met, they felt it afresh, as if they had planned a picnic, Alex arriving with all the cutlery, Sarah with the mackintosh squares – where was the food?

Still, Alex (who like most young men remained convinced his mother was uncommonly beautiful even as she thickened and

91

greyed) was charmed by her physical presence, her floaty hippie skirts and scarves, her hands which looked like his, the matter-of-fact way she would suddenly hug him to her chest as one man hugs another man on a playing field. She had things to say.

She said, 'If I'm anything, darling, I'm probably a Buddhist.'

She said, 'You see, when I married your father . . .'

She said, 'I think it's probably important to *do* rather more, and maybe *think* a little less?'

She said, 'Where do you keep your cups?'

Before she left, she gave him a box of papers and stuff relating to the relations.

'You mean this sort of thing?' she said, placing it on his night-stand.

Sarah Hoffman's family. Trinkets and photographs and facts. Here was great-grandfather Hoffman as a young man in European pose, looking cocky, clutching two other young men by the shoulders, the three of them with their thin ties and legs apart, standing in front of some building, some new enterprise, never to be finished. In another, four pretty sisters stand in the snow. Their heads are pitched at various melancholy angles. Only their lean Afghan hound looks at the camera, as if he knows the future secret of their terrible deaths, the location and the order. Elsewhere, a sepia postcard shows Fat Uncle Saul as a young boy. It is a studio portrait of him with palm tree and pith helmet, his sausage legs astride a stuffed miniature pony. This same Saul had believed the Hoffmans were related to the Kafkas of Prague, through marriage. But what's marriage? Alex dug deeper. A tram ticket for a defunct line through a defunct city. Ten zlotys. A pair of sloppy socks of scarlet wool with lilac lozenges. The qualification certificates of an émigré Russian teacher, distant cousin. One bowler hat, crushed. But let somebody else make a mournful list, thought Alex. The same people who keep boxes like these are the types who follow ominous noises into the dark cellar, who build their very homes on top of Indian burial grounds. People from movies. Everyone in these photographs is dead, thought Alex wearily. Tiring, all of it.

3

The night at Adam's, the night in question, this was not the first time Alex meditated on the letters. He had been going more often in recent months, thinking it might help. The procedure was always the same. They got stoned. They sat on the floor, holding big blank drawing pads. Pens at the ready. Staring at the walls. On the far wall, ten years ago, Adam had painted a crude Kabbalistic diagram, ten circles in strange formation. These were, according to Adam, the ten holy spheres, each containing a divine attribute, one of the *sefirot*. Or else they were the ten branches on the Tree of Life, each showing an aspect of divine power. Or they were the ten names of God, ten ways in which he is made manifest. They were also the ten body parts of Adam, the first man. The Ten Commandments. The ten globes of light from which the world was made. Also known as the ten faces of the king. Also known as the Path of Spheres:

The Ten Sefirot

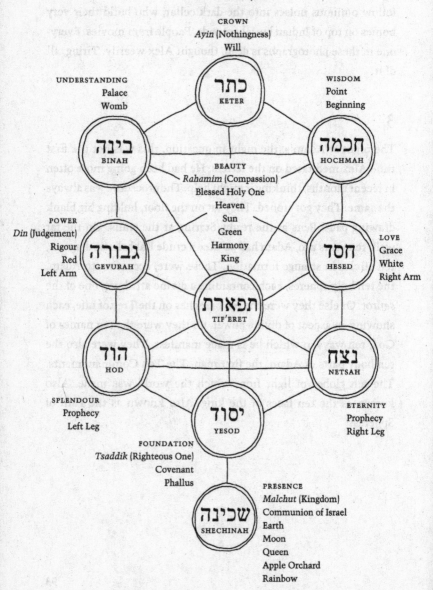

CROWN
Ayin (Nothingness)
Will

UNDERSTANDING
Palace
Womb

WISDOM
Point
Beginning

כתר
KETER

בינה
BINAH

חכמה
HOCHMAH

BEAUTY
Rahamim (Compassion)
Blessed Holy One
Heaven
Sun
Green
Harmony
King

POWER
Din (Judgement)
Rigour
Red
Left Arm

LOVE
Grace
White
Right Arm

גבורה
GEVURAH

חסד
HESED

תפארת
TIF'ERET

הוד
HOD

נצח
NETSAH

SPLENDOUR
Prophecy
Left Leg

ETERNITY
Prophecy
Right Leg

FOUNDATION
Tsaddik (Righteous One)
Covenant
Phallus

יסוד
YESOD

PRESENCE
Malchut (Kingdom)
Communion of Israel
Earth
Moon
Queen
Apple Orchard
Rainbow

שכינה
SHECHINAH

On the opposing wall, Adam had painted something simpler and, to Alex, more beautiful. All twenty-two letters of the Hebrew alphabet. The Path of Letters.

Fig. (b) Wall Two

יהוה

Twenty-two Foundation Letters

He ordained them, He hewed them, He combined them,
He weighed them, He interchanged them. And He
created with them the whole creation and everything to
be created in the future.

א	ב	ג	ד	ה	ו
ALEPH	BET	GIMEL	DALET	HE	VAV
ז	ח	ט	י	כ	ל
ZAYIN	HET	TET	YOD	KAF	LAMED
מ	נ	ס	ע	פ	צ
MEM	NUN	SAMECH	AYIN	PE	TSADI
ק	ר	ש	ת		
KUF	RESH	SHIN	TAV		

The world is broken

As far as this sort of thing goes, they were done very well, Adam having a real ability with a paintbrush. Staring at them for hours in silence, though: that takes a certain commitment. The Journey to God. It is very long. It is quite dull. And always at the moment when Alex was feeling ready to switch on the television and give it up, Adam would begin to visualize his spine as a palm leaf. Off he would go from there, travelling through the spheres, losing himself. But for Alex there was no merging, no loss of self. He didn't understand this idea of unity in nothingness. That sort of thing was beyond him. He felt no magic. Just the thick useless marijuana fug, staring at the letters, sensing nothing much, except vague anthropomorphisms: didn't that one look like a man waving his fist? A crown? Half a menorah? A table? A sleeping foetus? A long-haired sprite?

It was different for Adam. For him, the spheres and the letters put on their full show. Within each he saw worlds, souls, divinities. No doubt it helped to be able to read Hebrew, a trick Alex had never pulled off. But more: Adam did not forfeit wonder. Everything in Adam's world was wondrous. He read only a page of Torah a month, for each letter of it, to him, was a book in itself. In a single meditation session, Adam could copy down his six chosen letters at least twenty times, rearrange them, permutate them, make calculations relating to their numerical values, or their colours, or the prophets they symbolized, or the music they made. Sometimes his soul soared upward and materialized in Israel. It was the time of the glory of the Temple of Jerusalem. The letters were now many storeys high, like skyscrapers leaning over the land. He flew around them, examining every corner. He bathed in their light. He lay down at their feet. Lucky Adam.

'Take a seat,' Adam had said that Tuesday night, throwing Alex a velveteen cushion. The room was as ever: boxy, dark, candlelit. Joseph was cross-legged on the floor. Esther was stretched along the sofa, all legs, too high to move. A video was playing, a favourite of Esther's, an eighties romantic teen comedy with the sound turned down. Alex had no expectations.

'We're going to try something a bit different,' Adam said, opening his wooden box. He passed Alex a tiny pill. White, inviolate.

Sometime later, in the video (which was never different, in which people never changed and kept their beauty and did not die), the high-school boy realized that the plain and poor girl was beautiful and rich in her heart. There was a final, redemptive kiss in a car park. Without warning, Alex lifted Esther from the sofa, grasped her and kissed her.

'Get *off* me,' she said.

'Stop pushing me,' she said.

'Where are we going?' she said.

But they were in the car by then. Were they? Alex paused in the middle of this posh street and closed his eyes, trying to get – as the legal drama shows like to say – a mental picture. Was Esther with him? Did he have the Kitty by then? Had he clipped her to the windscreen like a parking ticket?

He recalled that they had stopped in a garage for food. It had seemed to Alex that everyone in the garage was speaking Cantonese until he looked at them. Then they would speak English. Cantonese, English, English, Cantonese!

Back in the car he turned to Esther. 'Everyone's speaking Cantonese. Sometimes,' he said. He was giggling. But Esther was crying and looking at her thighs. 'I'm so *selfish*,' she said.

It seemed to Esther that the two foetuses she had aborted (one Alex's when she was only seventeen, the other some man's she met in college) were in her thighs, one in each, and she could see their fingers, pressing to get out. It must have been soon after this that a bus-stop dashed across the road like a lunatic and threw itself at Alex's car.

At this memory Alex felt his face wet with tears. He did a goyish mime, for nobody's benefit, to the effect that something had blown into his eye. He used his sleeve. He tried employing the same breathing techniques Adam had taught him to use during their meditations. In the middle of this performance, he was approached by a teenage French boy. Hurriedly, Alex gave fictional directions to a place neither of them had ever been to. The boy turned left into who knew where. The sun brightened a notch. It made the older grey city stone flash white, and, for the first time in a month of smog, a pair of distant palaces winked at each other, two friends at opposite ends of a party when the crowd suddenly thins. Alex tried humming. Some of the shopping women smiled at him but with strain, as one smiles at the elderly, infirm or disabled. Alex persevered, humming all the way to a bollard and round a corner. Now he was singing a famous song. He was walking to its rhythm. The song was morphing. This was often his way. In the past he had spontaneously composed 'Let's Go to Court', a song about his landlord, set to the tune of 'Let's Get It On'; 'I'm So Bored' (a synagogue favourite) to the tune of 'You're So Vain'; and 'Incompetency', a song for varied bureaucratic and work-related situations, thieved from Prince's 'Controversy'. Just now he was singing a radically altered version of 'Norwegian Wood' in which Esther appeared, sitting on the pavement next to what was left of the car. Biding her time. In the song, as in life, she accused him of loving Adam more than her. But it was not true. That is, she screamed it, but she was wrong. He adored her. He just wasn't always so good at showing it. In essence, the problem predated the car. Alex was careless, in small ways, in the ways that count. His inability to remember the title of her Ph.D. ('Modes of Something in the Development of the Iconography of African Jewry in the Something'). The state of his bathroom. The books she recommended and he never read. He had her in his heart, but not always in his mind.

They had been together as children (he was just seventeen when she, at fourteen, reached out a quick hand for his ankle, hustled him into a hedge and kissed him), she was as familiar to him as Mountjoy. He was capable of thinking of her in that very way – as a kind of wallpaper that he did not notice until a spotlight was thrown on it. Even her pacemaker – hard and square, across which her skin was tightly pulled – was to him now an everyday affair. He had been through every stage with it: fear, awe, affection, sexualization. He no longer even attached to it the idea of her mortality, but then, she had encouraged him to be free with it. To clutch it, to dig behind it and make his thumb touch his fingers, through her skin, on its other side. He was confident of her heart. Only when they attended their respective universities did he become panicked at the thought of losing it. While there she slept with other people – one man and one woman. Alex thought he might lose his mind. It took that sort of thing. More recently, if a friend of Alex from some unconnected world – work, college – met her for the first time and commented on her beauty, only then did he re-realize it. Re-realize? But what other word for it?

He didn't believe in therapy; he could do it himself. Yes, he imagined his love on a screen in front of a preview audience; he saw them watching her and ticking the boxes. Yes, he wanted his love at a distance, physically close but in some other way hard to reach. The stranger's initial impression of his love – as an African princess, or the look-alike of this or that actress – appealed to him in a way that her various realities could not. He wanted to meet her for the first time, over and over. He wanted to always be at the beginning of the movie – not in the car park but in the classroom. He was in awe of her beauty and he never wanted to lose that awe. Yes, Doctor, yes. I want to be her fan.

Esther's head was shaved like a boy's. Lying next to her, he felt he could hold that coconut head for the rest of his life. She could beat him in an arm wrestle and most arguments. She was bigger than he, and more beautiful. But he was tortured by the idea that she would grow old! He understood that in all likelihood this sort of thinking would lead him to die lonely, without anyone. He told himself the story that this was the great tragedy of his heart. The great tragedy of his heart was that it always needed to be told a story.

4

Pointlessly, Alex ran the very last hundred metres, the gallop of an uncoordinated man – like an animal recently shot in its flank. And then stopped on the sudden. Just next door to the auction house, the popular musician Leonard Cohen was looking bored by a boutique alongside a woman who was not. Alex was not a boy any more – he had no intention of going over and begging for an autograph. But Leonard certainly gave him pause. He did find himself hovering near by, discreetly; he did watch Leonard spit some gum on to the pavement, pat the woman on the shoulder and then walk towards a famous coffee shop. 'Suzanne'. That was a brilliant song. Something of Mercy. 'Sisters of Mercy'. An eternal classic. But he was almost an hour late for this auction.

A minute later Alex found himself in the coffee shop against his rational will, standing behind Leonard, admiring the foreverness of Leonard, his infinite nature, the fact that long after the physical Leonard was worm-food, somewhere the virtual Leonard would still be moving, singing and being interviewed. And he was balding. It was incredible. He had an in-built distance. Even standing beside him, Alex felt worlds away. Leonard's fame was going to save him. Alex felt resentment build. Why Leonard? He just looked like a guy. What was so special about him? And why was he in this coffee shop anyway? What kind of a famous person walks into a coffee shop full of ordinary people like Alex?

Alex stood behind him now, angrily watching. Resenting the splendour of his loafers, the jeans, the smart jacket, seeing Leonard drum his fingers against the counter, hearing Leonard say: 'A mocha, can you do that? But could you *not* put the chocolate on top? And two parts milk to one part cream? That's great. Thank you, yeah, that's perfect. Actually – yeah, could you put that in an extra . . . yeah, like another cup – they're *really* hot these – I don't wanna have to sue you, ha! Ah, that's great. That's fantastic.'

Goyish, thought Alex-Li.

FIVE / *Tif'eret*

Beauty • Praying in the workplace • Quote unquote • Jimmy Stewart was Jewish • The Kabbalah of Elvis Presley • Drinking games • Once upon a time in Europe • Brian Duchamp • Proceed calmly to the nearest exit

I

Auction Room 3 works like this: it is not a real place but a sort of cathedral or synagogue to which Alex comes every other week and speaks by rote. He counts ceiling tiles and thinks about God. He prays, after a fashion (*God Help Me; Jesus Christ Get Me Out of Here*). He hopes that the phone bidding will cease, he hopes someone will let him own the things he loves. But nothing changes. Alex says what he has said before, making the same silent curses, watching the prices soar and escape him. The auctioneer, with his fruity, theatrical voice and his gavel, hits a block of wood in precisely the same spot, no matter the day. And the American, Jason Lovelear, says: 'Leonard Cohen? You're kidding me – Leonard Cohen? Is he still out there? He's not coming in *here*, is he? Jesus. I used to date his sister, Chloe. Chloe Cohen. Big girl. Thyroid. Not when I met her. It developed later – then I had to end it. Leonard was *very* dismayed. A lot of bad feeling went down between me and that guy.'

No, it is not true. Lovelear didn't always say that. But, taking into account changing nouns and pronouns, he always said something *like* that.

*

'Alex-Li *Tandem*,' said Lovelear.

No one's physicality depressed Alex quite as much as this man's. Lovelear's hair was either black and he was dyeing it blond or vice versa, and if ever he had an upper lip, it was not in evidence now. Although he was not atrociously overweight in terms of pounds, his flab was ingeniously placed. He had side bellies. The small fold-up chair he sat on could not contain them all. One of the many things TV does not show you is the potential range and horror of the human form. For this alone, thought Alex, it is rightly celebrated.

'Hullo, Lovelear. Sorry – late.'

'At *last*. We saved a seat for you. Dove, move up, man. OK. So. You look like a *disaster*. Why you so late? That girl, right? *I'd* be late if I had a girl like that.' Here, Lovelear made an obscene International Gesture. 'Yes, *sir*. But didn't you drive?'

Alex took his place between Jason Lovelear and Ian Dove, two men who considered themselves friends of his. He got the relevant catalogue out of his case, opened it up on his lap. He circled Lot 159 in the catalogue, an alarm clock that came with a certificate of provenance confirming its residence in Graceland between 1965 and 1969. Ian Dove passed him a wooden paddle with the number 10 on it.

' 'Mazing, innit, the estimate on that. Two thousand quid for an alarm clock. Can't be right, can it?' murmured Dove with the exact same intonation with which a normal man might say the following sentence: *Terrible, innit. And she was only forty. Forty years old and she got hit by a bus. And we'd only been married the day before.*

'Yeah, amazing.'

'Do you know what I reckon?'

'No, Ian.'

'I reckon we've got a serious Elvis fan on the phones. That's why the prices are going mental.'

'Right.'

'Do you know who I reckon it is?'

'No, Ian.'

'I reckon it's Jackson.'

'LaToya?' queried Alex-Li, just for a change. 'Or – wait – not Jermaine?'

Ian Dove's kindly face creased up. He ran both hands through his prematurely salt-and-pepper hair. Ian Dove worked shifts on the shop floor of a plastics factory near Gatwick. Every so often his wife found him profoundly drunk, asleep in their airing cupboard, curled up by the boiler. He could only afford to be a part-time Autograph Man, but he took these auctions very seriously, as a hobbyist will. He was the only man Alex had ever met who envied Alex his life.

'No, Alex – I mean –'

'I know, Ian,' said Alex softly. 'It's all right. You're probably right. I'm not feeling myself today. Ignore me.'

'Otherwise known as *shut the hell up, Dove, you're boring us*.'

Ian wrapped his arms around himself. 'Sorry I spoke.'

'*Sorry I spoke?*' echoed Lovelear, wide-eyed. 'Is that a phrase – *sorry I spoke?*'

Lovelear had spent ten years in England and grew no fonder of it. Alex often wondered what it must be like, to be stranded in a little country that seems a shrunken parody of your own, like Lilliput.

'*Anyway*,' said Lovelear, turning to him, 'you missed some choice items. And I can tell you this: no kids' stuff today. Uh-uhno. Naturally, John Baguley took maybe, I don't know, like 70 per cent of the rock memorabilia? Such an *incredible* asshole. You know he just opened another shop. In Neville Court? He's like the goddamn

Ronald McDonald of autographs now. *Asshole*. And everything else has been going on the phones. And then, get this, then they start into eighties film stuff and who comes up?'

'Ally Sheedy,' said Alex.

'Right. And which insensitive *loser*,' said Lovelear, turning to Ian, 'suggests I buy it, like it wasn't already hard enough ending that relationship? Like it doesn't just rip me up, seeing her face.'

Alex, unfairly, was making a certain pointed International Gesture (tongue tucked in front of lower teeth, long, invisible chin, tickled by fingers of right hand). Ian accidentally smiled. Lovelear let out a four-tiered expletive. It was a line from a movie. Ian shivered. Alex suspected that there was something about being sworn at by an American in the cinematic setting of an auction house (*North by Northwest, Octopussy*) that was cathartic for Ian Dove, who lived in Little Marlow, a small English village in which no film has ever been made or set. Something about it moved Alex too. He was so familiar with the dialogue between Lovelear and Dove that he no longer heard the specific words themselves but only their vibrations, their constant ringing bass note. He knew, for instance, what the disapproving woman behind did not know and could not appreciate: that underneath the words, ugly and amateurish, there was a beautiful elegy going on which never changed. Every conversation between these two men was actually the same conversation, different words, same meaning. A sort of modern Kaddish, a religious chant:

LOVELEAR: *I am an American, in this world and the next, and you are not, and will never be.*

DOVE: *You are an American, in this world and the next, and I am not, and will never be.*

'Leave Ian alone, all right?' said Alex, snuffing out the candles.

'Yeah, well, whatever. *Breathe in the universe, breathe out love*,' said Lovelear, making that most goyish of all International Gestures, the quote unquote motion with his fingers. 'That's my motto. That's what I had to say to Leonard, in the end.'

As the lunch recess approached, only Dove kept his fingers firmly clenched around his paddle; he was hypnotized by the deliberate curves of a young lady in blue, holding up props from the film *Tommy*. She turned them this way and that for the public view. Alex had slumped in his chair some time ago. Now Lovelear joined him, throwing his paddle to the floor, ranting.

'No point,' Alex cut in, feeling, in comparison to Lovelear, serene; becoming, briefly, the *Zen Master*, a role that passed back and forth between them during any auction solely to irritate the other party. 'To be expected. Way of world. Look at Baguley. Twenty people, they work for him. This no business for sole trader any more. Not been for long time. This important acknowledge. Once acknowledge, risen above. Wax on, wax off. Fact simple.'

Lovelear drove his fist into the empty seat in front. 'It wasn't so long ago, man, I could come here, buy a Jennifer Jones for a reasonable price, right? And I'm not talking about for resale, Al, I'm talking about for the sheer *love* of it.'

Lovelear had never bought anything for the sheer love of it, and there wasn't a single item you couldn't buy off him for the right price. He was unusual among his kind for this very reason: he had no sentimental impulses. Within the business it was often said of him that he would exchange his own grandmother for two Jimmy Durantes and a forged Ernest Hemingway.

'I mean, I'm not in this business for the money. I'm a *fan*. This is coming from my *heart*. These things really *mean* something to me.'

Discreetly, Alex made the International Gesture for *Soon, if we are lucky, everything in this world, including the man I speak to now, will be reduced to dust* (lower teeth brought forward over upper, top lip drawn short above gums, nodding head, eyes closed).

'Yes,' he said. 'No question. Hard for everyone.'

Lovelear glared at the alert young men of the auction house. They sat above the crowd on their dais with their phones. Buying and selling to foreigners the American things Lovelear wanted but could not afford.

'And now it's like, *what are they going to <u>do</u> with them?* Well, I'll tell you and I don't want you to take offence. The truth is, it's like, oh, I just had some *sushi* and now I walk back into my huge corporate office and there's a Gary Cooper in my *hallway* and I don't even know who Cooper *was* – like, I've got absolutely no *love* for Cooper, I'm like this Jap businessman loser *asshole* and I haven't even seen *High Noon*. I'm like this little yellow *nip* who can't even pronounce Cooper's *name*. No offence.'

'I'm Chinese.'

'Right, no offence meant.'

'None taken, Lovelear, because I'm *Chinese*.'

'Right, no offence.'

Lovelear rolled up his copy of the catalogue and began whacking Alex across the knees with it. 'The thing is, the *thing is*, this is *part of my culture*. And it is *Just! Not! Possible!* to understand a lot of this stuff unless you come from the place where this stuff comes from! And you can put a *Jimmy Stewart* in your Hung Win Shan

Chin office in Tokyo or wherever, but you are *never – never!* –
going to understand what a Jimmy Stewart *means*. Nothing against
anyone but no nip can truly understand what a Jimmy Stewart
means truly in his heart of hearts. No offence. Oh, *Jesus*, will you
look at this?'

Alex followed Lovelear's finger to the back of the room. A family
of Anglo-Elvis hillbillies (duck-tailed, rhinestoned) stood huddled
and distressed in the doorway.

'Oh-oh,' said Lovelear, 'check it out. Heartbreak Hotel.'

Long-time residents of. They had not a chance of picking up any
of these high-end-of-the-market Elvis items. The smallest girl, with
her monstrous dentistry and thin hair; the two boys, legs placed
wide apart in Elvis imitation; the father, full of that poignant,
misplaced fat-man-in-a-caped-jumpsuit dignity; the phthisic wife
– it all got to Alex, somehow. The undaunted belief.

'Just leave them, Lovelear. They come in good faith. They're just
fans. Move away from the scene. Nothing to see.'

'Are you *blind*?'

There was a chapter in Alex's book about the goyishness of Elvis
fans, there was a subsection about the legendary Ben D. Goodall, a
man who collected the autographs of everyone who ever came into
contact with Elvis, from the midwife to the mortician (see Diagram
[a]). None of these things was worth a penny. Goodall's is a caution-
ary tale Autograph Men tell each other. It is meant to horrify any
atheist dealer who buys to sell and aims to make a living, for
Goodall was a religious man, religious about fame. He believed in
the aura it creates, in the tinny, cheap, reflected light it shines out.
Once Goodall and his life's work had horrified Alex. Now he found
himself intensely moved by it.

Diagram (a)

The Ten Sefirot of Elvis

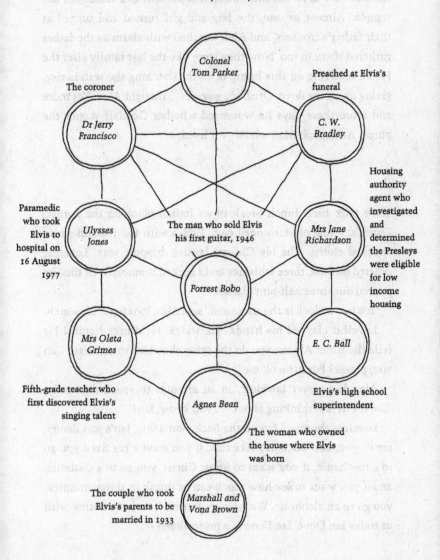

Colonel Tom Parker

The coroner

Preached at Elvis's funeral

Dr Jerry Francisco

C. W. Bradley

Housing authority agent who investigated and determined the Presleys were eligible for low income housing

Paramedic who took Elvis to hospital on 16 August 1977

Ulysses Jones

The man who sold Elvis his first guitar, 1946

Mrs Jane Richardson

Forrest Bobo

Mrs Oleta Grimes

E. C. Ball

Fifth-grade teacher who first discovered Elvis's singing talent

Agnes Bean

Elvis's high school superintendent

The woman who owned the house where Elvis was born

The couple who took Elvis's parents to be married in 1933

Marshall and Vona Brown

A cowboy shirt, with inlaid gems on each cuff, went under the hammer. The wife sighed. She laid her head on her husband's shoulder. He drew her into the arch of his arm and kissed her left temple. Almost as one, the boy and girl turned and tugged at their father's trousers, and Alex watched with alarm as the father gathered *them* in too. Now they were like the last family after the Flood, teetering on this hump of earth, watching the waters rise, giving up on the dove. *Of all the goyish* . . . thought Alex. Yet more and more these days he wondered whether Goodall wasn't the purest Autograph Man who'd ever lived.

2

They took their lunch break in an Italian place on the corner, Dante's, a real old-fashioned caff. Tables with the red-and-white checked cloths. The big Chianti bottles dripping wax. Lovelear ordered no food, three whiskies and a corked Beaujolais. Of this, he poured out three half-pint glasses.

'It's two o'clock in the afternoon,' said Alex, looking at his watch.

Lovelear clapped his hands. 'He walks! He drinks liquids! He tells the time! Al, can you do the tying shoe lace thing next? Can you, please? For little ol' me?'

Alex leant over Lovelear, in an attempt to speak discreetly. 'Look. I'm just thinking about . . . you know, Ian?'

Lovelear thumped Ian on the back. 'Ian's *fine*. Ian's just dandy, aren't you, Ian? Alex, it's like this: if you want a car fixed you go to a mechanic, if you want to know Christ, you go to a Catholic, and if you want to see how much can be drunk in thirty minutes, you go to an alcoholic. We are very fortunate to have sitting with us today Ian Dove. Ian Dove is a professional –'

'Pisshead,' said Ian Dove sadly.

Lovelear drew the three glasses into triangular formation in the middle of the table. 'Gentlemen?' said Lovelear in his best *Brideshead Revisited* voice. 'Shall we?'

They drank. Soon enough Kitty began to burn a hole in Alex's bag. Several times he almost reached for her, holding himself back only with great difficulty. Everything Alex had ever shown Lovelear, Lovelear had maintained to be a forgery, just for the hell of it. This time, he would not give him the satisfaction. He would not be demeaned, not today.

Instead he sank his half-pint of wine and led the cry for more. Through purple lips, the three of them swiftly itemized the best all-time musicals, the greatest Hollywood scandal, largest cast, biggest breasts, earliest nude scenes, infamous suicides.

'OK, OK, OK: name three vintage Hollywood decapitations,' said Lovelear, placing three new whisky shots on the table.

The room had started to shimmy by the time John Baguley walked in, bow-tie and everything. He went straight to the bar, but Alex knew he had seen them. The more successful Baguley got, the longer the period between Baguley spotting you and Baguley acknowledging you.

'Jayne Mansfield,' said Dove.

'Ding!' said Lovelear.

Alex began to pick wax off their bottle. Maybe he could show the thing to Baguley? Baguley knew his onions, after all! Baguley could verify, Baguley would see the truth! It would have to be done subtly, though. Lovelear didn't roll with the idea that Baguley knew more onions than Lovelear. *Also, probably best not to bring it up right now*, thought Alex carefully, unconsciously moving his lips, *not now when I'm a bit tight. That might make me look crazy.*

Alex watched the room rock some more and then roll. One and a half Baguleys stood at the bar ordering a ham sandwich. Alex considered the situation. On the one hand, Baguley definitely knew his onions. On the other, Lovelear hated Baguley. There was that onions issue. On the third hand, Ian also hated Baguley. Baguley made bad puns along the AA (Autograph Association/Alcoholics Anonymous) comic axis. Come to think of it, thought Alex, I hate Baguley too. How's that for a fourth hand! My God, I hate Baguley. I never realized how much! With his bow-tie. Thin moustache. The bastard. And now he's probably going to come over here. With his hate. Forfugssake. Who wears bastard hats like that, these days?

'Grace Kelly?' said Alex, and stood up. He felt delicate. He tried to ascertain whether Baguley was intending on the back of the bar or their corner of it.

'A point to Mr Tandem. Mr Dove and Mr Tandem now have one each. Tie-breaker.'

'I can't think,' gurgled Dove. 'Too pissed. All right, wait. Um . . . *God, er* . . . Montgomery Clift?'

'Baguley's coming,' said Alex as Baguley came.

'*Montgomery Clift*, Dove? That was *half* his face. As far as I remember, he still had his freaking *head* when he finished *Raintree* –'

'Baguley, shiddown,' said Alex as Baguley sat down. Alex was much, much drunker than he had hoped. With dread he watched Baguley take off his hat and put it on the table, the worst sort of bad luck in some countries.

'Do you know,' said Baguley loudly, 'what I've just successfully organized?'

'Own funeral?'

'Hullo, Lovelear. No, actually. A charity auction. A few nights ago. You boys should have come. We auctioned off character parts. In novels. Do you see? So you paid money and you got to be in this or that writer's book. Your own personal fifteen minutes, you see. I'm a good sport, me – I paid three hundred pounds. Lady writer.'

'What?' said Ian, who was, of course, tighter than all of them. 'What's he saying? Is it English? *Bastard*.'

'Look at that tie, dude,' said Lovelear, touching it. 'What *is* that tie *about*? Like, what does it *mean*? Does it mean something?'

'And the trouble is, I haven't decided,' said Baguley, trying to concentrate on Alex-Li, the one he thought sober, 'quite what I'd like to be in it. In the novel, I mean.'

'Amateur Satanist?' said Lovelear.

'Just a . . . like a . . . bastard?' offered Ian, and laughed a lot, dribbling wine down his chin.

'It's three, we're late,' said Alex smiling, looking at his watch. He almost didn't want to go, he was enjoying himself. There are friends you have who are only good when drunk. But that, according to the Kabbalah of Alex-Li Tandem, is not entirely a bad thing.

'Tandem . . . you're getting real flashy with that time-keeping shtick,' said Lovelear in Brooklynese, before judiciously switching to Yeoldechristmascarolese. 'My boy, I say you're hired. We'll take you on at two thrupp'ny bits a year, and I hope we ne'er regret it! And now –'

Ian made a trumpet noise. Alex contributed a lackadaisical drum roll.

'Baguley,' said Lovelear, lurching forward, 'it's been real. But *man* . . . we seriously have to go now. We have to go watch *you* buy some more of *Alex's* forgeries. Oh, *sure* – this auction is *full* of Tandem forgeries. That's all he does all day. Forge, forge, forge and forge again. That's why we don't bid. We rise above. We are Zen. Basically. Baguley.'

Ian tried to stand but staggered backwards. Alex laughed a lot through his nose.

'You know what you should ask for?' said Ian to Baguley as Baguley made to leave. 'You should ask that the writer lady makes you this bloke in the book who organizes an auction and then buys his place in, er . . . wait – no, yeah, in a book as a character who organizes an auction and then buys his place in a book and asks . . .'

For this little Jewish gem, Alex bought Ian two more pints.

When they returned, they were sincerely drunk in a melancholy way. Beneath the stark lights they rubbed their eyes like children. The popular movie actor George Sanders was under the hammer. Three thousand pounds for the 1972 suicide note in which he insisted he was too bored to continue.

'I empathize,' said Lovelear, stretching.

'A bird went in search of a cage,' murmured Alex.

'*Jesus.* What asshole said *that*?'

'Remember the scene, Lovelear,' said Ian, tugging at his sleeve. 'In *All about Eve* when –'

'Sure,' said Lovelear, batting him off.

They sat, they bid, but it was not their day. Bored, Alex looked around. Young burly lads in blue uniforms were heaving in pieces meant for a later auction. Statues, tables, gold things. It was easy to forget, as an Autograph Man, that names on paper are the very least of what is traded and shifted round the world. Autographs are a small blip in the desire network, historical flotsam. But look at this stuff, the big stuff. These cast-iron dogs with best paw forward. Bronze eagles drawing in their wings, preparing to land. Life-sized

marble Negroes, jolly and docile, holding by the paws the result of
somebody else's hunt. And, like a border running round it all,
many, many cold fireplaces ripped from great houses, laid on their
sides and overlapping each other, fallen dominoes of the gods. And
a moose. Towards the back. Stuffed, standing. Behind it, leaning
on its threadbare hindquarters, Alex now spotted Brian Duchamp.
A second later Lovelear had spotted him too.

'Ai yai *yai* – I *knew* this auction was going to get worse before it
got better. Dove, wake up, man. Look who it is.'

Dove unfurled like the dormouse. 'Bloody *hell*. Do you think
he's going to go for it, *again*?'

Alex wiped his glasses on his mohair.

'I spectso. He is still *mad*. I mean, unless you've heard something.'

'Hey, Al, I'll tell him to come over here, no?'

Alex thumped Lovelear in his right breast. '*Jesus*, I see him every
Thursday anyway – I don't need to see him more than that.'

'But don't you want him to like come over here' – Lovelear did
a stationary approximation of waddling with his upper body – 'you
know and then like sit down next to you' – Lovelear slunk down
into his seat until he was the sitting height of Duchamp, who stood
at around five foot four – 'and then put his face real close to your
face, and open his mouth wide and say –' Here Lovelear said *hello*
as a cockney gremlin might say, an accurate reproduction of Duchamp. He was not able to reproduce the halitosis, however, which
was so acute it probably could not be reproduced in a laboratory.

Brian Duchamp. He of the filthy shirts, the loneliness, the iso-
lated debt-ridden stall (from which, in his madness, he occasionally
tried to sell Alex items from his own house: toilet-roll holders,
lampshades), the supermarket trainers, skin issues, bad breath.

'What's he *doing*?' asked Lovelear.

Alex observed. 'Preparing.'

Out of his bag Duchamp was pulling a clipboard, several pens, some catalogues and a number of stray bits of paper, balancing them on the moose. He unfolded a pair of bifocals and thrust them as far up the bridge of his nose as possible, the result being a tremendous and terrifying magnification of milky, mad eyes.

'Oi-oi, look out,' said Ian. 'Curtain up.'

'We begin the bid at twenty pounds, twenty pounds, do I have any takers at twenty?'

The auctioneer was gesturing towards a pretty picture of Jeanette MacDonald and Nelson Eddy in what thirties Hollywood imagined the young people of Austria were wearing at the time (lederhosen, velvet collars, pigtails and wire through them, cow-bells). There were takers at twenty, forty, sixty and eighty and then there was Brian Duchamp. He surged forward, shouting, 'I'll give you for'ee!'

'Pardon me, sir – are you bidding?'

'For'ee!'

'Forty, sir? I'm afraid the bid is already at eighty.'

'I'll give yer,' said Duchamp, quieter now, and drowned out by what the newsreaders like to call 'general consternation', 'for'ee pence and a slap – 'cos that's how much it's worth. 'Cos it ain't bloody real!'

'*Brian*,' said Alex, as Duchamp came level with their row of chairs. 'Brian, for godssake sit down. Come here. Come on, come here.'

He stood up and made a grab for Duchamp, who cursed him like a sailor and stumbled; Lovelear and Ian wrestled him into a seat.

'Tandem? I see you Thursdays, not today. Thursday's when I see you.'

Alex marvelled at this ability of madness to be completely beside the point. He pressed Duchamp's shaky hands on to his knees. 'They won't let you back in, Brian, if you do this again. They threw you out last time, didn't they?'

Duchamp brought a handkerchief to his mouth and hacked something unspeakable into it. He fixed his sad, low-watt bulbs on Alex. 'These bloody experts, Tandem. But they don't know nothing! Barely out of fahkin short-trousers and they don't know nothing!'

A miniature bottle of whisky fell from Brian's pocket to the floor. He lunged after it. There was a mauve tinge to Brian's skin. He smelt terrible.

'Lovelear, I don't think he's well.'

'Newsflash.'

'I don't think you're well, Brian,' said Alex, bringing himself to put his hand on the poor man's bumpy forehead. 'I think I should probably get you out of here.'

But Duchamp pulled away from him, suddenly. For a moment he had broken from the shell of his world into Alex's; now he retreated. All his attention returned to the podium.

'Lot 182,' said the auctioneer, 'which is a preview programme signed by the cast of the film *42nd Street*, including the popular musical actress Ruby Keeler . . .'

The auctioneer kept talking, but so did Duchamp. A hum that had started softly was increasing in volume and pitch, becoming harder to ignore. Duchamp stood up. The auctioneer turned himself up: '*DO I HEAR TWO HUNDRED –*'

'If that's Ruby, *I'm* fahkin Jolson, mate.'

'Sir?' queried the auctioneer. 'I'm sorry, is there some sort of a problem?'

'That's not Ruby that's not Ruby that's not Ruby,' Duchamp was shouting, 'THAT'S NOT RUBY THAT'S NOT FAHKIN RUBY. THAT'S ME! I SIGNED THAT.'

Security was now finally being called, but Duchamp hadn't finished being mad yet, and there was something admirable – like a theatre crowd indulging a bad King Lear – in the way they were going to let him finish what he had started.

'I BLOODY WORKED FOR THESE STUDIOS, DINT-EYE? RUBY NEVER SIGNED A THING! I SIGNED ALL OF THIS STUFF!'

There was method in the madness, as all the Autograph Men present knew. Fresh out of the war, Duchamp had washed up in Hollywood, working in the publicity department of several studios. He signed thousands of items. In younger, less mad days, Duchamp had been invaluable to collectors who wanted to check on the authenticity of a purchase. He had always maintained that the British market was flooded with forgeries: he had a strong case. Still, Alex could think of better ways to air this issue than exposing oneself to the public, which Duchamp, fumbling furiously with belt buckle, seemed poised to do.

'RUBY, GRETA, MARLENE, RITA, KITTY, BETTE – THEY COULDN'T CLEAN THEIR OWN ARSES. I DID ALL THEIR DIRTY WORK.'

For his finale, Duchamp dropped his trousers, revealing a cotton canvas of heartbreaking, variegated stains.

3

How many moves, wondered Alex later, on his way out – that is, if this were a sophisticated game like mah-jong or chess – how many moves to get from where I am to where Brian Duchamp is? Because the people who buy the brass dogs and the billiard tables, they're not like this, are they? So why are *we* like this? What's *wrong* with us?

Who would ever choose this life? Alex stepped out into the centre of town. In the curved black glass of a superior clothes store he dropped his shoulders, placed his hands by his sides, itemized himself. No love, no transportation, no ambitions, no faith, no community, no expectation of forgiveness or reward, one bag, one thermos, one acid hangover, one alcohol hangover, one Kitty Alexander autograph, in pristine condition, written in dark ink, centrally placed on a postcard. Look at this. If this is a man. Look at him. *Never have I been more perfectly Jewish. I have embraced a perfect contradiction, like Job. I have nothing and, at the same time, everything. And if I am out of my mind*, thought Alex-Li Tandem, *it's all right by me.*

Alex believed in that God Chip in the brain, something created to process and trigger wonderment. It allows you to see beauty, to uncover beauty in the world. But it's not so well designed. It's a chip that has its problems. Sometimes it confuses a small man with a bad moustache and a uniform for an image of the infinite; sometimes an almond-eyed girl on a big screen for the stained-glass window in a church.

Maybe it is fatuous to think of steps, stages, *moves* between me and Duchamp, thought Alex. Maybe I am already there.

For I am an Autograph Man.

No choice, then, simply this: a closing down of options. This is a simpler game than chess. Simpler even than snakes and ladders. This is a slow, malicious game (Designed by whom? Controlled by whom?) of ticktacktoe.

SIX / *Hesed*

Love • Only he who hath the knowledge shall have the key • The Happy
Fried Chicken • Sex versus death • Fats Waller was Jewish • Talking
seriously • Movies versus Music • God needs us • The oldest joke

I

'Kofi *Annan*.'

'Boutros *Boutros*-Ghali.'

Finding the video shop closed, Alex-Li stepped to the right and
rang the doorbell for the upper flat. After the usual lengthy pause,
Adam appeared in the doorway, his face a perfect onyx sun framed
by short, skinny dreadlocks fanned out like rays, beaming on his
friend. And now they are in the middle of their ritual.

'Kofi, Kofi *Annan*,' says Alex, bowing deeply from the hip. The
pose is stately, the accent Nigerian. 'Kofi *Annan*,' he says. 'Annan,
Annan.'

Adam bows lower. 'Boutros. Boutros, Boutros-Boutros, *Boutros*-
Ghali.'

Alex brings his palms together in prayer. 'Oh, Kofi, Kofi, Kofi
Annan.'

'*Welcome*.' Adam straightens, grins. 'Welcome to my humble
yard. You best come in. Don't worry, Esther's not here.'

Alex inclines his head, resting it on the door-frame. 'Ads. Mate.
It's like I'm in some sort of Bermuda Triangle of goyishness today.
Honest to God. Tell me something.'

'Speak it.'

'Am I an Autograph Man? I mean, do I *look* like one to you?'

'Again?'

'Forget it. To be continued upstairs. Lead the way.'

It is no palace, Adam's place. The first front door opens on to a communal concrete space, like a corner of an underground car park, windowless, bulbless, and therefore always dark. On the left wall a grim miniature morgue of steel pull-out drawers spills useless mail (catalogues addressed to ex-tenants, electoral forms sent to Flat D's anarchists, electricity bills for the dead); further along, the iron railings of the staircase suspend three crucified bikes bound by chains and rope, in an attempt to counter the pervasive local belief that Adam's hallway is a 100 per cent credit, free-for-all, mountain-bike superstore.

On these stairs, Adam becomes morose. 'So. I take it you can smell it?'

Alex sniffs. 'Oh. Well, *yeah*. Different, though. *Spicy.*'

'Yes. I noticed that. New recipe. More sugar, more chillies. So, you *can* smell it –' Adam stops where he is. 'Like here? Before you're in? I swear I can't tell any more. I'm too close to the situation. Rubinfine said he couldn't smell it, but I think he was humouring me. He was three days late with a video so, you know, it was in his interest.'

'Ads, to be honest . . .'

How to put it? Alex places his hands on his best-friend's shoulders and delivers a quick consolatory squeeze. 'Sorry, but if anything, mate, it's *stronger*.'

'Well, there's a good reason for that . . .'

Solemnly, Adam ushers Alex through the door and on to the

long outdoor walkway. Here he lets his arms fall to his sides, palms open. International Gesture of the vanquished.

'Behold the Monster.'

'Oh. My. God.'

'Yes. Blasphemy aside, that was sort of my feeling.'

There is a new addition to the view. Not really part of the *view* as such. Too close to be effectively *viewed*. More like something that you're almost *in*. Two more steps to the left and its great mouth could swallow your head and still be hungry for more.

'Huge bloody pipe.'

'Yes. The Monster.'

'*Adam*. Huge bloody submarine-style *periscope* pumping smell of fried chicken *into your flat*. That's no *good*.'

'No, I *know* that.'

'Then, what are you *doing* about it?'

'Well, it's *done* now, isn't it?'

Agitated, Alex takes off his dirty glasses and begins to besmear them further with the corner of his shirt. 'No, Ads, no – this isn't a Zen issue. I mean, this is not an issue to which Zen should be applied. This is a private-property issue. This is an eye for an eye, tooth, etc., issue. This is a time for the application of Judaic law. You've got rights. You were here *before* them.'

Pacing down the walkway to get the plant-pot, Adam lets his lips vibrate with a sad exhale of air. 'Well, was I? That's up for debate . . . I don't know, any more . . . everyone's claiming, you know, something different . . .' Bending over the low wall, he empties the pot of its rainwater and drowned leaves, pouring the lot on to the lower roof of his adversaries. 'I mean, people who come for videos buy chicken from them and vice versa, so. I don't know, mate. It's like, I went to talk to them a while ago . . .' He moves the pot in front of the door. Alex kneels to hold it steady for him on the slippery asphalt. Adam climbs up. '. . . and I've got sympathy for their situation, you know? They're just trying to run a business, like me, and they've been there a long time, and the owner guy keeps giving it all this about do I want to ruin him and do I want his children to starve . . .'

'My knees are getting wet. *Please*, you're not going to ruin him – he's probably got eight more all over town.'

'No – wait – *where is it?* It's here somewhere. It slips along the gutter when it's been rainy – *ah!*'

Adam retrieves the Hooky-Thing (made out of two coat hangers, many elastic bands, the head and tines of a fork) from its hiding place in the lip of the gutter.

'Remind me again why you –'

'Look, mate, if you lost your key as often as I do, you'd do the same. Plant-pot back, please?'

Alex sploshes down the walkway hugging heavy clay. Comes back with a wet leaf pressed like a leech against his throat. Adam puts the Hooky-Thing through his own letter-box and begins the process of blind-feeling for his house key, marooned somewhere in the doormat.

Bored, Alex peers over the wall and down into the dismal cement backyard of Happy Fried Chicken. During the last summer, a brief détente in a six-year conflict, fun was had down there, Adam and Alex cautiously accepting an informal invitation (yelled up from below on a steaming day: *Play? Yes, yes – you want try?*) to take part in that mad game (is it Indian?) where everyone runs one way and then everyone runs another, and there's chalk lines everywhere but no ball. They got quite good at it. Lost weight too, also got tanned, until Alex was almost as brown and whippet-shaped as the bare-chested boys who worked there. Fun, yes. But no more. Now two of them stand against the huge black bins, drinking Cokes, clasping fags, looking back at Alex, returning insolence for insolence. Impulsively, Alex gives them the finger and hurriedly backs away from the wall, as the cans come flying.

'Ads, they're *laughing* at you. You do know anyone else would have sued them by now? Blown them up. Reported them to the bloody *health inspector*, that'd be a start. You should get on to Joseph about it.'

Adam's sweet face contorts as a dark thought passes over it. 'You know,' he says into the letter-box, 'the only thing that really got to me, that was *really* properly out of order' – his arm is very steady; carefully, and with great concentration, he draws the key through to his side of the door – 'is that they made sure the installation blokes turned up on Yom Kippur – *knowing* I wouldn't be here. *Knowing.* I just thought that was blatantly – *Ah! Got it!*' Key found, door opened. 'Enough about that, anyway. Too depressing. Open sesame. Tea?'

Everything in Adam's flat comes off the one, narrow hallway. One box living room, one box bedroom, one box kitchen and one box loo (actually a real box, this last one. If you were *giving a loo for a present* and you wanted a box to put it in, you would put it in this). No shower. No bath. No *sink* (except in the kitchen). If you were fortunate enough to spend an afternoon with Adam – you and he, two lazy, stoned flâneurs admiring the city – you would be treated, naturally, to the usual pyrotechnics of Adam's huge intellect (his incredible knowledge of pop-music trivia, and then its strange bedfellow, the various, sublime Judaic insights). You would also be given a tour of public utilities across town in which Adam showers and bathes. Swimming pools, gyms, homeless shelters, gay saunas, nunneries ('That's not *true*', 'Alex, all nuns *do* all day is *dream* that some smelly young man, preferably Jewish, will turn up on their doorstep begging to be cleaned'), retirement homes, schools.

2

The saving grace of Adam's flat is the living room. This is two boxes stuck together with a long window, the type you get on a London bus, stretching the length of one wall. The room has two modes: light for studying, dark for smoking. Just now, the curtain is drawn and it is dark. Finding his sight not sufficiently accommodated, Alex lights two more candles on the coffee table (plank of wood, supported by bricks). And there it all is, fabulous as ever. The Path of Spheres. The Path of Letters. The world is broken.

On the remaining wall, there are many shelves of books, mostly in Hebrew. Above them, a huge cross-shaped poster of the popular musician Isaac Hayes dressed in a dashiki and sunglasses, calling himself BLACK MOSES. Some photos of the popular musician Stevie Wonder. A badly framed print of the painter Klee's *Angelus Novus*. The director Steven Spielberg, the popular singer Michael Jackson and the styrofoam alien E.T. sitting on each other's laps. The martial artist Bruce Lee with nunchucks. The wise guy Walter Benjamin in need of a comb, a better tailor, a way out of France. A pin-board of notes and reminders, aphorisms ('All names and attributes are metaphoric with *us* but not with *Him*') and scraps of prayers. Most pleasing to Alex is a far corner of this wall, up near the cornice of the ceiling. Nine black and white photos in Kabbalah formation. The postcards are of famous faces. They go with the

autographs Adam sheepishly requests every now and then. They
look so pretty up there that Alex has almost forgiven him his
philistine mutilations (Adam pays good money for them, cuts the
names *out of* the documents, buys a postcard of the person in
question and then sticks the name with Blu-Tack *over* the postcard,
thus rendering them worthless to anyone but him. He did this with
Kafka. *Kafka*).

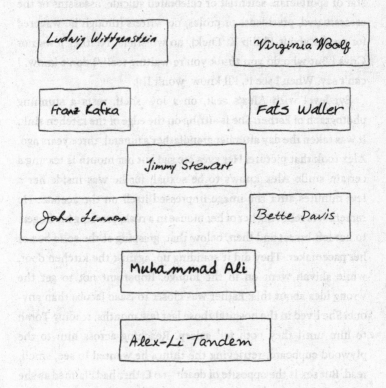

This represents the total of Adam's autograph collection, purchased
at the rate of about one a year. The collection seems to Alex one of

the most perfect he has ever known. Small, selfless, almost entirely arbitrary (his own inclusion, he presumes, is a joke) – and with so much time passing between one acquisition and the next!

If it is, indeed, a tree, then it is bonsai. Miniature, artificial, slowly tended. But with one branch missing. Adam insists there should be ten – a crown for the tree, a head for the body – and yet for almost a year now Alex has been unable to tempt him with star or sportsman, scientist or celebrated suicide, assassins or the assassinated, presidents or proles, no writers (though he wavered for weeks about Philip K. Dick), no wrestlers. Neither Jews nor Goys ('But who do you *think* you're waiting for?' 'I don't know. I can't say. When I see it, I'll know, won't I?').

Eye-level with Alex's seat, on a low shelf, rests a stunning photograph of Esther. She is sitting on the edge of the kitchen sink. It was taken the day after her grandfather's funeral, three years ago. Alex took that picture. Her eyes are sad but her mouth is teasing a certain smile Alex knows to be sexual, for he was inside her a few minutes after the image impressed itself on the acetate. He remembers relieving her of her blouse in a rush, pressing his fingers to her left breast and then, below that, grasping at the solid box of her pacemaker. They did it standing up, against the kitchen door, while shivah went on in the lounge. Important not to get the wrong idea about this: Esther was closer to Isaac Jacobs than anyone. She lived in the hospital those last few months, reading Torah to him until they both fell asleep. Reaching across him to the plywood cupboard, retrieving the things he wanted to see, smell, read. But sex is the opposite of death – so Esther had claimed as she pushed Alex up against the wall. *Sex is the reply to death.* They had replied.

*

Adam pops his head round the door.

'Fruit or normal?'

'Normal.'

'Milk? Sugar?'

'Both. Lots.'

'You'll get fat.'

Alex lifts his shirt and aims an exploratory poke into the fold of flesh where once he had a navel. 'Already happening.'

'Omphalos obfuscated.'

'By obesity in the offing. Yeah, yeah.'

Adam laughs and disappears and Alex looks after him, at the space where Adam has been. He feels a deep love. Also a kind of awe, something like: now, wait an ugging minute, *how did that happen?* Handsome, bright, enlightened, thin – what happened to that fat weird freak Black Jew kid? Who lurched from one ill-fitting 'identity' to another every summer; going through hippiedom, grunge, gangsta-lite, various *roots*isms (Ebonics, Repatriation, Rastafarianism), Anglo-philia, Americanization, afros, straightened, corn-rowed, shaved, baggy jeans, tight jeans, white girls, black girls, Jew girls, Goy girls, conservatism, Conservatism, socialism, anarchism, partying, drugging, hermiting, schizing, rehabbing – how did he get from there to *this*? How did he get so *happy*?

Adam will say *God*, of course. Except he won't say His name and if you ask him to write it down he will write YHWH, or, if he has a nice pen, יהוה. Yes, Adam will say God. Alex, on the other hand, is more inclined to say *weed*. Alex favours the argument: *marijuana*. Maybe, in truth, it is a split between the two, something like 60/40.

*

Alex reclines into the sofa, remembers something and opens up his bag. Drawing a folded piece of paper out from between the pages of a book, he opens it and begins to yell in the direction of the kitchen:
'LAST WEEK, BEFORE THE MESS. I FOUND SOME GOOD STUFF. IT'S STILL HERE IN MY BAG. LIST OF.'

'WHAT?'

'BLACK JEWS.'

'OH, YEAH?'

'I MEAN, PEOPLE WHO ARE. AUTOGRAPHS I COULD GET. TO COMPLETE YOUR COLLECTION MAYBE?'

'RIGHT. ANYONE GOOD?'

'SLASH.'

'YEAH, NO . . . I KNEW THAT. THAT'S LAME.'

'ALL RIGHT – WAIT – LENNY KRAVITZ, LISA BONET –'

'WHO?'

'LISA BONET. HIS EX-WIFE.'

'THAT'S PRONOUNCED BONN-NAY, MATE. FRENCH SPELLING.'

'ALL RIGHT, OK, LOOK, HERE – WHOOPI GOLD-BERG, PAULA ABDUL?'

'NO . . . I BET THEY'RE ALL NATION OF YAHWEH . . . OR ELSE THEY'RE FROM THE COMMANDMENT KEEPERS –'

'WHO?'

'MY OLD LOT, AL, MY OLD LOT. MY LOT NO LONGER.'

Alex thinks about this. After he's finished thinking, he says: 'YOU DON'T REALLY SEEM TO HAVE A "LOT" ANY MORE, ADS, DO YOU? I MEAN, YOU SEEM TO BE SORT OF DOING IT BY YOURSELF.'

'YEAH, I S'POSE.'

'BUT JUDAISM ISN'T THE SORT OF THING YOU CAN *DO* BY YOURSELF, IS IT? IT'S NOT LIKE BEING LIKE A JOGGER, SAY . . . OR A PROTESTANT.'

'IT'S LIKE THIS,' says Adam, and already Alex is regretting asking the question. 'THERE ARE TWO ASPECTS OF HASHEM, ALEX. HASHEM AS HE IS IN MANIFESTATION AND AS HE IS IN *HIMSELF*. THE FIRST FORMED A COVENANT WITH THE JEWISH PEOPLE AND THEY MUST TRY TO WALK TOGETHER TOWARDS HIM. THAT'S THE POINT OF COMMUNITY. THAT'S THE POINT OF HASIDIM, FOR EXAMPLE. BUT THE SECOND ASPECT – *EIN SOF*, *AYIN*, THE UNKNOWABLE, THE INFINITE NOTHING – THIS CAN ONLY BE APPROACHED BY THE SOLITARY TRAVELLER.'

'RIGHT. AND THAT'S YOU, IS IT?'

'AND THAT'S ME. ALEX?'

Adam reappeared, carrying two teas and a box of biscuits in the crook of his arm. His face had changed. 'I want to talk to you,' he said. 'Seriously.'

He sat down next to Alex, but leant forward. The picture of concentration, curved and precise, like Fats Waller at his piano. Alex leant forward. Now they were two pianists, poised for a duet.

'I spoke to your mum,' said Adam in an odd, cautious voice. He pushed Alex's tea towards him. 'A few days ago – don't get mad – I was just a bit worried about you . . .'

'No, fair enough, fair enough,' said Alex, and meant the exact opposite. 'And? How was she?'

'Oh, fine, she was fine. She always, you know . . . she's so relaxing to speak to. Very Zen, always.'

'Mmm . . . it's hard to believe we're related, I know. Have anything to say?'

'Um . . . well, you know, talked about Derek, and Shoshana's fleas – and now they've got a puppy apparently . . . she seems very happy. Went on about her pots a bit –'

Alex began to suspect where this was going and he didn't like it. As an Englishman he now exercised his right to fold his arms and smile and look as if he were enjoying it so damn much he might explode.

'Yeah,' he said, grinning, throwing his head back. 'Kuh! She'll do that. Get her started on clay and there's no end to it! I must actually call her – she's one of those people, Mum – she's so undemanding, and so you think you're in constant contact and then you realize you haven't phoned for –'

'Al,' broke in Adam, in that special tone of impending delicacy. 'She reminded me what date it is. Next Thursday.'

'Oh. Right.'

'It's the 26th.'

'Mmm.'

Alex got two biscuits and put one in each cheek. He shut his eyes and listened to Adam saying his piece, the same piece he said every year around this time. And despite its annual regularity, he felt more depressed by it this year than ever before. To have a religious best-friend is to expect (is to *resign yourself to the fact*) that there are certain fixed dates upon which a stilted, embarrassing argument will take place, climaxing in a tense and upsetting détente. Christmas, Passover, Ramadan. Whether you like it or not. But this doesn't make the argument any easier to have. For Alex and Adam the argument took place each year on and around the 26th of February. Usually, in the preceding weeks, Alex steeled himself with rationalist counter argument, but this time he had been caught off guard. Now he ate three more biscuits in morose silence before Adam, seeing he was getting nowhere, groaned and looked away.

'But *why*?' asked Alex, pressing a finger to the table. 'I *do* listen to everything you say, I *do*. But you never really tell me *why* I have to do this. What *good* it will do. I don't have any pretensions to being a religious man, do I? I mean, I'll turn up for Seder at a push – but that's just for Mum. I don't *want* to be a hypocrite. And I don't see *why* –'

'It's a ritual,' said Adam tersely. 'I think rituals are their own benefit.'

'OK, and I *don't*,' insisted Alex. 'Can't we just leave it at that?'

'Well, *obviously* you intend to.'

'I just . . . the whole thing is so *perverse*. He's been dead *fifteen* years, Ads. And he wasn't even Jewish. I know, I know, before you start – I am. We've been here before. Too many times. Please, now. Let's drop it.'

Adam shook his head and reached for the remote control. For a minute the two of them crabbily watched a yellow ball roll with agonizing slowness into the corner pocket.

'Look,' said Adam suddenly, swivelling round with renewed vigour, 'you, the son, are the atonement for where he rests. Don't you *get* that? *Thus does a child aquit the parent.* You bring him peace, you honour him. And all you have to do is go to shul and say Kaddish with ten friends around you. That's all it takes. Every year I do it and every time I do I realize the *value* of –'

'That's *you*,' replied Alex firmly, and opened the weed box, 'that's not *me*. I don't want a row, Ads. *Please*. I just want to have a smoke, all right?'

Adam did the International Gesture for the Jewish shrug. And Alex did it back.

3

Haggadah *(Pop Quiz #1)*

Q. When Alex and Adam had a smoke, how much of the fun
was in the rolling?

A. In the book it is written: *Oh, about 78 per cent.*

Of the L-shaped school. Always makes a roach, pretty coil of
coloured cardboard – and so Rizla packets are architectural disas-
ters; first no sides, then no back, then no roof, then no packet at
all. The rolling is slow, elaborate. Oh, about 78 per cent of the fun
is in the rolling.

Are you done yet, Ads?
                                   No, not yet. Just got to . . .
                      Any chance of that smoke, Ads?
                                   Wrong side of the paper, got to . . .
                            Did we already smoke that one?
No, haven't lit it yet.

So Alex just has to sit back and watch it happen. Attempts, second
attempts, best of five ('Adam, you do this *all* day. Why don't you get
any *better* at it?'). He walks over to the wine crates holding the LPs,
gets infuriated with the brutal Luddism of any man who still deals in
vinyl and needle. Sits back down and realizes the wrong tune has been
chosen. Too lively. You never know with Mr Gaye, that's his trouble.

'Black Jew, actually.'

'Marvin?'

'Yeah, no, well, not of a kind I recognize – kind of a Christian cult with a Hebrew fetish. Or the other way around. Can't remember the specifics. I read it somewhere. Liner notes?'

Adam sticks his face towards a candle, and the fat end of their smoke crackles like a bushfire. 'What a voice, though,' he says. He exhales magnificently. The smoke exits in two great curlicues from his nose like a phantom moustache. 'It's like God took Stevie's honey and poured it over gravel.'

For Adam, the world is music. It is a peculiar thing about Adam that films do nothing for him. He sells videos to people like a teetotal barman makes drinks, with an anthropological curiosity. Film is an artificial, circumscribed box to him – four walls and nothing but empty International Gestures inside it. Precisely the reason Alex loves it. It is *dealable* with. Whereas music is antennae, infinitely connected, impossible. Movies versus music. The last public entertainment these two men both enjoyed was a wrestling match, fifteen years ago.

'He's singing too fast,' says Alex, reaching, prematurely, for the smoke.

Adam sits back. He puts his feet on the table. 'You should get me Sammy Davis,' says Adam thoughtfully. '*There* was a Black Jew. He opened up Vegas for the blacks. He was a trailblazer.'

'Hmm,' says Alex, thinking of drugs.

'Oi. Where's my video? *The Girl from Peking*. Where is it? That's your tenth rental since I bought it. Why don't you just buy it off me? It'd be cheaper.'

Alex considers this. 'If I owned it,' he says gravely, 'I think I literally would not do anything else but watch it.'

'Only idiots use the word "literally" in conversation,' says Adam lightly. 'So, all right, then, give it back. You're late. You owe five quid on it already.'

'Let me keep it a bit longer. I think I feel like watching it tonight.'

Adam shakes his head, and applies one hand to his temple as if trying to ease the passage of an idea. 'Tell me, what is it about her, exactly? Not just her. All of them. It's not just work to you, is it? Or to Joseph. I mean, what goes on there?'

Alex waves vaguely at the record collection, wine crates that reach half the height of the room. 'No big deal. What are this lot to you?'

'Answer the question.'

Alex snatches the smoke, inhales to the pit of his lungs. He repeats the action three times and closes his eyes.

'I just want to know what the story is,' persists Adam. 'They're actors. And who cares about actors?'

'You have to understand,' begins Alex slowly. 'It's not the *new* ones. It's the old ones. I don't give a damn about the *new* ones. I don't care if so-and-so makes a convincing paraplegic. I couldn't give a damn about his stupid, ugly real name – he should change it. So he put on forty pounds and learnt to box. And? So he went and lived with chimpanzees for three months. And? I don't care if he climbed Everest. I don't care. All that is useless to me. I can't watch a film after 1969. They make me nauseous. I like the old ones.'

'Because?'

'Because . . . I don't know, something like because they just play themselves, they just play essences of themselves.'

'Explain.'

'It's like when you go on about Hollywood . . . like saying it's a false religion that only worships pleasure and the rest – then if that's the case, at *least do it properly*. Right? At least *be* a false god. Do you see what I'm getting at? Be *honest* about it. It's like: *be*

Clark Gable, *be* god of masculinity. *Be* Dietrich, the goddess of whatever, I dunno, easy virtue, say. *Be* Poitier, definitely god of all personal dignity. Etc. If you're going to be Bogart, *be Bogart*. Be the *essence of Bogart*. Ever notice how big Bogart's head was on his body? He looked like a caricature of *himself*.'

Adam frowns, nonplussed. 'And with Kitty – what is it with her?'

'She is the most beautiful thing,' says Alex sheepishly, 'that I have ever seen. That's it. I know that doesn't mean anything to you.'

'I think beauty, real beauty, is the realization of the divine on earth. A fresh-cut lawn. A canyon. A clean crack in the pavement. You're just talking about sex.'

'Look, I like trees too,' sighs Alex. 'And mountains. I like all of that stuff. But all I'm saying is that *beauty in women* is the realization of the divine in *human* life.'

Marvin, at last, is singing something suitable. Adam's eyes are big and sad. He is clenching his jaw. 'Esther said . . . she said that when you crashed the car, the first thing you did was check you still had the . . . whatever we're calling it – the *autograph*. The Kitty Alexander.'

Alex opens his mouth and shuts it again.

'Alex? Explain that to me, please. What's she the goddess of? Must be pretty important. You've been with Es for ten years, Al. *Ten years*.'

'That can't be true – Ads, I don't remember doing that.'

'That's what she said. She never lies, as you know. You're her whole life.'

'I *know*.'

'Imagine if she'd been thrown forward any harder – if her pacemaker had dislodged. I couldn't *defend* that. I can't defend *you*. It's like you think the world is made up of your name, over and over.'

'But – I mean, isn't that just the way *everyone* –'

Alex lets it go. Angry, Adam hunches over the coffee table to begin the rolling process again, although the first is not a quarter smoked. Alex hunches down next to him.

'Ads.'

'What.'

'Can I just ask something?'

'What.'

'Did you see me?'

'Did I see you what?'

'Fake it.'

'Jeez Louise, don't start this again, mate. Please.'

'Answer.'

'OK. No.'

'And Joseph?'

'You know what he says. He says you went to the kitchen and you came back with it.'

Alex whimpers.

'Is that all you're worried about?' asks Adam wonderingly. 'The name of someone you never met?'

Halachah *(Pop Quiz #2)*

Q. What is the law concerning the man who is very stoned and the man who is not as stoned as he? How shall these two behave towards each other?

A. The one who is less stoned shall make the tea and, eventually, seek out some food. The one who is more stoned shall have the right – for the period during which he is more stoned – to tell the other man exactly what his problem is.

'I'll tell you *exactly what your problem is*,' says Adam. His eyes are veiny blood oranges. It is late. The curtains are open. Alex has been trying to leave for about three years. He is hovering over the sofa in the pose of a cross-country skier. Outside the furious sun is plummeting behind the railway sidings. Red is everywhere.

'Ads, I should go, now, really. I've got to eat some food.'

'Do you or do you not want to know what your problem is?'

'No. I want to eat. I'm very stoned. Aren't you?'

'Yes,' says Adam. 'But in a very lucid way.' He stands, he walks to the far wall, he places his hands upon it like a healer. 'The world is broken, Alex.'

'Fine.'

'When the world was created,' says Adam, miming an orb with one hand, pointing to the biscuit tin with the other, 'He entered with His orbs of light; made from the letters, He filled the world with Himself. But HaShem is infinite – in order to create finite beings, He had to retract Himself, He had to *withdraw*. Creation is an act of withdrawal. But when He exited, He –'

'Screwed it up?'

'He did not exit fully. He left shards of Himself . . . specks of light and . . . bits –'

'Bits? Technical term, that, is it?'

'Bits of *essences*,' says Adam, pointing to the *sefirot*. Alex's head hurts. He could do without the lecture about the bits of the bits. He's had it before and he's never understood it. And for a while now, something sad has been creeping up on him, disguised in smoke. It may be Esther's face. It may be Kitty's. It is definitely the idea of woman, of a softness he might curl up into. He must get home. Find women. Call them, write to them. Get them to come and hold him, if only for an hour.

Adam says, 'And in the simplest terms in which it can be expressed, the problem is this: the godhead is incomplete. He *needs* us.'

There is biscuit all over the couch. It looks like Alex has been feeding the couch. His hunger is such that he doesn't have the patience to chew the biscuits any more. He just wants the biscuits to become part of him, to cleave unto him, by magic.

'To put it back together?' he asks, picking speculatively at one crumb. 'That's a big job, my friend.'

'To reunite,' says Adam, 'what has been dispersed. We do this by good actions. The godhead is not finished without us. We accrue merit to the godhead by good actions. The purpose is for *us* to reward *Him*, not for *Him* to reward *us* – if you don't get that, you can't understand Job. Job makes no sense without that. Remember Scholem? *A world without redemption – go explain that to the goyim!* The Jews heal the godhead, not vice versa. Kaddish is the same principle. Heal the father.'

Enough. Their time is up. Alex gets his friend by the elbow, Rubinfine-style, and moves them towards the exit. In the doorway, Adam presses a small bag of something to take home into Alex's hand, and for a minute they perform the I.G.s relating to *An undeserved gift between friends*.

'Do me a favour. Take this. And think about what we discussed. And call Esther. She has something to tell you. It's not for me to do it. Call her.'

Reluctantly, Alex pockets the small bag. 'I'll think about things, yes? And I'll call Esther this evening. Promise. On my note. OK?'

'Thank you. Thank you, Al, really.'

'Look, look – later –' Alex kisses his friend on the forehead. 'I'm leaving, and we haven't even talked about how it's going for you. I'll phone or – I'll mail . . .'

'That's fine. It's late – I need to study. Anyway, I'm guest-starring in *your* film today, right? I'm just here for the –'

'Enlightenment.'

'Actually, I was going to say entertainment.'

Adam opens the door. The rain is full again. A fist would barely hold ten droplets. He passes Alex an umbrella. 'Al, remember that thing? When I was going to study the letters of a joke, translate it into Hebrew – permute them? Meditate on them? You know, just to see. Like, the founding joke of all the others?'

Alex claps his hands. 'Got to be *"Shit Happens"*, surely?'

'No, I thought about that, but I wanted a longer joke. I knew I'd get more with a longer joke. It might take me the rest of my life, but I'll get more. I want to see if there's any patterns in the numerology. Can you tell it in 613 words, for an example? *That* would be a *trip*. Look, you've *got* to hear this joke, man – I've spent weeks choosing it – come *on* – it's not like you have a proper job, is it? Is it?' Adam does that little hopping dance of impatience on the doorstep. 'No? Yes? I'll even give you permission to use it in the book. Come on now, that's a good deal.'

'All right, but *quickly*. I've got rain coming down my collar.'

'OK, so it's about the Pope and the Chief Rabbi . . .'

The Joke about the Pope and the Chief Rabbi

Several centuries ago the Pope decreed that all the Jews had to
leave Italy. There was, of course, a huge outcry from the Jewish
community, so the Pope offered a deal. He would have a
religious debate with a leader of the Jewish community. If the
Jewish leader won the debate, the Jews would be permitted to
stay in Italy. If the Pope won, the Jews would have to leave.

The Jewish community met and picked an aged rabbi,
Moishe, to represent them in the debate. Rabbi Moishe,
however, could not speak Latin and the Pope could not speak
Yiddish. So it was decided that this would be a 'silent' debate.

On the day of the great debate the Pope and Rabbi Moishe sat
opposite each other for a full minute before the Pope raised his
hand and showed three fingers. Rabbi Moishe looked back and
raised one finger.

Next, the Pope waved his finger around his head. Rabbi
Moishe pointed to the ground where he sat. The Pope then
brought out a communion wafer and chalice of wine. Rabbi
Moishe pulled out an apple. With that, the Pope stood up and
said, 'I concede the debate. This man has bested me. The Jews
can stay.'

Later, the cardinals gathered around the Pope, asking him
what had happened. The Pope said, 'First I held up three fingers
to represent the Trinity. He responded by holding up one finger
to remind me that there was still one God common to both our
religions. Then I waved my finger around me to show him that
God was all around us. He responded by pointing to the ground
to show that God was also right here with us. I pulled out the
wine and the wafer to show that God absolves us of our sins.

He pulled out an apple to remind me of Original Sin. He had an answer for everything. What could I do?'

Meanwhile, the Jewish community crowded around Rabbi Moishe, asking what happened. 'Well,' said Moishe, 'first he said to me, "You Jews have three days to get out of here." So I said to him, "Not one of us is going to leave." Then he tells me the whole city would be cleared of Jews. So I said to him, "Listen here, Mr Pope, the Jews . . . we stay right here!"'

'And then?' asked a woman.

'Who knows?' said Rabbi Moishe. 'We broke for lunch.'

'Oh, *mate*,' says Alex, kicking the door, pushing tears away. 'Oh, Ads . . . now *that's* why I love you. That's really beautiful. Really.'

'Isn't it, though?'

SEVEN / *Gevurah*

Power • Anita versus Grace • Fingerprints • Modern life is rubbish and lonely • Eliot was goyish (he was also a prophet) • Artists versus workers • Kafka was Jewish • America • What do women want? • At the movies

I

'Look,' said Alex, to his downstairs neighbour Anita Chang, 'I'm not disagreeing with you. My cat, my responsibility. But I can't control everything Grace does. She's really her own person.'

Anita Chang bit the inside of her cheek, giving her lovely face something of a cold look. This evening she seemed all twisted out of shape. Why one shoulder up like that, and the arms crossed at such an angle and so tightly, the right ankle bent out of skew – why that high heel attacking the doormat?

'Cat,' said Anita, her mouth quick as a camera's shutter, 'not a person.'

A long, white, basically good-hearted coil of fluff twisted itself around Anita's peaceful ankle, speculated on the other one, thought better of it and slunk behind Alex in the doorway. He knelt down and scooped Grace up in his arms. 'Right. Cat.'

'And I don't want your cat,' said Anita, blinking rapidly, 'in my house. Any more.'

'O-*kay*,' said Alex very slowly. '*What. Ever. You. Say.*'

He tried to kiss Grace on the nose as a sort of seal on the deal, but Grace whipped her head round, flattened her ears and gave Anita the evil eye.

'And I don't want,' continued Anita, smacking her rolled-up evening paper on his kitchen windowsill, 'to come home to any more of your cat's mess.'

As she said this, the pink financial pages escaped the paper and landed on the floor in between the two of them. In her business skirt (But what business? He had always been too scared to ask), she bent down in a business-like fashion and inserted them back into the body of the newspaper, maintaining the overall crease. She was fantastic. Oh *Anita*!

'And what I *really* don't want,' said Anita, clicking open her attaché case and thrusting a sheet of paper at him, 'is to be treated like a fool on top of everything else. You might think this contract is a joke, but I took some time drawing it up, to solve precisely this problem, and everyone else in the building has signed it. Flats B, C, D and my own. It's just you left. My feeling is, if we all abide by certain rules regarding pets, then no one need lose the things they love. So. Please sign it properly.'

'Sign . . . ?'

'I pushed it under your door *three weeks ago*, with a note explaining the urgency, and then finally you push it back under my door like this? I don't find,' said Anita, underscoring with a pearl fingernail a line of strange doodles – a table, two long-haired sprites, another table on its side, a broken twig – 'this sort of thing funny. Please amend it, and then put it back through my door.'

Grace stretched out a paw of reconciliation, but Anita was gone.

In one economical movement Alex closed his front door, kicked off his shoes, removed his trousers, caught the back of Grace on the front of his foot and lightly drop-kicked her into the kitchen.

'I don't *know* why,' he said in answer to a quizzical miaow. 'I don't know what she has against us. We like *her*.'

Grace leapt up on to the kitchen counter, where Alex was preparing to heat up some soup. She put the wrong end of herself in his face.

'Well, *I* like her. You're weird about women.'

Anita Chang replaced Fat Roy (nice enough, obese) downstairs two years ago. Upon hearing her name in a leaseholders' meeting – even before his first sighting – Alex got carried away. Like a teenager, he shopped: new trousers, posh kettle, Chinese wall-hanging, impressive books. As the moving-van pulled up, he wrote reams of inkless fiction, fantasy scenarios: cups of sugar, lent and returned; *Well, since we're both stuck indoors tonight*; Oriental synergy; gentle ways to break the news to Esther . . .

It had not turned out that way, though. Anita wasn't sentimental like him, or interested in shared-race, or coincidence, or shared racial coincidence ('Yes, that is correct. Both Year of the Dog. Is it a reason for celebration? Shall we break out the Pedigree Chum?'). Sometimes he bumped into the boyfriend, a strapping South African who had that charming habit of asking a question and then looking elsewhere. So it goes.

Objecting to the bitter smell from the stove, Grace now made a big show of leaving the kitchen in disgust (tail up, piteous backward glance), only to return a minute later and slink back and forth in front of the cat-food cupboard. There are many Jewish cats in the world: his mother's sombre and *simpatica* tortoiseshell, Shoshana, had kittens constantly. He could have had one of those. What perversity, then, made him live with this goyish, humourless, pink-eyed fluffball?

Mre-surch, said Grace, sort of, while washing her face.

Yes, research. And now research had turned to love. He took two breakfast bowls out of a cupboard, put Grace's gunk in one and his own soup in the other. His was medicinal and disgusting. So was hers. Three weeks earlier she had been on a cat-drip in some sort of cat-hospital with suspected cat-AIDS. *Not* cat-AIDS as it turned out. Something else. He never saw the cat-drip, but was assured by his vet that it had been used. He had the image of the tiny bed, the tiny tube, the tiny bag. Three hundred pounds, he paid, for the treatment. Twenty pounds for the cat-gunk. Fifteen pounds for his own gunk. Grace's gunk had side-effects. It loosened her bowels and made her vomit, sometimes in Anita's flat (she came in through the window), or outside her door, left like a package she wasn't home to receive. On this very subject, Alex had once written: *The practice of medicine is at its most goyish when symptoms of a disease, and the side-effects caused by medicines given to <u>counter</u> those symptoms, are indistinguishable.* The side-effects of Alex's gunk seemed to be confusion, depression, forgetfulness, anger, weepiness, violence, feelings of worthlessness, dread of women and muscular aches. The medicine itself was meant to ward off the activation of what he believed was his genetic time bomb, his cancer gene. Two goys they were – Grace and her owner – trying to stave off the inevitable.

Ug, said Alex, as he spilt a bit of Grace's gunk into his own bowl. *Mrawh*, said Grace, *mwroo-euew*.

No one said anything about living alone. Or what it does to you. Outside, another man who lived alone in the same building tapped

amiably on Alex's window but did not pause. By the time Alex had
lifted a hand to wave, he was gone. Slowly, Alex brought his hand
back to the counter. A clean, slicing sound, like a guillotine, told
him that Anita Chang's contract had just been nudged into the
hair's-width chasm between washing machine and cooker. He bent
over. He could see it, down there. There was a whole gross *world*
down there. *Hello*. He could also smell –

Alex lunged to switch the gas off and stayed alive. He leant
against the counter, breathless. Thought of the other outcome had
he not (you live alone, you light a cigarette, BOOM! A modern
sort of tragedy). Then he put the lid back on the boiled soup,
deposited the empty cat-gunk-can in the bin under the sink. He
wiped down the surfaces, the front of the washing machine, the
edges of the shelves. He got a sponge and soaked up the week-old
gunge in the fridge. He swept something somewhere else where it
couldn't be seen. He got on his hands and knees and scrubbed at a
mound of red wax on a floor tile. After the greater part of it was
gone, he got a cheese knife and worked at the grooves in between
the tiles. Grace mooched by and knighted him with her tail. Once.
Twice. Third time he grabbed her by the head, examined her teeth
and cleaned those with the tip of his house-key. Satisfied, he stood
up. Switched off the light, and then switched it back on. The other
man who lived alone had left two fingerprints on his window,
visible from here. Reminiscent of murders, alibis.

2

In his bedroom, Alex sat at his desk and put Grace on his lap. He
scratched her behind the ears, and switched on the box of tricks.

Weialala leia went the music.

        Alex drummed his fingers, waiting –
Only fifteen seconds but it feels *so long* –

    (Teach us to care and not to care . . . Teach us to sit still)
Wallala leialala

A month or so ago, while Alex was drinking in a bar, a man claiming to be an artist projected this world-famous interface, this window, with its tinkly opening music, on to the wall. It was followed by other inanities, but nothing else had quite the effect of this. For a moment everyone in the bar was reminded, *compelled* to remember, the work undone. Documents unfinished. Letters half written. That game of suspended solitaire which sits at home, waiting for Alex-Li and his entire generation to return and finish it (and lose).

Wallala leialala.
      la la

Slowly Alex's window jerks into life. It has been designed, he knows, with the intention of ordering his thoughts and conserving his space. Thinking of this, Alex touches his fingertips to the plasma (concentric rainbows!) and takes some pride in how successfully he has thwarted these intentions. Icon overlaps icon, crowding out the wallpaper (the popular singer Madonna, naked, thumbing for a ride), pressing at the edges of the screen. All files incompetently named: ThisOne, ThisOne2, Alex1, AlexLi2, AlTandem4, Alexi3, Tandemimportant. He has a file called RUBINFINE-PHNENMBER which contains Rubinfine's phone number and nothing else. Important, he feels, not to let these interfaces have the power, not *all* the power.

And now Alex opens a folder called KITTYLETRS that represents the only evidence he has of thousands of words he has written over many years.

The Kitty Letters. They begin life as standard Autograph Man fare. They are fan letters and, at the same time, autograph requests. The letters come with self-addressed envelopes, interesting facts about their author and glossy 12 × 14s of Kitty herself.

A sample letter from this period, from when Alex-Li was only fifteen:

Alex-Li Tandem
37A Humboldt Avenue
Mountjoy
London N23

Dear Miss Alexander,

 I am your biggest fan. If there is a more beautiful vision than you as you appeared in the movie The Girl from Peking, *then I have yet to see it! As an avid Autograph Man, who is himself half Chinese and interested in the cinema, your signature would take pride of place in my collection. I am the kind of person who thinks of autographs as historical documents, and any museum of cinema would be deprived if it did not have you in it. I hope and pray that you might find the time to sign this photograph for me and return it in the self-addressed envelope enclosed within.*

 I remain your devoted admirer,
 Alex-Li Tandem
 P.S. May you rot in hell, Krauser.

Max Krauser being president of the KAAA (Kitty Alexander Association of America) and therefore Alex's nemesis. It is Krauser whom Alex holds responsible for denying him the true, the only, postal address. It is Krauser who sends him, on occasion, those humiliating form letters that open with the odious phrase *we thank you for your interest*. Krauser is the Wall of Jericho between Alex and what he wants, which would be fine if Alex's trumpet worked.

A few months after his seventeenth birthday, desperate at the silence from New York, Alex changed tactics. He felt the autograph guides had misled him when they advised that an Autograph Man should

talk interestingly about himself, show that he is more than just a fan, more than one of the hoy polloy [sic] . . . rather, try to show the celebrity of your choice that you are a unique individual!

– *The Autograph Adventurer*, no. 197

To Kitty, clearly, he was just like the rest of them. One day, he wrote the following line into a letter that was itself only three lines long: *From now on, I am going to tell you about <u>yourself</u>*. And that is what he is about to do now, in this new document he has opened. The same thing he has done for ten years. There are hundreds and hundreds of them and not one has ever been answered.

Dear Kitty,
   She walks into the store and winces at the age of the boy serving her. Even his knuckles have no lines. He should be in school, she thinks.

Love,
Alex-Li Tandem

Dear Kitty,

   While sitting on a bench in the park, she sees a man her own age doubled over as if in the middle of a painful crisis. She is alarmed (How can she help? What should she do?), but then she is freed from making a decision: he is only picking up a coin. She feels a sneaky relief and thinks of the old Zen joke: Don't just do something! Sit there!

Love,
Alex-Li Tandem

Dear Kitty,

   When behind a young man on a bus, she finds herself staring at his neck. The urge to touch it is almost overwhelming! And then he scratches it, as if he knew.

Love,
Alex-Li Tandem

Dear Kitty,

   She visits an area of town full of second-hand clothing stores. She smiles stupidly in a bakery, unable to suppress the thought that everyone is wearing everyone else's clothes.

Love,
Alex-Li Tandem

Over the years he has learnt that some of these letters come to him instantly, while others take longer to brew. Today, with the fake white page lit up in front of him, he doesn't know how to thank her. He reaches down to the floor, to his bag, and takes out the autograph. He rests it against the screen. And then the words come with no struggle at all.

Dear Kitty,

    It is pointed out to her at a family party (by someone she hates) that she crosses her legs as her father did. She protests, but then when she looks down, she can see for herself that it is true. A second later she remembers playing horse-and-rider on her father's boot. Smiling, she jiggles her own boot up and down.

Love and thanks,
Alex-Li Tandem
(Your greatest fan)

3

Kitty Letter done, Alex presses a button and the box of tricks begins to sing. With its screech. With its *jug jug*. With its dirty-bird song. In a few seconds he will be connected to the world. The world! One day he will take advantage of this incredible resource. He will find out about ancient Babylonia and gain a working knowledge of Estonian. He will learn how to make a bomb. One day. For now, he means to head straight for his corner of the world, an imaginary auction room where each day he checks on the progress of items he has put up for sale. That's his aim this evening – he is very serious and determined about it. This is his real business, after all, his bread and butter. And he will in *no way* be tempted by that friendly, clumsy woman, falling in and out of her bikini, beckoning to him from the corner of the screen . . .

Look, five minutes only, Alex said to Grace, who humoured him by nodding. She purred. He clicked. It opened. Grace brushed her paw down a list of she-males, plastic people, the elderly, the pregnant, the damaged, the tirelessly gynaecological, the twisted and restrained. Poor Alex; he only really wanted to see two young people, naked, together. Near the bottom he found something that would do. He unbuttoned himself and waited. Grace gave him her superior look. She disapproved. He disapproved too – but what were his options? He was lonely. In preparation, the muscles of his right arm flexed. *Go on*, he whispered, and one female leapt off his knees and crawled under the bed. The other pulled some strange pot-bellied man towards her and opened her legs.

Wallala leialala, cried the woman, after a while, *Oh baby!*

Ug, said Alex, after a while, *Oh, yeah. Uuug.*

In six minutes it was all over. The second after the ecstasy came the transformation. It was just one hairless animal stabbing another repeatedly through an open wound. Then it was gone, as if it had never been. Tissues in the bin, Grace reinstated, fag rolled. Back to business.

At the auction, Alex quickly and expertly raised the price of his own items with fake bids, and then swooped to claim a Mickey Carroll, one of the original Munchkins from the 1939 film. He meant to sell this to Rubinfine's wife, Rebecca, who had recently taken such a strong interest in the restricted nature of some people's growth. Rebecca's sudden, charitable urges represented a significant market for Alex. He had sold her three Helen Keller letters the month she was raising money for the deaf and dumb. When she became engrossed in the sufferings of Native Americans she relieved him of a very expensive chief. And when her father died, Alex took the opportunity to clear out his Judaica, he sold her *everything*: Israeli statesmen, Jewish humorists, postcards of synagogues, actors, inventors. All of which she made Rubinfine pay for in cash. Yes, the job had small pleasures in it, for the man who bothered to find them.

'Keep an eye on things,' muttered Alex, and left Grace in his seat as he went to the bathroom. When he returned he found Grace had successfully overseen the sale of a Dick Powell, a Carole Lombard and a Gary Cooper. A thousand pounds for the lot. This was the problem. It was too easy. Whenever he considered becoming more gainfully employed, he was forced to face that equation of money/time/work that is familiar to every stripper: in which other profession could I make so much money in so little time with so little effort? He had long ago confronted that very stark choice, so beloved by his generation:

1. Be a starving, but happy, artist.
2. Be an affluent, but depressed, professional.

Alex had chosen the less travelled, third path of ignored genius, the tenets of which are as follows: basically, the world doesn't like genius. The world tries to stifle genius, basically. If the world wanted genius, it would allow Alex a minute (just a minute!) to turn to the file named BOOKTHISONE.doc and start work. It would allow him to do nothing but work on *Jewishness and Goyishness* and starve while he did it. But no. Instead the world wanted, *demanded*, that he answer these flashing messages, sent by the emotionally stunted. And so he did. He assured Jeff Shinestein of Hoboken, New Jersey, that his Mata Hari was in the post. He calmed the raging Jim Streve of South Bend, Indiana, explaining once more that his Gina Lollobrigida was the real McCoy. He came to a gentleman's agreement with Texan Jim Eggerton: Veronica Lake and Viveca Lindfors in exchange for Jean Simmons, Alain Delon and Lassie.

Firing off bad-tempered mail (if only the real post were so quick, so sensationally *satisfying*), Alex reflected on the plight of poor Franz Kafka. All day long stuck in that office, drawing the mutilated hands of strangers, the victims of industrial accidents. His genius ignored for so long. Suffocated by colleagues. Ridiculed by friends and family. Almost directly, Alex felt better. Yes, there was always *Kafka*. Alex found examples of ignored genius from history very soothing.

Business done, Alex printed off this week's Kitty Letter and sealed it in a pretty pink envelope. Turning back to his screen, he checked quickly through the non-business material. A marvellous, technologically illiterate mail from his mother, asking if he'd got her last 'telegram'. Joseph had sent some poor jokes about people who work in telesales. What else? Adverts, porn, mass-mails.

Alex winced as he spotted a Mail of Doom. There is always one. This one was from Boot. Boot was a girl. She worked as an assistant in Cotterell's Autograph Emporium in Neville Court, a cobbled alley in the centre of town, the oldest part of the city. It was a posh shop, run by an elderly knight, Sir Edward Cotterell – but no one in it knew what they were doing. Once a week on a Thursday Alex went in and got paid three hundred pounds to tell them what was real and what was fake. And then he made the short trip to Chinatown to get some medicine. But on three occasions last year, instead of going to see Dr Huang, he had gone and had posh sex with Boot on her posh (very long) lunch break. Oh, Boot was posh (and *lovely*). But Boot had helped mess things up in his head regarding Esther. He was hiding from posh Boot. Had been, for three months. So, why mail me, Boot?

Subject: I suppose you're wondering why I'm mailing you.

Well, your due in the shop tommorow and Cotterell DEMANDS I be
in the shop tommorow and I can't get out of it and I cant be at all
bothered with arkwardness, alright? So don't be wierd. Or try to be
a little less wierd than usual.

That is all.

Boot xx

P.S. I know your avoiding me and I must say I just could'nt give a
monkeys.
P.P.S. I have cut off all my hair. with it has gone my GIRLHOOD,
apparently. Please don't go on about it when you see me.

He couldn't help it. He had his little goyish fetishes, one of which
was awe for anyone so posh she couldn't be bothered to be embarrassed. Or to *spell* properly.

Just as he is about to shut down, Alex spots a flashing mail in
the corner. The subject is AMERICA. The contents appear to be an
official confirmation of two tickets he has booked to New York: a
night flight, this coming Friday. Returning on the Tuesday. He has
no recollection of booking these flights. In a panic he smokes three
cigarettes back to back. He rips the room apart for his diary. Out of
February floats a flyer.

Oh. Yes. No. Right. The Autographicana Fair, an annual extrava-
ganza. Autograph Men from all over the world came to show off
their wares. Real-life celebrity guest stars turn up too, signing for
money. Last year, in Washington, the guest stars were Tom Ferebee
and Paul Tibbets, two of the men who dropped the bomb on Hiroshima. This year it is in New York. Guest stars to be announced. He

was going to surprise Esther and make some money on the side –
that had been the plan. But wasn't it *next* Saturday? And where
exactly was it? And who were his contacts there? Had he arranged
to have a stall? How could he cancel Esther's ticket? Does high-
grade acid really cause short-term memory loss?

Alex begins to mail people about all this, American people. He
waits for them to mail him back. While waiting, he visits a medical
site and diagnoses himself as having a rare blood disease and (in
all probability) the early stages of lymphatic cancer. He smokes
another despondent cigarette.

Americans are so efficient. Here come his replies, spelt correctly
and straight to the point. Honey Richardson, a lady in New York
with a substantial collection, e-mails him to say it sure is this
Saturday, and that the two of them can meet to trade, privately,
afterwards at the corner of something and something – one of those
cinematic coordinates. Don Keely, organizer of Autographicana,
says he has no record of Alex booking a stall and it's way too late,
buddy. Way too late now. Miss Alice McIntyre of American Airlines
says the tickets are strictly non-refundable. Strictly non-
refundable, asks Alex? Strictly non-refundable, says Alice. What
about, asks Alex, if I sell the ticket to a friend, I mean, can you
change the name on the ticket? Strictly non-refundable and non-
exchangeable, says Alice. And I suppose, says Alex, another
date . . . ? Strictly non-refundable, non-exchangeable and non-
switchable, says Alice. *Switchable*, repeats Alex, *now that's not
strictly a word, Alice.* Strictly, begins Alice –

But Alex hangs up on Alice and phones Esther.

'*Esther*,' he says, 'wait. Give me a minute.'

'No time, Alex. That's the point. Not even a minute.'

Her voice is harder than he has ever heard it.

'Wait, Es, wait. Please?'

She does not speak. She does not hang up.

'How've you been, Es?'

'I've been shit. And you?'

'Yeah, not the best. How's your finger?'

'Still broken. Rigid. I look like I'm giving everyone the finger all the time. Look – what do you want, Al?'

'Nothing. I miss you.'

She does not speak. She does not hang up.

'I wanted to explain, Es – about that night, and the thing, you know, with the autograph? I probably shouldn't have got so over the top about –'

Alex never got to finish that sentence. Apparently, it was not the point. The point, as Esther saw it, was not singular, it was not an incident. It was massive, amorphous. It was like a poisonous gas they were breathing. The problem, according to her, was everything. Alex rolled a cigarette and listened as she spoke the careful discourse of modern relationships – time apart, re-evaluation, my needs, your needs. He meant to follow, but he was easily distracted during abstract conversation. He found himself thinking of the way she could pull you into her by some interior muscle, and then, when you exited, you saw this flush of red neatly packed between two dark folds, like some crazy flower. Was that wrong?

She was saying, *You don't listen to me, you take me for granted*. She was saying, *And as for this other girl, the white girl, whoever she is* – which surprised him. He was truly knocked into silence by that. Had Adam told her about Boot? Alex felt consumed, furious about that possibility – now *he* felt the victim of an injustice. This new role was so much easier to play! He snapped at her. She snapped back. Now they were snapping. Towards the end she was crying.

The Autograph Man

She was saying, *All women are like just symbols to you? All you ever –*

And he was deeply regretful, saying, *No, no, no, you're wrong, I love you*, to nobody.

He rang again. She did not pick up. He waited five minutes, disguised his number and rang again. Now he was crying and she was perfectly collected. She said: 'I've got an operation on Sunday. They're taking the ticker out. It's past its sell-by date, apparently. I've known for a while, but I've been putting it off and now it's a bit of an emergency. No more time, though. Time for the next chapter. So I'm getting another.'

'Oh, no. Es, why didn't you –'

'Look: this is not *Terms of Endearment*, right? It's not a big deal. Routine. They cut me open, they take it out. Replace with new state-of-the-art number. I just want to know whether you're going to be there or not. It's St Christopher's.'

'But – why am I hearing about this so last minute –'

'Oh, Alex, forget it, just don't bother, OK –'

'No, wait – I'm just – which day? Just tell me the day.'

'Sunday. I just said. This Sunday.'

'Ri-ight. Sunday?'

'Yes, Alex. Sunday. Why – have you got an auction on? Is Kitty for sale? Is that a bad day for you?'

'Of *course* not.'

'Fine.'

'OK, Es? Es. Oh God. I know how this sounds . . . look, the only thing about this Sunday –'

With two little words, violently said, Esther terminated the conversation.

160

Alex went to the lounge, pushed the film in the player and took out Adam's little gift. He rolled. He smoked. He thought about that operation. Lifting that little box out of its home. Opening up that scar. Making another one. And black skin scars badly. What's left behind stays pink and angry, always.

He wept freely. After a while, he wiped his nose on his wrist. He could have played that conversation differently, he saw that. But you don't get no rewind in this life, as the black grandmothers in the movies like to say. Instead he pressed play. And God help him, God pass on judgement, but as the opening credits rose up, so did something inside him. He had always wondered: *can women do this too?* Can they switch from real people (Esther, only her, always) to fantasy people (Kitty, Anita, Boot, porn girls, shop girls, girl girls) and feel soothed by them? Will they ever tell? They don't tell. Women don't tell the truth about themselves. About love, about the *way they love*. Or else the truth is genuinely pure, involving no second-guessing – in which case, who could stand to hear it? Grace walked in and settled herself over his feet. Alex sank into his chair.

In the film Kitty's eyes were taped down as ever, and she was lost in New York, again, a Peking girl with no friends. In less than an hour she will be the toast of Broadway and then Hollywood, but of course she doesn't know that yet. Soon everybody will know her name. She will be famous. Soon. For now, she can only walk the streets, a nobody, fearing every shadow. Lonely. Alex's heart cleaves to her as he watches her slender form slipping into cinemas, sitting in the dark. You see, it is only at the movies that May-Ling Han finds comfort. From his elevated booth, Jules Munshin, who plays Joey Kay the projectionist, looks down. He is in love with her, of course. He thinks he has no hope. He is dumb-looking, poor.

But he'll get her. Things are moving faster than he knows. In one hour twenty minutes it will all be over. In between, there will be some tears. And then the laughter. He will become her manager, her husband, her everything. It is called a happy ending. The miracle of cinema is how rarely the convention of the happy ending is broken. The bigger miracle is that the convention of the ending is never broken at all. Alex watches Joey watching Kitty watching the huge flickering faces of people she presumes to be gods.

EIGHT / *Hochmah*

I

'So,' said Rubinfine, 'what are we going to do about *this*?'

Alex checked his watch. It was Thursday. It was nine in the
morning. Rabbis Darvick and Green looked exhausted. Darvick
had specks of white gloop in the corners of his eyes. Green had
both hands against the Mountjoy memorial, one knee bent, puffing
like he'd run a marathon. Rubinfine looked just fine. Parked in
front of them all was a small Italian car. Next to that, a huge
dining-room table fashioned from walnut.

'What are you *doing* out here?' asked Alex. 'Again? It's nine in
the morning.'

'What are *you* doing?'

'Look, I *live* round here. And now I'm going to work.'

Darvick's fat face started to shake. He laughed with his shoulders
forward and his mouth wide open. He grabbed Alex by the wrist to
steady himself. 'I thought you didn't *have* a job. I thought you were
just this schloompy guy with no job.'

'Well, Rabbi, you've been misinformed. I *have* a job. I'm heading
for Pemberton Hill. I have work. That needs to be done.'

'Of *course* you do,' said Green soothingly. 'Everybody has things they need to do.'

'Aaa-lex?' asked Rubinfine softly, studying the sky. 'What's the law concerning sun-roofs? By which I mean: if we put the table in through the boot, but let its forelegs, as it were, protrude from the roof . . . would I be violating any road regulations you're aware of?'

'Rubinfine,' said Alex with his eyes closed, 'that table is not going in that car.'

'On the contrary,' said Rubinfine.

'It must,' said Darvick.

'Fine. That's fine,' said Alex and turned to go, walking straight into a wall of flesh shaped like Green.

'You see, *Rebecca*,' said Rubinfine, crouching down beside the table, 'needs it. At the barn-dance, on Sunday. For the . . . small people. It's for the refreshments. She wants a buffet rather than a sit-down meal. She thinks it will be more . . . suitable. You know how she thinks of everything. Also, this table is particularly low and, as you know, their growth is . . .' Rubinfine sighed.

Green leant forward. 'Restricted,' he said.

'You'll come to the barn-dance?' asked Rubinfine.

'Uh-uh,' replied Alex firmly. 'I'll go to America. Sorry. I've got business.'

'Rebecca will be *very* disappointed,' said Rubinfine, his hands fussing with the air. 'She hoped to see you. Didn't she, Rabbi Darvick? She won't be happy.'

Despite himself, Alex felt for him. 'Tell her,' he said kindly, 'that I have an autograph for her. A Munchkin. Mickey Carroll. He was one of the Lollipop Guild, I think. That'll pacify her.'

'Maybe, maybe not,' said Darvick. He was staying in the

Rubinfines' over-decorated spare room. Rebecca liked to charge in unannounced to force-feed her guests. Alex had been there once when his own flat flooded. It was like living inside a violent tea-cosy.

'I shall come this evening, pick it up,' said Rubinfine. 'I shall bring Joseph.'

'Shall you indeed,' said Alex.

'I shall. I know that Joseph wants to talk to you, seriously.'

'Still?'

'So!' said Rubinfine. 'You don't think the table will go!'

'I *know* it won't go.'

'*Faith*, Alex,' rumbled Rubinfine, becoming purple. 'My colleagues will know this story by heart, but if they don't mind I will retell it. It is a story told by Bahya ben Joseph Ibn Paquda.'

'Ah, yes,' said Green, hugging himself.

'*Yes*,' said Darvick.

'HOPING,' said Rubinfine loudly, 'to create a path across a stream, a traveller threw all his silver coins in the water. All the coins sank except one. Catching this one in time, the traveller used it to pay the ferryman, who rowed him across. *Faith*, says Bahya, is like that last coin. When all of life's treasures are gone –'

'It alone will help a man across the waters of life!' said Green, with a radiant smile.

'Yes,' said Rubinfine irritably. 'It alone, you see? Well?'

'Right,' said Alex. 'Well, I have to go.'

Throughout this Darvick had been massaging his chin. Now he said, 'You know, I don't think that one's about *faith*. As I remember it, the coin is *good judgement*. I'm almost certain of it.'

'Well, either way –'

'Also,' said Darvick, shaking his head in concern, 'Bahya was one of the Sephardim mystics – that's right, isn't it? And you know *Kabbalah* . . .'

Darvick laid his hand flat in mid-air and turned it from side to side. Green nodded.

'Yes, well, I meant it as a . . . warning, more than a literal . . .' said Rubinfine, struggling. 'If you recall what Rabbi Zeeman said in conference only yesterday . . .'

Resolutely, Alex shook hands with the three rabbis.

'Off, are we?' asked Rubinfine, holding him fast. 'Taking that Kitty to market, hmm? Joseph seems to think you'll get a very nice price.'

'Joseph shouldn't be discussing my business. As it happens, I'm going to get it verified this morning, that's all. Not everything in life is for sale. Goodbye, Rabbi Rubinfine. Rabbi Darvick. Rabbi Green.'

'Of course,' said Rubinfine, as Alex released himself, 'we *saw* Esther.'

Alex squinted.

'Oh, *yes*,' said Green. 'The pretty black girl? Yes, she passed by here moments before you. She told us about her heart. So affecting! Like something from a film!'

Alex considered stabbing Green to death with a broken biro he had in his pocket, but he needed the information. 'Well? How *was* she?'

Three blank faces.

'I mean, how did she act?'

More nothing.

'Did she look all right?'

'Oh, she looked – she really looked –' stuttered Darvick.

'Oh, yes. She *did*,' murmured Green.

'What?'

Rubinfine opened his mouth, closed it and opened it again. '*Beautiful*,' he said.

There is South London. And then there is *South* London. And then there is *South London*. And then there is Pemberton Hill. And Pemberton Hill made Alex feel unwell. He couldn't help it. He knew he didn't have a leg to stand on. But you feel how you feel. And Alex had always felt like a North London boy, though it was an affiliation out of character. His instinct was to detest groupings of all kinds – social, racial, national or political – he had never joined so much as a swimming club. But for this corner of the world he felt that irrational something which enabled him to almost understand why people behave as they do in the contentious, blood-slick places of the world.

North versus South. Huge row about it once, nuclear row, sitting in a park one summer with Ads, during a heatwave. Shorts rolled up, legs in the air, decimated picnic. A troop of ants determined to cross a tea-cup into a land of pâté. A perfect London summer's day, in short, marred by this ancient row over North versus South. *Stupid and offensive pose*, Adam had said, furiously demolishing Alex's defences one by one (houses, parks, schools, pints, girls, weed, public transport), revealing them for the shibboleths they were. Soon enough the ants found a short-cut over their bellies. Finally, tired of rowing, Alex had stretched out in the high grass to bleat the only honest reason he had: *I think it's because nobody knows me in South London. And I don't know anyone. It's like being dead*.

Every Thursday morning, Alex died. Every Thursday morning, Duchamp was the only mourner. In a covered market in Pemberton

Hill, covered by concrete, under an underpass. Plants, old books and chipped china for sale, the sunlight breaking over all this in columns, a ballet of dust in these columns. Unspeakably sad, the whole place. Old women, rain hats tied in girlish bows under their chins, walked up and down lines of stalls, in a fretful, lonely way, looking for something; like war-widows threading through a cemetery of unmarked graves. Alex always held his breath as he passed through, only releasing when he got to the end of it all: three school-desks pushed together, Duchamp, his autographs, his toxic smell.

'Now ... it's Alex, innit? The Chinaman. My eyes...' said Duchamp coming up close. Alex stepped back, reeling. 'What can I do you for, squire?'

Duchamp looked dreadful. The deterioration, even from the day before, was terrible to see. His mind had given up some time ago, obviously, but now his body was giving up. And there's no way back from that. He didn't look scared, though. That's the safety net of madness, Alex supposed, that's its gift. Duchamp had no goyish fears, thanks to that net. It was only Alex who was feeling a terror grip him. A selfish terror. *How few Thursdays Duchamp has left to him! How many do I have?*

'Nothing, really,' said Alex, moving to the other side of Duchamp, the side without the mouth. 'Actually, I'm not buying at the moment, Brian. I'm selling.'

'Sorry, chief, didn't catch that –'

'I said, I'm not *buying* right now, Brian. I'm selling.'

Duchamp took out a handkerchief, the more frankly to pick his nose. Exploring his bare gums with a fat tongue, he waddled down the line of desks, finished fiddling with his nose and now held the handkerchief to his mouth. While he spoke he coughed up yellowish stuff flecked with red, and would not or could not stop shaking his head.

'Oh, now look, Tandem, look, I can't help you, mate ... You can't sheriously expect me ... I ain't buying, Tandem – I've gorra *sell* if I want to live. You can't ask an old git like me to buy, now, with the market like it is, flooded with fakes – I'm selling, Tandem, I ain't *buying*. I'm like whassisname.'

Alex made the International Gesture for *Sorry, Brian?* (hands holding invisible football, squinty eyes, head at an angle).

'Oh, don't give me that – come on, *whassisname* ... oh, bugger it – him, the fat one, oh, come on, squire! It's Alex, innit? Tandem – it's you, innit? Well, *Tandem'll know*. Nuffing Tandem don't know about this business. He's the *innellekchewl*, inny? Every bugger knows *that*. You should ask *'im*.'

'Brian ... I don't –'

'Yes, you do, come on, now, in the films ... don't be a nonce all your life –'

'Brian, I don't *know* ...'

Duchamp's nodding grew faster, frightening.

'Oh, God, Brian, I don't know ... is it Oliver Hardy?'

'Piss *off*.'

'Brian, I *just don't* have time for this, today – no, all right all right all right ... Charles Laughton? Sydney Greenstreet?'

'No, it weren't no one like that ... funnier than them; a funny one, you know. Fat, like. Huge!'

'Brian – *please*. Could we just –'

'W. C. Fields! In that one he did, you know that one, the Dickens one ... I'm like 'im, watching me money ... come on, you know it! What was it he said? Funny, it was. Come *on*. It was, er – oh, now I know it, it was something a bit like: "*Expenditure twelve pounds and three shillings. Result: happiness. Income* – no wait, how'd it go, no wait – bloody 'ell – it's the other way round innit, it's *Income, twelve* –'

People who are about to die and the insane. These people speak into the middle-distance, eyes clouded by some sort of a film, like a thick uncryable tear, and with their hands going, distractedly picking at their chests. In Lauren Bacall's autobiography, one of Alex's all-time favourite books, she described Bogie's death that way. The odour (*I realized it was decay*), the hands picking at the hairs on his chest *as though things were closing in, and he wanted to get out*. The fight to die. Duchamp was still on his feet, by some miracle, but death was on him. Alex could smell it, see it, feel it, just as Lauren did. Lauren Bacall: *not* the goddess of all sex (as has been claimed) but the goddess of all compassion. And now, remembering Lauren's honest book made Alex step forward and take Duchamp's busy hands, and place them by his sides and say, *All right, Brian, all right. What have you got for me, then?*

A 1936 MGM fan album, unsigned, photo of the actress Angela Lansbury, unsigned, a toothbrush holder, one slipper (*Danny Kaye's slipper, mate. He gave it me*), six stills signed by the horror actor Vincent Price, all forged, a picture of Brian's sister, June. And more. And more.

It began to rain heavily. Alex helped Brian move his three school-desks out of the range of errant raindrops. After they'd lifted every-thing ten yards and picked up whatever had fallen, Brian offered him a small plastic school-chair to sit on and took one for himself.

'Stay here a bit, eh?' said Brian, shivering.

Alex stayed. He brought up a box from under the stall and began working through the folders. There was good stuff in that box. Quite a lot of it. Duchamp had a cracking Harold Lloyd, for example. Some good mid-range forties studio stars: Tyrone Power, Mary Astor, Van Heflin, Joel McCrea. And a very nice Merle Oberon. All under the desk. On top of the desk, he was offering the public a broken anglepoise lamp. With no real hope of a reaction, Alex suggested that this situation might be reversed.

Brian breathed on him and then rubbed his eyes, over and over.

'But Brian, it would be better if –'

'Have you a lady-friend at present, Tandem?'

'Sort of. She doesn't want to be my friend much right now.'

'Well, there you are,' said Duchamp firmly. 'Women are the answer. They are. If you'll only let them into the story. Women. They are the answer.'

'What's the question?'

Duchamp laughed at this as if Alex had just told the oldest joke.

Duchamp had a flask under his chair and a spare cup. Alex now poured out tea for both of them. He spotted a stall for home-made cakes and came back with two fruit slices, moist and fat with raisins.

'Ta. *Well*. This is a bit of a turn-up. Fruit *slice*. Dear me.'

Duchamp turned it over in his hands a few times and smiled at it with a mixture of fondness and awe, as at a family heirloom. It was a few minutes before he seemed willing to eat it. They sat side by side. To make his fruit slice soft enough for his gummy mouth, Duchamp had to soak each piece in tea and then slurp it from the cup.

'That was a *treat*,' said Duchamp finally.

'Brian,' said Alex, 'there *is* actually something you can do for me. I wondered if you could take a look at this for me.'

Duchamp neither moved nor made any sign of comprehension.

Alex leant forward and removed his Kitty Alexander from the pocket of his bag. He took Duchamp's cup out of his hands. He placed the autograph on Duchamp's lap.

'Brian, could you . . . ?'

Brian brought the autograph within inches of his eyes. 'Oh, *yes*.'

'Brian?'

'Yes, *yes*.'

'What, Brian?'

'Kitty Alexander. Worth a bundle.'

'You think it's real,' said Alex very quickly.

Duchamp shrugged. 'Looks real. But needn't be. 'Slike you said. Sometimes birds ain't the answer, they're the fahkin question. Ha!'

'But in your opinion, do you *think* it's real?'

'I think I've seen some bloody good forgeries in my time. See that lot?'

Duchamp pointed to the box Alex had just been working through. Alex picked it up.

'This?'

'Mostly forged.'

Alex raised his eyebrows.

'*Your* forgeries?'

Duchamp nodded.

'Well, they're bloody good, Brian. *I* couldn't tell the difference.'

'Yeah, well . . . there's not many that can. I've sold *you* a few in the past. Ha! Now . . .' he said, not looking at Alex but reaching out to him with his stubby arm, physically trying to connect him to a memory, 'you . . . you're the Kitty man, int ya?'

He bent over the box Alex held on his lap, thumbing through the papers in it with a real expertise. He pulled one out. A photograph.

'A Kitty Alexander, squire . . . forged, of course, I did it meself –

but I did it back then . . . back in fifty . . . summink . . . so the age of the ink is fine. No bugger in the world spot that for a fake.'

Alex studied the thing closely. Taking it out of its sheath and bringing it under the light. He placed his own Kitty by its side. They were almost too close, and with dread he placed them now one on top of the other and held them up to the light. Maybe Brian was confused – maybe Brian's was a later forgery, an Autopen? And if Alex's fitted Brian's perfectly, then they were both Autopens, for no one can sign exactly the same way twice over. We are not so precise. But no. Alex's *A* slanted a little further to the left. The sweeping, Elizabethan tail of Brian's *x* came lower than it did on Alex's.

'Looks so real,' said Alex with admiration.

''Tisn't, mate. I did it meself. You forget, Tandem, I worked in these studios. There weren't no one better than me.' Duchamp wiped down the photo with a piece of chamois from his pocket. 'I met her once. Beauty. None like her. But, mate, you're twenty-five and then' – Duchamp clicked his fingers, incompetently – 'you're sixty. Nobody told you that, did they?' He laughed, grimly. 'People like her should disappear. Poof! Them on the screen like that, they ain't meant to get old. No one wants to see an old bitch, do they? The people don't want that.'

They're not too keen on old buggers like you either, said Alex's brain, but he shut his mouth and stretched out his fingertips for the treasure. Duchamp drew it back from him with an unpleasant smile.

'I know what you're thinking. Bet you could sell this on to them mugs in Neville Court, eh? Or down Jimmy's Antiques? If *you* can't tell, they ain't gonna be able to, is they? Three thousand quid or more, no doubt! Cut yourself a percentage, eh?'

'Well?' said Alex, blushing. '*You're* not even allowed into those shops any more, are you? I could sell it for you. I'll just take 15 per cent of whatever I get.'

'Why don't you sell your own if you're so keen, eh?'

'Brian, mine's the real thing. I'm a big fan. The biggest. I'd like to keep it.'

Duchamp tutted. 'Oh dear, oh *dear*. That's no good in this business. You can't get sentimental. Just ink. Just letters. The *real thing* . . .' he said. 'As if it mattered! The little difference that makes all the difference. What a way to make a living, eh?'

'I'll take it, then?'

'You sign an agreement first. I know this business, mate. Here – here's some paper. I'll write it. You sign it. So. I, Alex-Li Tandem, agree to keep no more than ten per cent –'

'Ten per cent?'

'Ten – of the sale of Brian Duchamp's Kitty Alexander. That'll do, wunnit? Ain't the bloody Magna Carta but it'll do. There – sign it, then.'

Alex took the piece of paper. The handwriting was atrocious. 'Just – read me that bit, Brian.'

'Bloody hell, you deaf as well as stupid? Ten per cent – and that's all you're getting, so just sign it.'

Alex signed his name. As soon as he was finished, Duchamp whipped the paper away from him.

'Call that a signature? Looks like a bloody scrawl to me. Never trust an Israelite. In Hebrew, is it? Eh? Ha! Ha! Ha! Ha!'

Alex felt a heave of disgust. He stood up.

'All right, all right – that's enough. Give me the Kitty. Ten per cent. You canny bastard.'

And for a moment, he did look canny. Ugly, smelly, laughing that filthy death-rattle – but still here. Still dominating the scenes.

Not yet accepting the role we all get cast in, eventually: the walk-on (fall-down) part with no lines.

2

Somebody at a tube station wanted to be famous. They wanted to be known, all over the city, if only for fifteen minutes. They let their heels cross the white line, they took a quick breath, they leapt into for ever. Thanks to this *passenger action* (a truly majestic new euphemism, emphasizing the inconsideration), it took Alex almost two hours to get from the South to the centre of town. At the mouth of the tube exit an unsmiling Adam met him, opened a giant candy-striped golfing umbrella and gruffly instructed Alex to take his arm. And so they set off through a downpour, dependent on a colourful piece of canvas like two men in a balloon. Past a grand theatre and a seedy bar, straight past the girls paid to beckon at them, the Left-Handed Shop (*Yes, Al, very goyish. You can make a note later, all right?*), the gay bars, the mixed bars, the strippers – like two determined Hasidim, straight past all temptation! They reached a favourite cake shop. Adam stood in the doorway to draw in the umbrella while Alex hunted for an indoor table. A minute later they were back outside, being led to a miserable archipelago of tables standing in dirty water, their tops barely covered by the awning of a barber-shop. A lean Italian waiter tried to make a run for it the second the two young men were seated. People in the centre of the city were known to be callous and impatient.

The cakes and coffee arrived. Soon they were speaking quickly, with nothing extraneous, in the semaphore of old friends. Except they were not merry today. They were off-key. It had begun with lateness and now stretched to a lack of choreography – each took his turn spilling a perfectly solid sugar bowl – and then the same disease spread to the conversation. Neither could make himself understood. Each seemed to the other vain and self-centred. To each it seemed as if this man sitting opposite spoke only about himself. Adam talked excitedly and incomprehensibly about his latest studies. He stood up to demonstrate to Alex how the ten *sefirot* also corresponded to points of the body; he stretched his arms out like a madman. Alex cringed.

'You see, my *spine*,' said Adam, 'runs where Tif'eret – that's Beauty, Compassion – my spine runs where Tif'eret lies. So to get from Netsah – which is my right leg – to Tif'eret I meditate on the idea of my spine. That's the path of Yod. There are thirty-two paths, according to Ari. But *here*' – he thrust the base of his spine, and with it his backside, into the air; the pretty boys across the road smiled, pointed – 'here is where the soul goes beyond its earthly place to find better seed. I feel I'm halfway there, man. After all these years.' He pointed to the air above his head. 'I'm moving towards the crown, to Ayin, to Nothingness. To the *essence* of God.'

'Yep. That must be great for you. Waiter! A bottle of red please, two glasses.'

They sat without talking. A wind was getting going. Adam looked wistfully at another table as if he wished he were at it. Alex took out his tobacco and tried to roll a cigarette in the manner of a man who has been unjustly wronged. He had been betrayed – this is how he felt. Why tell Esther about Boot? What kind of friend does that?

Just as he was about to make this accusation, the wine arrived. Adam sent his glass back; Alex filled and drained his as if it were grape juice. Adam watched him, one hand scratching his head violently between two dreads. Alex poured himself another and began to speak of the Boot development, subtly, hoping to detect some guilt in Adam's gestures. Nothing. Not a dicky bird. But maybe the total absence of guilt was in itself a sign. No one can appear so innocent all of the time, can they? Can they? *Someone* must have traduced Alex T. And if it wasn't Adam, then who?

Alex continued to drink, talking rapidly about he knew not what. Fifteen minutes later he knew his mouth was still moving but it had been a while since his brain was attached to the words. Bored, Adam exploded a glazed strawberry under his fork.

'But all these women,' he said, cutting Alex off, 'they're all the same woman, really. Don't you *see* that? Kitty, Boot, Anita – they just overlap each other. Think of an art restorer peeling the paint off a portrait to find other portraits underneath. You ruin a perfectly good painting out of some misplaced curiosity – the possibility of other portraits. It's a kind of endless substitution – and all because you don't know how to deal with things as they are.'

Alex made an International Gesture: the throwing back of head, the slight indent of front teeth on lower lip, the making of the sound *pfui*. He raised a glass, his third.

'Thanks, Sigmund.'

Adam shrugged. 'Take it as you like.'

'No, no, it's fascinating. And Esther – the first face? The last?'

'Well, that's obvious, mate,' said Adam coldly. 'She's the paint.'

Alex dug with his tongue at a sludge of pastry on his molars. 'Right. Beautiful analogy. It's truly your style: everything's a symbol of everything else. Which helps me *how*?'

Adam looked quizzically at Alex. 'You have the weirdest idea,' he said, shaking his head, 'that everybody's here to help *you*!'

For a while they spoke of the Trouble with Other People, an aggressive substitute for the conversation they wanted to have, namely: the Trouble with *You*. Rubinfine was obsessive. Joseph was repressed and miserable. Alex looked at his watch. He was due in Neville Court in ten minutes.

'Late are we?'

'Bit.'

Alex upturned the rest of the bottle into his glass and then went through the motions of swirling and sniffing, as if only now realizing what it was.

'Is that necessary? Really?' asked Adam, mopping up a puddle of red where Alex swirled too hard.

'Oh ... *Jesus* ... you know? Why d'you bother coming out if you're ... I mean, why aren't you drinking? You just gonner watch me? What is this? I feel like a bloody painting: Fat Man with Red in Rain. Study of Loser in Process of –'

'You're drunk, stop it.'

'Can't stop being drunk, Ads. One-way journey. Chug chug chug to the end of the line.'

'Slow down, then.'

'Aye-aye, Cap'n.'

'You're angry with me. Why?'

'Because. Next question.'

'Esther tells me you're not going to be with her on Sunday. I'm trying to understand that, but I'm having difficulties.'

'Not my fault – I've got to go to New York. It's booked – I can't get out of it. I'm *sorry*.'

'When do you leave?'

'On Friday night. Look – why don't you come?' asked Alex in the spirit of peaceful resolution. But Adam looked away to where a man wrapped in a duvet was doing a jig in the rain.

'The centre of *this* city is hard enough. I don't want to be in the centre of the centre. Too hard for this bredrin.'

'Right, well. No one's forcing you. Just an offer.'

'It's your father's yahrzeit on Thursday,' said Adam, turning back. 'Are you intending to be in the country?'

'Not that it's any concern of yours, but I'm back on Tuesday.'

'Well,' said Adam, tapping a spoon on the rim of Alex's glass, 'I've spoken to Rubinfine. His shul can't do it on the day you need, but he thinks he knows one that will. For the minyan you could have me – though you don't deserve me – you could have Joseph, Rubinfine, your mum, Esther, maybe if she can make it. People are happy to do it – all you have to do is just stop pissing everybody off for *one second*. So you're not going to her operation, is that right?'

By some horrible accident Alex had lifted his wrist to look at his watch at the moment of this word, 'operation'. He opened his mouth now to explain, but then could think of nothing and closed it again. He couldn't see how there could be any accidents in the world of gestures. Don't our bodies say exactly what they mean to?

'No. If you have to go, get on with it,' said Adam unhappily, 'I've got to find a shower, anyway. I've just been sitting in that room. I haven't washed in days. I'll call you later.'

They split the bill.

Stumbling down a famous road to a monument, and then turning back on himself, up a forgotten lane. But before going where he needs to go, Alex slips into an alleyway called Goodwins, slides down a wet wall until he is crouching. In this position he is covered by the protruding windowsill of somebody's flat. Here he rolls a joint, a really big joint, and smokes it. Instead of relaxing him, it adds a new dimension to his drunkenness, a thicker layer of smog between him and the world. Soon enough, with stinging eyes and a manic, stammering heart, he takes out a pencil and succumbs to paranoia. He makes notes in his pad about the lunch he has just had, the scraps of conversation he is already forgetting, the perceived deviousness of his best-friend, the significances of this and this, the symbolism of that and the other. It is all a sort of horrible betrayal of himself, of his whole life. Life is not just symbol, Jewish or Goyish. Life is more than just a Chinese puzzle. Not everything fits. Not every road leads to epiphany. This isn't TV, Alex, this isn't TV.

Oh, so now, thinks Alex, *you're having an epiphany about the importance of not having epiphanies. That's great.*

Feeling glum and muddled, Alex begins walking at a clip, wishing he could get over himself, get out of himself, out of this skin, just for a *minute*. That's probably all that they want, those famous passengers who take action. But they can't get just a minute – not by means of extraordinary strong skunk like this, or alcohol, or a Microdot, or anything else. There are no short-cuts. You're always *there*. So instead they cut their losses. They opt for for ever. 'And that's something *else*,' says Alex to himself, feeling for the first time the *weight* of suicide, the depth of that proposition. 'That takes some serious *balls*.'

Alex sways down the street, under the enormous sky, feeling humbled by those passengers who leap into the path of trains. The very least he can do, *in the face of this kind of serious balls*, is be a person of substance himself. At the roundabout, waiting for a safe moment to cross the street, Alex tries to imagine his defence if his life were on trial, that is, if he had to prove its worth. It is a kind of imaginary text he carries around with him, along with his obituary, because somewhere in Alex's head he is the greatest, most famous person you never heard of. And as such must defend himself from both slander and obscurity. Who else is going to do it? After all, he has no fans.

Please remember, please? Please remember this. Life is more
than just a Chinese puzzle [YOU ARE NOT WATCHING
TV]. It's more than that. You're angry because I'm failing,
but I'm *telling you* that life is more than this – more than –

Please. Things cannot in reality fit together the way the
evidence does when I write it down – please remember this,
please. The lunch wasn't just so, so tidy; I didn't walk down
a street to divert you; the scenes didn't follow one to the
other, flawless and meaningful – please remember this is my
life [YOU ARE NOT WATCHING TV]. This is the
description of a struggle. Judge it accordingly. One second of
it is as long as all the books that have ever been written. It is
also as short as the name of God. Please remember this.
Forgive the twin lies of entertainment and enlightenment
[YOU ARE NOT WATCHING TV]; please remember I
just walked, like you walk, with crooked elbows and my
back bent till my hands touched the seams of my jeans,
terrified occasionally by death and other matters that would
neither entertain you nor enlighten – remember that I
cannot organize things for you the way you want them
organized. Please remember that I just walked pointlessly,
that's all I could do, for life is more than just a Chinese
puzzle, more than this, more than this, please remember
that you are not – that I am not –

that this is just me walking totally stoned (this weed is
strong, this weed is psychotropic) down a narrow alley and
finding the next place I am meant to be and knocking on the
window –

Tandem is knocking on the window of Cotterell's Autograph Emporium, a charming little gabled shop located halfway down Neville Court in London's fashionable centre. Inside he sees first editions, collectable glassware, signed portraits and the worn brocade of a chair-seat upon which a stitched Chinese dragon leaps to freedom. Inside he sees cigarette cards and stamps. Theatre programmes and Christmas cards. Birth certificates and mono-grammed handkerchiefs. On the walls he can see photographs of the very famous, photographs which the very famous them-selves had touched and marked and which a man might purchase. A man could own these photographs and partake (in however minor a way) of the famousness of these people and their remarkable ability to cheat Death of its satisfaction: obscurity. A man wavers between awe and rage at the very famous, as he does at the idea of God. This afternoon Alex feels rage. He is having a psychotic interlude.

Inside he sees some people, real people. A tall handsome girl with a strip of black velvet round her white throat. A red-faced fat man in tweed wearing a pocket-watch and waving his arms. Inside he sees an audience.

3

So. One moment you are very pissed and stoned, you are having a psychotic interlude. The next – particularly if it is raining and you have a pretty girl screaming at you in the middle of the street – you are not. And Boot was full of questions today. Questions like:

What was *that* about?
Are you *completely* mad?

Are you trying to get me *sacked*?

What kind of a person turns up in that state?

Do you realize he could press charges?

What goes through your *mind* when you're like that?

Do you think that *insulting* people helps *anything*?

Is it broken?

Do you need a doctor?

'What was that last one, again?' asked Alex, pinching his nose to stop the blood.

'Oh, *Jesus*. Look, come *on*. I'll take you. I've got an uncle in Harley Street. You complete *nutter*.'

She grabbed his hand and took a stride forward, but Alex wouldn't move.

'What? What's the matter? Are your legs hurt?'

'I don't go to Western doctors,' said Alex gruffly, maddeningly aware of himself bleeding, red-eyed and soaking wet before a girl who wished all this and more upon him. 'I know a place in Chinatown. Be better. We'll go there.'

Leaning on Boot's impressive biceps, Alex negotiated the raised cobblestones, moaning softly to himself. How strong Boot was, and how beautiful! Since he'd last seen her, her hair had been cut short like a young boy's, emphasizing her rather masculine jaw. Her skirt was made out of a rough brown material that itself resembled hair, and her legs were controlled by a pair of long black boots which squeaked when the two sides met. A tall girl, well-bred like a posh horse. She could take almost all of his weight and trot along at full speed, unhampered by the raindrops streaming down her face.

'What I don't understand,' she said furiously, as they reached the commotion of a popular square, framed on every side by giant cinemas, 'is how you had the bare-faced gall to come into the shop so messed up, make such a total *fool* of yourself – and then – *and then* – try to sell him an Alexander. God knows, you *deserved* a punch for that. Really, Alex. After the last time!'

Two years ago Alex had successfully sold on to some suckers a group of forged Kittys he had himself been suckered into buying. He had forgotten that Sir Edward had been one of these secondary suckers.

'*Ug*,' said Alex. 'That was two years ago.'

'Leopard, spots.'

Boot stopped. The rain was easing off. She pushed him up against a wall. Above them, the movie houses pressed down, lit up like royal cities, cathedrals. Huge across the street, over Boot's shoulder, Alex could see the twenty-foot face of the popular actress Julia Roberts, the persistent vein in her forehead, the smile more radiant than Buddha's. Alex had a strong urge to kneel, but Boot held him fast by the elbows. Alex stared at Boot, trying to get a sense of what she looked like. The nearer you get to adverts for the cinema, he found, the harder it is to understand people's faces. But the sight of Boot was not as disappointing as one might have imagined. There were corresponding points: something similar around the jaw, the eyes.

She said: 'Well, you can kiss me now, if you like.'

'Excuse me?' said Alex.

Very close to him now was Boot's wide, angular, open face, a pair of extravagantly lashed brown eyes, a hundred faint freckles and a big striking nose. She touched her teeth with her tongue.

'I said, you can kiss me. I *presume* that's what this is all about. Your way of expressing your love etc. Your awkward way.'

'Boot,' pleaded Alex, putting his arms up in defence, 'I may have broken my nose.'

Boot retracted her head in genuine surprise and bit her bottom lip. She was a great movie-goer, Boot. She always expected to get kissed, sooner or later.

'Oh. OK. No, no, that's fine, really. That's *fine*. Actually, I'm not embarrassed. I suppose you think I should feel . . . Oh dear. I don't know. I just *thought* –'

'No, it's OK, Boot, really –'

'It's just . . . you know, I thought you really –'

'Yes, I see that, Boot. I'm –'

'Well, anyway,' she snapped, taking control of her wobbling chin, 'this is just like when she tried to kiss Lytton once – or was it Lytton who tried to kiss her? Anyway, *they* didn't bother feeling silly about it. So don't *you* think that I will.'

Alex's face was aching. '*Who?*'

'*Virginia Woolf*. Her diaries. I've been reading them. Do you listen to *anything* I say?'

Yeah, some things. Say, about 25 per cent on a good day. And much more than that, much more, when he was trying to convince her to lie down with him somewhere and do the beast with two backs. But this was not one of those occasions. She grabbed his hand again and marched him under the fake Oriental archway that heralded the beginning of Chinatown.

'I must say, for somebody who's meant to be in love with me, you don't make much effort.'

'But Boot . . . Boot, I'm *not* in love with you. I never said I was. We barely know each other. I have a girlfriend.'

Boot gave him an indulgent smile. Two cross-currents of blood met at Alex's chin. Boot took a tissue from her purse and dabbed at it.

'Silly. You don't have to *say* it. It's all in the eyes. In your funny Chinese eyes. And where *is* this girlfriend? No one ever *sees* her. She's the ghost in the machine, if you ask me. I've been thinking a lot about suicide recently,' mused Boot, in one of the frequent conversational U-turns she was famed for. 'Because of Virginia and everything. And because of Sylvia. Why *are* brilliant women always doing that? And then I was thinking about your book – oh! Can you smell that! *Gorgeous* duck thingy with pancakes. I'm *so* hungry.'

She stopped again and looked longingly through a window at a duck, glazed and hanging from a hook.

'What was I saying?'

Alex leant over an outdoor menu and spat blood on to the floor. Opposite him a cat-faced Peruvian played a pop ballad on an ancient pipe.

'Oh, I remember. You know how you split things into Jewishy type things and the other type things? You know, in that funny little book you're writing?'

And you *had* to say yes. Even if she asked: *You know how the sky's blue? You know how I'm a human being?*

'You know, in that book of yours?'

'Yes, Boot.'

'So, I was wondering which one it was. Which category it fell into. Suicide, I mean.'

Now, that was a pretty good question. Alex pointed to Dr Huang's medical centre, its little sign, jutting out from the wall one storey above a restaurant called Peking Nights.

'That's a good question.'

Boot smiled, showing a line of huge, perfect teeth, her Panavision smile.

'Yes, I *know*.'

They reached the side entrance. Boot pressed the bell and a second later Dr Huang's terrorized, screaming falsetto told them to push the door and come up.

'Goyish, on the whole . . .' said Alex slowly, as Boot helped him up the stairs, 'stones in pocket, head in oven, all of that. But there's another kind, I think. A sort of rapture . . . your death runs towards you with her arms open, and sort of . . . embraces you. You leap over a fence to meet her. You dance towards her. She explodes over you like a raincloud or a burst of sunshine. You don't have to do any shabby struggling. No complicated knots or car exhausts – you know – with the Hoover tubes. It's more like a, sort of a, *melding*.'

By the time he'd finished this little speech – really off the top of his head – he found he was beaming. Boot's face was scrunched up in the frown of a child. 'Right. I don't know if I under*stand* that. Sounds a bit . . . sexy. And that's Jewish, is it?'

Alex nodded his heavy head. Dr Huang opened his office door.

4

'You take this,' said Huang and passed Boot a cold compress. It was a damp muslin stuffed with something unidentifiable, smelling dimly of mint. It was not closed apart from the twist at its neck. A naturally enterprising girl, Boot removed the piece of black velvet from her throat and used it to bind the package. She held it to Alex's cheek. Her hand was shaking from the cold.

'You put it on his nose, on bridge of nose!' cried Huang, and shuttled towards his dingy backrooms, from which, soon after, the sound of a flush could be heard.

'The things I do for you!' trilled Boot gaily.

Head tilted back, Alex looked at the ceiling. He had been coming here since he was a teenager and knew the progress of the damp; it had long risen, saturating the plaster. Nodules of dripping water and stalagmites of mould were everywhere. It was a room which seemed always to be crying. He came here first a week after Li-Jin had died, when the room was fit for the feeling. In the morning Sarah had found a bottle of Dr Huang's in the house, and that same afternoon Dr Huang found himself confronted by a beautiful young woman, hysterical, in tears. She wanted to know why Mr Huang had poisoned her husband. *Look at my son!* she said. *Explain it to him!* she said. Her hair was everywhere. Her socks did not match. In her left hand, she held the paw of a sullen, odd-looking boy, in her right, a herbal remedy Huang had not prescribed in years. It took some time to straighten things out. For Dr Huang to explain how long it had been since he had seen Li-Jin, for Sarah to fall into a chair and weep and accept an offer of tea. That was the first time Alex drank green tea, or at least the first occasion he remembered. He remembered too that Dr Huang had told his visitors a story. After hearing it, Alex had felt confused, both by the story and by the sight of his mother, weeping afresh:

Mr Huang's Story as Told to Alex and Sarah

A rich man, famous throughout the court, asked Sengai to write something for the continued prosperity of his family so that it might be treasured from generation to generation.

On a sheet of paper Sengai wrote:

Father dies, son dies, grandson dies.

The rich man was angry.

'I asked you to write something for the happiness of my family! Why do you make it into a joke!'

'No joke is intended,' explained Sengai. 'If before you yourself die your son should die, this would grieve you greatly. If your grandson should pass away before your son, both of you would be broken-hearted. If your family, generation after generation, passes away in the order I have named, it will be the natural course of life. I call this real prosperity.'

He seemed not to have aged since then, the doctor. He remained spritely, slim, with tight skin. He wore a faded blue jumper celebrating a Vienna Jazz Festival at which the last horn sounded some twenty years previous, a pair of jeans covered in logos for imaginary racetracks and ski lodges, and an orange baseball cap so old and worn that the famous winged heel of the victorious goddess had been obliterated.

Now he pushed back through the curtain of coloured plastic strips that marked the partition between his surgery and his home.

'Young lady. Your name is?'

'Boot. My name's Boot.'

'Boot? Like shoe?'

'It's actually Roberta, but everyone just says Boot. Boot's fine.'

'Well, Miss Boot,' said Dr Huang sharply, 'you friend of Alex. Very well. So you have money to pay?'

Boot, who had grown up in the countryside, had an instinctive, inherited fear of the Chinese in any situation other than food delivery. She shifted back a step. 'Why on earth should *I* pay when Alex just gave you that cheque?'

Keeping hold of Alex's nose with one hand, Boot reached out for what Dr Huang was trying to show her.

'He not very well,' said Huang quietly.

It was a cheque. But where a signature should be Boot saw a shaky table, a catcher's mitt, the bottom half of a chair.

NINE / *Binah*

Understanding • Everyone in England has been on a quiz show •
Identifying objects • A Bogart/Henreid situation • Wittgenstein was
Jewish • Rubinfine carries things forward • Typing letters • Marvin
explains • Anita says no • Adam says yes • Who cut the plants?

I

Alex's fifth-year maths teacher was on television. He had 184
points. He needed only one more answer to get on the champion
scoreboard and guarantee a place in the quarter-finals. Keeping his
eyes on the screen, convalescent Alex tried to dip and eat a nacho
without using his hands. He secured himself by hooking his feet
round the far curl of the sofa. He began leaning towards the floor.

The quiz master said: 'Which philosopher was delighted when
he heard that his student had given up philosophy to work in a
canning factory?'

Alex said the answer eight times very quickly, and then said it
once in slow motion and then sang it. The maths teacher gave an
answer that revealed alarming beliefs regarding food production in
fifth-century Greece. Alex dipped his sore nose in salsa and let it stay
there for a while. The sorrow was upon him. The doorbell rang.

'DOOR!' screamed Boot from the kitchen. 'DOOR. DOOR.
DOOR!'

This is a door. Here is some salsa. That was my maths teacher.
This is a door.

'Can I help you?'

'Other way round,' said Rubinfine, making the International Gesture of reversal. He was wearing a puffy, salmon-coloured jumper that had written across it TO ERR IS HUMAN, TO REALLY *???!@# UP TAKES A COMPUTER.

Alex stood firm in the doorway. 'If it's Torahs you're selling, I've got one.'

'Hullo, Alex,' said Joseph. 'Can we come in? We just want to talk.'

'What happened to the schnozz?' asked Rubinfine, pushing past him into the hall. 'You have an argument with someone's fist? Somebody not like the cut of your . . . *Hello*.'

Boot had just emerged from the kitchen looking both strident and coquettish, a combination she had perfected in childhood to get her way.

'And your name is?'

'Boot.'

'Of *course* it is. A friend of Esther?' asked confused Rubinfine, whose last female friendship ended when the girl in question micturated in his sand pit. 'Or . . . ?'

'Alex's, actually. I mean we – we – that is, we have business together.'

Even for Boot, Alex thought, this B-movie guilty voice, this stuttering Other Woman shtick – it was all a great disappointment.

'Boot, this is Rabbi Rubinfine, an old friend, and this . . .'

Alex quickly understood that his next introduction was unnecessary. Boot and Joseph were moving clumsily towards each other (a gauche ballet of elbows and soft places as a coat was removed) and now converged in an awkward kiss, where neither the cheek nor the proposed quantity could be settled upon, another

B-movie convention. Alex felt a fury rush through him as he put the last piece in an offensively simple puzzle. He had not ever imagined that they knew each other.

'You two already . . . ?' said Rubinfine as they progressed to the lounge. Here he smiled and dropped into a chair, indifferent to both the end of his own question and the scarlet flush travelling up Joseph's neck, engulfing his pointed ears. Rubinfine picked up the first book to hand – a popular history of the scallop – and flicked to the central photos.

'For at *least*, what, three months?' said Boot, perching on the edge of the sofa. 'I never *thought* that you two might be friends too. But of course you would. It's not a very big world, ours, is it, really? I s'pose everyone who comes into the shop knows each other, really. Isn't this funny! Joe and Alex! It's like a bad play. Gosh. Joe, by the way, I'm glad you didn't buy that Nicholas Brothers. It is a nice piece, but it isn't worth *half* of what Cotterell's trying to flog it for. He's just too pig-headed to bring it down, admit the mistake . . . He thinks the market in musical stuff's about to explode, you see . . .'

Boot was no fool; she sensed the astonishing tension in the room. With disgust Alex watched her silently conclude that it was desire for her that must have caused it. He pressed his thumbnails into the soft of his palm, as she prattled on, shaping her body into a deliberate echo of the famous silhouette, the Marilyn hourglass. Back arched, abdomen retracted, turning out the lips like blushing petals, tilting the head low but looking to the ceiling – what an incredibly powerful gift! The ultimate in International Sexual Gestures: the metamorphosis from woman to vase.

'You just wouldn't think it *possible*,' said Rubinfine, lifting an eyebrow but turning his eyes back to the book that lay open on his knees. 'Two hundred and something pages about the scallop. About a shellfish. You have to admire the writer. Where does he get the *will*?'

'Joseph,' said poor Alex, shaking with rage, 'tea – could you? Help me? Carry some things in? And some drink – maybe we'll have some drink – rabbis excepted.'

'Rabbis *included*, thank you very much. The *day* I've had.'

Joseph, who had not yet sat down, began to move forward with the pigeon steps of a condemned man. Alex hustled up behind him.

'Well,' Alex heard Boot say, as he gave Joseph a little surreptitious jab in the back on the way out, 'you don't *look* much like a rabbi to me . . .'

In the kitchen, Alex found Grace and picked her up, clutching the reluctant cat close to his chest so that he might not throw a punch. 'I understand,' he said darkly.

'Alex,' said Joseph, glancing at the door to check it was shut, 'I'm not sure you *do*.'

Alex reached a hand from under Grace to thrust out a finger. 'You informed on me. For your own advantage.'

'That's a little dramatic, isn't it?' said Joseph, fiddling with his tie. With downcast, pretty eyes, he reached out for the kettle and put the water on. 'That's a little bit sub-Garbo, isn't it?'

'You told Esther about Boot,' said shrill Tandem, 'not Adam. *You*. It'll probably be the end of us. That's a ten-year relationship you've just destroyed. Ta very much.'

'Alex –'

'And I'm standing here trying to figure out *why*. Do you really think, Joe, do you really think Es would leave me for *you*?'

Joseph looked alarmed – his head shot up, he seemed amazed. He laughed, rather desperately.

'*Esther?* No, Alex, you've got the wrong – what are you *talking* about – Esther's like a *sister* to me.'

'You've always been competitive with me,' said Alex, talking over him. 'Was that the point? Were you just going to take her for the *sake* – why are you laughing? What's so bloody funny?'

'Nothing!' shouted Joseph, stamping his little foot. 'Look, just give me a second to get myself . . . I *want* to explain – this has got *nothing* to do with Esther – I mean, not in *that* way.'

Alex shook his head, as if trying to straighten out an idea. '*Boot?* Is that it? Are you having a laugh? Look, Joe, you can bloody *have* Boot, mate, you don't have to screw *my* life up in the process.'

'No, look, wait, this is going too fast,' said Joseph, taking both hands and pushing downwards, the International Gesture for calm. 'I just thought – she's my *friend*, Esther's *my* friend too – and I just thought she deserved to know, that's all. Really, I'm sorry – I just – she kept *asking* and she suspected *something* – Please, let's just forget the whole thing. I'm *sorry*. I made a mistake, obviously.'

Alex swore viciously and Joseph vibrated and put one hand to the sideboard.

'It's really not actually what you think,' began Joseph, and this made Alex laugh – the awful movie phrasing.

'Joseph,' he said, 'I don't *believe* you. You've *always* been competitive with me. You can't *stand* to see me – wait a bloody minute, *wait*' – Alex dropped Grace to the floor – '*God*, I'm an idiot. You told Cotterell to expect me with that Alexander, right? Am I right? You told him I was wandering round town with a forgery. You *bastard*. Well, for your *information*, I was selling one for Brian Duchamp. Who actually really needs the money. So well done there. Joseph, what's *wrong* with you? You're trying to mess me up –'

Joseph choked a little attempting a scornful laugh. 'Come on, now – I can't take all the credit for that – not at the moment –'

Alex punched an overhead cupboard. 'You *told* Esther. And I treated Adam like crap today, because of you. You *informed* on me.'

Joseph bit his lip. He seemed ready to cry. 'I gave her,' he began unsteadily, 'the information she deserved and would have received anyway, in the end. Everyone knew. Really, Al, it shows such *contempt* for her, as if she didn't exist –'

'Look, mate – one thing I don't need is relationship advice from *you*. When you actually manage to *have* a relationship, Joe, then get back to me.'

'Contempt, really,' continued Joseph quietly, taking a step back, 'and bloody hell, you know . . . as far as Boot goes, as you so nicely remind me, I'm a single man. You're not. Look, I don't even . . . I don't think I'm seriously interested in her anyway and . . . Alex, this really isn't the issue. This is uncivilized. We came here tonight, Rubinfine and I, as your friends, to try to –'

Alex picked up a huge bottle of Polish vodka from the sideboard, grasped it by its neck and pointed it at Joseph Klein. Inside floated a yellow thread of bison grass, bobbing at the neck. 'See this? Starter for ten. What's this?'

'It's Polish vodka. What? What am I meant to say? What – it's a drink? What?'

'Yes, but not only. It's a drink, yes. But think again. Let's remember our university degrees. Let's remember our *Ludwig Wittgenstein*. Tell me about the nature of a proposition.'

'*Alex* – get a grip – no, no, all right – calm *down* – OK, OK, the meaning of a proposition is in its *use*.'

'So?'

'So it could also be a weapon.'

'Ten points! We're going to drink this until we get uncivilized. And then, when we are uncivilized, I'm going to beat the air out of you. With this. My friend. My dear, childhood friend. Do you understand? Do we understand each other? We're going to have a sort of wrestling match. That's a note-promise, Joe. That's a commandment.'

'Alex . . . you don't *understand*. You *don't*.'

'But first we're going to drink. We're going to get tight. Middle of the movie stuff. We'll drink to Esther – she's having an operation on Sunday, did you know? There's a fact for you. Now, I'll take this, and this – there's some more down there, there we are. You open that cupboard. Get some munchies. There're mixers in the fridge. Hold that. And that. No, give me that one. Get a tray for those . . .'

'Ooh la la!' said Boot a few minutes later, now perched on the arm of Rubinfine's chair. 'Look at you two. Is all that for me?'

'We're having a party in inverted commas,' said grim Alex-Li.

'It's funny,' said Boot some time later, and more loudly than she knew, 'I actually wanted to be an actress. But we can't all be actresses. I mean, not *everyone* in the world can be an actress. It's like in the end it's just the luck of the Irish, no, sorry, what do I mean? Oh, *you* know, wotsit – of the *draw*.'

She was leaning against the fake fire with its glowing plastic coals, a glass of red wine, her third, cupped in both hands. Rubinfine kept nodding even after she had finished, and continued to pick up personal greetings cards from the mantelpiece to read their inscriptions.

'Did you ever want to be anything, Rabbi? I mean, apart from, you know, a rabbi?'

Rubinfine lifted up a tiny Mexican idol by the penis for the fifth time. He began to turn it over in his hands. 'Here's an interesting fact,' he said brightly, jerking his head up. 'I went to talk to some schoolchildren recently about the meaning of Purim – turned out my presentation didn't fill the whole hour, had problems with the PowerPoint presentation and there were other complications – that's not actually relevant to this story – anyway, to fill time I asked them what they wanted to be when they grew up and –'

Boot laughed suddenly and then looked tearful. Rubinfine frowned but pressed on.

'Yes, and in a class of thirty-five, nine wanted to be models, four wanted to be actors, two wanted to be pop stars, ten wanted to be footballers and the remaining ten wanted to be "entertainers", just "entertainers". I tried to get some specifics out of them – nothing doing. You never saw so many ambitious little – just a touch more, thank you, that's fine – ambitious little human beings.'

Boot gulped the end of her glass and began to pour herself another. 'Rabbi, honestly, I have to tell you – I'll know you'll understand – but when I was at school –'

'You'll excuse me for a moment, won't you?' said Rubinfine, who abhorred confessions. He had to call Rebecca about the arrangements, now that a third of the midgets (the term had become lodged in his brain, there was no shifting it) had proved to be vegetarian.

'And how are you two?' said Boot rather desperately, hitching her elbows on the mantelpiece, turning to the sofa. Here, Joseph and Alex had sat since the beginning of the festivities, drinking vodka shots, locked in a morose discussion of their childhood acquaintance. They had wiped out good times and distorted the order and severity of personal slights according to each man's taste. Now they turned to Boot like a hostile, woozy matinee crowd.

'Never been better,' said Joseph, dropping his head.

Boot bit her thumbnail. 'This isn't much of a *party*, is it? I keep feeling I want to *cry*. It's rather like a whatdyacallit – a wake, or something. It's as if somebody died but no one really knows who. I always think there's only so much Leonard Cohen a party can stand. Actually,' she said, swigging her wine and taking a stumbling step forward, 'I think I might go, actually, Alex, if that's OK. I might just toddle home.'

'Don't go, Boot,' said Joseph flatly, still looking at the low coffee table in front of him. 'It'll just be boys left if you leave. No good if it's just boys. Let's watch a movie or something. Be fun.'

'Thanks, Joe, but I think I better . . .'

Alex licked the joint he was rolling and looked around him. 'Where'd the Rabbi piss off to, then?'

Boot shrugged. 'Don't know. Upstairs, I think.'

'Missing,' said Joseph. 'Presumed dead.'

'You leave,' said Alex in the drawl of the popular actor John Wayne, 'and the Rabbi gets it.'

Upstairs, Rabbi Mark Rubinfine contrived to go missing for some time. He had phoned Rebecca but the conversation proved short and ill-tempered thanks to his inability to take the phrase 'novelty chicken swizzle-sticks' in the serious spirit in which it was meant. He had drunk a little too much wine, possibly. And he had reached that point which anyone who has organized even so much as a four-person dinner party reaches in the end: *why can they not cook their own food, hire their own DJ, eat and dance in their own damn homes?* For Rubinfine this feeling was now magnified exactly forty-eight times, once for each of these miniature trouble-makers he was being railroaded into entertaining.

He'd replaced the receiver with Rebecca still talking. Now, instead of returning downstairs, he found himself sitting aimlessly on Alex's bed. Reaching for the chocolate coins, he got a good quantity in his palm and began the fiddly process of relieving them of their metallic skins. Imagine living like this! Rubinfine shuddered and placed his free hand in the yellow hand-shaped stain on the wall. His fondness for Alex had never stopped him from being frank with himself about the inherent superiority of his own situation next to poor Tandem's. Rabbi Mark Rubinfine had a patio and a wife, curtains and carpets, a power shower and a twelve-seater dinner table. As soon as Dr Guy Glass cured Rebecca of her toko-phobia, the place would be full of children. See? He had collected things in his life, which is what you're meant to do, placing them carefully between you and death, as on an obstacle course. Alex's room was like a student's bedsit. There was no discernible difference between Alex's room when he was sixteen and Alex's room now. Pants still formed a mountain. Socks still cried out for their fellows.

Rubinfine leant forward to look out at Mountjoy. Out there, that was his world. He couldn't conceive of having no power in Mountjoy, no audience. Alex and Adam, like Akiva, hiding in their caves! Rabbi Rubinfine smiled affectionately at the eccentricity of his oldest friends. He spotted the famous note, lying on Alex's desk next to an overnight bag. It had been torture for Rubinfine, remembering not to spend his note. And then they discontinued pound notes altogether, and relieved him of the responsibility.

Now he kicked off his slip-on shoes, grabbed his right foot and brought the hard skin on his heel up for inspection. He peeled off a thick ridge and flicked it in the direction of an overflowing bin.

Will you look at this place! Some of the posters were fifteen years old. Still here, above the bed, the fake advertisement that promised four young matadors – *Mark y Joseph y Alex y Adam* – against a huge Spanish bull. Gulping down his last chocolate coin, he walked over to peer at a reproduction of a sixteenth-century Mantuan Kabbalistic text, a single page from the Zohar, maybe, or the Sefer Yetsirah. Rubinfine, to himself at least, did not pretend to be an expert. The text was written inside a pair of hands with pointed thumbs. Birds in rose bushes fluttered up the margins on either side. God's name, circled by flowers, sat at the top. It was delicate, superb. *And what things we have done, over the ages!* murmured Rubinfine's happy heart, for, no matter what Mountjoy thought, he had not become a rabbi solely to please his father. In his own small way he had wanted to *carry things forward*. Like the continuity man on a film set. At the time, this was an analogy that had not satisfied Adam, who thought the call to the rabbinate should be entirely pure, a discussion a man has with God. But God had never spoken to Rubinfine, really. Rubinfine was simply, and honestly, a fan of the people he had come from. He loved and admired them. The books they wrote, the films they made, the songs they had sung, the things they had discovered, the jokes they told. This was the only way he had ever found to show it, that affection. His childhood therapy had pinpointed the Rubinfine problem: personal relationships were not his strength. He was always happiest dealing with a crowd. The people of Mountjoy! The people! He never expected to add anything to them, to the people, never imagined he could offer any great rabbinical insight – he hoped only to carry them for a short time. Between the rabbi who came before him and the one who would come after.

Tripping backwards over his feet, Rubinfine hiccuped, giggled, righted himself and shadow-boxed the Ali poster, picking up Alex's bag from the floor and heaving it to the bed. Checking the door every few minutes, he hurried through the pockets, looking. He thought for a moment that Louise Brooks was Kitty, but Kitty was later, no? And her face was different. More modern. So many in here. There is so much fame in the world. Taylor, Pickford, Grayson, Cagney, Chevalier. And here we are.

Rubinfine drew Duchamp's photograph out of its plastic sheath and took a moment to concede that the woman was astonishing. If one were to become dangerously delusional about a woman and her signature, one could do worse. He looked a little longer, marvelling at the architecture of her cheeks. And then he ripped the thing into six pieces.

The exhilaration was considerable. It was what he and Joseph had agreed on during the drive here, though they had never imagined it would be so easy. They had envisioned an all-nighter, a twelve-tissue bout with tears and drama. They were going to walk right in and harass him until he handed it over. Because until the thing was gone, he would not be able to stop fixating on it. That was Joseph's formulation, and Rubinfine had agreed with it or decided to agree with it. So. Now it was gone.

Enormously pleased with himself, Rubinfine gathered the scraps into his hands and stood up. He toyed with the analogy of the parents who force their heroin-ravaged child into cold turkey. He reflected with pleasure upon the axioms 'tough love' and 'all for the best'. He was just about to leave the room, when three photographs on the near wall caught his eye: Norma Shearer, Debbie Reynolds and Deanna Durbin. Which reminds me, thought Rubinfine (Debbie Reynolds→Eddie Fisher→Carrie Fisher→Princess Leia→Han Solo→Harrison Ford): I bet he's not telling me something. Bet the sneaky bastard's hiding a Ford, waiting to sell it to someone else, someone richer.

Rubinfine went back to the bed and opened the bag. He found a Ford quickly enough. Silently, he cursed Alex. Then he looked closer. Rubinfine rocked back on the bed, yelped ecstatically behind his hand. To Mark! For a long minute Rubinfine thought he might cry. He had a birthday coming up, two weeks from now. And to think how Alex had hidden this from him, and so well! The trouble he must have gone to, getting this for him, personalized, perfect! Rubinfine was more than touched. He felt like taking this autograph and showing it to every one of those teachers and therapists and rabbis who had told him he had no interpersonal skills. Look what my friend has done for me! Look what my good friend Alex-Li Tandem has done for *me*! Reluctantly, Rubinfine put it back where he had found it. He would act surprised next time he saw it. Surprised and overjoyed, which was the truth, even if he had to replay it one more time for an audience.

On the bed, a small mound of torn photograph. For a minute, he had forgotten all about it, but there it was, reproaching him. Rubinfine collected it and shoved it in his pockets and left the room. Standing in the hallway, he could hear Joseph and Alex, all guns blazing. Boot was, unsuccessfully, trying to calm them down. The gist was *give it to me*. And the other gist was *over my dead body. If this house was burning*, Alex was saying, *I'd take my autographs before anything else here, including you.*

Agonized Rubinfine took a step forward and then one back and then slowly walked down the stairs. Now he stood at the threshold. As clear as the world he heard his friend say: 'Look, you have your work, Joseph, yes? And Rubinfine has his family. And Adam has his God. And this is what I have. My little obsessions. You used to have them too, but you grew out of them. Lucky you. But I didn't, all right? Do you understand? This is what is between me and my grave. This is what I *have*.'

Poor Rubinfine. He tucked his head round the door, told the assembled company that Rebecca's eczema had flared up again, that Joseph should come now if he wanted a lift, and disappeared out of the front door.

2

A much later stage of the party; only two people are in attendance. The video is rolling. Alex and Boot are collapsed on the sofa, having a silent misunderstanding about sex. Boot has removed her tights and is waiting to be groped, for no reason she can put her finger on. (Certainly not out of *desire*, for example. More out of a kind of *indignation*.) Alex is resolute in his intention not to grope, for no reason he can understand. (Not really out of *lack of desire*, as such. Maybe it is a moral objection. Maybe it's the drink.) Boot is pretending to be asleep, although she's wide awake. Alex is pretending to be awake, although he can barely keep his eyes open. Boot is perfectly comfortable, but keeps shifting her position in an attempt to reignite the debate. Alex has terrible cramp but daren't move. Kitty is in the final minutes of her journey, her closing song:

You were my lucky star . . .
You said that I'd go far . . .

Finally, as the credits roll, Boot turns her back to him. This is one of the great unequivocal International Gestures, the kind that cannot be misread.

autographman has enabled messenger (02.03)

autographman: Es, I can see your icon. Are u there?

autographman: Esther?

autographman: I'm not totally beneath contempt, am I?

autographman: I can be spoken to, can't I? I CAN BE TYPED 2 at least???

Missticktock: You can be spoken to.

autographman: Hi!

Missticktock: Hi

autographman: You're up late. hello.

autographman: Knock knock.

Missticktock: Not interested.

autographman: horse walks into a bar . . .

Missticktock: Ads says he saw u today. says u were acting like

autographman: barman says: why the long face?

Missticktock: a complete fool.

autographman: Hmm . . .

Missticktock: I have to go 2 bed.

Missticktock: tired, feddup

Missticktock: Adam's had me staring at walls all night

Missticktock: freaking madmen, all of you

autographman: wait –

Missticktock: goodnight Alex

autographman: wait!

autographman: PLEASE!

Missticktock: what?

autographman: just wait a minute.

Missticktock: ....?

autographman: going to NY tomorrow. Haven't even packed.

Missticktock: having surgery on Sunday. haven't even submitted to the principles of a major religion.

autographman: hello. My name is Alex-Li. I am a total waste of space. *Sorry*

Missticktock: At least it means I miss Rubinfine's barndance.

autographman: thank heavens

autographman: for small mercies.

Missticktock: very small. Four foot three.

Missticktock: Badoom boom boom.

Missticktock: thanguuuuverymuch

autographman: u funny. I miss u.

autographman: so much.

Missticktock: say hello to Ny for me

autographman: everything stinks

Missticktock: say hello to Kitty for me (she lives there right? 109 years old –

autographman: without you. Seriously. nothing works.

Missticktock: on 109th street.

autographman: I'm serious. The world is broken.

Missticktock: my centagenerian (sp?) white woman competition.

Missticktock: goodnight alex.

Missticktock: yeah, but who's gonna fix it, baby?

Missticktock has disabled messenger (02.18)

autographman: esther??

autographman has disabled messenger (02.19)

3

Friday morning was blue and without blemish. The long shadows made the coy pastel houses lean forward and kiss each other. The trees reached out for a fight with the fingers of wrestlers.

'That? That was Boot,' explained Alex to his milk operative, Marvin, who was on the doorstep.

'And? Does she fit?'

'What?'

'Boot. Does she fit?'

'Oh, got you. No. Not quite. Nice woman, though. Great, really.'

Turning together, Marvin and Alex watched Boot, in yesterday's clothes, mooch down the street and vanish at that point where Alex's pretty yellow road met Mountjoy's high street and all the dark, contesting facts of the world.

'Mate, if I had what you have . . .' said Marvin and whistled. Marvin was a great fan of Esther and pursued her frankly and relentlessly. He was one of those who called her 'African Princess', a description she considered an insult, along with the rest of the feminine diminutives: Baby-doll, Hot-stuff, Glamour-puss, Sex-kitten, Girlfriend.

Alex snapped his fingers. 'Oh! Marvin, before I forget – I won't be needing any milk until next week. I'm going to New York.'

Marvin returned his order book to the pocket of his uniform. 'Going to New York. No milk. Hold the phone. Be still my beating etc.'

Now he reached into a bag on his shoulder and brought out a medium-sized package. 'Before *I* forget, you got another one of these. Gary Fitz – I know him from way back, *way* back – he does the Mail Ex round here, but he can't be arsed with this street – too out of his way and up a hill and the rest of it – so he's started giving them to me when he gets 'em. 'Member? I gave you that one las' week, back whenever.'

'Gave me?' said Alex absently, taking the spongy packet in his hands and ripping along the red thread. He looked over at his dead car, musing whether he should pop in on Hollywood Alphabet, apologize to Ads, find Esther.

'How's your head, anyway? Where's your head at, Alex? Did it come home?'

From a sleeve of cardboard Alex drew out a pristine signed

photograph of the popular actress Kitty Alexander, signed boldly to the lighter portion. He reached out an arm for Marvin, to steady himself.

'You all right?'

'I don't understand,' whispered Alex, looking about wildly.

'It's not rocket science, mate. It's just the post. Someone sends it, you get it. Nice photo. Who's that, then? Hey, *hey* – don't close the door on me – you've got to sign for it, Alex – wait, man – otherwise I don't get my commission, you get me? There's no moolah for meelah, otherwise.'

Alex held the photo to his chest and then out in front of him. If it wasn't real, he wasn't Alex-Li Tandem. The inscription: *To Alex, finally – Kitty Alexander.* Alex's face exploded into Technicolor.

'Was this Adam? Jacobs – the video guy, you know, down the road? My friend? Or Rubinfine, the rabbi? Did someone put you up to this? Where did this *come* from?'

Marvin sighed, took the package from Alex and turned it back over. 'Return address American, envelope . . . American. I'd say America, man. Look, I can't stand here all day. It's just a package. It looks just like the one I gave you last week –'

'Why do you keep saying that? When?'

'Last week – a package from America, I gave you one. My name is Marvin. This is a house. That was your car. There is the sky. Laters, man.'

Marvin did his traditional mosey down the path, but just before the gate Alex braved the cold ground and raced barefoot after him.

'Wait, Marvin, wait. When you gave this other package to me – did you – did I open it? I mean, did you *see* me open it?'

Marvin did the International Gesture for memory retrieval: the furrowed brow. 'Er . . . *Jesus*, man, I don't remember. Nah, I don't think so. You were in a hurry, innit? You were off somewhere, going somewhere – I dunno. I didn't *see* you for five days after that, anyway. You were *sleeping it off*, if you get me, yeah? Oh, man – I forgot – sign here, please.'

Alex signed Marvin's clipboard, thunderously dotting his *i*. He grabbed Marvin's cheeks and kissed Marvin full on the lips.

'*Oi!* Get out of it. I'm not that kind of delivery boy. I'm a milk operative, man. A milk operative. And dat's it. Wait – *that's* your signature? That's not even English. Is that Chinese, man?'

'Now, you see, Marvin,' said beaming Alex-Li, 'this is a good fact. You didn't see me open it. That's the most important fact yet. Because it means – don't you see? I'm not insane. I must have opened it at Ads', when I was high. Which is reckless. But it's not insane. I am not insane. On the contrary, I understand. I *understand*.'

'Bit early in the morning for epiphanies,' said Marvin disapprovingly. He gave his shirt one thorough, valedictory shake and shut the gate behind him.

'Anita,' said breathless Alex-Li Tandem, patting down his bed-hair and placing the cat-box on the ground by his feet. 'God, you look great. Look, I'm glad I caught you before you left . . . you see, this is a bit awkward, but the thing is, I'm going to New York tonight, bit last minute, you see – and I was just wondering, really – as it's only for a few days – whether, you might consider taking –'

'No,' said Anita Chang.

At Hollywood Alphabet the fools of the world were trying to force their late videos into the slot before opening hours. Except Adam was wise to them. He had fashioned the slot to be precisely an inch too small for the videos. It was the gateway through which no man could pass, unless he was truly determined. At nine, then, each morning, Adam calmly took up his position by the slot, sitting on a fold-up chair with the Zohar on his knees. His smooth black fingertips striking against the coarse white grain of the page. He read aloud and in Hebrew.

> *Rabbi Shim'on said*
> *'This one is not known by any name in the world,*
> *for something sublime is inside him.*
> *It is a secret!*
> *The flowing light of his father shines upon him!*
> *This secret has not spread among the Comrades.'*

Alex had the knack, though. He knew how to angle his video in such a way that it took a sliver of paint off the door's woodwork and fell rattling into the waiting cage.

'Tandem?'

'Always.'

Alex's manic excitement this morning made the opening of the door a trial. It also made the making of tea a trial, and the hearing of the incredible tale – by the time Adam was asked to take Grace, he had been worn down. He said yes as they sat on the three steps that formed the split-level of the borrowing area, hugging mugs of green tea, looking out upon a sea of stories.

'You'll tell Esther, right? Just as I told it to you? You'll tell her the facts. The whole story.'

'Soon as she's back from the library. Promise. The whole story. Alex, have you thought any more about –?'

'Doesn't it feel good,' said Alex happily, 'when everything gets tied up?'

Grace curled round Adam's ankles. Adam picked her up and held her to him.

'When Lovelear sees this!' said Alex, hugging the package. 'There's a return address, clear as day!'

'Hmm.'

They sat quietly for a time, listening to the morning.

'Adam,' asked Alex suddenly, 'what do you think's wrong with Joseph?'

Adam visibly brightened, and turned to face him. 'What do *you* think is wrong with him?'

Alex frowned. 'Well, I don't know, do I, that's why I'm asking you.'

'I see,' said Adam quietly.

Adam stood up, with Grace in one hand and *The Girl from Peking* in the other. With a sigh, he put Kitty back in her rightful place between *Gilda* and *The Glenn Miller Story*.

'You seem disappointed in me,' said Alex.

Adam shrugged. 'So this story of Torah,' he said, 'is merely the garment of Torah. Whoever thinks that the garment is the real Torah – may his spirit deflate! The Torah has a body: this body is clothed in garments: the stories of this world. Fools of the world look only at the garment, the story of Torah; they know nothing more. Beneath the garment is the true Torah, the soul of the soul. They do not look at what is under that garment. As wine must sit in a jar, so Torah must sit in this garment. The Zohar helps us look under this garment. So look only at what is under the garment! So all those words and those stories – they are garments!' Adam said all of this in Hebrew. The only word Alex understood was Torah.

4

'No, can't stop, no way,' said Alex, stepping over the iron bed frame. 'Train. And I intend to catch it.'

But Rubinfine, Darvick and Green spread their arms and formed a wall. 'It's as important as hell, if you'll pardon my French,' said Darvick, and grabbed on to the waistband of Alex's jeans.

'You see, the thing is that Rabbi Rubinfine,' said Green pleadingly, taking Alex's face in his hands, 'well, he has something very important to explain to you – he wants to give you his reasons. For doing what he did. Which, though essentially good, may not be immediately apparent. Do you see?'

'Excuse me?'

'It's *important*,' insisted Darvick, getting a firmer grip, 'that the Rabbi should be allowed to give a proper account of himself – to say his piece, like any defendant!'

Alex shook himself free and held up his package and drew Kitty from her sheath like a sword. He held her above his head. He felt like the popular film actor John Cusack. He said, 'You see this?' – Rubinfine screamed like a woman – 'Today this is more important. OK? *OK?* Rubinfine – what's going on?' asked Alex, as Rubinfine sat down where he was and knocked the back of his head three times feebly against the monument.

'You see what we're trying to achieve here?' barked Darvick, motioning to the bedstead and the 2CV it was bound for.

'I see it,' said Alex simply. 'I'm just not interested. Erm . . . hey . . . Rubinfine, are you –'

'Four rabbis,' broke in Green, looking pointedly at Rubinfine, 'entered the Pardes, the paradisal garden. One gazed and died, one became demented, one cut the plants, and only one, Rabbi Akiva, survived unharmed.'

Rubinfine looked devastated. Darvick chuckled softly. Green smiled his beatific, full-lipped smile and stepped aside to let Alex pass.

'Rubinfine – did I –'

'Go,' said Green. 'You're late already.'

His heart full of gratitude, Alex began his sprint to catch the train, just audible as it came down from the east, over the peak of the artificial mount from which the great suburb of Mountjoy receives its name. He could hear Rubinfine, his voice carried on the tail-end of that same easterly wind, his tone deeply aggrieved. 'Cut the plants? And that's meant to mean *what*?'

TEN / *Keter*

Crown • Jimmy's Antiques • Highballs with Lola-Lola • Conspiracy
theories • The Youth Brand • Zen Radio • Flying into nothing • Zen
Casablanca • The collector saves

I

Late that night, in the queue to check-in, Alex-Li reflected with
pleasure on the glories of the day. After seeing the rabbis, he had
caught the train to the east of the city and walked into Jimmy's
Antique Market (est. 1926) feeling every inch the conquering hero.
Through the covered arches he walked, past the ratty stalls hawking
every kind of nostalgia: clothes, glassware, records, posters, stamps,
badges, coins, autographs. He had known some of these traders for
almost fifteen years, from the days when he came as a boy to spend
his pocket money. He had always felt a kinship with them, however
reluctant. But today he felt different. He had been set apart. How
many of them had found the item they dreamt of, their personal
grails? Had Lola-Lola worn Marilyn's air-vent dress? Had Stuart
Pike played Hendrix's guitar? Had the popular writer J. D. Salinger
ever once penned poor, devoted Oliver McSweeney a friendly note?

The peculiar thing about such obsessions is their specificity.
Just as a man with a fetish for slight, downy-armed Japanese women
is left cold by a big, brassy blonde, so the man who has spent his
life in the pursuit of the tap shoes worn by the popular musical star
Donald O'Connor can muster no real enthusiasm when the man

at the stall to his right shows him the ruffled shirt Henry Daniell wore in *Camille*. All fandom is a form of tunnel vision: warm and dark and infinite in one direction.

Alex tramped through the market, looking for interested parties. Jimmy himself (grandson of original Jimmy) informed him that Lovelear and Dove were around here someplace, but he couldn't find them. For the first time in his life, he really wanted to see Lovelear, or at least he wanted to show Kitty to someone who would fall to his knees and clasp his hands together in prayer.

But Stuart Pike spotted him first. Under duress, Alex stopped at Pike's stall with its mountain of twentieth-century tat (Beatles wigs, cocktail shakers in the shape of hula girls) and sat with him a while, looking through his serial-killer correspondence. One of the more infamous of Stuart's 'friends' had recently been executed in the state of Texas. The man's trademark had been to carve the name of his victim into her own forehead. On death row he was married twice and proposed to a dozen times. Stuart was inconsolable. 'Every letter he sent me,' said Stuart, showing him an example, 'I could get an American to buy it. Four, five hundred dollars. Roaring bloody trade.'

Stuart was a Yorkshireman of good family. He had been in a glam rock band, once. He owned three paintings by the popular psychopath John Wayne Gacy.

'Do you know who Kitty Alexander is, Stu?'

'Is she the Arizona baby murderer?'

'No, no, she's, she *was*, an actress. In the fifties. Russian Italian American. Very beautiful. Actress.'

'Actresses,' said Pike, as if considering an unusual species variation. 'Never been much into actresses. Got the bail-bond that

Lana signed for her daughter. Actually, I know a feller who's got Judy's tranquillizer prescriptions, only signed by the doctor, but still. Better than a kick in the head. Any good to yer?'

It was in Lola-Lola's fifties boutique that Alex found Lovelear and satisfaction. Lola-Lola, a peroxide, top-heavy, Muscovite divorcee, was sitting on her pink pouffe, drinking highballs, entertaining Lovelear and Dove with a set of Bettie Page playing cards. Misha, her overworked young man ('*moy malchik!*'), was out front, frantically looking for the left hand of some white kid gloves a customer had set her heart on. In the backroom, the popular singer Bobby Darin sang of an underwater date he'd planned. A buzzing lightbulb cast a red light over distressed minks and limp fox-furs, UFO toasters, skirts like open umbrellas. On the back wall, a grainy projection of some unknown American family on a sun-spotted lawn, reliving their heyday at an eternal barbecue.

Alex sat cross-legged on the floor next to Dove. He laid Kitty in front of them all. He began his story – shortened by this point and refined. Lola-Lola gave a shriek of pleasure at the key moment and placed her flat palm over her cocktail glass. Lovelear opened his mouth to say something, looked closer and remained silent. Dove thumped Alex on the back and gave him a hug, which affected Alex more than he would admit.

'She just sent it to you,' said Dove respectfully. 'No note. No explanation.'

'No note,' said Alex, choking up. 'No explanation. It's just a gift. It's a *gift*. I think she wants to see me. I think she wants me to go there.'

'Ahlex,' purred Lola-Lola, from the very curl of her throat, 'zis is fantastic – after all zis time you deserve it. But still it is not heep to be always smiling like the hep-cat who is eating of all the cream!'

'If you give me and Dove the return address,' Lovelear said, with some grace in defeat, 'we'll look her up for you when we go. How'd that be? Tell you all about it when we get back.'

'Thanks, Lovelear,' said Alex, a few seconds before the penny, as the journalists say, dropped. 'Nice thought – but you mightn't be there for months – and I'm actually I'm off right now, no, I mean, actually tonight, for this Autographicana thing, so – yep – flying across – the – great – big –'

The glories of the day, then, had been tarnished somewhat. Lovelear and Dove were, at present, exactly twenty-three people behind him in the snake that led to check-in. At every bend they waved their arms like a French mime act, an attempt to get simple messages across, stuff like: *Bag unzipped* and *Better not have weed in that suitcase* and *Look at that fat woman*. It caused Lovelear pain not to be able to deliver to Alex his commentary on every stage of this queue and everybody in it. In the final stretch, it seemed to become too much for him; with despair Alex watched him pushing his way through, negotiating his gut around the public's matching luggage. He was wearing a tight white shirt and some famous blue jeans, having read in a magazine that no man can go wrong in such a combination. The article had been illustrated by photographs of the popular film players Marlon Brando and James Dean. Alex would like to send a picture of Lovelear to that journalist.

'So!' says Lovelear, releasing his massive bag, 'what do you think her deal is?' Lovelear's bag flumps to the floor and spreads itself over Alex's feet. Lovelear kicks it but it only shunts an inch into somebody else's way. Swearing obscenely, he drags it back up, rests it on his hip like a child and then lunges forward, swinging it on to his back. Lovelear is one of the few in this queue with a bag that requires picking up. Everyone else's have got the wheels and the cases with the stiff armature, the handle. The goyish guys like Lovelear who lug holdalls might as well be walking around clasping the necks of dodos. Alex reaches for his notebook but he has left it at home. And as soon as his fingers register the emptiness of his pocket, he feels that he does not wish to make a note, not today. Maybe not ever again. This may be the death of the book. He has grown tired of filing.

'I was back there,' says Lovelear, 'thinking it over, right? And I'm thinking: is it a *trap* or something? I mean, could it be? Like her guy Krauser's got some trumped-up harassment charge against you or something? That *totally* happened to a collector I knew. And then that thing with me and Miss Sheedy, now known as the party of the second part – I'm not saying that's how it *is*. I'm just saying we don't *know*. We don't have all the facts. You're really just flying into the unknown, that's all I'm trying to say.'

Since the afternoon, Lovelear had been growing conspiracy-crazy. He did not understand an object's status as a 'gift'. He did not believe, for example, that a film is any more than its publicity, a painting any more than an abstruse way to make a buck. He did not believe that songs or books were in any way substantially different from sandwiches or tyres. Product is product. And he did not believe in free lunches. And he does not believe a woman just –

'You know, like just turns *round* and does this thing that she's refused to do for *anyone* for twenty *years* without a reason? I mean does that even make *sense* to you?'

Alex tells him the same thing he told him three hours ago and has tried, in one way or another, to tell him since their acquaintance began: this is not a film.

*

In the plane, Alex is relieved to find he has been seated on his own. He is in an aisle seat with Esther's absence next to him. Illegally reclining, he opens his plastic bag, a gift from the plane. The plane is a famous brand of plane, part of a worldwide brand that reaches as low as cola and as high as a jumbo-jet. This is a plane for young people and/or the young at heart. With intellectual leanings. And natural style. It is a brand that employs the most shameless flattery to get what it wants.

Our youth is but a brief night: fill it with rapture!

So it is written in a peculiar font on the plastic bag. Alex feels no rapture when he opens this bag; he feels nothing, nothing, not even recognition. Who is this bag for? Who *is* this youth? What does he want with individually wrapped facial cleansing wipes? Why does he like all fonts to be bold, and all colours in flat, uncompromising blocks? What does he do with such a little writing pad – what notes is he making?

Alex tries the earphones. Over the radio the youth can choose from three genres of music, none of which Alex enjoys. Then a comedy channel whose comedy derives from a feeling of familiarity with a youthful comedian's life (*So you're doing the washing up, yeah? And your girl walks in, yeah?*), the recognition of which resemblance makes Alex feel suicidal. Finally, a sub-Zen relaxation tape that consists of an LA therapist whispering koans over the sound of the sea. The sea has been enhanced in some way so as to lend it a musicality it never seems to possess when you are standing at its edge worrying about pollutants.

'*A distraught mother,*' says the lady, 'begged Buddha to heal the dead child in her arms. He did not perform a miracle. He said, "Bring me a mustard seed from a house where no one – "'

'Could you please do your belt up, sir? The light hasn't gone off yet,' says a stewardess to Alex, who has not even noticed they are in the air.

2

The autumnal quilt retreats (England is always autumnal from the air); now they are above the clouds. Alex sits in the plane imagining himself from the perspective of a bored child sitting in a car, looking up. They should swap; this plane is designed for the very young and the very bored. All Alex is required to do for the next six and a half hours is eat and watch television and fall asleep for a while. All this is so earnestly wanted for him, *of* him. No one has desired his comfort and sleep this badly since he was a baby.

Everything possible is being done to make him feel that nothing momentous, like flight, is occurring. At no point does anyone suggest that he and four hundred other strangers of unknown mental-health status are trapped in a 400-tonne aircraft flying thirty-five thousand feet up in the air relying on equations of energy and velocity that no one aboard could sketch out in even their most basic form. Everything in this plane is an interface, like the windows on his computer. Nothing on this plane has anything to do with flying, just as his desktop doesn't have anything to do with the processing of information. Pretty, pretty pictures. Lovely, distracting stories we tell each other. If Alex leans far out into the aisle he can get a glimpse of the brilliance of the illusion: this private experience he is meant to be having is replicated as far as the eye can see. The same meals, the same detritus (the missing sock, the broken biro, the twisted blanket, the plastic water glass quite exploded), the same angle of recline, the same TV screen showing the same father and son playing catch, the same vigilant mindfulness of one's personal space. In this context, leaving the interface, crossing over the white line, is pretty unthinkable. It's a hero's job – or a madman's. Accompanied by birdsong, the Zen lady says, 'Knowledge is the reward of action, because it is by doing things that we are transformed. Executing a symbolic gesture, truly living through a role, this is when we come to realize the truth inherent in the role. When we suffer its consequences, we fathom and exhaust its contents.' Alex turns to channel six in preparation for watching the popular cinema classic *Casablanca*.

God knows (thinks Alex, about an hour and a half later when he is washed in joy), Europe has made many American movies, but America has only ever made one European film: *Casablanca*. Ah, Casablanca! Rick plays chess, not cards. Every European immigrant actor who was in town at the time is in the cast. The music, the script, the cinematography – European ears, and minds, and eyes. Look at the miracle of it! An American movie with no happy ending, made by Europeans, mostly European Jews, in the middle of a World War! Alex can think of no better example of the accidental nature of great art. He knows all the legends. The chaotic set where the script was written daily, the actors who did not know what their lines would be until they were handed them. Alex puts his chair back one more notch (he has been saving this notch) and marvels at the size of Bogart's head. He mimes along with lines that seem, to him, almost Zen-like in their purity:

RENAULT: *I've often speculated why you don't return to America. Did you abscond with the church funds? Did you run off with a senator's wife? I like to think that you killed a man. It's the romantic in me.*

RICK: *It's a combination of all three.*
RENAULT: *And what in heaven's name brought you to Casablanca?*
RICK: *My health. I came to Casablanca for the waters.*
RENAULT: *The waters? What waters? We're in the desert.*
RICK (laconically): *I was misinformed.*

Facts. When Bergman and Bogart kiss, what looks like a moon turns out to be a searchlight. When Lorre is up against the wall his eyes completely revolve. Did you know that Ronald Reagan was seriously considered for the role of Rick? That *play it again, Sam* is never said? That Bergman thought Bogart a bore?

'That the mechanics – you see the guys round the airplane? In the final scene? They were midgets, actually. People don't know – the facts just get lost. Seriously, it's a fact. The plane was just a cardboard cut-out and they couldn't get the perspective right so they hired midgets to play the mechanics, can you *believe* that?' Alex asks his right-hand neighbour, who is simply trying to watch the film in peace. The collector is the saviour of objects that might otherwise be lost.

BOOK TWO

Roebling Heights
The Zen of Alex-Li Tandem

You see, this is my life. It always will be. There's nothing else. Just us, and the cameras – and those wonderful people out there in the dark.

– *Sunset Boulevard*, Charles Brackett, Billy Wilder and D. M. Marshman Jr

In the twelfth century the Chinese master Kakuan drew the pictures of ten bulls with a written commentary. The bull is the eternal principle of life, truth in action. The ten bulls represent sequent steps in the realization of one's true nature.

– *Zen Flesh, Zen Bones*, Paul Repps and Nyogen Senzaki

ONE / *The Search for the Bull*

I

'The longest Sabbath of my life,' concluded Tandem, and cursed Lovelear, whose bag he was carrying. Pausing, he dropped it to the floor, opened his hand and peered into a swollen landscape of red ridges, bloodless islets, like an aerial view of Japan. For the second time today, it was very early on a chilly and unforgiving Saturday morning. What more confirmation does a man need of the bitter futility of international travel?

He bent down once more and seized the bag. Dove beside him was on autopilot, pushing a trolley with his eyes closed through a dead president's airport. Lovelear, despite the bravado, was in fact deeply terrified of flight and had repaired to a nearby restroom to vomit with relief.

'Look, Ian: New York,' said Alex, as they approached the huge revolving door.

'New York, yeah,' said Ian.

'Ever been to New York, Ian?'

'Can't say I have, no.'

'Interested in looking at it?'

'Everything looks . . .' muttered Ian, and stepped out. It was snowing. Alex opened his mouth to ask a question, but a sweep of it met him full in the face, lacing his tongue with a dirty, metallic taste of heaven.

'. . . the same at two in the morning,' said Ian softly, laying his head along the trolley's bar. 'Everything does.'

Amid the snow-blown interference of the scene, Alex could make out the famous taxis, coming and going so that there was never a lack or an abundance and no man had to wait very long.

'Feel like I've been here before, a bit,' said Ian, levering his eyes open at the moment a cab stopped before them and wound down its window. 'Familiar, like from another life or something. That's weird, innit? Considering I –'

'Taxi Driver,' said Alex flatly, removing bags from the trolley. 'Manhattan, Last Exit to Brooklyn, On the Waterfront, Mean Streets, Miracle on 34th Street, West Side Story, On the Town, Serpico, The Sunshine Boys, Sophie's Choice –'

'All about Eve,' broke in the driver, 'King Kong, Wall Street, Moonstruck, The Producers, Plaza Suite, The Out of Towners original and re-make, The Godfather parts one and two, Kramer vs Kramer and freakin' Ghostbusters. We can do this all morning, my friend. The meter's running.'

'Everyone's been here before, Dove,' said Alex, opening the cab door.

'Are you *kidding*?' cried Lovelear, spat out suddenly by the revolving doors and thinking of a different film altogether. 'You can get *limousines* around the corner.'

'Ah, this is the *life*,' said Lovelear emphatically, making the awkward International Gesture of luxury (hands behind head, legs extended with feet crossed). 'I mean, this is *the* life.'

Alex was unsure. Somehow, the limousine, though improbably long on the outside, did not seem, once you were inside, to be any roomier than a normal yellow cab. It was dirty too; the worn upholstery stained many times over by other thrill-seekers (How many blow-jobs, thought Alex, and how many champagne corks? How did so many people come to believe that these things are to be done in limousines?). From two dusty decanters, pale, warm whisky came, to which Lovelear was gleefully adding flat, warm cola. He raised his glass for regular toasts to the snow, the city, the cops, the skyline, the ideal hotdog and the curvy girl in the toll-booth who had not yet killed herself. Lovelear was from Minnesota.

And they were not there yet. The last of the suburbs was still passing by, hunkered down for the winter and still as Sunday. Alex felt a particular yearning for the suburbs between an airport and a city; he wanted to stop the car and knock on one of those pine doors, and squeeze in between the fireman and his wife until someone rose to make breakfast and the kids started to yell. But you need a specific address for the suburbs. Only in the city can you be dropped off in front of statues and behind opera houses. The suburbs are by invitation only. And here came the city anyway, insistent, unavoidable. Lovelear grabbed the back of Dove's head and pointed it in the right direction.

'OK, OK, OK, Dove – get ready, no, come closer to the window, OK, are you ready? OK . . . look . . . now!'

The car achieved the hump in the road and the city appeared miraculously before them, outlined in moonlight, the concrete ECG of an ecstatic vision people have of themselves. Alex was as moved by it as the next man, more than – it was the only other town in the world for which he had ever felt desire. But sometimes you have to turn your eyes from a mistress or you'll never go home to your wife; Alex turned now, to look out of the other window, to the harbour and beyond that to melancholy Brooklyn (from the Dutch, *Breuckelen*, broken land), and to a glimpse of the stone lady herself. The sword in her hand seemed only just to have been raised aloft and the snow swirled about her form.

2

Out of the traffic, into the town. To the Rothendale Hotel, a massive, forlorn building. Its old brick had been covered in new paint, and two unsightly extensions built on each side. The street had gentrified; the Rothendale had been forced to keep pace. From the outside it seemed dazed at its own sudden respectability, like a dissolute grandfather forced into a suit and dragged to a wedding.

Inside, a corporate virus had spread from the red and gold trim wallpaper, to the odourless flowers, to the fake marble water feature, to the repeating monogram pattern in the carpet, to the professional smile that was being laid on Alex right now.

'And the gentlemen,' said the meticulous young man, 'are here for the Autographicana Fair?'

Alex considered his walk across the lobby. Which gesture had given him away? Cheerlessly, he took his Autographicana goodie bag and listened to Lovelear interrogate the young man about the hotel's facilities.

'It's 3 a.m.,' said Lovelear, triumphant in the hallway a few minutes later, 'and I could go for a jacuzzi on the *roof*. You think you could do that in any of those London dumps? Hmm? I could go for a jacuzzi on the roof *right now*.'

'Then why don't you?'

'What?'

'Then why don't you?'

The lift arrived. They got in it.

'I'll come with you, if you like,' said amiable Dove as the sixth floor sank beneath them. 'I'm feeling quite awake actually, now.'

'It's 3 a.m., Dove,' said Lovelear wearily, then shook his head and got out on the seventh.

''Course, there's no thirteenth, you know,' said Dove, who always took silence in a confined space as a personal failure. 'In American lifts – elevators, I should say. They don't have a thirteenth floor.'

It was rare in the extreme for Dove to produce any fact that Alex did not already know, but he did not know that one. He looked up without expectation at the sequential lights – he was surprised.

'Imagine,' said Dove sleepily, 'ancient superstition like that in a big modern country like this. Mental. 'Slike believing in the tooth-fairy. Or bloody resurrection.'

'Goodnight, Dove,' said Alex, with a generous smile.

'Yeah. Night, Tandem.'

From his bedroom window, Alex could see more famous sights than any Autograph Man has a right to expect. He was being invited to marvel at the withdrawing darkness, at the dawn, the daily count of enchanted objects: green glass, spires that seemed to pierce fat clouds, theatrical débuts, notorious murders, men going about their days. Tentatively, Alex dug about in his bag for his camera. As his fingers brushed the lens cap, he caught sight of a complimentary magazine on the dresser which had chosen as its cover image the view from his hotel window. Feeling oddly oppressed, he closed the curtain and opened a map.

He was looking for Roebling Heights, Brooklyn, the return address on his package. There was no house number, no other details. He would simply have to go up there and ask around, like the popular detective Philip Marlowe. If that didn't work he had plan B, which consisted of going to the Lower East Side, finding Kitty's fan-club president Krauser and beating it out of him, like the popular actor Jimmy Cagney. Yeah, like Jimmy Cagney, god of all scrappers.

What da ya hear?

What da ya say?

On the map he found tiny abbreviated Roebling squeezed between the Black area, the Hipster area, the Hasid area and the Polish area, at the end of a subway line he had never used and never heard of. In the index of his guide book Roebling Heights made only one appearance and warranted only one comment. *Roebling*, Alex read, *has seen better days. It has also seen so-so days and worse days. Now it's settling for just 'days'*. Everybody thinks they're a comedian, even the writers of guide books.

Alex stood in the middle of his room and took some deep breaths. He was far from home, far. The only way he could travel this kind of distance was to make wherever he went as much like Mountjoy as possible. To this end, when he packed to leave, he took what everybody takes – clothes and essentials – but he also placed his extended arm upon his desk and swept whatever was there into a carrier-bag, which he emptied now on to his hotel bed with the intention of spreading the items around the place. This was travelling without moving. Receipts, bills, unread books with snapped spines, push-pins, Post-its, the famous pound note (this he Blu-Tacked above the door), a very old hairclip of Esther's, an ageing muffin, half a joint. The joint was a surprise and he pounced on it, smoking it in and out of the shower, during his brief bathroom perfunctories, and then reaching its coiled tip as he nipped naked into the tightly made bed and fought the sheets for the space he had paid for. By his eye, a red light on the phone flashed on, off. He picked up the receiver, but that didn't stop it, so he phoned reception.

'The light, sir? That would be the light that indicates you have some messages to pick up on your voice-mail.'

'I just got to the hotel.'

'Yes, sir, but your voice-mail has been active since noon.'

'My voice-mail precedes me.'

'It sure does, sir.'

Alex had three messages. He was halfway through the first before he recognized the speaker – that low, throaty New York sound. Something in the timbre of her voice told you she was black. Honey Richardson. He had never met her in the flesh, but they had traded four or five times over the past two years, by phone or computer. And now he remembered he had arranged to meet her at noon, before the big show. Alex put out his joint on the leg of the side table. Her voice was terrific. Like being smacked and stroked at the same time.

Sinking into his pillow, he listened to the music of it without listening to any of the words. Then it was over. He had to play it again to discover that she wished to change their meeting place: instead of the corner of such and such, she would prefer it if they met at the corner of somewhere else. This would be, she said, more appropriate. Appropriate?

Alex hitched up on one elbow, intrigued, and hit the button. It was Honey again, this time with a further explanation of why the previous arrangement had been found wanting. Too busy an area, such a *damn rush of everyone*, and in her situation ... But this sentence was left unfinished. She seemed to think Alex knew something of her situation that he did not. He knew only that she was an inexperienced dealer, a *woman* dealer, who bought stuff from Alex that he couldn't give away to anyone else. In the dark, Alex felt around for a pen to take down her number, but it was gone before he put pencil to complimentary pad. And she was still talking – the message was *endless*. Alex sat himself up in bed as she told an ambulatory tale about a recent shopping trip with her sister, Trudy, who was a dental technician, see, getting married in July, and they had wandered into a crowded area and two people came out of nowhere and started yelling and trying to – but here the beep sounded loud in Alex's ear. Bemused, Alex pressed the button to listen to the third. Honey said: 'Look, here's how it is. I think the best for everybody concerned is if I meet you in the lobby of the hotel and we just come right into the restaurant, do our business and then leave and I don't want anything else suggested or implied and my story is mine and it's yesterday's news and I'm just here for the business, as anyone in this business will tell you. I've been everybody's goddamn anecdote and I won't be yours. I'll be wearing gloves. Goodnight.'

Alex phoned reception to find out if Honey Richardson was staying at the hotel. She was staying in the next room.

TWO / *Discovering the Footprints*

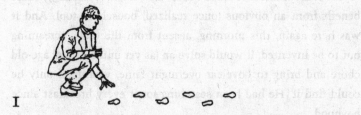

I

It was quite a spread. The white linen cloth, as pristine as the morning, presented breakfasts from around the world. Here boiled eggs sat in their china cups, pretty as Buddhas. Half a pig, sliced up and fried, had been arranged into a mountain around which scrambled egg shimmied and shook. Porridge, in a huge cauldron, sat on a piece of tartan, waiting to be ladled. Endless choice. Thin slices of waxy Dutch cheese, Italian baloney or German hams, conserves claiming Cornwall in *ye olde* earthenware jars, Philadelphia cream cheese, melted Swiss chocolate, fluffy Caribbean ackee or twelve hot English kippers, like dismal shoe soles, laid out in star formation. On the side, a swan-necked jug of maple syrup, a pancake tower, baskets of croissants and moist muffins, sizzling grits, the yang of bagels split conveniently from their yings, strips of smoked salmon re-formed into the silhouette of a fish (open-mouthed, so it seemed to eat a shiny mound of its own red roe), dried cereals for the serious, unlimited coffee (but no tea), all the juices of the known world and a resplendent four-tier fruit display, kept cool by an ice sculpture of Mount Rushmore.

It had taken three return visits, but finally the battle of the buffet was drawing to a close. Tandem and Dove were doing coffee shots with tobacco chasers. Lovelear was scanning the remnants of their breakfasts while holding forth on one of his favourite topics: the Overlooked Invention. He always believed some aspect of his breakfast could be made simpler by technology, could benefit from an obvious (once realized) household tool. And it was here again, this morning, absent from the table, screaming out to be invented. It would solve an (as yet unidentified) age-old chore and bring to Lovelear overnight fame, wealth. If only he could find it. He had been searching for it every breakfast since boyhood.

'Did you ever think,' said Alex-Li, checking his watch, 'that historically we may have reached a saturation point as far as *ease* is concerned? So there's actually no way you could've made that breakfast any easier than it was? Unless we, like, took it intra-venously.'

Lovelear reached out for the guava juice and poured himself a pint of it. 'Tandem, nobody thought they could improve on matchbox design? And then some guy went to the factory –'

Alex pushed for a name, any form of corroborating detail.

'*A* factory, OK? 'Snot important to the overall scenario – and it's 1926 and the guy walks into big man's office and he's like – I mean, the *guy's* like – I'm gonna sit down here and tell you how you could save millions of dollars every year, but in *exchange* I want twenty thousand dollars a year for the rest of my natural-born life – that was a lot of money back then – wouldn't cover a year's groceries now, but on with the story – and they're like, what the hell – thinking this guy's a crackhead or whatever – so, they just sit back and say OK, whatever, let's hear it. 'Cos they got nothing to lose. And he says, *put the sandpapery shit on one side*. Because, they were putting that shit on both sides, up to that point. Put it one side, man. Lived like a king till he died.'

'I have to go,' said Alex.

'You don't have to go anywhere. Fair's not for another hour. Where you gonna go? You don't know nobody in New York.'

Dove had been nose to nose these last few minutes with a milk carton, reading its side as he polished off a final bowl of cereal. Just as Alex pushed back from the table, he raised his head, slid the carton towards Alex and pointed at an image printed on its side. A fourteen-year-old missing person, one Polly Mo of the Upper East Side. Snaggle-toothed and eager against an unearthly lapis lazuli; detached, as in all school photos, from family and furniture. Alone in the big blue world. Last seen by the CCTV of a candy store, buying ten lottery tickets. Fondly, Ian wiped a splatter of milk from her face.

'They'll find her soon, prob'ly. Hopefully. Poor love. She must be on a million of these things. 'Sgood idea, mind – they should do it back home. Oi, what do you reckon?' he said to Lovelear, lifting the carton and placing the girl's face alongside Alex's own. 'The missing twin sister? A bit, don't you think? Around the eyes?'

'Dove, if that's your criterion, there's another half billion girls in the world who could be Tandem's missing twin sister. *Jesus Christ*,' Lovelear scowled, grabbing the carton out of Dove's hands. 'What a way to become a household name. Depressing the hell out of people when they're trying to eat breakfast.'

'Got to meet this weird woman person dealer thing,' said Alex, snatching his bag from under his chair. 'Late already. A bit of business, hopefully. Not expecting much. I don't think she knows what she's doing. You go on ahead, I'll see you in there.'

'Whatever. You're no great loss. Me and the Doveman, here:

235

we're Zen, we're down for whatever. Wax on, wax off,' said Lovelear, harpooning the remnants of a Mexican sausage with the tip of
his knife, holding it up. 'Just remember to put a rubber on it.'

He knew instantly that he recognized her. He had no idea why. He
strained to get a better look from behind the maître d's podium, he
stepped in front of it and waved – but at that moment she rested
her head against the solid, silent glass, beyond which it snowed
and snowed and things looked less like themselves and more like
another note in a symphony of white. This was her backdrop, this
was the scene she was stealing. She was black in a red dress. She
sat completely alone at the very back of the sea-themed restaurant,
amid papier-mâché starfish and plastic shrimp, the tentacles of an
octopus mural stretching out to get her. Alex approached. At closer
range, he could see that the dress was quite ordinary, with a high
neck and motherly overtones, the earrings larvae-like clusters of
pearls. There was a certain statuesque weight to her; she was maybe
thirty-five or so. Alex fixed on a set of large, mesmeric, glossy lips,
the same colour as the dress, a luxurious addition to a face that had
its lines and troubles. She was holding a vast pocked California
orange in her right hand, and had almost succeeded in peeling the
thing in one, fluent, corkscrew gesture.

'Hey, there. This enough fish for you? This enough *snow* for
you?'

Alex took the hand she offered. If he lived to be a hundred he
never expected to meet another woman wearing skin-tight black
rubber gloves in a public restaurant. As he went for his seat, she
made a low noise of triumph and held the orange peel up by one
end. She bounced its coil above the tabletop.

'That's nicely done.'

'I always think it's so much *nicer* that way. Like the orange got free itself. Just went right on and slipped its skin.'

Alex smiled feebly, and continued the battle to make his coat stay draped over the hunched shoulders of his chair. She spoke, therefore, to his back. She had a husky voice, but an orotund, serious one. There was no element of flirtation in it, nor anything overtly mad. He turned and sat. There was a pause. It was all he could do not to look at the gloves and it wasn't working: he was looking at the gloves.

'I told you I'd be wearing these on the phone, right?' she asked sharply. All the warmth bled from her face. She pushed her chair back from the table.

'I'm sorry? I don't under –'

'Look, if you don't want to do business in my fashion, then we don't need to waste each other's time, do we? I thought I made that clear on the telephone yesterday.'

Alex was as intimidated as he could ever remember being. He shrank in his chair and discreetly clutched the tablecloth. 'No, you misunderstand –'

'I like,' she said firmly, 'to get the jokes and the curiosity out of the way before the business starts, because when I do business I do *not* enjoy comedy.'

Honey brought back her chair, looking him dead straight in the eyes, like a cowboy. Alex had the sense that she had made all these gestures, in the same order, many times before. Either that, or she had seen them in a film.

She said: 'So before you ask, the answers are: about average, cut, he approached me, twenty-five dollars for the whole thing, and no, I never made much money out of it in the end. Why the hell would I be doing this if I did? As for this, I always been a movie fan, and I just kind of fell into autograph work, and therefore here I am. So. Business now?' she asked wearily, lifting a large black folder from her lap. 'I'm sure the other guys have already told you, but the rules are, one, no touching any of the product, unless you're wearing gloves, which I can provide to you; two, if you give me cash that you've touched with your hands, which I'm presuming you have, I'll have to spray it, and if it's a lot of cash, I'd appreciate it if you helped me; three, when I'm handling *your* items –'

She stopped and lifted her eyes from the spot on the table where she had been encircling her points with a rubber finger. Alex was nodding in that meek English way, quickly and about nothing.

'Hey. You OK?'

Alex opened his mouth, couldn't think where to begin, and closed it again.

'Hey. Ohhh . . .'

She raised an eyebrow as her face passed rapidly through suspicion, to recognition, to something like humorous regret.

'You got no damn idea who I am. Am I right?'

'You're Ms Richardson,' said Alex slowly. It was his even-toned voice, designed for the deaf, disabled, insane, irretrievably foreign. 'I sold you a Flowers McCrae – a two-reeler contract she signed, dated 1927? Last month, I think it was. And some cigarette cards featuring the Wheelerettes. And a lot of different things last October. I'm Alex-Li Tandem.' He reached for his card. 'I hope that's not – I mean, oh *Jesus*,' he said, rising in his chair, instantly red at the possibility that it was he and not she who had a problem, '*tell* me I'm at the right table –'

She opened her eyes wide, smiled, took his card and motioned for him to sit. 'You're fine, you're fine. I know who you are. See, I forget,' she said, looking across the room and hailing a waiter with a quick finger, 'that not everybody spends all their damn lives reading the papers. I'm gonna order us an English tea. I'm sorry I was so . . .' The sentence got lost in a movement of her hands, a quiet bouncing gesture, as if she were weighing two identical packets of flour.

'Anyway, anyway,' she said, almost to herself. She picked up a bottle of water and filled both their glasses. '*Damn*. We should start again. I'm Honey and you're Alex-Li. Hello, Alex-Li.'

She turned back to face him and smiled. She had a lot of teeth. She offered him the black rubber again. He shook it.

'Just it's usually the English who're the worse. One woman I met in Mar-lee-bone – is that how you say it? I always get those tube things mixed up – Mary-lee-bone?'

Alex corrected her. She tried it out twice, gave up with a little sigh.

'However you say it, but I was there on business, minding my *own* damn business too – this bitch spat right in my face. In the middle of the *street*.'

'Christ – I'm sorry,' said Alex, and concluded that he had just had a long and unusually opaque conversation about racism. It was at this point he began to feel more comfortable. It was like reaching the twenty-seventh minute of a French film, the point at which he usually began to have some hazy idea of what was going on.

'What you sorry about?' said Honey with a frown, and opened the folder. 'You didn't do nothing. Shall we?'

Honey pushed an Erich Von Stroheim towards him, a good studio portrait, signed boldly, in excellent condition, a quality autograph item. It was the first thing Alex had truly understood since he sat down. He moved to touch it, but she snatched it away.

'Let me explain again. You can't touch nothing of *mine*, until it's definitely *yours*. If you want this, and you're sure, then take it, but if you change your mind I'll have to spray it, which is a little tiresome, you know?'

Alex didn't know.

'If you're worried about *germs* or something –' he began, amazed; she cut him short with a low growl.

'I know, I know, you ain't got cooties, right?'

'Excuse me?'

'*Every*body's got cooties. You better take these gloves.'

It was a bewildering hour. Whenever he decided on an item, she would take the cash and leave with it, heading for the bathroom. When she returned the money seemed to glisten – it had a funny smell. At one point Alex's forearm brushed Honey's. She leapt from her chair. It was twenty minutes before she came back, smelling like a hospital corridor and with a wild, exhausted look in her eye.

'I guess you know,' she said, on her return from the bathroom, holding his freshly slick money, 'the definition of a movie producer.'

'Uh-uh, no. Tell me.'

'A man who knows what he wants but don't know how to spell it.'

'That's good, funny,' said Alex, laughing through a mouthful of scone. She had that disinterested charm that Alex envied in people whenever he came across it. The talent of not caring what is thought of you. He watched his own new rubber hands reaching up to his face as if someone else were feeding him.

'Hmm, it's OK. My favourite's Sam Goldwyn, though. He had *all* the zingers. This one time, he had some foreign actress in his office, and she was hassling him about making more political movies –'

' "*Look, sugar,*" ' broke in Alex, accent and hands and everything. ' "*Pictures are for entertainment. Messages should be delivered by Western Union.*" I like that one too. I'm sure it's apocryphal.'

'Come again?' Honey was glaring at him as if he had broken a trust between them. 'You're sure it's *what*?'

'No – sorry – all I meant was – he probably never *said* it . . . like a, you know, *Play it again, Sam* – just a saying, that's all.'

'Oh . . .'

She lowered her head and looked up from beneath her brow – a soulful, penetrative stare, like a blues singer finding her note.

'Why don't you just say that, then? I hate people who talk like they swallowed a dictionary.'

'Me too. Sorry. Point taken.'

'See her?'

She pointed to one from the pile Alex had just sold her – a box full of random items he had picked up at Jimmy's Antiques and barely looked through. Just put a five hundred dollar tag on it and called it a collection.

'Know who she is?'

'Theda . . . Bara,' said Alex, and he had to dig for the name. 'Vamp? Silent vamp?'

'Yeah, that's it – her name was like ARAB DEATH but all switched around – what do you call that again?'

'An anagram?'

'Yes, Mr Dictionary, *anagram*. And she was born in the shadow of the Sphinx, weaned on serpent's blood, etc., etc. According to the publicity. She was supposed to be sex on legs. Hard to believe.'

Together, they looked at the photo. A plain, big woman with heavily kohled eyes and pudgy arms. A suffocating asp pressed to her bosom.

'Her real name was Theodosia Goodman,' said Honey, perfectly dead-pan. 'The woman was from Cincinnati. She was fat-faced with bad circulation. When her folks in Ohio heard she was born by the Nile, they were pretty damn surprised.'

Alex laughed gleefully.

'See? I know things too. And Miss Beavers here' – Honey pointed to the photo of Louise Beavers, whom Alex dimly recognized as the black maid from a dozen movies – 'she wasn't fat naturally so she had to eat all the time, you know, to get fat? She wasn't Southern either so she had to fake a Southern accent, and when she played Aunt Delilah someone had to teach that poor bitch to make flapjacks.'

'Really?' said Alex, truly beginning to enjoy himself. 'Seems a lot of work. Couldn't they have just *hired* a fat black Southern woman? I mean, if that's what they wanted.'

'Wasn't about what they could get, it was about what people'll do to be famous. It's about humiliation. That's nothing on Stepin Fetchit.'

'Who?'

'Rolling eyes, usually saying *yessuh* in an elevator or a cotton field or su'in like that? Every person in Hollywood turned up with some nasty old name and the studios changed it: Frances Gumm, Archibald Leach, Lucille LeSueur, Phyllis Isley – they all got nice new names, everybody did. Black man turns up in Hollywood by the name of Lincoln Theodore Monroe Perry they rename him Stepin Fetchit. It's *tiring*, you know?'

This thought seemed to take away her laughter. She stared despondently at her fingers. 'Makes me want to throw up my hands and say MU! to the whole thing. MUUUU!'

Alex looked quickly about the restaurant, but there was no one to be embarrassed but him.

'That's a Buddhist word,' said Honey, retrieving her hands from the air, placing them neatly on her lap. 'It's how I let go of things.'

'You're a Buddhist.'

'In my own way. Why? That so strange? What the hell are you?'

Alex retracted his turtle head. 'Er . . . nothing, really. Jewish. I mean, by birth.'

Honey made a sound of satisfaction. Alex made it back at her.

'You're fairly confrontational for a Buddhist, that's all I meant. No offence.'

'Yeah, well, it's in my own way, like I said. I'm *far* from satori, that's the truth. So. I'm learning, it's a long road, next question.' She leant in towards him, expectant. 'Come on, come *on* – you so full of questions – nothing else you wanna know?'

Her face was a brazen challenge, the kind no woman in England ever wears unless drunk and talking to her mother.

'Look, I haven't *got* any other questions. *Man*,' said Alex, folding his arms, 'you're very . . . you know? I mean . . . you're quite . . .'

Honey smiled hugely, so that Alex was shown every one of her claret gums. 'Yeah, I am, ain't I?' She patted his hand. 'I'm just kidding with you, Alex-Li, really. I'm just a little upfront. That's the word you looking for. Know who that is?' she said, pointing to a picture that lay between the two of them, a bosomy girl with a tower of dark hair. Alex identified her correctly.

'Right,' said Honey, 'an' I'm a little like Gypsy. Her real name was Louise Hovick, by the way – but that's all she lied about. She never pretended she wasn't what she was. That's like me.'

Alex, who had no idea what they were talking about again, nodded amiably and started collecting up his things. As she began to do the same, a piece of hair from her bun fell into her face, and suddenly she was familiar all over again.

'Do I . . . ?' began Alex, bringing up his bag from the floor and placing it on the table.

'Do you *what*?'

'Nothing – I just . . . Do I . . . *recognize* you? Or . . . ?'

'I don't know,' said Honey flatly. 'Do you?'

It seemed very quiet. Alex searched for an appropriate facial gesture but could find nothing suitable.

'We better get going,' said Honey, looking away from him. 'We're done here. And it's time.'

'Right, right,' said Alex, and put up a hand for the bill. He peeled off the gloves she had given him, but she wouldn't have them back, so he shoved them in his bag. Outside, a riot of car-horns started up. As Honey looked out, a waiter passed, and Alex fumbled with the tea tray trying to pass it to him. He tilted to one side, the waiter tried to steady things. Accidentally, Alex touched Honey's arm.

She sprang from her chair once more and headed for the bathroom, and over Alex's flurried apology she called out, over her shoulder, 'You go in, go on, go in. I'll see you in there. Don't worry about it. Shit happens. That's Buddhism too. Nice doing business with you, Alex-Li Tandem.'

2

The tiny blonde at the threshold furnished Alex with a name-tag and a plan of the venue. With a high-mooned nail, she pointed out the must-see rooms at Autographicana this year: the Jedicon Room (in which minor players from the popular films held court), an Apollo Astronauts Room (an undistinguished mission that Alex had never heard of and suspected had never taken place) and an alcove where one might queue for the autographs of two of the men who had blown up Hiroshima, here again for the second year running. These all came off the main room, the Rothendale Hotel's huge, airless 'Miami Dream' ballroom. Plastic palms, murals of tropical scenes (the Rothendale was very big on murals), a timetable of events. Tomorrow Autographicana had to make way for Lorna Berkowitz's bat mitzvah. There were a hundred stalls or more. There were at least a thousand Autograph Men, milling. In their bad trousers. Alex's first instinct was to turn and run, screaming *MUUUUUUUUU* through the streets of the city.

Only there were things in here he wanted. Things which worked on him at a subterranean level, far beneath his rational mind – he needed them. So. Welcome to the twentieth century in miniature. Castro's signature, Oswald's shirt, Connery's cheque stubs, Streisand's concert programme, the AT-AT (still in its original box), Ali's gloves, an envelope Joyce forgot to post, a photo of Darth signed by both the voice and the body, Dorothy's ruby slippers (rhinestones, but as expensive as rubies, now), Kennedy's Christmas card, Himmler's exercise book –

'Himmler's exercise book?' repeated Alex, craning forward.

Karl and Anna, the pleasant young German couple whose stall it was, smiled. Anna brushed some dust from the plastic flyleaf.

'Oh, yes,' said Karl, shrugging. 'Very rare. He was fifteen. This is where he did his workings, you see? And here he got one wrong, you see? Very funny when people see this, you know?' Karl laughed, as if demonstrating what laughter sounds like. 'They like this in a way because it is more personal, you know, like this. And the price on it is about fourteen hundred dollars, you know? Rare, rare.'

'Some people have a problem with this,' said Anna, smiling. 'But we do not.'

The Autograph Man

'Right,' said Alex.

'Some people, you know,' said Anna, although Alex did not know, 'some people make a rule, so they say, you know, no Nazis and no serial killers. But . . .' Anna smiled again. She had the kind of wholly symmetrical face for which smiling is ill-advised. The more she did it, the closer the resemblance to an advert for home insurance.

'History is history,' said Karl decisively, and turned the page. There, pressed between plastic, was a napkin Sinatra had signed.

'Right,' said Alex.

Karl turned the page again. There, pressed between plastic, was Hitler's tiny signature under a routine policy document. Karl frowned.

'Sinatra's in the wrong section,' he said. 'Should be in fifties crooners.'

'Don't you think –' began Alex, but then came a terrific thud at his back. It was Lovelear.

'Hey, hombre, see anything you like?'

They began to amble around the room, Autograph Men lost in a crowd of their fellows. As a survival technique, Alex persisted with the idea that he was not one of them. That he walked among them, but was not of their nature.

'Lovelear . . .'

'Uhuh?'

'How do you feel about . . . I don't know . . . about stuff like Himmler's exercise book . . . assorted Nazis. Lot of Nazi stuff this year. Did you notice? It's like it's the year of the fascists or something.'

'Oh, sure,' said Lovelear earnestly. 'And who knew? I had Goering ten years ago, but nobody'd take it off me, everybody made me feel bad about it . . . finally I sold it for, like, nothing. You know

246

how much that's worth now? Goes to show you, man, these things go in cycles.'

Alex hugged himself. He felt nauseous. The air-conditioning kept coming despite the snow outside. He felt himself breathing the artificial air of a chiller cabinet, like he was being refrigerated, artificially preserved for something. He could feel himself growing hysterical. And they just kept on collecting! As if the world could be saved this way! As if impermanence were not the golden rule! And can I get Death's autograph too? Have you got a plastic sheath for that, Mr Autograph Man?

'Dove's still in line for the Hiroshima guys,' said Lovelear cheerfully; he had just discovered a muffin in his pocket. 'Pretty nice guys, actually. Golfers. That's not where the action is, though. Hey, Tandem, you're hurting my arm! *Jesus*. Chill out a little – it's not so bad. It's kind of fun. No, the *action* is in the Playboy corner. Trust me, they're pretty ripe, but they're signing pictures of back in the day for twenty-five bucks a pop. You wanna meet Miss January 1974? I just met her, man. Samantha Budnitz. She's a little leathery but she looks pretty good still.'

They queued for the Bunnies who no longer looked like themselves. They queued for the accidental agents of mass destruction. They queued for the five ancient astronauts, heartbreaking in their bright bomber jackets. A nervy woman with Republican hair made everybody write their names on Post-its, which were then passed to the astronauts, who, with watery eyes, looked from the Post-it to the person, back and forth, waiting for the alchemy of cognition, too near-sighted to read the names . . . In the Jedicon Room, Lovelear had a fight with an Ewok over an obscure scrap of dialogue while Alex watched the Ewok's ten-year-old daughter, Lo (already a head taller than her father), do a bored cross-eyed tongue-out headstand against the wall in her little white socks. A disgruntled Ewok told Alex that he made only 25 per cent of the retail price of a signed picture because Ewoks had to buy the pictures in the first place, off the studio. Another told Alex that personally, as a person of restricted growth, yes as a ha ha, yes it's OK, you can say it, as a *midget*, he considered the popular cinema director George Lucas to be one of the great liberators of his people.

But after the kids' stuff was finished, the business got done. The business was everywhere. The mood turned from carnival to conference. You couldn't cross the room without making a deal or overhearing one done. People Alex had met only virtually appeared before him now in hideous material form: Freek Ulmann from Philadelphia, Albie Gottelmeyer from Denmark, Pip Thomas from Maine, Richard Young from Birmingham. All these people now had their bodies, their faces. He traded with them all, listened to them. They needed to talk. Maybe the business itself was simply an excuse for this need. Alex learnt of the dissatisfactions of wives in towns he had never visited and never wanted to. The grade averages of various children passed under review. Richard Young told him he could never truly love a flat-chested woman, no matter how kind she might be to him. A stranger called Ernie Popper told him that most days he wished he were dead.

Familiar faces too. Alex and Lovelear ran into Baguley, negotiating to buy, of all things, a forged Kitty from a notorious Swedish crook. At the point Alex arrived, each man believed himself to be on the verge of pulling off a magnificent sting. The Swede knew he was selling a fake. Baguley thought he was buying the real thing for a steal.

'The Swede,' said Baguley, turning from the stall and stage-whispering in Alex's ear, 'is a total dullard. Used to be a bloody gynaecologist. Before that he rode a *bike* or something. Doesn't know a thing. Doesn't realize what he's got. Found four Kittys in an attic, some old director's house – doesn't even know who she is! He's going to take eight hundred dollars for each Kitty and be none the wiser. *Marvellous*.'

'Ah, Mr Tandem,' said the Swede, with a terror-stricken flick of his strawberry-blond head, 'the expert. Good to see you. And you are well?'

Weighing up his dislike for these men, Alex decided to give the break to the Swede.

'Fine. I'm fine. And that's a very fine Alexander. Very nice piece. Lucky Baguley.'

'Yes, yes, I am glad you think so' – the Swede patted at his sweaty face with a monogrammed handkerchief, on which an *H* and an *I* wrapped around each other – 'Baguley is indeed lucky.'

'The rumour's going round,' drawled Baguley, pushing the brim of his hat up with a finger, 'that you're in New York to find her. Find Kitty. That's the rumour. I've got ten bob says you'll be arrested at the gates. She'll set the dogs –'

'Hey,' yelled Alex across the room. *'Hey.'* He could see Honey over by the Suffragette table, flicking through a wine-box of filed postcards.

'Who you waving at?' asked Lovelear, turning. 'Dove out there?'

Alex caught her eye, she grinned at him and raised her hand; but then her face altered. The smile vanished, that look of terrible injury returned; she turned her back, hurried through a tourist group of kindly oval women from the Midwest. She disappeared into a room dedicated to that popular disaster, the sinking of the RMS *Titanic*.

'What the –' began Lovelear.

'That's so *weird* . . . I had a meeting with her an hour ago – I really thought we –'

'Rewind: you *know* Honey Smith?'

'Honey who? That's Honey Richardson. That's the dealer I met this morning.'

The Swede cupped his hands to his mouth and guffawed like an English schoolboy.

'Honey Smith – this is a name I do not hear in a while. Boy, the Swedes loved that story, yes, sir, they did. Though personally I would have paid her more, yes? Twenty-five does not seem very much for such a service. And he had much money, of course.'

'You do know,' said Baguley eagerly, 'that she's in the business now? Yes, *yes*. A colleague of mine bought a Fatty Arbuckle off her in Berlin. My hand on my heart. Said she did him under the bloody table too. Lucky bastard.'

'I just *saw* her, man,' squealed Lovelear, pointing at the space where she had been. 'I swear to God it was her. Tandem was waving to her! Tandem's getting the goods from *Honey Smith*! Tandem, are you boning Honey Smith? She's like the most famous whore in the *world*. OK, so I need the whole story, *now*.'

The name gave up its secret. Alex now recalled the two mug-shots: the ruffled Scottish actor, squinting in the flashbulb, the hooker, unbowed, familiar with this kind of camera. Front page for a week? Two weeks? And then it had struggled on for a time in all its lurid instalments: her story, his, the girlfriend's, the pimp's, the public's, the confessional interview, and then, finally, the tidy resolution: her return to obscurity.

3

Hotel rooms are the godless places. You don't care for anything in there. Nothing in there cares for you. In his room, drunk, lonely Tandem phoned home. But in Mountjoy it was 5 a.m. – the resilient silence of answering machines. On Esther's machine, he sang 'All the Things You Are' in four different keys to avoid high notes; on Rubinfine's he grew offensive and then, on Adam's, grossly sentimental. Joseph picked up, but by then Alex had become ashamed. He opened his mouth and nothing happened. Joseph put the phone down. It got late. After drinking everything it contained, Tandem approached the final phase of his relationship with his mini-bar: surreal optimism. He was reaching out for a chilled can of caramelized peanuts when there was a knock at the door. He was expecting a neighbouring irate Christian (sex was on the television at high volume), but through the spy-hole saw a convex Honey, all forehead and eyeballs, looming out from the hall on a pair of tiny feet. Alex hunted for his trousers, the remote control. He switched the channel. She knocked again, louder.

'I don't think it's polite to keep a lady –'

'Hi,' said Alex, lunging for the door-handle, fastening his fly. 'Honey. *Hi*. It's late.'

'Now, you . . .' she whispered, narrowing her eyes for confirmation of her initial diagnosis, 'you're drunk. Yes, you are. Don't even try to deny it. You're a *drunk*.'

'You're a Buddhist.'

'You're a Jew.'

'That's a chair,' said Alex, pointing to the fold-up director's chair in Honey's rubber hand. She was wearing red satin Chinese pyjamas, her hair parted in the middle and drawn back in two thick plaited ropes.

'I always bring my own. Step aside.'

She walked unsteadily past him and unfolded the chair in front of the television. It said HONEY on its back-supporting canvas strip. She sat down. Alex perched on the end of the bed, a few feet from her.

'So,' he said.

'I thought I told you,' said the television, 'you're off this damn case. You're too close to it, McLaine.'

'Got any liquor?' asked Honey.

Alex tried to think: 'No . . . noooo, actually – wait . . . *wait* . . . maybe. Maybe . . . red. In the cupboard? There's wine, small size, definitely wine, though . . . Yes, wine. Two of them! Screw-cap – hurrah! Just unscrew . . . this . . . like this . . .'

'Got any glasses? Actually, forget it. This is fine.'

Honey took her bottle and put it to her mouth in such a way that one couldn't help but have thoughts. Her eyes wheeled round the room, as if she had just this moment recognized she was not in her own.

'Little bigger than mine. Smells funny. What's that? Stuck up by the door.'

'Um . . . a note. A bill. English money. Thing my father gave me.'

'All my father ever gave me was a concussion,' said Honey dramatically, and drank half her bottle in one swig.

'Honey, was there something –'

'Shhh. I like this guy, this guy's good. He's got range.'

In silence they watched the last twenty-five minutes of a film. Unsustainable ideas of sex floated in and out of Alex's head, none of them very determined.

'Anything else on?' she asked, as the moody saxophone played and the credits replaced a city skyline.

'Well, of *course* there's something else on . . . there's something like seventy-two channels. Look, Honey –'

'Why bother with painful exercise routines?' asked the television.

'Honey,' said Alex, switching it off, 'it's awfully late. Did you want to . . . talk about something? Or something?'

'Well,' said Honey, talking to the wall, 'I sucked this famous dick once – caused a whole lot of fuss – but I guess you heard that about, I mean, *about that*, today.'

The silence that followed seemed like an Alice-hole they were falling through, the two of them tumbling after something curious. Honey closed her eyes for a moment and out of each came a weighty tear.

'Remember me now?' she said finally.

'Honey, I really don't –'

'Want my autograph? See, trick is, to get mine on a corner of a big old sheet of paper and then go door-stop the actor in Marr-lee however you say it, in London, and get him to sign the same piece without him knowing? That goes for a hundred dollars. Me by myself – doesn't push much more than twenty-five.'

He had not noticed until now how intensely drunk she was. She wore only one glove. He was reminded of Lady Day in those final recording sessions – eyeballs out of control, lip hitched up for a fight.

'Yep. Been on TV and everything. Talk shows. Made a movie.' She dealt with those two tears now, clamping one hand to her chin and smearing them across her fingers. 'Actually, sounded like you were watching my movie when I knocked. I understand it plays a lot in hotel rooms.'

She laughed darkly and clapped her hands.

'You know Richard Young?' she asked, taking a whisky miniature from her pocket and unscrewing it. 'Meticulous son-of-bitch?
English? Jewish? His pants are always just so. Real successful.'

Alex filed through the faces he had met today and came up with
a black-haired, handsome, careful young man who had about
him the air of the wunderkind, a quality that depressed Tandem
beyond measure now that his own wunderkind days were behind
him.

'From Birmingham. Yeah, he's up and coming. He's got a fantastic collection, Rich.'

'Yeah, well, *Rich* heard from some guy who heard from some
other guy who heard from some asshole that you're in New York
to find Kitty Alexander. Kitty Al-ex-ander. Zat true?'

Alex tried to gulp at his wine in a carefree way, and sent it on a
catastrophic journey down his t-shirt. 'Ug . . . You know . . . It's
just . . . she sent me an autograph. It's not really . . . it's not a big
deal. It's not like I *came here* to find her. It's not like that. I'm not
some lunatic stalker. I just wanted to thank her for it. I'm just
another fan.'

Honey stuck an improbably curved nail in his face. 'No, no, no
– *biggest* fan – that's what I heard. An' I must say I was surprised.
You don't seem like a fan of anything to me. I thought you were
totally Zen – you know, rising above it all.'

Honey stood up and stumbled towards the window, stepping
ineptly over the repeating monograms. She rested against the curtain and pointed out.

'Lives in Brooklyn. I grew up in Brooklyn. Sunday sitting on
the stoop. Everybody knew who you were. Before church, after
church . . .'

'I'm going to make some coffee, I think,' said Alex, crawling up the bed and stretching for the kettle on his side table.

'More people know you than you know people . . . see, that's all it is. Ain't nothing more than that, really. It's for amputee people, fame. I mean, people who're missing something vital. That's all. I'll tell you what's messed up too. In my neighbourhood, *I'm* a celebrity. Do you believe that? In certain areas of Brooklyn, I'm Elizabeth Taylor.'

'I met her once,' said Alex, missing the electrical socket for the plug and falling off the bed.

Honey swivelled on her heel, and laughed until she needed the bathroom. Soon he could hear her vomiting in there, despite the sound of running taps. He stood at the door with a towel and offered to help, but she wouldn't let him in.

After that, they had coffee. Talked until the light came over the city in two incoherent stages, electric orange, followed by a thin, sulky blue. Honey didn't believe in abortion any more, although she used to. Alex thought televised charities were run by crooks. Honey didn't see why she should touch things if she didn't know where they came from. Alex couldn't see the point of fake nails or figure-skating. Honey thought there was something weird about English children. They both wondered why there had to be so much mayonnaise on everything.

'I know Roebling. Roebling knows me. I can show you where Roebling is, show you around,' said Honey, folding up her chair.

'Fine. You're on.'

'Huh? I'm on what?' asked Honey.

'Let's do it,' said Alex-Li.

THREE / *Perceiving the Bull*

I

In the event, Honey reversed the plan. Practically minded, she voted for the Lower East Side first, to find Krauser, and then on to Roebling. Despite its map-proportions, she remembered Roebling from her working days as a complicated sprawl, where the grid system employed in much of the city finds itself replaced by the ancient way of things. Chaotic roads with peculiar names, roads that dip and curve and hide the door numbers of apartments from the public view.

'*And* it's cold as hell out there,' said Honey, pulling on some leather gloves in the lobby. 'And I don't feel to be wandering around with a bitch of a hangover and no idea where we're going. I just *know* this guy Krauser is going to help us out. No question. We're going to show what a nice guy you are. We'll *charm* his ass.'

Alex struggled with the zip of his duffel and then succumbed like a toddler when Honey, bored with the performance, gripped him firmly by the toggles, zipped him to the neck and brought the huge bear-hood, trimmed with a halo of synthetic fur, over his head. Her own coat, close-fitting and camel-coloured, added and subtracted from her curves where necessary. She evened out the cord either side of her waist, tying it to the left in a bow.

'OK? So we done now?'

She gave a maternal pinch to his cheek, already pink from the concierge's premature flourish with the front doors.

'Yes. That's – you just touched me.'

'Strike up the band. Whatever you got, I got it by now, anyway.'

'I feel bad,' said Alex, as they took the fierce day full in the face. 'About my . . . colleagues. Lovelear, Dove. I should at least . . .'

Honey hooked her arm around his. 'They got room service, right? TV? And there's a maid to clean it up after. That's pretty much nirvana these days. Anyway, what is this, a school trip? Two of us is plenty, already.'

It was a five-minute walk to the subway, but long enough to bring out the tourist in Alex-Li. He walked like a visitor, face to the American heavens. When a taxi sounded its horn, he looked to see why. Just before the subway's entrance, a Japanese man in an orange boiler suit stepped out backwards from a doorway, caught his heel on a raised paving stone and dropped a crate of lychees across the sidewalk. Honey crushed a few under heel, out came their little white centres.

'Come *on*, let's get on with this?' she called back to Alex, who had meant to negotiate his way round but now took some pleasure in getting a dozen in a footfall. He hurried along behind her down the subway steps. This was her city, not his. He had to give himself up to the sensation of not knowing, of no-power. He felt like the boy who finds the treasure map and shows it to his more competent friend, seeing the X as well as he, but less able to find it.

'Cold,' said Honey, once they were underground. 'C.O.L.D. *Co-o-old*.'

Opening her mouth, she made the cigar-smoker's O, releasing a cloud of steam. Along from them, on the platform, two black boys made animated hand gestures at each other, different congregations of fingers, first two fingers divided from two, then three divided from one – Alex watched them and recalled diagrams he had seen, hand gestures of the high priests in the Temple.

'You do me a favour, OK?' said Honey over the train-rumble. 'You lay this out' – from her bag she produced a foot-long piece of material, a miniature rug decorated with a clan's tartan – 'like, wherever you see a spare seat. I don't like to sit directly on these things.'

Even in the short journey they had made thus far, Alex was thrilled to see how many people spotted her. As the train doors closed behind them, three pairs of eyes seized her immediately. One boy made an obscene International Mime to his friend (the groping tongue in the cheek); now a girl tried to replay the flit of an image that she had seen in some quick-firing neuron. Her mouth opened, she looked away and back once more, and then, with an indiscreet, triumphal flex of the fist she had it! She smiled and endeavoured to return to her bad novel. But her eyes wandered repeatedly off the top of the white page. Back to Honey's famous red mouth.

And so it went. When they got off at their stop, a gaggle of cruel-eyed schoolgirls sent one of their number leaping up the stairs, four reckless steps at a time, just to see her from the front. At street level, Honey crossed the road and bought a pretzel. She bit into it and Alex asked her: '*How* does it feel?' She stared at him for a spell, shrugged and unfolded the hotel's complimentary map of the island.

'This address you got here – it's in Chinatown. Two blocks from here. We need to take a left here – yeah, a left, definitely. OK, now,' she said, setting a quick pace, 'Alex-Li wants to know. He wants to know.'

'I want to know. Is that awful? I'm curious. Just about how it feels.'

'Curiouser and curiouser.'

She thrust her hands into her pockets and lengthened her stride, deliberately placing each step in the mushy imprints of an earlier stranger. No cars passed, barely any people.

'I hate it,' she said finally. 'I hate it, obviously I hate it. But it's weird. I hate, hate, hate it, and yet . . .'

They passed a chess game (two Russians, three dogs), got caught up in its cries and then strained to hear them. They walked another block without a word. The smell of duck was beginning. At the lights, Alex looked right, stepped out unthinkingly. Honey grabbed his wrist and saved his life.

'Every time, I feel sick,' said Honey a minute later, as they jogged across. 'But the weird thing is, if nobody looks, I notice. I just notice – and I feel . . . I don't even know how to explain it. Like, out of focus. Fuzzy.'

'Fuzzy?'

'You asked, I'm telling you. Fuzzy. Like I can't sense myself. It's sort of disgusting, isn't it?'

At the next corner an ancient advertisement for pianos, starting just above Alex's head and ending many miles away where a crane bent its interested head over the rooftops. Adverts become themselves when there's nothing left to sell: this one was especially moving. The faint, chalky letters of LAIRD & SON, their doomed musical venture.

'See, *she's* the real thing,' said Honey. Mistaking his interest, she pointed to a still larger billboard to the right. It was a full-colour photograph of a beautiful woman. She was selling a clothes store. Her colossal bronzed legs stretched the length of a deli and clear over the human fish-tank of a public gym where people were busy going exactly nowhere, running at great speeds towards impassive glass.

'That's when you go on to a different level,' said Honey respectfully. 'You're godly, then. You got a half million commuters looking at your you-know-what on a daily basis? People crashing they cars, people losing they lives? That's when you know you made it. Hey, you know what? That one, the red. That's the door.'

Alex stopped and looked blankly at the door, then the letter-box. The one-way correspondence of his boyhood had fallen through that hole. So many letters! He had turned into a man while he wrote them. Looking at it now, he felt terribly sad. If he had been alone, he would have walked away. But here was Honey pressing him forward to peer at the roll-call of apartments and their owners: businesses and private individuals, artists' studios and whole squashed families. Krauser they found under his trading name, president of the KAAA. Alex still wanted to turn back, but, as Honey went to press the bell, the door opened of its own accord, and a grocery delivery boy, still counting his stingy tip, let them in as he left.

'And what now?' whimpered Alex, shivering in the hallway. It was somehow colder than outside, because of the betrayal, because in here one *expected* warmth.

'What now is just what is,' said Honey.

A voice had been speaking without pause for a couple of minutes. Now it said: 'Am I speaking English? So scram. So drift. So take the air. Don't you get it? I'm not in the market for a goddamn shakedown.'

'No, wait,' said Honey, raising her voice and putting her lips against the panelled wood. 'Listen a minute. If you'll just . . . We don't want to sell you a thing, Mr Krauser – and we're not a charity. We – he, my friend, Alex, he just wants to talk to you, that's all.'

The dry voice behind the door started up again, a strange, breathy, scratched monotone, like one of those old gramophone records of inflectionless writers reading their own prose: 'And I'm saying I don't like onion ballads. Go sucker-bait somebody else. I'll give you a tip: this is a building full of schmucks. Try Castelli. Upstairs. He's the cliff dweller on the fifth. Boy, does Castelli love an oil merchant. Ha!'

'Mr Krauser, couldn't we just –'

'Go pick yourself an orchid.'

They heard footsteps leading away from the door, the sound of running water, a radio. Honey stepped back and Alex replaced her, ringing the doorbell once more, jamming it down. He waited a while and repeated his full name. The water stopped running. Slowly, the sequence of sounds reversed, and Alex could once again sense this man, close by on the other side. Alex set upon reciting his Krauser facts.

'Yeah, yeah, buddy,' cut in the scornful voice. 'I know who I am. Don't worry about me, I'm on the beam.'

But Alex pressed on: 'And before, in the fifties, you were her script editor, I believe . . . and after that, you acted basically as her agent, that's right isn't it?'

'Well, listen at you. You're a regular encyclopedia salesman.'

Here, the door opened. And one had to, as in the old cartoons, look a foot lower than expected, down to where the bald dome of President Max Krauser skimmed the mid-air between Alex's shoulders and Honey's breasts. This, the postal nemesis? The man's face was a nothing-much, dominated by a pair of bulky bifocal spectacles, tinted with rising orange mist like a TV sunset. He had a fleshy, pink, vulnerable mouth that deserved a younger man – a few wet, black, adolescent hairs grew around it. A zipped-up brown towelling jogging suit, the auteur's silken neck-scarf, sneakers. A belly like a present he was hiding from a nephew. He was not, on second glance, completely bald: very tightly curled silver hair edged round the back of his head like a fringing cloud.

'Max Krauser?'

'You can take that to the bank and cash it.'

Leaving the door wide open, yet without any hint of invitation, Krauser turned his back, walked into his apartment. The effect, from where Alex stood, was monkish, Krauser a silver-haired friar all in brown. And the room was a Kitty cave, naturally. Posters, movie stills, framed news clippings, magazine covers. One kitsch masterpiece: Kitty painted in thick sentimental oils on a stretched piece of black velvet, gilt framed. But Alex recognized at once that this church was interdenominational. A record player somewhere (the room was subsiding with the weight of rubbish) sang over and over of *Minnie the Moocher . . . a red-hot hoochie-coocher*, and all about the place were pictures of black men with clarinets, trumpets, sax, double-bass and microphone, also their records, also their biographies, their posters, their concert programmes, whatever they had left behind. Furniture was an after-thought. There were only four pieces of it: a small card table, bereft of the chairs it needed, a tall, stiff-necked brass lamp with nodding art deco head (weeping jangling, pea-green, cut-glass tears) and a pool table pressed up against one wall. Its baize was covered in junk-mail, pizza boxes and record sleeves. In the centre of the room, one barber-shop chair.

'OK, I'm captive,' said Krauser, turning and dropping himself into this. 'Go into your dance.'

Honey moved to the left, laid her rug over a corner of the pool table and cautiously perched upon it, her gloved left hand down a pocket. Alex pushed his glasses up his nose and peered at the small man in the swivelling chair.

'Look,' he said, shrugging as if to apologize for what he was about to say, 'my name is Alex-Li Tandem.'

At this, Krauser seemed to jolt; one foot slipped to the floor. He brought it back slowly and returned it to the footrest. Then, regathered, he introduced a new benevolent smile and sat forward. Alex, thus encouraged, began to speak his piece, forging a little path for himself between the spot he stood in and one at the threshold of the walk-through kitchen. He went back and forth. But Krauser was neither looking nor listening. Krauser was stretching his legs. Krauser was doing a soft-shoe shuffle on his carpet.

'Ta-ta ta ta-taaa,' scatted Krauser, spreading his arms like the men in the musicals, 'this is the sandman-shuffle, young man. I got a degree in Toeology. You still talking?'

Honey groaned, stood up and folded her rug, making the International Gesture for lunacy (temple, tapping finger). She pointed at the door. But Alex persisted.

'Java juice, java juice, java juice,' murmured Krauser meditatively, as Alex, with no special plan in mind, moved towards him. At the crucial moment, Krauser sprang from his chair, pushed past Alex and proceeded to the kitchen. Here, he leant over the breakfast bar and picked up two packets of coffee.

'This one,' he said, drawing his top lip tight over his gums, 'this one is just strong as hell. And this one here is less strong, but it's ethical. Everybody gets paid their folding green, including the brown ladies who get it out of the field, if indeed coffee even comes from a field – I'm just going by what my grandson tells me. But you're boring me into a wooden kimono, so I'm taking it strong and nix on the moo-juice. Keeps me lively. Anyone else?'

He hitched his little pot-belly up on the bar, lifted his feet off the floor and loomed in towards Honey, who shrank back, knocking a pyramid of pizza boxes to the floor.

'Hey, you. I know you? You in pictures? This guy over here, he could stand one more greasing, he's not slick enough – but *you*. You're a slinky piece of homework.'

Krauser turned his face to the ceiling, put his big lips to an invisible trumpet, played it, sang: '*Strutting . . . strutting with some barbecue, barbecuoooo . . .* Know what my grandson calls himself? Jamal Queeks. His mother looked just like you. And thereby hangs a tale. And there goes – say bye bye! – there goes two thousand years of tradition. It's a goddamn shame. Well, isn't it?'

Honey pressed her bag to her chest and walked over to the door, opened it, stood proudly, waiting. Alex persisted.

'Mr Krauser – please listen to me. I think Miss Alexander – I think she might be glad to see me. It's more than that: I need to see *her*. I know that sounds weird. I don't how to explain to you . . . I waited such a long time – and then she sent me her autograph. Twice.'

'Put that in wri-ting,' said Krauser to the rhythm of a sax solo, tapping out a beat with the hubs of his palms. 'And I'll pa-a-aste it in my scra-hap-book.'

'He has them right in his bag,' said impassioned Honey, stepping forward from the doorway. Her eyes were burning, her hands shook and Alex felt a startling throb of gratitude and love for this new friend, who would abandon her Zen for him in this way.

'Look,' she was saying, 'we came out here, you know? We came out here. This guy's from London, England. He didn't have to? Nobody *has* to? And I'll say it, he's too polite to say it: this boy's been writing your *crazy* ass for fifteen years –'

'Thirteen, actually,' said Alex, raising a hand. 'Thirteen years.'

'OK, so *thirteen* – and without no replies and so what? So this: so he *deserves* this. People like you don't signify without people like him – you get that much information? You understand that? *Asshole*,' said Honey, in response to a clownish face Krauser made. '*Racist* asshole. And let's get real here, anyway. It's not as if Miss Alexander is exactly prime-time these days. Am I lying? Am I saying something here which ain't the case?'

Krauser launched off the bar forwards into the room and landed four inches short of a serious man. A mountainous vein that ran from his temple to the back of his left ear stood raised and angry.

'Now,' said Krauser, 'don't you chew the scenery with me, Miss Thang. I'm no crazier than your mother was. It's like this: I lack patience when it comes to two kinds of people: Moochers and Autograph Hounds. Here are the facts: Miss Alexander does not send anything unless *I* send it for her. And I do not send anything. There it is, soup and nuts. Miss Alexander does not have *time* for Autograph Hounds. She is the greatest star in the firmament, as they used to say back when it meant something. A Hum Hum Dinger from Dingersville. Protecting Miss Alexander from people like you is what I do. And that rhymes. Ladies, Gentlemen.'

They were escorted to the door.

2

The centre of Roebling. Here a wide, pretty street steadily climbs its hill and shovelling a share of the snow is every man's civic responsibility. Honey and Alex have spent an afternoon walking up and down this street, asking questions in the local shops, wandering down side streets to no end. Each waiting for the other to give up. When a coffee shop presents itself for the eighth time, it is Alex who raises his shoulders, puts his arm round Honey's waist and moves them both into the warmth. And the world continues. A Spanish-speaking kid is running past screaming something. He dives behind a jeep, misses his big brother's ice-hearted snowball, pops back up and gets it in the neck. The black kids are starched for church. One rabbi, adrift. A few people are improbably fat, but no more than a few. A city truck disperses pink grit like industrial candy along the road. This is the desirable end of Roebling: the side streets are lined with dignified, crumbling brownstones that draw up their shabby skirts and disappear just before the black area and one block into the Jewish. At least one ageing American novelist is known to live here. He can be seen, prominently displayed in the bookshop window, and sometimes in the flesh, trying to convince young American men to shoot hoops with him.

At the hill's crest lies neglected Roebling Zoo. Here, a big-bottomed capybara or even a reclusive family of gophers can legitimately feel themselves star attractions. The snakes have all gone. There never were any tigers. And on a Sunday this zoo attracts only the Hipsters, looking to be distracted from their hangovers, maybe, or just charmed by the crazy dances of captive jackrabbits. From their coffee-shop window seats, Honey and Alex watch a steady drift of them, these lovely, sorrowful kids who are never in a hurry.

Gangly, sloping, beautiful, wearing a generation's forgotten coats, tramping uphill in the snow.

'And so,' says Honey, sprinkling chocolate, 'she's having it today, this operation? But it's not risky, right? 'Cos you wouldn't be here, obviously, if that was the deal.'

Alex is convincing Honey who is convincing Alex who is convincing Honey that removing a pacemaker is a routine procedure. They both use this phrase *routine procedure*, stolen from a long-running television show. Frantically, they agree with each other ('Right', 'Right', '*Right*').

'This is exactly it – I just want to have the relevant facts. Ask someone, have someone tell me. That's what I'm used to. I grew up . . . my dad was a doctor.'

'Yeah? What he do now?'

'Turns in grave, mostly. Dead.'

'Well. I'm sorry.'

'So you should be. It was your bloody fault in the first place. Oi,' said Tandem, dismissing his homely china cup and reaching out for Honey's steaming glass packed in sedimentary layers, beige, brown, deeper brown, white. 'What's that like? Why's it look better than mine?'

Honey gathered a spoonful of the highest level of fluff and held it out for him. 'See,' she said, bringing the steel to his lips, 'you got a black de-caf. Because you the kind who like depriving himself. You think you're going to benefit by drinking that. But the reality is, you're miserable. Ain't no benefit involved. Now *this*, it's got a chocolate, mocha and caramel dust on it – see, tastes good, don't it? – with half and half, whipped cream, a shot of Kahlúa, toffee pieces on top . . .'

Alex opened his mouth and closed it again around the spoon.

'See, now that's good, ain't it?'

Alex nodded helplessly.

'And it teaches me the impermanence of pleasure – that's my Zen again, you see? It won't do me no good, but it's a pleasure while it lasts. And when I die, I can add it to the list of pleasures that fleeted. Flighted. Is that a word, fleeted?'

Alex removed the spoon and assumed the hounded saucer-eyes of the popular comedian Buster Keaton.

'That was so good it *hurt*.'

Honey laughed, dipped her head and rose with a cream moustache. 'The funny thing is, once you've actually had pleasure, *real* pleasure, it's fine letting go of it. It ain't a thing. It's a *no*-thing.'

'You should go on the shopping channel. They need more Buddhists on that channel. I really think –'

'Krauser.'

'Huh?'

Honey took possession of another man's newspaper and spread it out against the shop's window. From behind the local headline (an unfortunate reprobate had vanished with his stepdaughter) Krauser materialized, a tricky mix of man and newsprint in the glassy sun. He was trying to cross the street at its most hazardous point, he had on a waxy green raincoat with wrinkled hood, his arms outstretched as if this were in some way useful for the passing traffic. He vanished for a moment behind a dark-inked advert claiming to improve your memory skills and reappeared in the middle of a political scandal.

It is impossible these days to follow a man or quit a job without an encyclopedia of cinematic gesture crowding you out. Honey snorted at Alex, who set out hugging walls and scuttling on tip-toe,

Perceiving the Bull

but soon enough she herself made use of a pair of shades and an unconvincing whistle. Then it turned out Krauser's hat was connected to a transistor radio – the wire went round the brim and behind his ear, an aerial protruded from his pocket – he was oblivious to them both, engrossed in a political news show of some kind ('Zimbabwe!', he was heard to shout, as he took a sudden left into a quiet road. 'Now he's on to Zimbabwe?').

Four doors from the end of this street, he stopped. Turned off the dial by his ear. Honey and Alex hung back by some rubbish bins. They watched him skip up the front steps of a turn-of-the-century brownstone, ring the bell and get let in by machinery. The door closed behind him. Like good detectives, they watched the spot where he had last been, jogging up and down and breathing on their hands. Alex rolled a cigarette.

'This is ridiculous – this *can't* be her place.'

'Why not?'

'It's too easy – it's ... this just doesn't happen that I want something and then it's just *there*. With no *effort*. That's not how it happens.'

Honey put her hands round his waist and squeezed. 'Baby, that's *exactly* how it happens. Somedays, shit just lands in your lap, believe me, I know. Gimme some of that smoke when it's ready, huh?'

'Is this the plan, this? Waiting?' he asked, trying to use the flank of Honey to light the thing out of the wind.

'The plan is no-plan. Waiting is what we're doing.'

'And when the waiting's finished?'

'Then something else'll be on, I guess.'

The wait was not long. Ten minutes later the door opened once more and Krauser stepped out. A pair of arms passed him a small,

269

FOUR / *Catching the Bull*

I

Not yet! He didn't want her caught, not yet! But the steps went up – wide, cold, mineral. Honey was already there, finger on the bell. She turned and grinned. He was on the stairs. Admiring a tuft of moss, the way it had pushed through stone. Green through the snow. Where were these steps going? He held out an arm, but Honey rang the doorbell anyway. Another step, icy. And taking him closer to a world with one less sacred thing in it. Because fans do this: they preserve something, like the swirl of colour in a marble, in the solid glass of their enthusiasm. He had done that, Alex. For thirteen years he had kept her as perfect and particular as a childhood memory.

A voice calls from an upper window, three storeys up at least. He can see nothing. The glittering windows of these brownstones share the sun, parcel it out. She calls to say she is coming. Honey turns again, grins again. Gives him the International Gesture for well-being, the vertical thumbs.

Alex squints at the crumbling plaster of this high-arched Roebling doorway. Then he closes his eyes. Now here is its replacement: Celebration Pictures' grand Palladian façade, splendid in the

California sunshine, a lifetime ago. It is a photograph Alex owns. At the moment it was taken, a Crawford or a Cooper swept by in a smudgy white Rolls-Royce. Three harried writers (sleeves rolled up, chewing cigarettes) leant against the right-hand pillar, and a headless costume girl was cropped out of shot. And, in the foreground, a new arrival: Kitty Alexander, smiling devotedly into a deceitful wide-angle lens that loved twelve starlets altogether. Second row, third on the right.

It's not a famous shot, but he loved it. Because this is the beginning of her. She had recently lost her real name, Katya Alessandro ('Too Russian,' said the producer, Lee J. Komsky. 'And also too damn Eye-talian'), and some weight (the studio put her on its infamous ACT diet: apples, coffee and tobacco), and the first assaults were made on her extravagant accent (this last never succeeded. She remained a Russian–Italian child of Capri).

That is the face. The one he loves. Why subject it to Buddha's rules of impermanence? This is the face. Her forehead melts into her nose like buttermilk down a ladle, as it did on Garbo. She has the bone structure of a nymph, heart-shaped and high cheekboned. Her eyes are green, her hair is black and bobbed. Her plucked brows can't hide their natural soulful curve, like two sighing bridges over Italian water. Alex has watched that face play everything from disenfranchised Russian princess to flighty Parisian ballerina to Chinese immigrant. Maybe it is precisely the fluidity of it that stopped her from being a star of the first order. It is a face that will do whatever you ask of it, so full of gesture and movement that the critics have offered the futile, consolatory comment that the silents died too early, before their greatest star was out of her nursery. It is a face, as Hedda Hopper had it (the alliteration itself brings on

nostalgia!), to be conjured with, it is made of magic, and it is no
more.

2

'Max? But you are not Max. Where is Max now? Are you coming
from Max?'

The sun is everywhere, a cosmic spotlight, and she grabs his
sleeve, a firm grip. Her face, folded over many times, still makes
sense. She remains a beautiful woman. Her make-up is not too
much, only a little cornflower-blue flaking from the eyelids. There
is no hotel robe, no black silk Parisian slippers with the exploded
dandelion toes. No sign of the white, queenly towel wrapping a
steeple of wet hair. Instead, a simple pair of high-waisted jeans with
red plimsolls and black shirt. The swell of her breasts is weird,
youthful. She has one plain clip in her thin, but still bobbed, grey
hair. The sole embellishment is the fabulous brooch that has landed
on her throat, a ruby-encrusted butterfly.

'Do you know something about computers? I am trying to send
the message and I do as I am told, all the instructions that I have,
and I *cannot* – I don't know what it is, but something is not correct.
I must have done something, *God* knows what. Can you imagine?
That I am having to fuss with this all afternoon by myself – Max
walks Lucia, so, that is this, I suppose, can you *imagine*?'

'Miss Alexander?' asked Honey, with a fantastic smile, and bent
in towards her, for Kitty was small, smaller than one would
imagine, as they always are.

Kitty looked up, confused, her palm still pressed to Alex's wrist.
Her skin here was puffy and risen, like pastry. Alex's leg was doing
something uncontrollable. So was the city. The city was carrying

on – he couldn't stop it. A boy in the street punched another boy in the arm even though the boy didn't exist and neither did his friend. And Alex saw it happen. And he could see her. This time there was no glass between them. The viewing was not one way. She could see him too. She was inspecting both him and Honey: a shrewd, amused study.

'Yes,' answered Kitty, genially. 'Yes, this is of course my name. But I think I don't know you – I would remember, you are very striking – so, I am sorry you must leave now, unless you have some idea of computers and you are not a psychopathic killer or the like which you could say – but how would I believe?'

She laughed quickly, and touched a shaking, involuntary finger to Honey's forearm.

'I think it is when *Lucia* goes,' she confided, 'I lose my concentration and things get unnecessarily complicated, and I tell Max, I can walk, I'm not an invalid, but the truth is that he is in love with Lucia himself a little, he is her *paramour* – or so I imagine, but look at me, eesh!' She released both of them, Honey and Alex, and brought her fluttering hands up to the delicate hollows of her cheeks. 'It is too cold, here, really, I cannot stand like this on the step to chew fat or otherwise to talk of Jesus and this sort of thing, so I say goodbye, I don't mean to be impolite, of course, but please excuse me –'

For Alex, speech was another minute away. It was Honey who put her hand to the door-frame.

'Miss Alexander, my name's Honey Richardson. We're here to see you.'

To this, Kitty made that superb little *oof!* of Russian exasperation and clasped her hands together.

'I understand this, but my dear . . . I am not here to be seen. I assure you, Jesus and I we are – how do you say? Entirely strange to each other.'

She gave a guileless smile of finality and took a step backwards, inwards, letting the door fall to.

'But I'm Alex-Li Tandem,' said Alex-Li Tandem and it swung back, like one of those doors in the old tales that are meant for only one man, for only one man's name will open them.

On the stairs the most that Alex could manage was to tell himself over and over that those are stairs, and these are my legs, and this action is called climbing. In the tight, mirrored hallway, he regressed back to physical mantra: don't touch, make space, step back. Reaching the lounge, he took a preparatory breath – but she had already left the room, insisting on making coffee. Honey yes-ed and no-ed to the questions of milk and sugar, called out from an unseen kitchen. Tandem attempted orientation. He was here. *He* was *here*. There was no feeling of disappointment. It was (as he had foreseen!) a home for European trinkets, rescued (he imagined) from fire and theft and revolution. It was the home of a collector. It had its New York touches, of course – capacious windows, indecipherable, modish art (from this lounge he could see down the mirrored hallway, straight through a bedroom to a New York bathroom, white tiled, with ancient, leaky shower fitting and aquamarine verdigris steadily eating the copper taps), but its heart, this was resolutely old world. An imposing stone Buddha, as big as an eight-year-old, sat by the doorway, bearing the loss of its nose with great fortitude. A wire and silk lotus flower at rest in its lap. A girl in an etching looked over her shoulder. The likenesses of dogs were everywhere – shaped as bookends, embodied in ornaments, embroidered on pillows, painted on mugs – and then when one

looked again they resolved themselves into the one dog, one aristo-
cratic breed: a stubby-legged, cream-coloured baton with abbreviated black snout, bulbous eyes and crumpled forehead. Two
mahogany cabinets with mother-of-pearl trim stood opposite each
other on eight wooden paws. Everywhere white linen throws,
Arabic arches and Venetian prints, beaten-thin cowhide rugs, and
pink silk shot through cream pillows, unravelling. Ornate silver
mirrors hung at dipping angles, seeming to catch the room just
before it fell through the floor. Everything made with care and
handled with same. Alex thought of his days and the rooms they
had always been spent in, where the furniture came packed flat,
requiring cajoling before it would stand upright and live. Now
he was in her room, her days. Because they were just as he had
anticipated, he began to feel very calm. His Zen came over him.
Honey was fumbling with a magazine; his own hands were still.
Soon, Kitty would come in here and they would talk and it would
be as it would be. *Spring comes, grass grows by itself.*

Then the sound of a minor calamity of china from the kitchen.
'I should help?' whispered Honey, and sprang up with her two sets
of glass twins, hurried down the mirrored hall and multiplied again,
accompanied now by an infinite amount of doppelgänger Honeys,
companions.

Time moved forwards.

'But I am telling it backwards!' Kitty complained, and put
another sugar, her third, into the cup. For a few minutes she had
been talking very quickly and (or so it seemed to Alex) in a number
of languages. Now, finally, she stopped fussing, and fell into an
armchair. She sat like a much younger woman, with one bare foot
tucked underneath her and one knee drawn up to her chin. Alex

and Honey sat on a neighbouring sofa. She beamed at them. Alex
couldn't be certain which face he did back. She picked up a hair
clasp from an empty silver fruit bowl on the coffee table, brought
her hair up behind her and fastened it in a tiny tight bun with this
clasp, which she took from her teeth.

'Wait, *wait*,' she said, and pulled a curl of hair forward to frame
her face. 'First things are first. Alex-Li Tandem! Alex-Li *Tandem*.
I cannot *believe* it is you. I am such a fan of yours, truly. But you
are not at *all* what I expected. Not at *all*. And meanwhile, I think I
sit just as you wrote it, no? One leg up, one leg down . . .' She
glanced down at herself and then back at him with a look that only
magicians and doctors rightly deserve. 'How could you *know* a
thing like this!'

Alex opened his mouth, but Kitty smacked her hands together
and caught whatever he had to say between them.

'And this one, you remember? *Dear Kitty, She is very proud of
her feet and touches them often. When standing she feels the air
under her arch and stubbornly believes she could have been a
dancer. Love, Alex-Li Tandem*. True, completely! It is my biggest
vanity, my feet,' she laughed, extending her left and pointing the
toes to the ceiling. 'Applause you deserve for this!' she said and
began to clap. Honey joined in at a sardonic pace. Alex, who had
no experience with applause, sat and smiled stupidly towards it.
His knee was going again. Kitty stopped, moved forward and put
both hands on it.

'Nervous. Don't be. Silly, to be, please,' she murmured, and her
face suggested she understood him all the way through, to the
marrow, as we all want to be understood. Alex, so grateful for this,
wanted to nod but couldn't. Any movement of the head might
cause chaos in the tear ducts. A small bell chimed somewhere in

the room. Alex found himself meditating on the gold-green spine of a gardening book. Kitty smiled at Honey and Honey smiled back. What had begun as an incidental silence between them all began stretching across the room like tarpaulin.

'You know,' began Honey, but Kitty had spoken at the same moment. Honey laughed, Kitty laughed.

'No, I was just –' said Honey.

'*Please*,' said Kitty, and put her coffee cup to her lips.

Across the street a sash window slammed shut. Alex put his hand up, something he hadn't done since school.

'I have to – I mean, you must let me –' he began, and thought with pain of what this speech had always been in his head, how glorious, how crystalline. 'No, start again – what I *mean* is – I'd really like to say – without, you know, going on – just how much I've *admired* you – I mean, not just like for the films – but more, you know, as a person who –'

Kitty took a deep, exasperated breath. 'Oh, no, no, no, no, *no*,' she said with amazement, 'you must know I don't care for any of this. Pfui! You write better than you speak, I think. But of course our dear Sirin said this was true of all the great writers, and he should've known. He was a *great* friend of my third husband. Now. Cookie?'

Alex shook his head. His mouth had taken on its six-in-the-morning state. So dry you just couldn't be sure if the words would come.

'What I was *trying* to say,' continued Kitty happily, 'though I get it backwards – look: I start again. I am trying to tell you about your letters, because I think the story is *very* unusual. Because you see, I get almost no letters ever on this topic. I mean, letters concerning my *cinematic career*' – she snorted at this – '*if* you can give it such a grand name. A few maybe, once a year from the Oscar people – *when* they remember. But I don't care for any of it, really. My life has moved on – I mean I *hope* it has moved on, I flatter myself it has, at least.'

Here she made a movement very familiar to Alex. It was from the dressing-room scene, in which May-Ling begs the stage-manager to make her an understudy. A quick forward thrust of her head, chin up, eyes pleading – and then an impossibly poignant retraction. Everything back in its box, including all feelings. Alex knew the next line (*I'm sorry, I just can't do it, honey*), and thought for a moment he might say it.

'Besides,' continued Kitty brightly, and with that air of ingenuous, childlike egotism that belongs to those who are used to an audience's attentions, 'it is like a garden, celebrity. It requires tending, do you see? I am seventy-seven now – I have only one kidney left. I have already had the cancer, and by some miracle I keep my treasures' – she placed both hands on her breasts – 'but I cannot always be so lucky. I have to get on with things while the time is here – I have time to tend a garden full of weeds? And more than this: to do as Max says, to pretend the garden takes care of itself?'

Honey, who had long lost the thread of this metaphor, nodded eagerly. She took a *biscotto* from the china plate that Kitty was holding up to her and chewed around the edge of it with that unique ineptitude we bring to food we do not recognize.

'I want to thank you for –' began Alex, and then closed his eyes and tried again. 'The autographs. Thank you for doing th –'

Kitty whooped, and put two fingers over his lips. 'My *God*, don't be *ridiculous*! The *least* I could do – but still you don't let me explain, so let me explain. And so then recently some bad things have been happening here – this we will come to in a moment –

but because of this bad things, you see, I don't like to be alone in the apartment. And on this night, three weeks ago, somehow, I get a panic!' she said, her face re-creating the feeling. 'I don't know why – I think I hear a thing on the stairs, I get a little crazy – and so I call for a car and Lucia and I, we go into town to Max's, and we have a key of course, but there is no sign of Max. Probably,' she said *sotto voce* to Honey, 'in one of these strange bathing places where they have all the sex with barmen they see never before . . . anyway, this is not my business . . . it was very late and cold, and I did not wish to go all the way back, I'm not so young to be galavanting around New York. So I am in Max's and I eat and Lucia eats and we wait, wait, wait, and nothing and we get rather bored, can you imagine? In this little, so dirty apartment which I have not been in in maybe fifteen years and Lucia has never been! So we are bored, and we nose around a little. And to make it short, this is where we find you! Lucia finds, actually. In cupboards in the kitchen – hundreds of these things! I never before seen or heard of these. Every one: Alex-Li Tandem, Alex-Li Tandem, Alex-Li Tandem – going back to I don't know when. Almost all the envelopes closed. Unread! And so I open, naturally because they are for me. They are for *me*. And what is inside . . . oh, it was so beautiful . . .'

She kept talking, Kitty. Alex was being praised. He was great and talented. Something he had written had affected someone, as surely as if he'd pushed them over with his hands. All this was said. And he heard the noise of it, the way she sang it, but it meant nothing to him. For thirteen years he had believed he had an audience, even if it was only Krauser, reading them and tearing them up. He had heard of those perfect Zen artists who write their books and paint their pictures with no expectation of audience, and set fire to their work when they are finished. But that is a choice they make.

Kitty stood up and moved to one of her dog-footed cabinets, took a small key from her jeans pocket and began fiddling with the lock. The front rucked, folding like a wooden fan, and a writing desk was revealed, ten slim drawers either side. These she began to open, looking for something.

'Wait – you never saw *any* of my letters?' asked Alex with what was left of his voice. 'In all that time?'

'Never! This is what I say. I am not so grand to ignore so many letters.'

Alex was turning a funny shade of purple. Honey put her hand on his and gave it a supportive squeeze.

'I don't understand,' said Honey, 'you mean he never showed you them?'

'Exactly. This is it, exactly. He hid them, I think. Can you imagine!' Kitty said and tutted, as if at a child's foible.

'But didn't you ask him?' pressed Honey. 'Didn't you ask him *why*?'

'No, I don't *ask* him, he doesn't know I found them – I abhor this, anyway, this *theatrical* exposure. Terribly cruel thing I think to reveal somebody like this, like it is television or something horrible. But of course I wonder why he would do . . . Ah, now here we are.'

From a drawer Kitty took a small bundle of letters in Alex's pink envelopes. She rested an elbow against her defunct fireplace. 'They are so lovely, really. I read almost all of them – it did not take very long, they are so brief. What it cost you in postage I can't imagine. I took a few only, so he doesn't notice. I like this very much: *Dear Kitty, Whenever she hugs children she looks over their little shoulders to the parents and smiles to prove she does not hate children. Love, Alex-Li Tandem.* This is too perfect! This is what I do, always!'

Alex tried to smile.

'I wish so much,' she said, 'I could have found them before, when my third husband was alive. He was a painter. Maybe you know of him?'

Kitty said a foreign name, and Alex, who was entirely paralysed with rage, made no sign of acknowledgement.

'Well, Alex, I think he would have *loved* you. He would have taken you to his heart, I know. He loved the writers who could say a lot with a little – and the people he would have introduced you to, oi! This apartment was full of writers and artists always – they adored this place, they felt at home here.' Kitty stroked the white stone wall behind her.

'Do you know why I like them?' she said wistfully. 'Your letters? They are nothing of movies. Nothing about that. They are just a woman, walking in the world. This is beautiful, I think.'

'What kind of a person,' began Alex loudly. Shaking, he rose from his seat.

'Alex,' said Honey sharply, '*sit down.*'

Alex sat back down and lowered his voice. 'What kind of person hides a kid's letters for thirteen *years*? That was thirteen years of *my life.*'

Kitty looked at him with concern and then turned her eyes to the window. 'I am so sorry for this. For *you*,' she said, and brought both sets of fingertips to her lips.

Alex hated her for that – the theatrical gesture at that moment when he was stripped clean, without gesture, without defence.

'The only reason I can think of, possibly, is that the few letters

I receive, they are very much the same, you know? It is always: *I
am your greatest fan* – so vulgar, this word, this "fan", I *hate* it in
the first place – but I think, maybe your letters . . . they are so
unique, and they seem to *know* me almost – and to Max, this an
affront, you understand? Because he thinks of himself this way.
As the only person who understands me. For him, this is very
important. I think he wished to maybe . . . *preserve* an idea, a
Platonic idea, he has of –'

Alex didn't want to hear the philosophy and thumped his fist on
the coffee table, toppling the cups.

'Let me understand this,' he said, pushing Honey's hand off his
shoulder. 'So, what? He just had a grudge? Against me? You got other
letters, sometimes, didn't you? He just screened mine or what? He
just did it for a laugh? Just wanted to waste thirteen years of –'

'No!' cried Kitty, holding the letters to her chest. 'He *protects*
me also. He is very *paranoid*, Max, he worries that some people get
a little crazy, very attached, like a Norman Bates or somebody.
People are strange about movies. He thinks it is his job to protect
me from the crazy people. This is an irony if you knew Max . . . he
is himself a little crazy, I married him once, so I know – for seven
days in Hawaii but it was enough – and he proved to be homosexual,
which in this business is rather common – oh, yes,' she said to
Honey's open mouth, 'my dear, everybody should marry a homosexual at least once. It robs a pretty girl of all her sexual vanity. It
is *very* healthy. And then, when I married again, Max lived with
us. I couldn't stop him, my dear,' she said, addressing Honey completely now, who was enthralled, 'this is how he is. He used to
bring drinks in at our parties like a butler!'

'That isn't . . .' said Alex, shaking his head. 'Could I just say
something without . . . If I could just say my piece? Please?'

Kitty looked distressed and reached her arms out towards him. 'But of course!'

Alex, given the stage, suddenly wanted to skulk by the curtains.

'Go on, please,' said Kitty beseechingly, putting a biscuit in his hand. 'You must speak your mind. In America, this is practically the law.'

'Well, look, I mean . . .' said Alex through an ignoble mouthful of crumbs, 'what did you need protecting *from*? My letters? Did I ever give you any bloody reason to –'

'Al,' said Honey, and got him by the back of the neck, 'you're being really rude, OK? Give it up. We'll go now, Miss Alexander. We've wasted pretty much enough of your time.'

Honey stood up, but Kitty, who was leaning against her fireplace, motioned for her to sit. Alex closed his eyes, and apologized for himself.

With a gentle, forgiving nod, Kitty went back to the cabinet and opened another drawer. With a new handful of letters she came and sat next to him, almost uncomfortably close. She sighed and scattered the letters on the table. 'Understand, please, of course I don't need protecting from *you*,' she said. 'But not all my so-called fans are like you.'

They sat in a line now on this small sofa, Honey, Alex, Kitty, a scenario he could not have imagined a week ago. Pressed on both sides by celebrity, the fantasy of every Autograph Man. Kitty lifted an envelope up and passed it to him.

'This is the bad thing. It started six months ago. The police say they can do nothing. Can you imagine? It is only Max who worries for me.'

'Can I?'

She nodded, and he peered into its torn fold and extracted a letter.

'It is so horrible,' said Kitty with a deliberate shudder. 'He seems to know everything. Where I go and what I buy and what I wear. Obviously he follows me. For me, it is not so scary as it is *tedious* – Max barely allows me to leave the house because of this. I am like a prisoner now because of this boring maniac who has nothing better to do than follow an old woman and her dog around New York. It is *ridiculous*.'

Alex scanned the letter quickly. It was in a childish script and cliché was so prevalent four movie projects might have been launched from this half-page alone. Aside from its problems of style, the thing was unpleasant. The detail obsessive and very particular.

'Where are these sent to? Are these all of them?'

Kitty pointed to the floor in a robust manner, but her eyes gave her away. Now her left hand, which Honey had impulsively taken in her own, was shaking.

'They come here. And I don't understand it – almost nobody has the address, really, except a few very dear friends. And, Max, of course.'

She knocked over a cow-shaped silver creamer and couldn't be stopped from rushing to the kitchen for something to sop up the milk. Honey and Alex barely had a chance to exchange an International Gesture with a long and noble history, the meaningful look. A minute later she was back and the three of them were an inefficient assembly line of moved cups and rescued books (the milk had surprised everybody by travelling in two directions) while Kitty outlined an impossible situation. Overprotective Max ('I am not even allowed outside with Lucia!'); an increasingly restricted, lonely life; a neighbourhood in which antisocial madness was so frequent a lunatic had to truly out-do himself to attract the serious attention of the law.

'Listen, Miss Alexander, I don't mean to be . . .' began Honey, which always meant she *did* mean to be. 'But didn't you ever think it might be this guy *Max* who's . . .'

Kitty lowered herself into her chair.

'Miss Richardson, I am not an idiot. Of course I think about it – especially when I find all of these fan-letters hidden – and not just Alex's, other things. A few requests, invitations and so forth – I am not saying I would have done these, but I should have liked to have had the opportunity to at least *think* about –'

She dipped her head, and blinked away a tear.

'But no, I can*not* believe Max wrote these letters. I don't *want* to believe it. We've been together forty years. He is my best-friend. What he does, he does always to protect me. This is what he thought he was doing, hiding your letters from me. There is nothing malicious in Max. I don't think he is capable of this, of hurting me.'

It took some effort, but Honey politely said no more.

'I'll take one of these,' said Alex firmly, pocketing a letter and feeling impossibly capable, like Charlie Chan. 'I know all the American dealers – maybe they received something from this bloke – maybe it's one of the dealers. I can compare handwriting. That's my job. It might be someone like that.'

Kitty made the relinquishing gesture.

At the sink, she started the taps and seemed to forget them. Alex walked in and shut them off just before the cascade.

'I want to get out of the city, sometimes,' she said, putting a finger to the oily surface of the water. 'This is so much a city for somebodies. Not as much as Hollywood, I used to think, but now I don't know . . .'

She rubbed her eyes and turned to face him. The smile was

identical to that moment when the Salvation Army woman offers May-Ling a bowl of chicken soup.

'And now, you have the revelation, now we have met. I am no one at all. Just an old woman with a big mouth and too many problems. A terrible deception has been practised on you, Mr Tandem –'

'Not true. Not *close* to true.'

She pointed to some yellow rubber gloves on a shelf, which Alex passed to her. 'Thank you – and you will dry. *Dear Kitty, She hopes for nothing except fine weather and a resolution. She wants to end properly, like a good sentence. Yours, Alex-Li Tandem.* This one I memorize – it's so lovely. And at the same time, Alex, if it is not too rude to say, it *worries* me that you write these. *Why* did you write? You are really too young even to remember my last film, no matter my first. I think,' she whispered playfully, 'it suggests a lack of sexual intrigue in your life, to be interested in this ancient history. There is no girlfriend, or she is not effective. There is a lack somewhere. I think this must be true.'

'Why don't you go away, if you want to?' asked Alex earnestly. 'I mean, if Max has you all cooped up here? That's no way for you to live.' He took a wet cup from her. 'You've got European fans up to the eyeballs, really. I could help you organize –'

'Wanna keep these, or?' said Honey, appearing at the door with a saucer of milk-damaged biscuits. Kitty beckoned her over and examined them.

'Lucia will have. Over there, do you see? This bowl. This bowl is English Wedgwood, but what can be done? She is a diva, my Lucia. She fills in for my inadequacies in that department. You know, my dear, you can take off your gloves in the house.'

'Why don't you go away?' persisted Alex.

'You . . . you are so familiar-looking. One feels like one knows you already – such a friendly, striking face. And almost terrifying what a tall girl you are. They say it is the additives. Americans – they are all so tall. Either this or they grow the other way. Or both.'

'You could open film festivals. It'd be like a comeback tour. Paris, Venice, London . . .'

His voice was unexpectedly passionate, angry, and it silenced the tiny room. Honey gave him a look and an International Gesture (index finger drawn across throat) but defiant Alex looked away. He felt irritated by Kitty's inability to stay on the subject of her own fame. It is an oddity of the Autograph Man that if he were a slave freed by his master, we would find him the next day back at work, self-flagellating.

Kitty had finished washing her cups. She held her gloves out to Alex. He removed them without a word, as if he had been in her service for twenty years.

'I have no money,' she said simply. 'This apartment is rent-controlled. And with whom will I go? Max would never agree. He has never left this country in his life. And now we are finished with washing, yes? What to do now? I know a thing – you are young, maybe you can help with this computer before I go crazy completely?'

They walked through to the bedroom. Honey excused herself and used the bathroom, while Alex was told to sit at the desk. He experienced a mortifying rogue sexual thought as the warm bulge of Kitty's chest descended and remained hovering by his face. She pointed to a key on the laptop. Pressed it and demonstrated its failure. Alex put his finger to the mouse-pad. The toilet flushed. The doorbell rang.

'Who's that?'

'It's Max!' gasped Kitty, backing away from the little window. 'But *oh* . . . this is too ridiculous . . . and I can't stop him, he has his own key.'

'Good,' said Alex resolutely. 'I want to talk to him.'

'No, no, no . . . wait . . . yes, it is OK – he won't know you. I will say you came to fix the computer. It is good, actually. Now you will meet Lucia! Now, *this* is the real honour.'

Short-lived. Alex saw only Lucia's backside; she was barely in the room when Max rushed her from the floor as if she were in danger, and, with the dog struggling gracelessly in his embrace, he started yelling and raised his comic little fists.

'You heard me, make like a tree. I'm not joking. How long you *been* in here anyways? Did you break in? How'd you find it?'

'Oh, Max, you are being ridiculous – please, don't shout like this, *Max*, one moment, you don't even know who is this – he is here to fix the computer – I am not in any danger, Max – I really apologize, I don't know why he is behaving so –'

Honey emerged from the bathroom, twisting her hem.

'What's all the – *oh*.'

'And here she is,' said Krauser, triumphant. 'Bonnie. Clyde. I know these two grifters, believe me. And they're hitting the bricks.'

An operatic argument followed, performed in four voices and three movements (the hallway, one lap of the lounge and then down the stairs, Italian style), in which no useful information was exchanged and a handful of lines was repeated over and over. With a finale on the doorstep.

FIVE / *Taming the Bull*

I

'That's very disappointing, Tandem,' said Lovelear solemnly. 'That's anticlimactic. I'm glad I didn't get out of *this* to listen to *that*.'

He slipped deeper into the churning water and assumed an expression of supreme tranquillity. Alex pulled his feet up on to his deckchair and hugged himself against the chill. The sun was not going down. It was simply leaving, evaporating, one of those days that fades to white before the night comes. In this dying light, he could see the damage the city had done to the snow. Everywhere it had been squelched and gritted and dirtied. Even on the roofs the hot air vents were creating islands where earlier there had been continents. And down there in the streets they persisted on stamping all over it. Millions of colleagues, tiny pointillist people, one blob for the head and one for the body. Jumping in taxis, doing the sidewalk race. Everyone was going home except Alex.

'You should really try this, mate, do yourself a favour,' remarked Dove, looking like a half-cooked lobster, red, with a blue tinge. ''Sbit like the best bath you ever had.'

'It's nothing like a goddamn bath,' said Lovelear. He clutched the curved sides and lay flat. 'This is godly. This is terrific. This is enlightenment right here. This is the tub in which cold and hot do not exist. This is always the right temperature. This is like being *born*.'

'I checked the letter she gave me,' said Alex, dragging his fingers through his hair. 'It matches Krauser's handwriting. I mean, it's obvious to anybody – you wouldn't have to be an expert. She must *know*.'

'Christ, Tandem, they're probably in it together – some scam to make you feel sorry for her and give her some money or something. *I* don't know, I don't really *care*. And that's another thing that smells to high heaven: how *can* she be broke, Tandem? How? Answer me that. She's sitting on a goddamn goldmine. She just has to sign her name and she makes six thousand dollars. That's money from air.'

And if I leapt, thought Alex, from this roof to that, from that to the next, and shed my body in Brooklyn and my mind in New Jersey, and reached England as my true self, my Buddha-nature, would you know me, my darling? Would you be the same, with your new heart? Would you take me to bed? In the office block opposite, a black girl with Esther's neatly bald head, but dressed quite differently, in an office suit. She put on a coat and pulled the blind. Everybody was going home except Alex.

'OK, here's another one,' said Lovelear, reaching for an absurd cocktail. 'What kind of an Autograph Man goes to the house of Kitty Alexander and fails to get her autograph? Is that normal? Doesn't ask her anything about anything, doesn't come back with a single interesting story about the films, doesn't even steal an item from the house – I'm not saying it had to be anything *big* –'

'Small, like,' explained Ian. 'From the bathroom. Something that wouldn't be missed.'

'Exactly – although the bathroom would not be my room of choice – and doesn't come back with anything *anything* that would help God-fearing people like me and the Doveman here believe you were ever there in the first place. And on top of this, to just totally ice the cake, you *fail* to sleep with Honey Smith, which is like, excuse me? If you can't sleep with Honey Smith, you have a dick malfunction. I'm sorry – you do. I mean, that's her *job*. She is actually *famous* for sucking dick. And you didn't manage it? Now what *precisely*,' pronounced Lovelear grandly, crossing his arms over his breasts, 'are we to make of an Autograph Man like that?'

'Answer me this,' said Alex, standing. 'What did my face look like before my parents were born?'

'Er, I'm gonna have to pass on that one, Al,' said Lovelear, blinking. 'Ask me another one.'

'OK. Can I go now?'

'Free bloody world,' said Dove, sniffily.

'For once,' said Lovelear, heaving himself out of the tub, 'our friend Dove is right. It is a free world. Free up here, anyhow,' he said, slapping his forehead. 'You can always go, Alex. You always *could*.'

He was massive, near hairless and completely naked, at once vulnerable and obscene. Alex felt compelled to hand him his towel.

Lovelear tucked his tongue into his cheek. 'You just have to make up your mind to leave, is all.'

Back in his room, Alex found a note from Honey, suggesting that they eat together, and a hotel questionnaire. The questionnaire, conscious of its own monstrous nature, was offering as its bribe a European vacation, the lucky winner to be chosen at random. Simply hand me in, said the questionnaire, at the front desk when you check out. Three times the questionnaire referred to itself as 'me'. Alex took it and a pen to the bathroom, removed his clothes and ran a bath that was too hot for human life. He returned to the bedroom for a bottle of wine and a glass. Sitting on the toilet lid, sweating from the steam, he briskly drank a huge glass of white and filled in his name, sex, racial profile and address. He had no problem giving out personal information. It was the thing he had in abundance. Once in the bath (a slow, stoic lowering), he found a perfectly placed phone just by his head, and a wooden rack by his left hand, designed, it would seem, for his wine glass, his questionnaire and his pen. He washed his penis with one hand, soaping gently under his balls, and finished the questionnaire with the other. At home, when in the bath, one always hoped for the entrance of Esther, rushing through half naked to grab a deodorant, or standing, for a moment, at the mirror, to put a lens in. And then, if you had pleased her, she might turn round and kiss you on the forehead, or run her finger down the seam of your wet belly, or find the soapy penis and kiss the tip of that. She loved you in the morning because the day was new. Argument was left on last night's pillows along with the wept mascara. Alex drank another glass of wine and found himself, at the end of it, moving his finger around the rim, over and over, waiting for it to sing. The drink, the hot water – these had relaxed him sufficiently. He phoned Adam. It was a crossed line. Two people somewhere were talking faint Japanese.

'No, you can't,' said Adam.

'Hi, it's me. I was just –'

'I know it's you, it's late, man. And no, you can't.'

'Can't?'

'Have her number. The ward closed at seven.'

'Please, Ads. I need to speak to her.'

'I know – but I'm telling you, she's fine. It went fine. I'll give you the number tomorrow.'

'She's all right? It all went all right?'

The relief came in a terrific swoop, as it will. His chin could not keep its shape, it stumbled and fell. Graceless tears carried on down his neck, ran down one arm.

'You saw her?'

'I went in this afternoon. She was groggy, but she was making jokes. I told her you couldn't get out of New York –'

'I *couldn't*, Ads. It was all paid for.'

'Right.'

'And . . . I don't know . . . she didn't seem to want me to be there much.'

'I think the point was that you were meant to *want* to be there.'

The line went quiet. Alex started gulping, loudly.

'Look,' said Adam with a sigh, 'her heart works. It always did. Better than most. Come on, Alex – you're fine, she's fine. Calm down. Have you been drinking?'

'Bit.'

'All the more reason to leave it, then. Call her tomorrow. OK? How's New York. Any better?'

'Again? I can't hear you.'

'Said: *any better?*'

'Oh. Hard to tell.'

'Well, you're home soon,' shouted Adam, over the increasingly crossed line. 'Tomorrow you leave, right? So. You'll live. Worse things happen at sea. Oh – and it's on Thursday, OK? So you best be learning it.'

'Oh, Ads, man . . . come on, I already told you –'

'You can buy it in any bookshop over there. Remember it's the *mourners* one. Kaddish Yatom. There're like four different ones. OK?'

'I can't hear you.'

'WHAT?'

'I'M NOT DOING IT. I TOLD YOU.'

'Look, I've got to go to bed, mate. This line's awful, and I'm knackered. I can barely hear you. Talk tomorrow, yeah?'

'Wait, *wait* –'

'And Esther's fine, I promise you. Groggy, that's all. Oh, and Grace is doing all right too. Shalom, Alex.'

'Adam?'

'Shalom aleichem, Alex.'

'Shalom, yeah.'

Alex slid down the bath, submerged and watched the ceiling swim. When he surfaced, he had wet his questionnaire and had to hang it over a radiator to dry.

Were the range of television channels sufficient for your needs?

.....*Television is always sufficient.*..

How did you find your sleeping arrangements?

.........*Lonely.*..

What changes would you make to the menu on offer?

.....*Less food.*..

What single thing would have most improved the standard of service you received during your stay?

.....*Monkey butlers.*..

Would you appreciate group activities scheduled for you and your fellow guests during your stay?

.....*I'd need more details before venturing an opinion.*...

Here at the Burns Baldwin Hotel Group we have a simple, homespun
philosophy, which we've taken as our promise to our guests:
  Every day is a new beginning.
We think each and every hotel room should be returned to a state of
perfection day after day, night after night, and we work hard to keep
that promise. We also like to know as much as possible about our guests
and their opinions and desires – that way we can give you more of what
you want! By taking the time to fill me out, you're helping the good
people of Burns Baldwin to help you. Please feel free to write your own
philosophy of life in the space below.

...... *Regret everything and always live in the past.* ....

By seven, Alex had finished with the wine and moved on to a bottle
of bourbon, sipping it like a girl. He started to watch an advert. Half
an hour later he was still watching it. He had been misled, now he
was late. He put on his approximation of evening wear (white
t-shirt, black jeans), left the room. The lift had moved. It was not
to the left and round the corner, its last known location. Nor was
it to the right. All arrows led to exit signs and bleak fire escapes,
and, although he was only on the second floor, Alex resented even
the *idea* of stairs in a hotel context. The point was ease. Always
ease. Even if it had to be the kind of ease that makes things more
difficult.

He found the lift, finally, to the left and around three corners in
a spot from which he could clearly see the door number of his own
room. An arrow lit up.

'Room for one more?' chirruped Alex, thinking himself suitably
amiable, American. He clapped his hands. There was a documentary team in there, four men in earphones and equipment, and a
girl with a clipboard. Unsmilingly, they took a collective step
backwards.

'Going down?'

'Nope,' said a man with a camera. 'Goin' up.'

Alex looked to his right and saw the number thirty-seven burning amber. He pressed L.

'You know,' he said to a man with a sound boom, 'when people are asked to choose a number between one and a hundred, most people choose thirty-seven.'

The boom mike slipped and bounced off Alex's shoulder. The man apologized. In the silence Alex wondered which part of him wanted to be in their documentary. How big was that part? Floor twelve elided into floor fourteen.

'Who's it about?'

'Excuse me?' said a man. Like the others he had the word TEAM written on the front of his t-shirt. Alex looked closer and spotted his laminate, the face of a famous adolescent.

'Shylar,' said Alex, nodding. 'She's *very* good. Amazing what she does with her . . .' Alex pointed to his own pot-belly. He moved it to the right and then the left. 'Almost improbable.'

They reached floor twenty-five. From this point onwards, thought Alex, a fall would be one hundred per cent unsurvivable. Just a splat, while a ring or a necklace kept its noble metal shape, because we are not as strong as things. Things win. The lift shuddered and stopped and opened. A woman and her young daughter squeezed in. Alex was now pressed close to the man with the boom, facing him, with the boom itself hanging overhead as if it were Alex's words it wanted to record. Now he became aware of a strong smell of alcohol coming from his own mouth.

'The three most – I read this somewhere, it's true – the three most typed words – typed, as in *entered* into the computers when they're . . . you know, the three most thingied words are: God,' said

Alex, showing an erect thumb, 'Shylar and –' Here Alex swore obscenely, and the American mother, in a proud display of puritan gestural technique, waited two beats into the following silence, made a noise of disgust and put her big pink hands over the child's ears.

She looked amazing. A plum-coloured, sleeveless satin dress this time, without arms, as once worn by the popular actress Rita Hayworth. The gloves were black satin and elbow length. Her hair seemed to be completely different from the hair of the day before. About five inches longer with a chestnut streak in it.

'You look *amazing*,' said Alex, tumbling into his chair.

'Thank you,' said Honey pertly, patting herself down. 'Took about five hours. Some of it was painful and the rest was just goddamn boring. I am *so* glad I'm a woman. And you look awful – how thoughtful of you.'

'Put the blame on Mame. So,' said Alex, picking up a long piece of card, 'what are we eating?'

'Lots of tiny-ass pieces of food piled on top of each other in the shape of a tower.'

'Good. We *love* tall food. I want the tallest thing on this menu.'

'That's the wine list, baby. An' it's upside-down. What's the matter with you? Why you so *nervous*?'

'I'm not nervous.'

'I'm not nervous,' parroted Honey in a passable accent. '*Bull*.'

'I think you'll find you're confusing the two states of "nervous" and "pissed".'

Alex took an ice-cube from a glass full of them and gripped it in his hand, an old sobering trick.

'Fairly weird day, no?'

'I've had weirder, to tell you the truth.'

'I checked the handwriting. It's Krauser's completely. I mean, you just have to look at it.'

'Yeah, I figured,' said Honey, putting her wine down before it reached her lips. '*God*, but that's sad, isn't it? I just think that's so *sad*. For both of them. *Jesus*. You can't say anything to her – she's clearly in denial. She doesn't *want* to know, obviously. Talk about living a lie, right? *Jesus*.'

She moved her hand across the table and laid it over his.

'Honey?'

'Oh – my – God, *please* don't say Honey like that, like we're in some bad TV movie. What? What is it? Just say it, whatever it is.'

'I really, really don't want you to take this the wrong way.'

Honey scowled and took back her hand.

'Lemme tell you something. There's no wrong or right way to take anything. There's just words and what they mean. Be an American. Say what you mean.'

Alex put his elbows on the table. 'I just wanted to – I mean, I want to make sure . . . rather, to establish, that this isn't – because, you know I leave tomorrow, and there's someone who – so, I wanted to, just to be clear, that this isn't –'

Honey got him by the neck and brought his face to hers and gave him one of the most luxurious kisses he had ever experienced. It was like eating. He was being given something rich and rare.

'No,' she said, drawing back and lifting her hand for the waiter. 'This isn't a date. Don't flatter yourself. That was just a period on the end of an unusual day.' Here, a breakdown in transatlantic communication, rare these days. 'You know, a period? The black spot at the end of sentence – what do you call them over there? That was *almost* one, but that was a question, that's not quite . . .

and that's not it either; and now here's the real thing, you know, look out, at the end of this.'

She curved her hands around the empty air and gave a sharp nod.

'We call that a full stop.'

'Really?' She smiled. 'That's nice. That's kind of more like what I meant.'

Just after the desserts came, Alex noticed the hotel tilt and all the air disappear from the room. Honey was telling him about a gallery exhibit 'of Jewish stuff' that she thought he might like, but everybody else in the room was being drawn into a vacuum that had just presented itself with its entourage at the circle bar.

'My daughter just *loves* her,' said the waitress and spilt the coffee. Alex held himself up a few inches from his chair. He could see the tiny girl, a bodyguard the size of a water-buffalo and about fifteen people of the kind the magazines call 'handlers'. The aura was being effectively handled. Though the girl was only a hundred yards from Alex, she seemed a galaxy away.

'You'd think she could afford a better hotel,' he said, feeling oddly offended that she had made herself so accessible to him.

'Well, *exactly*,' agreed the waitress.

'Am I *boring* you?' said Honey loudly. Alex scrutinized the black hole, its unusual nature. Everybody knew it was there, and there it sat in its uniform of hot-pants and haltertop; everybody was already inside it (in her skin, as the girl herself, or in some orifice, doing the girl), but not one person looked at it directly.

'We probably shouldn't stare,' said Alex, who had once spent three hours staring at pictures of this girl's head attached to the naked bodies of other girls.

'Oh, *man*. Are you serious? Don't you know what that *is* over there?' asked Honey, turning around finally. 'That's dry shit on a stick. That's the cypress tree in the garden. That's three pounds of flax. Buddha is Buddha is Buddha is Buddha. So what is the big deal, exactly?'

'Sexual vortex,' said Alex, feeling it as strongly as the next man. 'Symbolic sexual vortex, added to by means of infinite repetition, televisual sheen. Not necessarily prettier than the waitress. Or you. Or me. Irrelevant. She *is* the power of seventeen. You remember the power of seventeen? It's nuclear. She's seventeen for the whole world.'

Honey threw her napkin on to the table. 'I know there's not a thing a pretty girl can't have in America for a while. Until she can't have it no more. Symbol, my ass. MU! Come on, let's get out of here.'

As they made their way through the lobby, they passed the documentary team setting up a shot of the concierge welcoming Shylar to the hotel, although Shylar had been there three days already.

'That was Honey *Smith*,' said the cameraman to the clipboard girl and clapped one hand on the front desk.

2

Here goes the city. Here it goes. There it is. On television. In a magazine. Written on a towel. In a photograph that hangs above the bed in moody black and white, as you sit indoors in this Technicolor city. There it is again. On channel nine, on twenty-three, briefly on seven, in cartoon form on fourteen and always on number one, which is the channel of the city. And it is also out that window, or so you hear. Car-horn, Spanish yell, women's laughter, syncopated beat, barking. A swooping cop's siren, like a prehistoric bird, passing through. In here, laid out along the bed, are the secrets of the mini-bar, multicoloured bottles in descending order: we finish one, we knock it to the floor. We finish one, we knock it to the floor. Ten green bottles. And that's just the beers. This is fun! Honey has retired to her room. But who needs women? Look at this television! The channel of history offers history in neat half-hour segments. The only history is the history of Hitler. The channel of entertainment entertains, ruthlessly. It wants your laughter. It will do anything. The channel of sex looks like sex and sounds like sex but it doesn't do smells. Smells are important. The channel of nostalgia shows dead people up and walking, hour on hour, always. They tell corny jokes, they clutch the curtains and weep, they tap-dance sometimes. The channel of nostalgia is the channel of old films and – my God – there she is! *There she is.* Right there, on the screen. And that was her beauty and those are pearls that were her eyes, and yes, you *know* the problems of two people don't amount to a hill of beans in this crazy world but still. But *still.* Here is your coat and those are your shoes and that is the door.

And it is not a real plan, of course, until you are standing outside the hotel, swaying slightly, inebriated, and horrified by the cold, the snow. It's one in the morning. Where did all this white stuff come from? On channel fifteen it was late summer, leaves just beginning to curl and blush. The concierge, who understands incapacity, hails you a cab.

In your own city, a night-time cab ride is a dull box with your thoughts inside. In another, it's the only journey. There's not enough light to use your tourist eyes. Nothing can be seen until you are at its feet or by its side – there are no views, only shapes becoming themselves before you. The street-lamps are one continuous stripe. The cabs run through the town like a blood supply, taking drunk people to bars. He is surprised at himself, for doing this. But Honey told him he would, and she knows Autograph Men. The very definition of them might be that they find it hard to let go.

He reaches forward and asks a man called KRYCHEK, GARY to take him on a detour through a square famous for its museums and prostitutes. It has, Alex realizes for the first time, almost a metaphysical name. There is even an imposing electronic counter sitting on top of a tower, clicking backwards to some zero date that cannot be contemplated when one is this drunk. He can see all the doors of the museums are flung open. Byzantine art, Renaissance sculpture, Medieval French armour. The city is having a festival to encourage culture by opening museums (as they put it) twenty-four-seven. But the real crowds are still here, outside, letting those vile LEDs count their lives away. They eat popcorn while they wait and look up at the ticker-tape news, travelling round the edge of a skyscraper. A president has died: it's not theirs. The snow is timorous now, falling in light flakes that can't survive the wet ground. On a soap-box four black boys are screaming about reincarnation. Adverts shine and move and speak and transform. Stretched the length of a building, a mammoth moving-image of a white cat, licking at a bowl of milk. This last is very beautiful, like a dream everybody's having together. The days of the museums are numbered. A chubby red-headed whore stops Alex's cab from presuming to cross her path with one flick of her ass. She shows them the International Gesture of contempt (middle finger) and trots into an exhibition of Chinese ancestor painting.

'See, this area ain't really ideal for driving tours,' says Krychek drily. 'Lot of pedestrians. With big asses.'

'Roebling, then,' says Alex-Li, at which Krychek laughs and stops the cab and Alex has to give him twenty dollars to start the engine again.

And so they pass over a bridge and its water.

3

All the opening lines he can think of call for a younger woman in the role ('*I couldn't leave without seeing you again*', '*We've got to talk*'). He ends up standing in the doorway with his mouth open. But there is no noise from either of them, only the sibilant swish of a silk dressing gown as she accepts him into her apartment, leads him to the lounge. Here she picks up a pocket-watch from the top of a cabinet and holds it up in her hands like a baby bird.

'A peculiar time, I think. To call on a lady. But maybe I am not fashionable.'

Alex squints, trying to focus.

'Is Max here? Will you throw me out?'

'Pfui! You talk as if I were a force of nature.'

'I think you are,' he says in a breaking voice, and has to kick off his shoes or go crazy from the damp coming through them. His legs give in, the sofa catches him. Kitty sits down opposite him. They sit like this for a minute, Alex unconscious with his head against the back wall, his eyes closed and his mouth an open cave; Kitty watching. She takes one of his feet in her hands, removes the sock and massages his instep.

'No,' she murmurs. 'You make a mistake: nature is *fascista*, the big bully is nature. I am the very opposite. I am not the fittest, and

I will not survive. I am cultivated. I pretend I am quite calm when I have strange men in my little house at one twenty-six in the morning.'

Alex squeezes an eye open. 'That's my foot. What's the time? Christ, I'm sorry' – he takes his foot back, her hands feel dry – 'I'm a bit drunk. I shouldn't have –'

'Oh . . .' says Kitty archly. 'I see. You didn't come for a foot massage? You came for passion?'

The bedroom door swings wide and a yellow wedge of light encompasses the hall, a luminous path for a panting, quick-stepping animal, hot and alive and suddenly among them.

Kitty turns on her stool, opening her arms to receive it.

'Lucia, see our visitor, yes! Oh! *Lucia, Lulu, Lo-Lo*, yes, we wake you with our noise – and see how she likes you too – you must pick her up and make some love to her, she is a really a *prostitute* for affection, any affection – look at how she throws herself at him!'

Alex, finding himself with a sinewy handful of dog, stops its writhing with a firm grip and looks in its peculiar face. The eyes, huge and protruding, are an oily black with bloody specks in the vitreous. Both are covered in a film of mucus, like two unborn things.

'She is my angel, of course . . .' says Kitty, knotting her fingers together. It is hard for her not to touch this dog. 'And we are glad you come – the truth is, we do not sleep so well. Coffee?'

Here they are again, in the kitchen. She asks him where he is from, what he is, exactly. When he tells her she says well, I must say you *look* Jewish. One of the great unanswerable Goyisms of modern times. But Alex has no capacity to be angry with her. He keeps seeing her young face. Maybe he is here to see her young face for her.

'Lucia is Chinese also,' she says, passing him a tray. 'Her family were all imperial dogs, back through history. This is what the dealer tells me, anyway. It is interesting to me that she is a great fan of Peking duck. She becomes crazy for it, truly!'

Alex takes the biscuits he is passed, and accepts a tea-towel laid over his arm.

'That's . . . nice.'

'I don't know if it's nice – it is certainly expensive. And now we will watch the television,' she says, pushing briskly past him with Lucia right behind, dancing through her legs. 'Do you know the American television? It is like all the finest food in the world put into a bucket and stirred with a stick. Come.'

By some accident, or because it is played on a loop, they watch the same informercial that duped Alex earlier.

'You will excuse me,' says Kitty wrapping a blanket round her shoulders and climbing into her bed. 'A breeze will kill me – I am finally of the age of the lethal breeze. When I think how my *tedious* Russian aunts used to complain of it, complain, complain – they couldn't sit here, they couldn't sit there, and I had no pity, none, and now I reach the terrible age. No, no, you stay there, don't worry. How anybody can believe a cream in the jar do this to your bosom, I can't imagine. You will take control of the whatever-it-is?'

She passes him the remote, and he slips off the end of the bed to the floor, where he sits cross-legged. Though the television will not stay quite still in his vision (it triplicates, or dances drunkenly to the left), Alex does his best to control it. He flicks. He lands. The popular actor Jimmy Stewart is desperately clutching two handfuls of paper and looking in the godly direction.

'I hate this channel,' says Kitty with vehemence. 'For me it is too morbid. Graveyard of my friends.'

Alex kneels up and looks down the bed. An obnoxious night-light has picked out the patches of scalp revealed by thinning hair and now catches her stricken expression with no sympathy, no care. He would protect her from close-ups. Lucia lies against her chest like a baby.

'I have lunch with him, once.'

'Really?'

The position is tiring. Alex lays his head next to her feet.

'Yes, really. We had a mutual friend in Charlie Laughton, and his wife, Elsa, who was lovely. Odd-looking, but never jealous or this sort of thing. They were both very English, very elegant – which was something for me because everybody in Hollywood was terribly *vulgar* and I missed my home, and they knew a little of Capri and so on – so, one day, Mr Stewart came to Texas, I don't know why, and I was there getting married to an *idiot*, and Mr Stewart, he knew nobody, and Charlie, he remember that I am there, and he give him the number for my hotel, and we meet for lunch. Very tall man, with the most unusual voice pattern. He loved me a little, I think – but I was too flattered really to even know what to do. And also there was this marriage to the ridiculous oil man with the terrible feet . . .'

And this is the touchstone. They talk about the films, about single moments in the films, gestures. He goes to the lounge and looks where she has told him to and returns with a tape. Expertly, he fast-forwards to a single frame.

'This?' she exclaims, putting on a pair of glasses. 'What is it? What is special?'

On the screen Joey Kay, agent, husband, is on stage with May-Ling Han, as they accept the applause after the première of her first film. The curtain is a landscape of red velvet folds. Flowers are being thrown, great open-throated lilies. Even the orchestra in the pit have laid down their brass to clap. She is a smash! And he reaches out for her, his face full of love, but she does not turn to him. Her focus is now purely on the first three rows. Something has changed. There is a tiny pulse in this wrist that he grips. It speaks a bible. She has made her choice. Between a man she has loved and those wonderful people out there in the dark.

'I see nothing here,' says Kitty, peering, 'just a lot of dumbshow. The film is ridiculous to begin with. I look as Chinese as my shoe.'

They go through films like this, fast-forwarding, freeze-framing. Kitty's laughter is hearty and at odds with her small mouth. Tales of lascivious co-stars, cruel directors, diva tantrums.

'You are a library of me,' she says, shaking her head, as he extracts another tape. 'Nobody asked you to keep a library. And of such absurdities!'

'One more,' pleads Alex.

Later, the light comes through.

'My God, do you see this! The night is finished. I have to close this blind.' She pulls back the blanket and slowly stands. He sees more than he should: a piece of her thigh, the skin candle-white and glutinous, without muscle, falling off the bone. Purple veins, thick as pencils. She closes her robe. As she passes the television, Alex seizes a scene. Kitty in a two-piece, drying her hair. She stops. Stands above it, looking down at the image from an oblique angle, scorning it, almost.

'Look at this. Can you imagine?'

'You are *so* beautiful. Beyond . . .'

'No, no, no, no. You can't know, what it is to see.'

'It's amazing. You get to see this, always. It's on film. You sort of live for –'

'Now you are being ridiculous,' she says severely, and walks across the room to the window. 'People don't tell the truth. As if we pass easily from one to another. Youth to age. No – it is not true, one is yanked. And the *fear*, this they lie about too. I can't sleep for thinking that it is all almost finished. My life. And I will go alone. And in America. This I never planned. Nobody with me, except Max.'

'Kitty, don't you think that Max . . . has, *Christ* – maybe a bit too much *control* of –'

'I'm so tired now,' mutters Kitty, going back to her bed. 'You must forgive me.'

'I'll sleep here,' says Alex decisively. He thinks he will stay here like a sentry, one eye out for death. He switches off the screen. She closes the blind. A warm fuzzy grey fills the room, making the two of them black, indistinct shapes, their own shadows.

'Of course you will,' says Kitty with equal firmness, and gives him whispered instructions to find a blanket, pillows. 'And your lady-friend?' she asks. 'She will not miss you? She was maybe a little too tall for you, I thought.'

'Why,' asks Alex, throwing a blanket over his shoulder, 'are we whispering suddenly?'

Kitty gets into her bed and points to Lucia, who has somehow shunted all the way down and lies like a bolster at its edge. Alex makes his bed. Kitty lies down. Alex lies down. Their breathing begins to fall in sync, because he is tracking her inhalations, following them exactly. Alex's heart strains at the sound of a stray cough from her, or a wheeze. Of all the possible deaths that stalk everyone every day, at this moment hers feels the most unbearable. This must be, he thinks with satisfaction, the top and bottom of love.

*

It is 5 a.m. In a passionate, dramatic gesture, he stands up in his grey underwear that refuses to conform to the passion and drama of the moment (stuck all to one leg and disappearing up the back) and tells her that she must come with him and leave this place because there's no other way for her to be free, and besides, he has a plan. He's been thinking of this speech for an hour in the dark.

'We talk at breakfast, hmm?' she says as neutrally as she can, turning to find him kneeling by her side in an artificial panic, and with a cast to his face that she has played opposite, many times. 'We sleep now. It's terribly late – too late to play a B-movie.'

She rolls away from him and grips the coverlet. Her fingers have gone cold. Even when making those films, even as a know-nothing girl, she had slept badly on the suspicion of just how many of these people, these movie-goers, take a line, take a look and use it on a loved one.

SIX / *Riding the Bull Home*

I

The park resembles a Russian prospect. A gold-leaf Orthodox basilica peeps through the trees, a Soviet-style running-track sits at its centre. Banks of dirty grey ice are heaped up against tree-trunks and benches and around the water-fountain, and there is one odd island of it on the running-track that the joggers jump over. Alex would not have believed there could be jogging in February, but here it is. It is 11 a.m. exactly. Roebling has shaded into somewhere else and he is on his way to find a subway to take him back into town. He has made plans today, and purchases: food, an air ticket, an improving book. He has had, as the advertising executives like to say, a hell of a morning.

He finds a seat and watches a mixture of Hipsters and Poles mark out a beat in a perfect circle. The Hipsters run in towelling sportswear, in seventies brand-names and sweat-bands. The Poles do too, though in a different spirit. These two groups do not meet on the race-track or chat by the fountain, they keep to themselves. It was the same deal, Alex noticed, in the shop where he bought this muffin. Herring, latkes, kilbasa and perogi on one side, lattes, falafels and cheesecake on the other. And in the bookshop a shelf of the popular writer Charles Bukowski stood across from a table piled high with Polish-language bibles.

On the street the Poles seem to understand the snow and dress for it. The Hipsters think they can accessorize the cold away, or simply ignore it. The Polish girls are waxy skinned, cat-eyed. They don't know Alex is alive. The Hipster girls are apple-cheeked with erratic hair and may be interested, depending on how much interest you show in the art that they are making. Though he has only been in the area twenty minutes, Alex feels qualified to further probe this weird cohabitation of Hipster and Pole, to puzzle the relations between them, the laws. Is it like-that or like-this? He sips his coffee. He resurfaces with the following:

The Realm of Like – This

1. Poles need Hipsters because Hipsters bring new money to the area.
   Spring comes, grass grows by itself.
2. Hipsters need Poles because Poles are proof that Hipsters – despite their increasing financial stability – are still bohemian. Living near Poles is a Hipster's sole remaining mark of authenticity.
   The blue mountain does not move.
3. Hipsters are Poles. Poles are Hipsters. Poles sell 1950s retro gas-station t-shirts. Hipsters eat pickled herring.
   White clouds float back and forth.

Contented with this, Alex stretched his arms along the cold bench. In his pocket, an air ticket, on his lap an open book.

'Yitgadal ve'yitkadash,' he read out loud, and then repeated the same phrase more confidently in English. He glared at the Aramaic letters, of which he comprehended only their basic forms (*yod, tav, gimel, dalet, lamed*), but nothing of these attendant dots and dashes. Infuriating. He laid his hands over the text. Breathed from his diaphragm. There was no good reason to be doing this unless one accepted that the very lack of reason made it worth doing – a perfect Jewish formulation. But that wasn't it. She had said something, that was it.

He was in the shower at the time and she stood at the bathroom mirror, openly watching. And this had felt almost normal. She applied her make-up, asked him about his family.

'My father also,' she replied to his reflection, 'although at my age, of course, this is more to be expected. But I know what is it, to feel this. My mother, she died when I was very young, eleven. She was my beloved.'

Alex prepared to exchange those perfunctory TV consolations that everyone of his generation learns by heart. But without a pause, Kitty had already begun to tell a story, as if everything up to this point was prologue to the telling of it.

'A *Romanian*,' she said meaningfully. 'Terrible! I hated her so! This is the woman, you see, that he remarried. Like in a novel or a fairy-tale, this was the proportion of her wickedness. A thief and an adulterer and a climber, socially. And she *hated* me. I was so pretty, of course, and she was *awful*, like a gargoyle or something like this. She beat me whenever he was not looking. But the worst is, we had a summer *palace* almost, in St Petersburg – well, what do you think? She took everything from it when he died, from the paintings, to the cabinets, to the pink English saucers underneath the cups! Everything was sold to the highest bidder, really, this is how it was! These things that were in my family some of them for three hundred years, can you imagine?'

This detail about the saucers, spoken with such horror, made Alex inadvertently smile, and he turned his face to the wall. Indefatigable Kitty carried on talking, dipping her head to one shoulder and then the other to put in a pair of pearl-drop earrings. Alex shut off the shower, and stepped back from its final cold dribble.

'And see that is one of the most precious items, right in front of you,' she said, turning and pointing. 'This is the result of my labours.'

Alex looked at the circular, gold-framed, seventeenth-century miniature resting against the window. Kitty's great-great-great-great-great Russian grandmother, damaged slightly by fire and missing one eye. Kitty had spent these last years paying Max to pay other people to shuttle round Europe retrieving the objects of her childhood.

Alex accepted the towel she passed him.

'And that's where your money went.'

'Of course, where else? I have no champagne, no gigolos. It is odd to me because I always believe I hate my father for marrying this woman, and now I spend my time and all of this money saving his things. Most of them I don't even like. But in its way it is a gesture, I think. You never know, until it happens, what you will owe the dead.'

'Magnified and sanctified,' said Alex loudly, 'be His great name.'

He noted with regret that this last came out in the voice of the popular actor James Earl Jones, a rich basso that often appeared in his throat when he attempted religion. He looked up from his book.

What you owe the dead.

What you owe the dead.

What you owe the dead.

A luminous Hipster girl, with long yellow hair, rucksack and roller-skates, had been flying around the track like a goddess. Now she knelt down three feet away from him to tie her lace. She wore a famous skirt from the eighties. Her knees were scuffed and blue. It seemed deeply unlikely to Alex that she would ever have to figure out how to mourn a father dead for fifteen years in a dead language.

'YITGADAL VE'YITKADASH!' he said, too stridently, and the girl flushed purple, apologized. She rolled away before he could explain. He saw her a few minutes later walking out of the gate in a pair of trainers, a human girl again on two human feet.

2

But rewind: who woke first? Or had they really, as it seemed, woken together, roused by the same curtain-flutter, the stab of intrusive light? Alex had hoped to surprise her in bed, had imagined himself walking in with a tray of fresh OJ and eggs-over-easy, and a flute glass with a single rose and the rest of the movie props, but, as his eyes opened, so did hers. They sat up. And then somehow she was out of her bed before he could stop her ('Can you imagine, at this age, if it is not done immediately it is not done at all!'), and gone. He found her in the kitchen opening a can of sardines for frantic

Lucia, whose tongue lay out of her mouth, panting and curled at the tip.

'Ug,' said Alex, and held his head to stop his brain leaking from his ear.

'Like Karloff, you look,' said Kitty.

They ate boiled eggs and bowls of cereal in the lounge window-seats, and watched a young couple in the brownstone opposite have an argument. Alex took the two paracetamol Kitty had given him and dropped them into the final pool of milk at the end of his muesli.

'You see that she is in a suit,' said Kitty, tapping the window with a knuckle, 'and he is in pyjamas. She is *very* high-flying, in publishing I believe – see, there are books in every corner – and he I always see in bed until the afternoons. Occasionally he sits on a mat for three hours and crosses his legs. Can you imagine! And once a week they have a huge row, and sometimes he makes a pretence of packing bags, but he never goes. But his body is *incredible* . . . so we forgive him, I think.'

'I want you to come to London with me,' said Alex.

Kitty laughed shrilly as if she had been tickled. She stood up to clear away the breakfast things, but he grabbed her hand. She took her seat again and lifted a cool eyebrow.

'What it is you would like me to say to this?'

Alex let go, sulkily set about his cereal again.

'It's just –'

'What is it just?'

'You said you wanted to see Europe again.'

'I would also like to be twenty-six again. But things are not so miraculous.'

Alex looked up, moved towards her and held her elbows. 'Just to get away. From Max, from being stuck in the house all day. It's just a holiday. It's not the end of the world. It's easy. We'll go tonight.'

'You are very sweet,' said Kitty, smiling and standing once more, 'and very unstable. You sound like Trevor Howard or somebody. And everything with you is done at maximum speed. I have known you precisely twenty-four hours. Pass me this and the egg-cup, please.'

Across the road, a huge sash window jerked open and the young lady in the suit thrust her hand out, pointing to the street.

'Out there!' she shouted. 'Out there in the world!'

'Ooh la la,' said Kitty, whistling and heading for the hall. 'And finally it explodes.'

'Listen to me,' said Alex, following her. 'I know you don't have any money. But you *do*, I mean – you could have. So easily. Put that stuff down, wait – just put it down for a second.'

With a good-humoured groan Kitty left her tray on the cabinet. Alex scanned the room for a pen and found one on the mantelpiece. He grabbed an old magazine.

'Just write it here – your name.'

Kitty took the magazine and pen from him and dropped them on the sofa.

'Oh, *Alex*. This is your plan? You think I never think of this? But am I to sell my own autograph, fifty dollars here, there, a stoop sale of my life – Max tells me about this sordid business – I'm sorry, Alex, it is rather too undignified. Look at how I live, alone, eating breakfast with a stranger. My life is quite undignified enough.'

'Wait, *wait*. *Fifty* dollars? Is that what Max told you? He doesn't know what he's *talking* about. I've seen people buy a letter of yours for eight thousand dollars, Kitty. Eight *thousand*.'

And this did stop her. Her mouth opened and closed again. She sat down.

'*Eight?*'

'Eight.'

'This is quite serious, this money. I could do very much with this. And you,' she murmured, looking up at him and tucking a stray wisp of hair behind her ear. 'You are quite serious too, I think.'

Alex sat down by her. 'I thought about it. All night. It makes sense.'

They heard the window across the way close again, and there was something conclusive in it. The end of something over there, the beginning of something over here.

'But what can be done? It must be illegal. And how anyway am I to sell my own –'

'That's what I'm telling you. You don't do anything. I'll do it, all of it. There's nothing dodgy about it. I'll take a percentage, like any agent –'

'Ha! This I hear before, and then they run off with everything –'

'Just 10 per cent, standard. I want to help you –'

'You want to help *somebody*,' she flashed, moving away from him. 'You feel guilty about something, I see it in you – I am a Catholic, I know about guilt also. It gives you the Samaritan disease! I don't want any charity!'

'Right, well, then you can just owe me for the air ticket. Listen to me, please. It's not charity. It's a gift, back to you, for what you've given me. The point here is you could have a nice holiday. Make some money. Then, if you liked, you could live anywhere. You could live in Italy. Anywhere. If we did it right.'

'Lucia, please' – the dog scurried up on to her knees – 'do you listen to this fantastical business! Where do you feature in such a plan, hmm? And then Max – oy! Max would love all of this, no?'

'Max Shmax,' said Alex, and swore colourfully, making Kitty laugh. 'It'll just be a week or so. We'll tell Max when you get back. He won't complain when he sees the money. And if you fly first class – well, how big is Lucia. She'll fit in a bag, won't she?'

Lucia settled into Kitty's lap and made a noise of approval as the extra skin of her neck was kneaded between two attentive fingers.

'Kitty?'

'Yes, I listen, I listen. But it is a lot to be taking in all at once. And what does this mean, doing it right? How would "right" be?'

'Incrementally.'

'This word I don't know.'

'Slowly. In bits. If we flood the market, the value will disappear. We'll sign old photos – we could try dating the ink, even – but most private buyers, they don't even check. And old letters, if you have any. I'll do it through open markets, auctions, on the computer, through agents . . .'

The plan, for Alex, was formulating as he spoke it. The size of it was growing as he spoke it. His own perceived heroism was filling the room like a giant airbag. He couldn't see any way that either of them might be hurt.

3

A late lunch was taken in the piano bar of the hotel. Lovelear and Dove sat on painful stools waiting for two slovenly blonde waitresses to clock off. They had been pleading with these women, Alex was informed, since breakfast. As evidence of this, a stack of empty tissue-lined raffia bowls, soaked in the sweat of thirty chilli-chicken wings, awaited collection. To this, industrious Alex had since added one empty bottle of red wine, three glasses sticky with the residue of whisky, a cocktail that had only managed to save its cherry and a can of beer with a cigarette in it. A dimpled red arm and a sallow pinch of cleavage swung into view, come to collect the ketchup.

'They're something, aren't they?' said Lovelear.

Alex took Lovelear's violent nudge in the ribs silently, and then released a musical burp, for he alone was the Zen Master. He patted his belly. Across the room, a very old gentleman called Mister Martins fatally extended the final chords of 'Some Enchanted Evening' meaning to wring some applause out of what was left of his audience: three drunk men, two waitresses and one bus-boy. Alex clapped, gamely, and with some accuracy, considering. The old guy turned and bowed, only for Alex. Tugging at his raggedy purple tuxedo like a butler. And this is what an audience is, when you get down to it, thought Alex, this gruesome, banal exchange. No-talent applauded by no-taste. Martins closed the lid of his piano with unsteady hands, removed his name card from the top and replaced it with one which said BACK AT 5:30PM! One of Lovelear's waitresses wheeled in an ice sculpture, freshly cut. A heavy-hipped Venus in her shell.

'We're going skating,' said Lovelear, licking round his fingers for fugitive sauce, 'when Della and Maude get off. We're all skating. It's our last afternoon. You're coming. We're skating and then, very quickly, we're getting laid, and then we've got a flight outta here so we're gonna have to love 'em and leave 'em. *Literally*. That's the plan.'

Alex had not told them of his own plan; the thought of Lovelear's redoubtable enthusiasm was too much. And he didn't feel that he could trust either of them to keep quiet. Beyond these two facts, Alex had not progressed. He had booked Kitty on a flight an hour earlier than his own. He meant to drop her off at the airport and then pick her up at the other end. In the interim, as the consultants like to say, skating seemed viable.

'Oh. Fine,' said Lovelear, wrong-footed by lack of resistance. 'Well, you're gonna need a sweater.'

'Fine.'

'And a girl – you can't have ours. Get Honey Smith, and then if our two don't put out, you know, we can always get her to –'

Dove, who adored slapstick, had already begun to snigger as Alex reached into a neighbouring umbrella-stand. Alex pulled out one of the golfing breed and thwacked Lovelear across the shoulders with it.

'You've got dog-mind,' said Alex, still wielding the umbrella, as Lovelear stared at him like cinema. 'Dog-mind. All you do is howl after the moon. Chase your own tail. Thasswhayoudo. That's the dog – see,' stumbled Alex, alcohol flooding his moral high-ground, 'a dog – like this is a dog – and just chasing, chasing, its tail, that's you.'

'Damn right I chase tail,' asserted Lovelear, slipping off his stool and switching all his dead-eyed attention to Della, the fat one, who had just thrown her apron over the bar.

In his room, Alex washed his hands and head. With his hair wet there was something of the Russian monk about him. It fell, the hair, in two black uneven sections, flat against his head, and through this poked his fanatic's ears, pointed and prominent. Unable to improve things, he left the room and went next door.

'Skating?' queried Honey, stepping back from the doorway. 'With you?'

321

'And others, yes.'

'Are you OK? You look funny.'

'Yes. My hair is wet. I'll meet you in the lobby in ten minutes. Bring a jumper.'

'A what?'

'A sweater. The snow keeps coming. Oh, how it comes.'

'Uh-huh. It's a little early to be this drunk, isn't it?'

'No, no, *no*, Mrs Buddhist, let me ask *you* a question. Did you know in a book by a famous Jew someone asks someone what his name is and the person says "Negro"?'

'Excuse me?'

'And here's another question,' said Alex, leaning into the door, 'do you think that because you are a woman of black – no, start again: I mean, a black woman, that I can't understand what you, you know, *are* or something?'

Honey put a rubber finger to his sternum and pushed. 'Do you wanna try moving your breath back a little? Please?'

'Because you know actually as it happens my girlfriend is black. My best-friend is. Too. You know? So. There's that. To consider.'

'Congratulations,' said Honey, smiling. 'Well, I guess it's our last few hours together, *darling*. I'll meet you in the lobby in ten minutes, OK? Try putting your head back in the water again.'

Returning, Alex noticed what he had missed the first time: his room had been returned to its pre-Tandem state. Two days perfectly rewound.

It turned out the girls were not natural skaters. Della was the worse of the two, collapsing spectacularly, every few minutes, into Lovelear, who struggled to put the quaking giggler together again, like a man setting jelly back in its mould. Maude, in Ian's stiff and adulterous arms, lifted each foot as if walking through sludge and let out a birdy screech if ever he tried to coax her from the safety barrier. Honey did not need Alex. A stately skater, she made her way round the circle smoothly and without incident, occasionally executing a turn with a neat flourish. Alex himself sat on the side and smoked a cigarette. The edges of skates are very thin and very sharp, he felt, the opposite of human feet. It takes an optimistic man to put them on. Skating is not to be undertaken lightly.

But there existed pleasures for the non-skater at this rink. Not normally moved by a scene, he was provoked into admiration by this ingenious piece of city planning, up on its hill with panoramic views. It gave to you a sensation you never even knew you wanted: skating on top of the world. From here he could see Roebling. He thought of an open suitcase with Kitty bent over it, folding her dressing gown. He could see the airport, he could see the top of the hotel. Briefly, he considered his mini-bar bill. He could see where the Jews lived and the Poles and the Hispanics and the Blacks and the Russians and the Indians and the Punks and the Lunching Ladies. He could see flags, silk, being carried on the breeze.

Over on the rink, he could see Honey in the centre of a crowd of kids. They were tugging at her. One of them kept putting something long and sharp looking into her face. Alex lifted a hand to see if she was OK, but she waved him off and smiled. Two kids tumbled to the ice and now he could see what she was doing. She was signing. There were about ten of them, arguing over a pen and looking for receipts to write on. It got larger. Husbands came, then wives. She had to skate to the barrier and take them in a messy kind of queue. Alex felt something wet and brought his hand down from the air. On the crease of his lifeline, one of those unlikely snowflakes had landed, the size of a sweet. He watched it melt. Laughed. He laughed

like a loon. Then the trees were kings in ermine, and every building
was an achievement, and the sun was demanding the clouds move,
and light made film stars of everyone, and Della's breasts became
marvels, and the sky grew pink, and Sinatra was singing! Sinatra
was making a list of the things he loved. A fireside. Potato chips.
Good books.

Conditions were favourable. Alex threw his finished cigarette
into a bush, laced his boot and stomped on to the ice. He'd made
barely a step when Honey came behind him and he was away.

'Did you see that?' she asked hotly in his ear.

'I feared for the lives of those children. I thought you were going
to stab them with their own pens.'

'Nah, I decided to give 'em a break. It's just a name,' she said,
guiding the two of them through the arch made by another couple's
stretched arms. 'It's not me. It doesn't take from me. It's just ink.'

'That's very enlightened of you, Miss Richardson.'

'I thought so. Now. Mr Tandem. If you were staying in town, this
could be the beginning of a beautiful friendship, don't you think?'

After that they took one more revolution perfectly, uninterrupted, performing that fantasy of flight. Both knew this was their
version of goodbye and the bottom line is there was something
godly in it and here is Alex's (partial) list:

Sinatra's voice between 1948 and 1956
Donald O'Connor's right foot
The old route to school on a March morning
The letter א
Being inside her with her legs crossed round my hips
People falling over
Jokes

Overweight cats
Food
The films of Kitty Alexander
Relationships that do not involve blood or other fluids
Tobacco
Telling children that all life is suffering
Alcohol
God
Smell of cinnamon
Esther

4

Last call. That ominous point where only the right piece of paper will let you go a step further.

'Now,' she said, holding his chin, 'you will be there, this you promise me.'

'I'll be there. An hour later. I'll be there.'

'An hour, can you imagine? What is one to do in an airport for an hour?'

'Watch people come,' suggested Alex. 'Watch people go.'

Kitty shuddered. 'This I've seen plenty, including the version where they don't come back.'

Alex gave Kitty a kiss on her powdery forehead. She smelt of theatrical make-up. She was dressed in a red suit with diamonds in her ears and a sparkle of green on her eyelids. Her hair was curled. Inside her holdall, even Lucia had a nice tartan jacket. The two of them are from that age when travel was still performance.

'Poor Lucia. In a bag for seven hours. It is indecent for a lady to travel this way.'

'She'll be all right,' said Alex, sneaking a hand in to stroke Lucia's back. 'Just keep her quiet.'

'Max has probably already called the police department. He will think the stalker take me away to rape me or something crazy.'

'I'll deal with Max,' said Alex, and, without any confidence in this final proposition, kissed her once more and said goodbye.

An hour later a piece of good luck befell him: he got bumped up to business class. He had never been there before, and, though he understood he was meant to take it with good humour, something about it terrified him. The *effort* that had been taken. And all to identify and assert a few tiny differences: between orange juices, serviettes (cotton or paper), thickness of blanket, sharpness of pencil. The distinctions between coach and business class seemed to him worldly manifestations of the goyish conception of heaven. Which is a place for the kind of child who exults in his own lofty tower of ice cream the instant his friend's cone falls to the ground.

On the other hand, in business class you got phones. Alex swept his credit card through one and at a rate of nine dollars a minute listened to Esther tell him that while she was being operated on, during a lucid spell, she had felt his father's presence at the end of her bed.

'I s'pose,' she said, her voice almost unrecognizable, weak, 'that sounds completely mental.'

Alex was silent. Esther had her moments of what she called 'spirituality', which ranged from inconstant trust in back-page star signs all the way to creative discussions with her African ancestors via poetry. In this area, Alex kept his counsel. He was barely capable of faith. Confronted with spiritualism, he found only humour.

'Go on,' she said. 'Say it. Whatever it is.'

'No, I . . . nothing. Just. *My* father? Not *your* father?'

'Your father. He was holding my feet.'

'Right, because he was a big foot-holder in life, feet were a very important –'

'Oh, forget it. Forget it. Look, I can't raise my voice, I'm all bruised. I've got to go.'

A stewardess brought her face very close to Alex's and asked if he wanted cocoa.

'Esther, wait. Wait. When are you getting out?'

'Morning. Soon. I'm ready. I want to get out.'

'I've got something huge to tell you.'

'Save it for tomorrow. I've got a load of stitches to show you. We can play Show and Tell. Where are you anyway?'

'Direct course to Mountjoy. I'm flying over water. In the event of a crash, what do you think's a better chance – water or land?'

'Alex, what's wrong with you? Touch wood right now.'

'None about – I'm in business, it's all high-tech. Flash.'

'Touch it.'

'OK, OK, chill. How about wood derivative?'

'That'll do.'

Alex touched his menu, from which he had the choice of five kinds of mushroom.

SEVEN / *The Bull Transcended*

I

It was a three-seater couch, covered in red velvet. Rabbi Darvick held one end and Rabbi Green the other, the two of them in lively conversation. As Alex approached, they positioned the thing squarely in front of Mountjoy's war memorial, placed it on the ground and sat on it.

'And of course, the marvel is they did it all indoors,' Rabbi Green was saying, pointing at the busy road. 'The whole street made from scratch!'

It was Darvick who spotted Alex first. He stood up to shake his hand.

'Tandem! Home! What a city, right? So! Good morning, or should I say' – he looked at a bare patch on his wrist – 'good afternoon?'

'Where's Rubinfine?' asked Alex, looking around.

'As a matter of fact, the Rabbi has taken the car to run an errand for *you*,' said Green, and from his sitting position he seized Alex's hand, which Alex did not withdraw quickly enough. 'He's gone to the Mulberry Road synagogue to talk to Rabbi Burston. About Thursday. And how things shall proceed.'

'He didn't have to do that,' said Alex irritably. 'I could have done that.'

'Yes, of course,' said Green, smiling. 'Only you didn't.'

The clock above the station struck noon, and an unruly crocodile of schoolboys passed under it. The trees, newly cut back, thrust their twisted fists into the air. Alex could see that it was Mountjoy, only it was outlined and strange to him, more sharply defined, as if he had just left an optician.

'You look bad,' said Darvick, whistling. 'Jet-lag. Better sit down for a moment.'

'Actually, I'm just nipping to the shops –'

'Sit down a moment, *please*,' said Green, and patted a space on the sofa between him and Darvick. Alex complied, but sat cross-legged and kept his eyes set on his feet.

'We – Rabbi Green and I – we will be joining the minyan on Thursday evening, did you know that?' said Darvick, placing a hand on Alex's knee. 'As will many of your friends. At every side, familiar faces.'

'That's great,' said Alex, trying to remember the brand of dog food Kitty had sent him out for. 'Really. I appreciate it a lot, because, you know, a minyan with less than ten people, it's not really on. It's not kosher. As I understand it. So, thanks. Tell Rubinfine thanks.'

'It's much better than that other stuff, for you,' said Darvick, in a conspiratorial whisper. '*This* is true faith. This is getting something *done*.'

'Yes. I see that,' said Alex, rising to go.

'Living,' said Green, his voice gaining the pitch of quotation, 'is the little that is left over from dying. Do you know the poet?'

'I don't read poetry, Rabbi. I can't find the time.'

'Attend to the dead,' said Green, in a quite different, frosty tone.

'I'll do what's required of me,' said Alex, with equal froideur.

'And how's that book of yours?' inquired Darvick, very jolly in his voice, but unmoving in every other way. 'The one about this is the opposite of that, yada yada, and so on.'

'I got tired of it, finished it,' said Alex, performing a mock salute before walking away.

Back indoors, he passed her a coffee and apologized once again for his flat.

'In Iran,' said Kitty brightly, 'I live in a tent for three weeks. In Ethiopia, a building made out of nothing, of animal waste! You don't know but I am a great traveller. When the movies were finished I drag my third husband around the globe from boredom. Your bedroom is no great adventure, believe me. The only thing we want to know, Lucia and I, is the whereabouts of this famous cat of yours.'

'I can't explain to you,' said Alex, taking the seat opposite her, getting her in frame, 'how bizarre it is, to have you sitting there. Right there. Just *there*.'

Kitty drew her legs up into her armchair and shook her head. 'What is bizarre? Think of it like a grandmother comes to stay. And now, please, stop this avoidance – where is this Jewish cat? You talk about her so vigorously in the taxi! I sense the possibility,' she said, nodding at Lucia, busy running a frenzied circle round the coffee table after a broken-necked cloth mouse of Grace's, 'of a friendship between opposites, ying and yang, which is something –'

But here the telephone in the hall demanded attention, and Kitty, with adamant hands, motioned him out of the room.

'*Alex*,' said Adam's voice, as if he had found him in a maze.

'Back. And in time. We're having lunch. Joseph's on his way from the office to pick you up.'

'Joseph? What? No, I can't go for lunch, Ads – I'm busy. I'm completely – no, look – can I call you later, or something?'

Three thuds came through the earpiece, Adam striking his phone against the table in frustration.

'Hello? Mr Gaylord? No, you can't call me later. It's lunch. It's a summit meeting, I've called it – and everyone's coming. Including Grace – you've got to pick her up, we've had enough of each other. It's too late anyway, Joseph'll be at yours any minute –'

'No, Ads, listen, I can't – lunch is just not – I've got to – well, see Esther, apart from anything –' began Alex, and had the unpleasant realization that this was the first time he had considered her since he landed.

'She's napping at home. Let her sleep. Come to lunch.'

'Look, a sort of thing has happened. I've got to talk to you –'

'You're talking to me.'

'In person.'

'Then come to bloody lunch!'

The phone switched to its humiliating monotone.

'Go, of course,' said blushing Kitty, the second he appeared at the door. 'Go to lunch. I am so jet-lagged I was soon to excuse myself, anyway. Please, go, go. Take Lucia – she goes crazy for a walk. She is terribly overexcited.'

Compulsively apologizing, Alex gripped the banister and watched Kitty climb the stairs. Lucia, scuttling behind her, got halfway up before he grabbed her round her middle, pressed her to his chest and with one hand held her mouth shut.

'Just so. Be a man with her, otherwise she does not take seriously anything. Her lead is hanging from the banister.'

The doorbell, in which the battery was coming loose, gave out its strangulated whine.

'Whose dog is that?' asked Joseph. He wore a grey suit with a long black coat and a black briefcase. His hair was slicked back, he was absolutely clean-shaven. He looked like an undertaker.

'Mine,' said Alex, affixing the lead. 'I felt it was time. For a dog.'

'Interesting decision,' said Joseph, closing the door behind them. 'Good to see you both. What's his name?'

'Endelmann.'

'Pretty.'

Joseph walked down the path and opened the front gate. 'Come on, Endelmann, let's go, there's a good boy.'

The three of them crossed the street.

'Surprise,' said Joseph without inflection, and walked directly to the driver's side of a perfectly beautiful red MG. He put his key in the lock.

Alex picked Lucia up, pressing his and the dog's head up to the window.

'Joseph, whose car is this?'

'Yours,' replied Joseph, opening the door. He paused, looked up and over Alex's head. 'Alex, who's that old woman at your window?'

'You know . . .' said Alex vaguely, waving back to Kitty, who was waving at Lucia. 'Mum's mum. Like, my grandmother. Whose car is this?'

'Yours. Shall we go round one more time or is that enough?'

'Fixed?' murmured Alex, stepping back from it as Lucia dived to the ground and sniffed the wheels.

'No, new. Adam is a prophet. He insured the old one three weeks ago, with me, at Heller's. He didn't tell you because he wanted you to stew for a while. And he got this relatively cheap, I understand, so there's some money left over. For a religious man he has a business nose. I'm going to drive it, you take shotgun – jet-lag and heavy machinery don't go. We'll have the top down, don't you think? And rap music, yes?'

'It's immoral, of course,' said Alex a few minutes later, as they passed down Mountjoy's high street to appreciative looks. 'The whole idea of insurance. Things break. People die. It's paganism, basically; insurance is like this mystic rite we throw at the inevitable.'

'You're wrong. Part of the inevitable,' said Joseph, taking a right turn, 'is the need for compensation. It's a sin to get it, but an act of faith to want it. That's where God is. In the wanting.'

'But it's still a lie,' said Alex stubbornly.

'It's a moment of grace, like your health, or a woman. It's not yours by right – it's a loan, a partial repayment on the everyday misery.'

'Where are we going?' asked Alex, grumpy and out of practice as far as a Jewish argument was concerned.

The rapper on the stereo explained how he felt about The Real. He was attached to it. He'd never give it up.

Alex put his foot on Lucia's backside to make her sit still down there. 'Why lunch anyway?'

'Russian restaurant in the East. Lunch because it's been a while, I suppose. Because you wait for one and three come along at once. Because Adam's learning Russian. Because if it doesn't rain, it pours. Etc.'

'It'd be nice to get a bit of forewarning. Instead of being bloody *summoned*. How's Boot?' Alex asked cruelly, and looked away. Joseph blushed.

'There was never any progression,' he said quietly. 'I wrote her a few letters. The more I write, the less physical resolve I seem to have. I've only embarrassed myself in that department, if that pleases you.'

''Course it doesn't *please* me,' muttered Alex, suddenly ashamed. 'Seems a pity, really. She's nice, Boot. What *is* it, anyway, with you and women? Never seems to get off the ground.'

To this there was no reply. Alex turned a little in his seat and watched the walking people get sucked backwards into where they had just been. Lucia yapped.

'I don't know what's been wrong with you and me lately,' said Alex at last. 'You've been acting . . . just weirdly.'

Joseph smiled bitterly. He tapped his fingers on the leather wheel.

'We've turned into abstractions of each other, it's obvious,' he said, rather high-handedly. 'We fear each other as symbols of one thing or another. We don't tell the truth.'

'Look, it's *exactly* that sort of thing,' said Alex, exasperated, 'that's just what I'm talking about. I don't know what you mean. Part of the problem is the way you express yourself. We used to be friends. There was none of . . . this. It used to be easy, between us.'

'I used to be an Autograph Man,' said Joseph coolly, adjusting his wing mirror. 'And that dog has no male genitalia. And your grandmother died the day the Germans marched into Paris.'

He turned his eyes completely from the road to look at Alex.

'Well, I think you resent me,' said Alex evenly, not looking back, brazening the moment out, 'because I don't suffer like you or something. Specially recently. You've completely had it in for me, like I'm being judged. And punished. I feel like you're furious at me for being able to do this thing, to do this thing that I *love*, well, at least, if I don't exactly love it, you know . . . it's something I can tolerate. And I know you loved to do it, I mean it was you who *started* me – and now you're stuck in that office. But that's not my *fault*, Joe. That's not my bloody *fault*.'

One of Alex's words hung infuriatingly in the air as surely as if he had placed it in a cartoon bubble. And now Joseph took one hand off the wheel and laid it speculatively over Alex's, restoring, with this one touch, a knowledge Alex had possessed from the beginning. A responsibility he had never wanted, never been equal to.

'It's the opposite of resentment,' said Joseph, in a low, breaking voice. 'It's *wonder*. You don't see it. You have the *power* with things. I document the acts of God. I give out the insurance when things mess up. But you're *in* the world, with things. You sell them, you exchange them, you deal with them, you identify them, name them, categorize them' – Alex freed his hand and slapped the dashboard in protest, amazed, like most people, by another man's laudatory description of the accident we call our lives – 'you write a bloody *book* about them. I'm sort of horrified by it, actually – you're so determined to shape what to me is fundamentally without any shape – and the joke is, you don't even realize it. You always go on about despair, but you don't even know what colour it is. You have Esther, apart from anything else. You *have* someone. Try,' said Joseph, with a choking laugh, 'fifteen years of unrequited.'

'There are a million other girls in the –'

'Unrequited,' repeated Joseph loudly. 'For a man who barely knows you're alive. Try that.'

They stopped at the traffic lights. The larger part of Alex had always stood resistant to any story in which he was not the victim, but now the stone rolled away from the mouth of the cave and he looked in. An indigo parade of memories went by with the cross traffic, snapshots of a passionate, difficult friendship, performed almost entirely in gesture over the years (as two boys in a red bathroom, bent over a sink full of developing photographs; as teenagers, pressing up against the purple velvet rope outside a cinema, clutching the brass posts, waiting for a star; as men, turning simultaneously the pages of two green leather-bound albums, exchanging this for that and back again). In all these reminiscences Joseph seemed in the edge of the frame, with his hands open, waiting for something to come to him. All that had happened these last few years was that the gestures grew further apart, less frequent and, consequently, more violent. Photographs to end the film.

'This has been,' said Alex, bowing his head, 'the weirdest week of my life.'

Joseph let out that awful, mirthless laugh that had begun to belong to him. 'It's fantastic – it's melodrama. It's wasted on *you*, though. If only you knew how to dress for it. *Mr De Mille, I'm ready for my close –*'

'But it's so masochistic, Klein,' blurted Alex, feeling now the full sadness of it. 'To choose *me*. Of all people.'

'That's one thing, Tandem,' said Joseph, pressing down on the pedal with a dull smile, 'that you have never been. From the day I met you, however buggered you were, you were always looking for pleasure, not pain.'

'See, that's it again, that really irritates me – like I don't suffer, so I'm the goy, I'm the putz –'

'No,' said Joseph passionately, 'I never said that, never felt it. Life is a negation already. It's pointless and vain to negate the negation. *I'm* vain. Adam said from the start –'

'Adam knows?'

'Adam guessed. He sees everything. He knew when we were kids. He said I need to find somebody else to love, that's all. It's not an accident. It's a decision I made, he says. A vain decision to suffer.'

A car in front of them slowed to almost a halt, and Joseph turned again to look at Alex, who couldn't quite bear it. Both their eyes moved stupidly to the dog.

'How about Endelmann. He need any? Love?'

Alex wished to all the gods he knew that Joseph would stop saying that word.

He pulled Lucia up on to his lap, where she proceeded to eat the leather ball of the gear-stick.

'I would say he's over-indulged, actually.'

'Shame,' said Joseph, pulling a hand through his hair and exhaling everything. 'Okaaay,' he sighed. 'Done, done, done. That's enough for one day, I should think. Let's try to concentrate. Look out for the signs now. We're looking for anything that says To the East.'

2

'That?' said Joseph, slipping into the crescent booth. 'That is Endelmann. The eunuch.'

'Does he want to meet Grace?' queried Adam, pushing a cat-box with his foot from under the table. 'Or is he the replacement?'

Rubinfine squeezed up to let Alex in on his left. He was wearing a pair of tight jeans, gruesome in their restrictions, and a jumper advertising the 1989 Mountjoy Israeli Dance Championships in which he met Rebecca and took third place.

'Am I just being an *appalling* cultural philistine,' Rubinfine asked the assembled, 'or can I mention that there's a raw egg floating in this soup?'

'*Alex*,' said Adam, and reached impetuously across the table. Alex gave him his hands.

'Ads. How *are* you?'

'Good. You look good, man. I think you're going to like this restaurant. The waiters are real Russians. I don't think they ever had a person of the Negro persuasion in here before. I ordered the starters – one of them almost fell in the bortsch when I opened my mouth – oh, look, here we are; OK, OK, beer, is it? Beer, Joseph? Izvinitye . . . da, OK, dva botillky peevo, pojalsta . . . spasibo, spasibo, da. So,' he said turning back to the table, 'are we ready for Thursday?'

'The car, Ads . . .' began Alex, but had to end there with just a smile.

Adam shrugged. 'The car is the car. The important thing is we're going to do this thing on Thursday, and it's going to be wicked – really, just *great* – everything's organized, you just have to turn up – we don't even have to talk about it, we can just sit here and drink the vodka. OK? Is that cool?'

Alex nodded and picked a hunk of bread from a grubby china bowl, rimmed with the flaking gold-leaf pattern that appeared on every single item in the room. He took a bite from the bread and then held it up with a question as to its Russian name.

Adam made a ridiculous explosion in his throat.

'Why are you learning this language? There's so much *phlegm* involved,' asked Rubinfine with distaste. He passed his full soup-bowl back to a passing waiter.

'Rubinfine,' said Alex, feeling a rush of goodwill and thumping him on the back, 'long time. So, I hear I owe you. Thanks for

organizing . . . well, Green and Darvick told me you've been working behind the scenes, etc. Rabbi Burston, is that right?'

'I do what I can,' said Rubinfine piously, lowering his head back
and inadvertently knocking it lightly against a giant samovar. 'He's
meant to be at a wedding that day, he's very in demand – it wasn't
easy. Favours had to be offered.'

Adam, never the sort of man to waste much time with table
etiquette, put his butter knife into a little pot of iridescent fish eggs
and delivered a line of them on to his tongue.

'Oh, *good*,' he said with relief, 'I'm glad you don't mind about
Rabbi Burston – I mean, not that there's any reason to mind, really
– and it's a bit of a schlep to get to, but no one in Mountjoy was
really available, and he is progressive, so the women thing wasn't
an issue, and we've to be grateful to him for doing it at short notice
and all that.'

Joseph seemed to suppress a giggle, and Alex, who was in the
process of freeing Grace from her box, looked up.

'Mind? What's there to mind?'

'*Exactly*, nothing, really – I knew you'd see it like that. Joseph,
get that waiter, man – we're going to need to get the dog something
to eat other than the cat.'

Grace was circling Alex's lap, one paw trailing to goad Lucia.
Now she stretched up and licked Alex's nose with her tiny coarse
tongue.

'I don't get you. Is there something wrong with Burston?'

'But didn't Green? Or –'

Here a waiter with an epic jaw came and pleaded with Adam in
Russian, pointing sporadically at the animals.

'Ooh-litsa,' murmured Adam, as the waiter turned on his heel
and marched back towards the kitchens. 'That's definitely "street".'

I really want to know what the long word was, though – I think it might have been zoo, or menagerie, as in, *this is not a –*'

'Adam, what's wrong with Rabbi Burston?'

'Nothing, really,' said Joseph, his sorrowful dark eyes taking on some of the mischievousness of his boyhood. 'I met him on Sunday at the barn-dance and he seemed really capable, interesting. I had a conversation with him about Preston Sturges, he was really interesting on that, about Jewish subtexts in Hollywood film of the era, really sharp, I thought –'

'What was he doing at the barn-dance?'

'Do you know what he said to me, Al?' said Adam, wiping his mouth with a napkin. 'We were having the old Kabbalah debate, but he said this one fantastic thing: *God is a verb*. He said, I'll agree with you on one thing – God is a verb. That's *great*, isn't it?'

'The man can also line-dance,' said Joseph. 'Honest to God. He danced everybody else off the –'

'He's a midget, isn't he?' concluded Alex, letting his chin fall to his chest.

The table went quiet.

'No, actually, his growth is –' began Rubinfine, but Alex held a hand up to stop him.

'How tall? Come on, how tall?'

'Very reasonable, mate, really,' said Adam, looking concernedly across the room at the approach of the earlier waiter and a man with a managerial forehead. 'I don't think he's much under, like, four-six?'

Lucia ran to greet the manager, licking his shoes that smelt of the kitchen. A scene followed. Adam begged them all to stick to Russian, this being great conversational practice for him, but the manager's face took on that look of undiluted pessimism concerning the rationality of others, a look that is every Russian's birth-right. With a shake of his wrist, he turned away a second waiter, who was heading for their table with his high-held tray of beer and blintzes.

'And it is now,' he said, exercising the foreigner's clout with the present tense, 'that I am asking you to leave.'

'It'll be like a feature,' offered Joseph, once they were out on the street. 'You know. No one's likely to forget it. It'll be memorable.'

'It's not a garden pond,' said Alex stiffly, taking Grace's box from him. 'It's Kaddish. I don't want any features. I'm not likely to forget it, am I? I mean, am I? Really?'

'I'm so glad to hear you say that,' said Adam, linking arms with him, pointing in the direction of other lunch possibilities.

It started to rain hard. After two restaurants refused to be arks, the sheen rubbed off lunch somehow. Joseph had to get back to work, Rubinfine wanted to buy a pair of those socks with the friction soles.

'Am I being forsaken?' asked Adam, shaking his little dreads of water.

'Can I give you a lift?' said Alex, opening the door of –

'Hey,' he said, putting Grace on the seat, 'I need a new name. It's a new car.'

'Kitty. She was always Kitty. She was only Greta because you're afraid of being obvious. Nothing wrong with the obvious. It's sustaining.'

'Oi, don't start. It's raining. Lift or no?'

'No,' said Adam, drawing his coat over his head like a panto-mime hunchback. 'I think I'm heading other way, library. I'll get the tube. Tell Esther I'll be back late.'

Alex got behind the wheel and wondered why he hadn't told him.

3

Opening the front gate for Lucia, he saw a curtain twitch. He was halfway up the path when Anita Chang came down it, clutching a handbag in front of her, a clumsy prop meant to encourage the misconception that she was just on her way out.

'Alex!' she said without pleasure.

'Anita,' he said without hope.

'And how did you find New York?'

'Pilot knew the way.'

Her fixed smile flat-lined.

'*Your* dog?'

'*A* dog.'

'A dog that belongs to you?'

'A new dog in town. Visiting friends in the area. Trying out,' said Alex, as Lucia attacked a patch where Anita was growing daffodils, 'the local cuisine.'

'I see.'

'And I hear. And Endelmann, that's the dog, he touches. Grace smells, but you know that. We find someone with taste, we could make a band.'

Taking off his coat in the hallway, Alex heard two voices together, two opposite voices, and from such extreme poles of his mind that for a moment his brain refused to reconcile them. And then, at the threshold of the living room, the obvious stated itself: these were not voices from his brain at all but two people in the world, living. He had no business reconciling them.

'Hey, stranger,' said Esther.

She was stretched out on the floor before Kitty, dressed unseasonably in cream-coloured culottes and a thin, red cashmere vest.

'This,' she said, lifting up on one hip, 'is the most amazing woman in the world.'

Kitty reached forward and rubbed her freshly shaved head.

'She listens to my stories, this is all. I think she likes them. I tell her all about our meeting in New York, and your tall American friend, *Harvey*,' said Kitty, very pleased with this basic subterfuge. 'But, *Alex*, you never explain she was like this, such a beauty! To look at her causes disaster – I am surprised you survive.'

'Barely,' said Esther quietly, and with a smile, trying to give him a private look. He turned away.

'What is this?' asked Kitty, cupping her ear.

'She said barely,' said Alex bluntly. He felt that mad cold one sometimes feels upon seeing an absent loved one, a kind of dysrecognition: is this really her? Are we really lovers? Is this where I put all of my life? Does she know me? Do I –

'Tea,' he said, and left the room.

In the kitchen he put the kettle on and placed both hands on the sideboard.

'Are you angry?'

He turned and saw her in the doorway.

'No, Es, of course not. 'S just –'

She folded her arms.

'It's nothing. It's just I haven't even told *Adam*. And it's a bit much, all at once. Seeing you and . . . Look, are you OK? How's your finger?'

'Cast off. Fine. It was just a fracture, really.'

'And? . . .'

'Bruised, that's all.' She put her hand to her chest and pressed it softly. 'They did a really good job. Put everything back where they found it. *Alex*,' she said, putting her hands behind her head and opening her eyes wide. 'Kitty Alexander is sitting in your living room. In *your* living room.'

'Yeah, I know.'

'Well, is it a secret? Aren't you going to tell Adam? I mean – *Jesus*, man – what's she *doing* here? In *Mountjoy*?'

'Es, please, *please*,' he said, reaching for her like a blind man, 'let me just – can we talk about all that later? I mean, can I get a kiss or something? I've *missed* you.'

'Oh, come here,' she said at last. He walked forward and she enfolded him in her rangy arms. 'I don't understand – you should be over the moon. What's *wrong* with you?'

'Almost everything?'

The smell was as ever: cocoa butter, a perfume she had used since college and the aftershave she put on her head.

'Al, I've been talking to her all afternoon. She's just *amazing*. Did you know,' she said, between kisses, 'that she went to bed with Clark Gable and Carole Lombard? At the same *time*?'

'Hmm . . . That's a lot of movie star in one bed. Kiss me over here.'

'But – I don't understand – I mean, how does it *feel*?' she said, her plum lips buzzing each word on his earlobe. 'She's *here*, you met her. Ever since I've *known* you you've wanted –'

'Come to bed with me,' he murmured, pushing one hand past her culottes and some aggressive knicker elastic. 'It's just me, but we would call some actors . . .'

'Alex, stop it . . . She's so much *nicer* than I imagined? She seems such a *diva* in the films, but she's so *normal*. She's just incredibly frank, and she's a feminist – really, I'm telling you, man, she's *inspirational*. The things she says – I could listen to her *all – Alex!*'

His middle finger had been trying to get past cotton so it could touch her there. She drew back from him and straightened her clothes.

'Look, I'm going to go back in there. It's too rude to leave her there alone. And also – *please* tidy your room properly. You can't put her in there like that. There's rubbish everywhere. She's a freaking *movie star*. Actually, I can't *believe* it,' said Esther, losing her control, breaking into her awesome smile, the flash-bulb eyes, 'Kitty Alexander. Kitty Alexander! Kit-ty-Al-ex-and-*er*. In your living room. In *your* living room. It's *surreal*.'

'Yes,' said Alex, unable to feel it.

She kissed him on the nose. Ten years is a long time to have the same person kissing you in the same places, but he still felt some portion of the thrill. And the gratitude.

'Oi,' he said, as she turned to leave. 'You've seen my news. I want to see yours. We had a deal, didn't we?'

She stopped, and he approached, taking the vest by its ragged edge and lifting it slowly over her head. As her arms lifted to help him, the box lurched forward, pushing at the skin. He could see stitches and the outline of a wire. He took one hand to her right breast, one to this new heart. The kettle knew how to whistle.

Fact. Women have an endless capacity for anecdote. Men prefer jokes and stories. Alex didn't mind any of the above, as long as he was doing the telling, but Kitty and Esther had set off, before he arrived, on their open-topped bus, on their nostalgia tour. They rolled round the deserted sound stages of old studio lots, the penthouses of closed hotels. They did not pause, and there was no opportunity for Alex to get on board. His exit from the room, after a pronounced sulk, went unnoticed. Only when he returned five minutes later to requisition Grace did he get some attention.

'Oh,' complained Kitty, 'but she and Lucia, they are in love.'

Alex grabbed a disinclined Grace, shoving her head through his armpit. 'She likes it upstairs with me. She likes watching me work.'

'*Work?*' asked Esther, laughing. He glowered, disliking her when she was like this, performing, he felt, for somebody else's benefit.

'Preparation,' was his curt reply.

'You will call?' suggested Kitty, hopefully stretching her arms up in expectation of a hug like an aunt. 'Maybe you will call Max for me. Just to say I am all right. I leave the number on the noticeboard in the kitchen. Call him, I think. Make sure he is not angry with me.'

'Sure,' said Alex, stepping back and closing the door behind him.

Upstairs, Alex picked up the case from his trip and emptied the contents on to the bed. The clothes he lifted in one stinking bundle and dropped into the bathroom's washing basket. Books he put on the floor and then kicked into a reasonable pile in a corner. He filed through the paper by hand, throwing every other piece of it into the bin including all receipts, for he had long ago decided that he would rather pay the tax in full than allow himself to be the type of man who remembers a beautiful day by the expenses he ran up on it.

A dealer's card. A Playboy Bunny's signature. A ticket to skate. A yellow envelope. Alex takes out the stalker's letter and rereads it. Poor, crazy Max. But Alex is compelled by the tone; there is something in it that he recognizes. Great love, adoration, yes. But also cauterized resentment. It is a quality present in Alex's own letters too, although there it is better disguised. He didn't realize it at first. And then an epiphany when he was still a teenager, one very rainy première, stuck against an iron barrier, soaking wet, watching the French actress he had come to see sweep down a red carpet under a giant umbrella, without giving him a second glance. He had written up the incident in his book under the subheading: 'Jewish Fame and Goyish Fanhood'.

Groupies hate musicians. Movie-goers hate movie stars. Autograph Men hate celebrities. We love our gods. But we do not love our subjection.

Alex sat down and switched on the box of tricks. He made a quick mental list, to be expanded later, of the various auctions in the ether he would put Kitty on. Back in New York, she had given him access to eight cardboard boxes of her private correspondence with the proviso that he could take anything he liked except letters to her family. As far as the other material was concerned, she was entirely unsentimental. On his desk now sat a selection of love letters. She had had an affair with a famous actor, his widow had returned her letters when he died. And talk about content! In one she describes a Vegas hotel room, early in the morning, with yet another lover, a black actor. She remembers the colour of the uniform the maid wore when she came in unannounced and spat on their duvet. Alex didn't really dare to think how much such a thing would be worth, how much all of them were worth. From New York he had already sent a bundle of four to his London auction house. They would be sold tomorrow. He barely allowed himself the transcendent mental picture of sitting there in front of everyone with the Autograph Scoop of the century.

It was not the money that excited him. Not entirely the money. He told himself it was the joy of giving a gift, a gift back to Kitty,

EIGHT / *Both Bull and Self Transcended*

I

It had been a wonderful night, that was the tragedy of it. Nirvana should be judged not by the quality of vulgar passions but by the subsequent repose, and they had slept together beautifully, curled around each other on the sofa as if they were part of its design. He awoke with his face at home in the cleft of her shoulder blade, his hair stuck to her skin. He was happy! Daylight swelled behind a closed blind. He squeezed her waist, kissed the back of her neck. This was happiness! But then she stretched, and her hand found its way into a fault-line in the sofa.

'What's this?'

'Hmm? What's what?'

She drew it out with theatrical slowness. In the half-light it seemed to Alex that she was skinning a snake.

'Alex, whose are these?'

Alex opened his mouth.

'Don't say Kitty's,' said Esther firmly, and, with that, their closeness was over, she was ripped from him, suddenly sitting up. 'They're fishnets. Old women don't wear fishnets.'

And that was a fact.

'Es, wait –'

She swore quietly, expressively, and grabbed the remote control. The TV trembled into life, almost cautious to intrude. She put on her underwear. A talking piece of furniture willingly filled the sound-gap, one of its most useful functions. Alex opened his mouth.

'And please,' said Esther, ramming her feet into her shoes, even before her trousers were on, 'don't use the phrase *innocent explanation*. Or, *she's just a friend*. Don't tell me you'd *never do anything to hurt me*. Please. Please try not to say anything you've heard on television.'

In the middle of the East a man had boarded a bus with a bomb pressed to his navel. In Parliament a man accused another man of deceit. A child was missing. Her parents rocked and gulped and couldn't finish their sentences. 'Do you think you can *play it out*?' she asked. She had those tears, waiting. She stood in front of the screen. He didn't know what she meant by these words. He knew, however, what her body meant, naked except for knickers and shoes. Those fierce bulges that were her thigh muscles: she could walk away. She would.

'There will never be that moment, don't you get it?' she asked, punching the arm of the sofa. 'When you've had all the different people you want, when you're done, when you *settle* for me. People don't *settle* for people. They resolve to be with them. It takes faith. You draw a circle in the sand and you agree to stand in it and believe in it. It's *faith*, you idiot.'

A musical was closing. Various songs would never be sung again on this stage.

'And so,' said the television, 'after five thousand performances –'

'Boot,' offered mumbling Alex, sitting below her in apish pose, hairy, limp, hands hanging to the floor. 'The one from before. 'Cept it's not happening any more. She slept here, that's all.'

'I see,' said Esther.

The ceiling was thin. From upstairs, they could hear Kitty's brisk steps, followed by Lucia's, like a stutter. Esther was getting dressed as if it were a fight she was having with her clothes.

'Es, calm down – for one minute –'

'My dear –' came Kitty's voice from the landing. 'Esther, I wonder if you could help me, possibly, just for a minute? It is a little awkward – Lucia, stop this, please – *Esther!*'

With one shoe on and one in her hand, Esther pushed by Alex and started on the stairs. Grace, whose support Alex had hoped for, waited an indecent ten seconds before following her up.

Alex turned back to the television. He sat on the floor and tried to achieve *vajrasana* posture, but, short of breaking and resetting his bones, he couldn't see how this might be achieved. Instead, he settled for half-lotus. He found a hairy mint in the carpet and began to suck it. The news turned financial. Numbers went by on a ticker-tape. Alex closed his eyes and tried to remember the rules of meditation.

  1. Sit quietly in the meditation posture.
Yes, thought Alex, yes, got that. Yes, and I'm bloody sat quietly. So? Next. *Next.*

  2. Become aware of being in the present, here and now, and relax into this space.
Relax into the here and now? Relax *into* it? But I'm in it, aren't I? That's what I'm *doing*, I'm bloody in the present, bloody relaxing. *Christ.*

3. Resolve to let go of your thoughts, fantasies about the future, nostalgia about the past, mulling over problems, etc.

Finally, something you could get your teeth into. Alex opened one eye, stretched one arm and grabbed the end of a bottle of red sitting on the coffee table. He polished it off and resumed the position. *I am resolving*, he thought, *to let go of my thoughts*.

'And now finally . . .' said the television.

Alex tried to rid himself of all nostalgia about the past. Every time he felt nostalgic about the past, he had to begin his breathing again as punishment, starting from one and counting to ten on the exhale. As a result, he was close to hyperventilation.

'Alex,' came Esther's voice, 'Alex, stop that, it's a pain. Look, I've got to get to college, but you need to buy a separate towel for Kitty – she's got nothing clean up there – Alex, I'm talking to you. Will you stop that, please? You sound like a bloody . . .' Esther's voice disappeared. When it came back, Alex couldn't locate it in the room. It had become a whisper.

'Oh my *God*,' she said.

'Died peacefully in New York last night . . .' said the television.

'Alex, Alex – *open your eyes* – Alex, look at this! Are you *listening* to this?'

Alex felt a kick in his flank, but refused to allow it to break his concentration. Because Alex-Li Tandem was a Zen Master. *I am letting go*, thought Alex, *of my fantasies about the –*

Meanwhile, the television, well aware of the median age of its viewers, spent barely a minute on this new death, 152,460th of the day. Here is a picture of the actress when young:

Here is one of the men she loved (he is broken now, and on wheels):

Here is the most famous moment of her most famous film:

Reclusive, in recent years. She was a talent. Joy to so many. Private funeral. Sorely missed. And now for the weather.

'Oh my God,' said Alex.

'Oh my *God*,' said Esther. They sat, she and Alex, side by side on the floor, freeze-framed. An attractive woman took the opportunity to try to sell them an air-freshener.

'It's Max,' said Alex, at last speaking aloud an earlier, silent conclusion. 'He's mad. He must have told them that she – '

'You have to call somebody,' said Esther, not listening, standing up and looking for the phone. 'You have to correct this. This is *terrible*, she can't see this. It's *incredibly* bad karma.'

'No – wait, let me *think*.'

'What do you mean, *no*? What the hell is there to think about? She's *upstairs*.'

Kitty was calling Esther again, quietly, apologetically, from the top of the stairs.

'I'm coming! Look, here's the phone. Just call the papers. A paper. Just let them know a stupid mistake has been made, that's all. It's not hard.'

Alex took the phone and stood up. He closed the door after Esther. He bounced the cordless phone in his palm for a minute, thinking. Then he dialled, listening to the numbers sing an eleven-note song he knew by heart. Esther burst back through the door.

'She just wanted to know where the shampoo – are you calling them now?'

Alex put his hand over the receiver and held out a hand for Esther to be silent.

'Hello? Yes, could you put me through to the Columbard Room, thanks. No, listen,' he said, covering the receiver again, 'look, Es, hear me out – '

'Alex, who is that? Why are you calling – '

'No, Es, wait. Before you – it's not for me. I could make her some serious money today –'

'*Excuse* me?'

'No, *think*. That's what she wanted. Right? She needs to be independent – especially of that lunatic – I can make her independent.'

Esther sat down in an armchair with her mouth open. She made the International Gesture of disbelief (eyes closed for three long seconds and then opened with pupils dilated).

'*Esther?* It makes *sense*.'

'Don't give me that,' she said stiffly. 'You just want your big day. You just want to show all those freaks –'

'Look,' said Alex, 'tomorrow we can do the big truth thing and everyone can be confronted with their sins and a duke can come on at the end and marry everybody off – the whole works – I *swear*. Es, the stuff I put in the lot, yesterday – it will have *tripled*. It'll be – wait, hello? Yes, is that Martin? Is he there? Martin Sands? Yes, it's Alex-Li Tandem, thanks, yes I'll wait. *Es*, we just have to keep it quiet for a day. Nobody gets hurt, and she benefits most, right? Right?'

Down the phone came one of Bach's cello things, to Alex always the music of judgement. Esther said something. Elsewhere, Alex's mobile phone was ringing. It stopped, then Esther's started, and then his began once more. What vultures used to do on the outskirts of a village is now the business of the telephone exchange, satellites. What comes after death happens on the phones.

'What did you say? Es? I didn't hear you.'

'I said OK,' repeated Esther, and seemed to him defeated, small and unlike herself in his armchair. 'Obviously, taken as read – not for you. For her. Not for you. But you can't let people think it for any longer than necessary. She might have family – you don't know. When the auction's done, then – '

'*Thank* you. Please, take her out – get her out of the house, don't let her see the television. Please, thanks. We'll talk properly, later. Thanks.'

He threw her the keys. He told her something he hadn't told her in a while.

'I know. It's going to kill me,' she replied.

2

Something akin to a welcome committee awaited Alex that afternoon at the auction house. The gathered smokers on the funny front steps whistled and stamped and jeered as he illegally parked before them.

'Body not even cold!' cried a man he had never liked. Quite a few Autograph Men of his acquaintance were turning to each other to make one of two gestures: either reaching into their pockets or holding out their open palms.

'*Tandem*,' complained Lovelear, appearing at his passenger window. 'Well, I bet against. Never picked you for a mercenary. I thought you'd at least wait a *week*. I'm a sentimentalist, I guess. You just lost me twenty-five pounds, man.'

Alex shut off the engine and got out of the car. 'Has it started yet? Have you seen the catalogue? How far into the auction are they?'

'Hi there, Lovelear,' said Lovelear, trying to keep pace with Alex's light jog into the building. 'Nice to see you, how's it going? I'm fine, Tandem, thanks for asking.'

'Not now – later.'

They sprinted through the hallway.

'I've got some sorta sad news,' said Lovelear breathlessly on the stairs. 'Tried to call you earlier, but –'

'*Later.*'

Just as they took a left at the cafeteria, an arm reached out for Alex, attached to Baguley. With the other hand Baguley removed his hat and held it to his chest. His face, grotesquely contorted, carried the suggestion of tears. To ward this off, Alex smiled as broadly as he could manage.

'Baguley. Good to see you. Coming in?'

'And death,' said Baguley, looking up, inexplicably, at the fake fresco on the ceiling, 'shall have no dominion.'

He put his hand on Alex's shoulder and painfully squeezed it.

'When I heard,' said Baguley, 'the first thing I did was to put on *Rich Pickings*, and all right, OK, it's not one of her best, but I just watched that and you can see her there so young and beautiful . . . well, I can tell you, I just felt: *death has no dominion*. She will literally live for ever. In our hearts, and our minds. And on film, of course – that's the big one.'

'That's terrific,' said Lovelear. 'Now, if you'll excuse us –'

'Of course, your thoughts,' continued Baguley, 'go to her family, naturally. She was young, really. In real terms. Your thoughts go to the loved ones. Personally, I think it only decent to wait a while before . . . can't just jump in there. Besides, I'm still waiting for verification of my pieces, so . . . But I think what you take away from it is just, well, one moment you're here, starring in the film of your life, and the next the great director in the –'

Here, Alex feigned a coughing fit as a last resort. Baguley came close into him, alternately rubbing and thumping his back.

'He's upset, just upset – we *all* are,' whispered Baguley to Lovelear. 'It's always hard, and of course he *met* her . . .'

357

Alex righted himself and looked quizzically at Baguley. Just looking at him produced a sweat of anxiety, palpitations of the heart. Baguley was a mass hallucination. Baguley was something bad the world had eaten.

'Where were you,' resumed Baguley softly, folding his arms, 'when you heard?'

'Holding the smoking gun,' said Alex, taking off his jacket. He had not drunk nearly enough, not yet, but still he thought he might hit this man, out of curiosity if nothing more. Then the stream of Autograph Men heading for the Columbard Room became a flood and Alex let it take him. He was almost lifted from the floor at one point by two impressive bellies. At the doorway he found Dove twisting his catalogue into a cone, eating his bottom lip. It had just gone three but the smell of cooking sherry stuck stubbornly to him.

'Been waiting *for ever*!' he burst out, hitting an accidental falsetto. 'Seats over there. Your lots are in, Tandem. Coming up any bloody minute.'

'And now,' rumbled the auctioneer.

'I don't *believe* this,' wailed Lovelear fifteen minutes later. He turned and stared at Alex as if he had never met the man before. He was not alone. As the bidding continued to ping-pong from an obese man in the front row to a mystery buyer on the phones, more eyes – awestruck, incredulous – turned on Alex, and that very special whisper of an auction room, the one that sounds like money being counted in a vault, rippled once, twice, three times round the room. Alex couldn't stay in his body, it tingled so. Esther had been right, he *had* wanted this – he hadn't realized how much. Ten years in this place watching the big boys. He did want to be a big boy, if only for an afternoon. He wanted to know what that *felt* like. And it felt, for a moment, incredible. He felt himself rise up, actually *rise*. He was part of that crazy number the auctioneer had just called out, and that one, and the one after that, and some element of him was in the intricate interlocking hexagons on the ceiling, the royal blue plush of the carpet, other people's eyes. But the feeling was only good, was only transcendental, for a moment, and in a moment it turned.

Ten minutes in and he knew he wanted the whole thing off. He wanted to stand up and tell them it wasn't even his money but he could only sit there and take this celebrity that was being given to him, his fifteen minutes with its fusion of wonder and hatred. He wanted to put his arms up in the air and say *Guys, guys – I'm still one of you, this isn't my . . . you mustn't think this is my . . .*

Instead, he sat with his head between his knees as the numbers climbed. Up, up. And he knew he should be happy, thinking of Kitty, who could now sail to freedom on this rising tide of money. Only he could feel himself transforming, in the eyes of this audience, into a symbol of his century's collective dream: *He'll never work again.* Part of the fame dream, this – maybe the largest part. The lottery ticket, the windfall, the mad hope that fate might permanently separate one man from the lives of every man ever born . . .

He could hear them: not whispers in the room but whispers in the world. It was so sad, a chorus of moans. Because luck is a sort of insult to the world. Li-Jin had said that. The cinema is full of fathers and their wisdom, but Alex remembered only this one example: as a boy, watching a Chinese earthquake on the television, he had turned to his father and congratulated him on his luck for being here, instead of there. Li-Jin smacked him for his impertinence and told him that luck is an insult to the world. The unlucky dead begrudge you it. And now he could *hear* them, in this room, that sorrowful fellowship of ghosts (was Li-Jin among them?) who have suffered and died trying to get what was coming to Alex-Li Tandem with gross ease and for no reason whatsoever.

For the fourth time the auctioneer knocked his little gavel against Alex's heart. It was over. The signed photo she had sent him went for fifteen grand. The love letter to a star went for thirty-eight thousand. Another for forty. The final lot, the copy of a letter (of outrageous sexual content) sent to J. Edgar Hoover went for sixty-five thousand pounds. A man from a London evening paper told him to look surprised and took his photograph.

An eventful Hollywood auction always wound up in Dante's, where the Autograph Men went to pick wax, pick over the big sales. On this occasion Alex could not join the faithful right away. He *was* the big sale. He still had business in the auction house. There were forms to sign, a cheque to collect. He did these things like a man in a dream pretending to be a rabbi. People spoke to him, a journalist among them, and in all these transactions he felt a new order of fraudulence. He was not only not the person they thought he was (rich, lucky, shrewd), he was not the person *he* thought he was either (useless, damaged, doomed). The truth was somewhere midway, and for the first time in his life he realized that he did not own it.

When, finally, he was let back into the world, the great crowd of his people had thinned – no one stood on the pavement resting a beer on the windowsill – but inside Dante's the atmosphere was still convivial, boisterous, at least until Alex-Li Tandem walked in. It is important to get this correct. It was not that people ceased to talk or even that they stared at him directly. The jukebox, playing its limited selection of opera favourites, did not fall silent. This was not TV. Simply, the quality of attentiveness changed. The *vibe* (and this was a word he had never found a use for until now) changed. It shifted in direction. Instead of pursuing its many natural and chaotic paths, it streamlined. All arrows pointed to Alex. He was a desire magnet. He was ever so slightly famous. He was the centre of everything.

Feeling the suggestion of a new type of loneliness, one harder to shake than its predecessor, Alex made his way to the bar. Everyone he passed congratulated him; there was suddenly no other subject than his success, no form of conversation but those formal felicitations one overhears at bar mitzvahs and weddings, the ones that sound like bells. But they're just valedictions, thought Alex with horror. Valedictions wearing a different garment! These people are saying goodbye to me. I am no longer of them. I am dead to them. I have passed on. And certainly by the time he arrived at the beer mats and pumps, he felt emptied, slapped so many times on the back he was winded. He tried to order a triple gin and tonic, but now Dove was tugging at his coat.

'Tandem,' he hissed, stinking of one sweet meth plied on top of another, 'what you doing here? Should be somewhere better than *here*. Can't drink in *here* no more. This place's for *losers*, mate.'

'And I'll have a bucket of champagne, big man,' said Lovelear, appearing to the left. He had rented a smile off somebody and it was the wrong size.

'Lovelear,' said Alex quietly, and felt his whole body apologize. 'Well. That was all a bit weird, eh?'

Lovelear whistled. He was still smiling this alien smile. His movements were trying to push towards some vision of Lovelear's regarding *jollity*.

'A hundred and fifty *thou-sand*. That's not a bit of weird, my friend, that's a whole *lot* of weird.'

'Yeah . . . It's weird. It's very . . .'

'I just think it's great,' said bombastic Lovelear. 'I just think it's *so great*. I mean if you're asking me, couldn't have happened to a nicer guy. Damn straight.'

'*Thanks*, Lovelear. Really, I appreciate that. Champagne, was it?'

'Hmm? Oh, yeah,' said Lovelear, thumping the bar. 'I mean, you deserve it. No question. How long you been in this business? Never really made much out of it, right? And now! I think it's incredible – what a story. You know what? I think we have to blow this place, man. I'm with Dove on that one. This is really not up to your newfound status, not any more. Different club you're in now. Whole different society.'

'I happen to like this place,' said Alex, looking around and wondering whether that had ever been true. He watched the only woman in the place, the Slovenian barmaid, pick her way through the bottom-pinchers with a bowl of ravioli held above her head. She delivered it to the far corner where a man was sitting, his face down on the table's surface, not making any audible noise but still, one assumed, crying. A hat sat beside him. His great rolling shoulders were going.

'Isn't that Baguley?'

'Sure. He doesn't have your luck. Turns out he bought not one but *five* phoney Kittys from the Swede at eight hundred dollars each. Mark Sands just told him they're about as real as Adolf's diaries. Swede has disappeared. Vamoosed. Got on his bike and cycled into the sunset. Leaving Baguley with one monogrammed handkerchief and not much else.'

'Good,' said Alex, catching a barman by the sleeve. 'Triple gin and tonic, please, and whatever these two –'

'Now, what do you mean, exactly, "good"?' asked Lovelear, losing his smile.

'I mean, *good*. You know. Good that Baguley got screwed.'

'Oh, I *see*,' said Lovelear, nodding at Dove. 'Oh, so it's good when other people get screwed? Is that it? Just as long as *you* don't get screwed.'

Alex shrugged, confused. 'It's Baguley,' he said. 'We're happy when Baguley gets screwed. The screwing of Baguley brings us joy. Remember? Has always done. Since time etc.'

'All right for some,' said Dove in a little voice.

'Excuse me?'

'Newspaper takes your picture, huh?' began Lovelear, with a Tourette's nod. 'Feeling like the *big man*. Step on everybody you see, make everybody feel small, is that it? Guess you're feeling like the big old *man*. Bet you got a few more of those Kittys too. Stashed away. Of course, you never let *us* go and meet her, you told *us* she didn't even sign anything for ya, but then, you can lie to *us*, *we've* never done anything for you, have we? Well, Tandem, I am just so goddamn happy for you. Aren't you, Dove? Aren't you just so goddamn happy?'

Alex gulped at his gin, and prepared an elaborate chain of expletives, laying them ready along his tongue like the setting of a Seder table. But then he felt oddly constrained; even though the noise in the bar had not decreased, he knew people were listening to him. He was making a scene. There was nothing unusual in this. Except this time it was being watched.

'Look,' he began, more reasonably, 'I don't particularly want to turn out like –'

'What? Like me? Like Dove? Lucky those love letters came out of the blue, then, ain't it? No more messing around with twenty quid autographs for Tandem! So – wait, explain it to me – you're now too good for –'

Alex slammed his drink on the counter. 'What are you *talking* about? You think I forged them?'

'You tell me, man.'

'*Christ*. Look, let's start again. There's no need for a row. It's just a hundred and fifty grand, it doesn't mean –'

'Listen to 'im!' cooed Dove, from over the rim of his pint. 'Only a hundred and fifty!'

'All I *meant*,' tried Alex again, 'is that this business, you know . . . it's insecure. Now, as it happens, I'm just the agent on those Kittys, you can believe that or not –' bellowed Alex over a flurry of International Gestures for incredulity. 'Look, I'm not really fussed – but yes, if this puts me in the big league, it puts me in the big league. You've got to make something at this game, haven't you? It's not a vocation. I don't want to turn out like bloody Duchamp, or something, minus a pot to bloody piss in.'

Here the vibe changed once more, it changed distinctly. It got quieter. Not just among the three of them, but to a radius of about twelve feet.

'What?' asked Alex.

Lovelear shook his head and rolled his eyes. Dove had on a certain kind of English face which is that island's mild substitute for the wordless disgust of the Spanish fist, or the excoriating Italian glare, or the French gasp, or the Russian wail. The face that says: *That's not really on, now, is it?*

'*What?* What is it?' asked Alex.

'I actually tried to tell you earlier?' said Lovelear snootily, look-ing away. 'But big man couldn't be bothered to listen.'

'Will you just –'

'Duchamp's dying,' said Dove.

3

Alex, like everybody, held hospitals in the highest, purest, dread and loathing. To come in with a bump and leave with the baby – this is the only grace available in a hospital. Other than that, there is only pain. The *concentration of pain*. Hospitals are unique in this concentration. There are no areas in the world dedicated to the concentration of pleasure (theme parks and their like are a concen-tration of the *symbols* of pleasure, not pleasure itself), there are no buildings dedicated to laughter, friendship or love. They'd probably be pretty gruesome if they existed, but would they smell of decay's argument with disinfectant? Would people walk through the hall-ways, weeping? Would the shops sell only flowers and slippers and mints? Would the beds (so ominous, this!) have wheels?

'Brian,' said Alex, lowering himself into that too low, too orange, awkward plastic chair. 'I brought you some mints. And some flowers. Daffs.' From the head to the chest, Alex's old trading partner was almost unchanged, but after this he radically tapered off. When you're for it, your childhood legs come back to you, but they can't take you anywhere. Brian's were twiggish, white, without hair or muscle.

'I had a dream,' said Brian faintly. 'Or maybe ... and Kerry, the nurse, she was marrying Leon, in Holland somewhere, or Belgium. Flowers, all over, and cheese and pastries, like. Lovely. Feast, it was. Went on for days, seemed liked days anyway. She wore peach – I can't remember about him. But you weren't there, were you? Weren't many there, really. Weren't enough. Flowers and bells and cheeses. Beautiful.'

'Daffs, Brian,' said Alex helplessly. He was unmanned by tubes. Going in, going out. And beeping machines. And that pool of dried blood trapped under colourless tape that sat in a hollow of Brian's pulsing neck.

'It was funny,' said Brian, opening one eye. 'I thought he was queer, see. But there he was wiv her, dancing in the hall! Flowers on the floor!'

Now he undertook a series of burps, each one followed by a terrible wince. His hands were up on his chest, picking at the hairs, that final self-groom. He burped for the tenth time and this one was too much, it seemed; he moaned – pure, concentrated pain – and thrust his face into the pillow.

'Shall I get someone, Brian? Shall I –'

The ward was open-plan, men, women, and Alex stood and searched it for help, for he was still in that world where pain, even the smallest hint of pain, is front-page news. It deserves attention from all quarters, it demands the laying on of hands. Alex went to Dr Huang for knee ache, for the *suggestion* of knee ache, for the *twinge*. And then you pass over into this world where the pain of Duchamp, acute as it may be, is graded on a rising scale against the man by the window who cannot breathe without assistance. The woman with no breasts watching TV. This, the cardiac ward, brought all sorts. People who had been travelling along their own singular road of pain – cancer, road accident, brain accident – now united in suffering as their hearts decided to stop or skip or explode. Brian Duchamp, as the matron had explained to Alex on arrival, had been undergoing the removal of his sole remaining, cancerous kidney, when ten minutes from the end of the operation his heart objected. 'Lucky, really,' she had said, reaching for a ringing phone. 'Now we know he has a bad heart. We wouldn't have known otherwise, now would we?' *Lucky?*

'Excuse me . . .' began Alex to a passing nurse, but something was bleeping on the other side of the room and she rushed to it. Brian burped again, moaned and seized Alex's hand.

'I don't fink I'm gonner make Thursday, mate,' he said, closing his eyes. A very pretty young man in white came and stood by them and watched a machine, suspended above the bed, where the pain of Brian, fed down various tubes, was represented in lines and numbers and beeps.

'He's making these weird burps,' said Alex beseechingly. The boy turned, in no great hurry. His name tag said LEON. He was camp in the strict sense that none of his gestures was useful or necessary. With a pronounced lisp, he explained to Alex that without kidneys, stomach juices have nowhere to go. The toxins attack. A machine would come later to clean Brian's blood for him.

'When? When will it come?'

'When the doctor says.'

'But he's in pain. He's in a lot of pain.'

'He's got a button. That has painkillers in it. He just has to press it.'

'But he's *pressing* it, isn't he. And it obviously isn't bloody *enough*, is it.'

'Enough would be too much,' said the boy primly, and walked away.

'I was dreaming it, about Leon,' said Duchamp sadly.

'What, Brian?' said Alex, still glaring at the ironed creases in

Leon's trousers, still contemplating running through the ward with one of the emergency fire extinguishers and using it to put an unholy dent in the boy's skull.

'I didn't go to no Belgium. I won't be out of this bed, Tandem. Not in this life. That's a fact. It's jumped out of the kidney, you know. 'Sall over me body. *In* it, I should say. They wos gonner come up with a cure, at one point, as I remember,' said Brian, and tried to smile. One of those vicious burps came reeking from him again. 'Oooh . . . oh, *God*. Years ago, they were gonner cure it. What happened to that, eh? Iron lungs and pigs' hearts and miracle cures. Who arsed all that up?'

He drew one arm from under the cover and Alex was horrified afresh by a roaming bruise, purple-hearted, yellow-edged, that covered the underside of his forearm. Brian studied this, and the raised fistula that lay under the skin, with disinterested eyes.

'You go to the market,' said Brian bullishly. 'Tell 'em my pitch is still my pitch, tell 'em to keep it for me, that's all.'

''Course, Brian. I'll do that, of course.'

'What they sayin' about me, then, them nurses?'

Nothing good. On Thursday night, as Nurse Wilkes told it, he had collapsed in his stairwell. That same night he was in hospital. On Friday they scanned him. On Saturday he had final-stage renal failure (you don't have it, really, until you *know* you have it). On Sunday at five they operated to remove the cancerous kidney. During that he had a heart attack. Today, on Wednesday, the cancer was touring his body. His chance of becoming a full-time dialysis patient (itself only half a life, a life half lived by a machine) was minimal. All Alex could think of as he sat on a gaudy sofa in a quiet corner ('Shall we go to a quiet corner?'), listening to this staggering list, was this: religious war. This was Jerusalem of the cells. This was Belfast of the lower belly. The escalation. The concentration of pain.

'They're saying you're all right. They're saying Duchamp, he's . . . he'll be all right. With some dialysis and . . .'

Something yellow came from Duchamp's mouth and had body enough to wriggle wormishly down his chin. Alex passed him tissues and, with heaving stomach, took back the package a moment later. Unable to see a bin, he placed it in his coat pocket.

'Like a snowflake in a fahkin' fire, I'll be all right,' said Duchamp, and started a laugh soon cut short by a mighty groan, and a jolt. He was looking, with real panic, at his groin area, and Alex in response lifted in his seat, his hands hovering above the area of corresponding blanket, as if this might help.

'Dick on a pipe,' explained Duchamp once the crisis was over, and Alex did not inquire any further.

'Have you filled in your lunch preferences, Mr Duchamp?' asked a curvy nurse who had materialized at the end of the bed. 'Do you know what you'd like for lunch?'

'Your tits,' said Duchamp and laughed a great deal. Despite himself, Alex joined in.

Nurses are famous stoics, but they are not above revenge. There was something very clear in her face that said a price would be extracted for this later, once Alex had left, a physical humiliation of some kind. Duchamp too seemed to sense this, and bowed his head.

'No, really, Nurse, nuffing, nuffing, nuffing. Can't. Won't go down.'

'We'll see about that,' she said curtly and moved on. Alex watched Duchamp's face complete its transformation from leering bully to fearful child.

'They're nice in here,' said Brian meekly, pressing his button. 'Do their best, you know. I like the black ones better, though. More cheerful. Oh *gawd . . . awww . . .*'

Alex sat silently for another ten minutes, an effort of the most colossal will. He would be anywhere but here. He was unable to take his mind or eyes off the man in the next bed, who was much, much too young to be in this place. It was an affront to Alex's own sense of himself, this out of place youth. It was obscene. There is a time and a place for youth and it's not in a cardiac ward. *Excuse me* – this is what you wanted to demand of the nearest nurse – *exactly why is that man dying? Doesn't he have anything better to do? Shouldn't he be in school?* Hospitals are called St Mary's, St Stephen's, St Somebody's. This one was St Christopher's. They should all be called Job's. Job is the rightful patron of hospitals. Job has guts. Job would ask: why this young man? Why the children's ward? Why (and this last one is almost impossible) the babies in intensive? Why do babies get intensively sick? What is going *on* here?

'Brian,' said Alex, recovering his breath from this uphill train of thought, 'Brian, I have to go, I think.'

Brian had just concluded another tiny unit of sleep, the stuff which comes between the pain. He opened his eyes.

'Tandem. 'Fore I forget. That Kitty. Make anything on that Kitty?'

'Yes,' said Alex. He had no idea where that Kitty had gone. It had evaporated. It had spiralled away, like burnt paper up a chimney, along with the rest of last week.

'Yeah? You managed to sell it, then?'

'*Yes,*' said Alex emphatically, and reached for his bag. He drew out his chequebook from a pocket and dug around in Brian's dark cupboard for a pen.

'How much? A lot?'

'Fifteen grand.'

'Fifteen *grand*?'

'Yes. She died yesterday.'

'Yesterday?'

'Yes. Prices rocketed. I went to the Columbard. Flogged it. Should have mentioned it earlier.'

'*Fifteen*?'

'Fifteen.'

'Bloody *hell*.'

They were Autograph Men again, for a moment. Just doing business.

'So, fifteen, minus my fifteen per –'

'Oi! Ten, more like.'

'Right. You're right, Brian. You know what? Forget my commission. I've had a bit of a windfall myself today.'

'You sure?'

'Certain.'

'Stone the *crows*. And they never figured it? Never 'ad a doubt?'

'Not for a second. You're too good, Brian.'

Alex wrote out the cheque. He signed it. Held it up over Brian's face.

'Fifteen thousand pounds and no pence,' read Brian, slowly, grandly. 'Bloody *'ell*. Paid to the order of Brian Duchamp. That's me. Though *gawd* only knows when I'll 'ave a chance to spend it. Signed by Alex-Li Tandem,' he said, taking a finger and pressing it gently to Alex's wrist. 'That's *you*.'

371

4

Couldn't face the Underground, *being under ground*. Couldn't face a cab either, those black theatres playing cockney monologues. Spat out by the hospital into the middle of nowhere, Alex finds instead an Overground station and a line that will take him tolerably close to Mountjoy. The platform is all cigarettes and schoolgirls. This feels like travelling. The train does not simply *appear* as it does under ground. Under ground you get impatient with lateness, because essentially you don't believe the tube has any real distance to travel. It should just *be* here, and then *be* there. But with the Overground, you will wait, and quite happily wait, and smile when you can see it coming, the train, rounding the corner under the vast azure sky, chuffing past trees and houses.

The doors open. Everybody in the North of London knows this line affectionately as the Free Train. There are no machines and no one ever pays. Kids smoke on it, tramps live on it, and the mad like to sit in the lotus position and strike up conversations. It takes you to the big parks at the top of the city and the ghettos at the bottom. Teachers ride it because admin and essays can be laid out on the many empty seats and calmly dealt with. Nurses sleep on it. Buskers play concerts uninterrupted. Dogs are welcome. Sometimes you walk into a carriage and the clouds of marijuana smoke make your eyes sore. To look out of the windows at the passing world is to think that the city consists only of forests and schools and sporting arenas and swimming pools. The dark satanic mills must be somewhere else. The whole place looks like the Promised Land.

Alex phones Esther and speaks to Kitty. He tells her his news.

'But this is *incredible*!' she says, gasping and swearing in Italian. 'Why so much money? My *God*! You are like the Wizard of Oz or something incredible like this. I am completely speechless. Completely. I have not a thing to say! It is *amazing*! I never hear such a thing! I would kiss you now if you were here. But I don't understand – *how* could it *be*?'

'Kitty –' begins Alex, but there is no one there. He waits.

'Alex,' says Esther, 'I can't walk around any longer. It's cold. You need to come home. You've got to tell her. I'm going to tell her if you don't. I should never have agreed, it's bloody ridiculous – can you imagine how she's going to feel, when we tell her? Correction: when *you* tell her. I feel sick that I said yes to this. Look, I have to go. Get home *now*.'

As Alex gets closer to Mountjoy, he feels a shadow cast itself over his heart. Maybe he can get off at one of these other stations? Start again? There is no Kitty in Larkin Green, for example, and no Esther and no unkeepable promises, no *muddle*, no life of Tandem with its facts and obligations. He takes out his pouch of tobacco and puts his feet on the opposite seat. A very unusual feeling has come over him, one he has never had before in his life. He doesn't want to go home.

At Mulberry Road a woman wheels a mountain bike on to the train. About a year after Li-Jin died, Adam had turned up at the old Tandem house, amused about something.

– What? What's so funny?

Alex kept quizzing Adam as he walked silently through to the kitchen. Sarah offered him a cup of tea. He took a seat at the little plastic table they had back then, still smiling. And no one had dared smile in that house, not for a year, not since it happened. Alex remembered how shocked he'd been, to see that smile.

– Come *on*. Out with it. Mum, tell him to come out with it. *What!*

– It's just . . . I was on that train, the Free Train. Just now.

– Yeah?

– And this guy walks on with a bike missing a wheel. And then at the next stop, this other guy gets in, in the same carriage, with a bike wheel but no bike. Everybody noticed, everyone in the carriage. It was driving us all crazy. Except these two gaylords. They didn't even *look* at each other.

– *And?*

– And nothing!

The radiance of the laugh came back to Alex now. The repeated dawn of the smile. He was thoughtful, Adam, and knew even then that one person's capacity for joy can pinch those people who can't manage it. Sarah and Alex, still shot-through, still heart-whacked by grief, could only look back at him blankly. Adam had tried hard to force that smile to lie flat, but it only rose again.

NINE / *Reaching the Source*

I

Men who don't want to go home, go to a bar. Alex knew this because he'd seen it in the films. They go to a bar, and the barman, who is an American, who is a New Yorker, makes a certain gesture of reluctance – a frown, followed by a gentle, tolerant shrug – as he is asked to pour another glass of whisky. Alex wanted a bar like this, but Mountjoy could not provide one. If people drank here, they ate Chinese food with it and sat at a table with napkins on their knees.

There was only Bubbles at the top of the high street with its blacked-out windows and frequent name changes (you could effectively age the inhabitants of Mountjoy by the way they referred to this bar. It was Bubbles, the Mount, Ben's, or Follies to the under thirties, it was Bar Zero to the new arrivals, and there were a few ancient souls who remembered eating cakes at this location or posting letters). It had a bad reputation, Bubbles. There were murmurings about drugs. The people who drank there didn't know when to stop. And on most week nights Mountjoy's sole celebrity could be seen stumbling from its doors, lavender-faced and plum-nosed. (A 'national treasure', this man; an ursine, physical, marvellous actor who had spent thirty years bringing the tragic gestures of Antony, of Brutus, of Othello, to a series of small-screen policemen, doctors and farmers. A Thursday night found him doing his raging Lear down the high street, gripped on either side by two unsmiling television producers, sent by the soap opera to get him out of Bubbles and on to set, sober.)

Like most people in Mountjoy, Alex had never been in Bubbles. He had no idea what it looked like inside (outside, its sign famously struggled to light up, and failed, at each pulse, in a different way: now no stem on the glass, now no pink bubbles gurgling over the edge, now no luminous red cherry). He had no more idea, really, once he opened the door. It was so dark. It was five in the afternoon on the pavement, perpetual midnight inside Bubbles. There were four or five people moving in the shadows. No music. A small glum disco-ball revolved, its million little searchlights climbing the walls, vainly seeking those dancers it sprinkled with stardust twenty years ago. Elsewhere, an attempt had been made at a painted beach scene, a topless brown beauty was coloured in only so far as her navel. Her legs were empty, sketched. The palm tree's eight wide leaves shimmered with green sequins, sadly depleted. In another corner a hole in the wall for a DJ, now boarded up. Something that looked like a barman and a bar. Alex walked towards this and began.

Whose idea was it to drink alphabetically? Alex did not come to Bubbles with that intention. He merely came to have a drink, maybe drinks, maybe *drinkseses*. After five swift whiskies, though, the idea just sort of *presented* itself. And Roy, who was the barman and must take some of the blame, Roy did no frowning, no reluctant shrugging. Oh, no.

Roy said: *Go for it, my son.*

And Tommy, a pregnant Irishman, whose idea it may have been, said: *Twenty says you don't get beyond fookin' haich.*

Which was a dare. And drunk men take dares like they take breaths.

Absinthe, then, set it off with a bang. Alex felt a mulberry cloud envelop each eyeball, and had an abortive conversation about famous artists and their absinthe.

''Cos in a way, Roy, you see, the art and the absinthe were sort of *inextricably intertwined*, weren't they? It brought the muse on, it got them all fired up –'

'Got 'em bloody shit-faced, is what it got them.'

Beer and Cointreau passed like a heavy orange brick through his system. At this point cautious Roy reached over the bar, looked into Alex's wallet and shook his head. A few minutes later Alex found himself round the corner, swaying impatiently in a cash-point queue. It was daytime still, out here, and he was not ready for it and fell over. Two women, a mother and daughter, watched him do it and nodded at each other. Back in Bubbles, scuffed but rich, he whacked his wad on the bar.

'D . . .' ruminated Roy, fully in the spirit of things now. 'D, Phil? Got any ideas for D?'

Phil, an older man with a leather jacket and glasses on a chain round his neck, came very slowly out of the fruit-machine corner, took a lingering look out the door at his neglected black taxi and then, finally, approached the bar.

'D? No, no ideas, Roy. No ideas on D.'

'Daiquiri,' said Alex, thumping a fist into a palm.

'Draught beer,' corrected Roy gently.

Beer turned up again in brand-name form for F, then spiteful, familiar Gin followed by a volcanic Hot Toddy, made by Tommy who (with unguessed at athleticism) vaulted over the bar to make it.

I gave them pause. I stuffed them, for a while.

'Iberia . . . *Iberian* . . .' began Phil, who was doing a crossword.

'I could make something iced,' offered Roy. 'Iced something. Or another.'

But it was Irish whiskey, a warming candle in the throat. Another beer with a German name served for J, and Kahlúa, sweet and thick, painted itself in a coating on his tongue, not to be removed. Lager and Muscadet were poured into the same glass in the spirit of a 'spritzer'. And then things got messy. Tommy, who had been drinking whisky all along, matching Alex shot for shot, started talking about the problem with these bloody Jews is they always want to run everything. Alex swung a punch at Tommy, missed and lay on the floor a while, impugning his Catholicism. After a bit of back and forth, Tommy agreed there were none more evil than nuns and personally he hated God anyway. Roy gave a quite moving speech about tolerance ('Well, it's all fahkin bollocks, isn't it, I mean, *really*,'), and Tommy bought Alex an Irish whiskey and Alex bought Tommy one too. And then a woman walked in. She was forty-something, and not much flesh on her, but what was there (as the actor Spencer Tracy said of his love) was choice. Her haircut was historical, and all her many denim items resolutely tight and stone-washed. She looked to Alex like a tall blue felt-tip pen, low on ink, topped by the wrong cap (yellow).

'Thasserwo . . .' confirmed Alex, and hobbled to the bathroom to make himself respectable. When he came back his hair was wet and he looked like Rasputin. The woman was behind the bar.

'Stella, Alex, Alex, Stella,' said Roy, while Stella lugubriously dried a glass as if this were the first of five thousand. 'She comes in for the rush.'

Half an hour later the rush – four men from the betting shop across the street – were cheering Alex on from one end of the bar as Stella lined up a Rum, a Sherry and a Tia Maria in front of him.

'Why you doin' this, exactly?' asked Stella.

None of the men present had thought this worth asking.

'I mean,' said Stella, propping herself up on one sharp, pink elbow, 'why don't you just go 'ome?'

''Cus,' said Alex, standing on the raised edge of the bar, pointing a lot, 'I don't *wanna* go home. NORRINNERSTED IN GOWEEHOME TO GEJUSBOLLKT BYIMMIN *LIE KEUW*.'

'Please yourself,' said Stella.

The argument about U weaved in and out of things, like a loose stitch in the conversation. It was forgotten finally when Phil made the jukebox work, and Alex tormented Stella until she danced with him, or, more accurately, until she allowed him to fall unconscious on her shoulder blade while she shifted quietly from foot to foot.

'Dad's yaar-zite tomorrow!' he said, waking without warning, his head springing up.

'Last night doing what?' asked Stella, and then stepped away with the speed of a woman who's seen it before as Alex slipped to the floor.

He had his pride; he got to the bathroom without assistance and threw up there in the quietude of a cubicle. When he returned, Roy was standing in the middle of the floor, holding Alex's mobile.

'Adam,' said Roy stiffly, reading from the little screen. 'Boot?

Carl. Dr ... Huwang? Look, which one of these do I call to take you away?'

They came, they came. Somewhere, beneath the drink, he understood what it meant, them coming. That they would always come. That this was godly. He felt a great swell of feeling, and, like most young men, he feared it, and converted it into aggression.

'Friends!' he cried, as Joseph took his left leg, Adam his right. 'Romans! Autograph Men! Lend me your money.'

They carried him like this, like a man on an invisible chair, out on to the street.

'Don't call *me* an Autograph Man,' said Adam gruffly. 'That's *your* game. That's his. Not mine. You got any idea what *time* it is, friend?'

'Ri-*ight*, yes, yes, yes, *of course* – no, 'cos you're *superior* – you just want *God's* autograph. *'Scuse me*, can I just trouble you, jusforramo ... You want him to turn up with his wotsit – his lightning finger, finger with lightning in it, like a bolt – WHAM! Zzzzzz! Ha! Hahahahahaha! Write in on your forehead!'

'No,' said Adam, patiently bringing back Alex's lolling head as it swung backwards towards the ground. 'That'd make me a golem. Alex, stand up. *Stand. Up.*'

'Alex,' said Joseph, 'help us to help you. All right?'

'*Help us,*' repeated Alex, '*to help you! Help us to help you?* Does that like, come with the job like, you learn it, like and they say, right learn this, in a Heller Insurance ... handbook or something? *Guide to speaking like a cretin? We can* literally *change your life. We want* you *to sleep easy knowing that* your *loved ones are protected. Help us to help you.*'

'You're the cretin.'

'Oh, *I'm* the cretin?'

'Yes, Alex, right now you are the cretin.'

'Me.'

'You.'

'I may have to ask you to step outside.'

'We are outside.'

Alex swivelled round until he was facing Adam, gripping him by the neck with both hands, for balance as much as for intimacy.

'Shall I fight him?'

'To what *end*?'

'To the end of breaking his stupid face.'

'Do you think that's likely?' said Adam, moving his face out of the range of Alex's breath. 'That outcome?'

Alex's head dropped, and his brain slipped forward to rest on his eyes. He closed them. The hour was late.

'Probably go home now,' he said tenderly, reaching out one arm for Joseph, who took it with equal tenderness and wrapped it round his own shoulder.

'So,' said Adam, as they started down the high street, 'what was the occasion anyway?'

'Fear, and . . .' said Alex, and then thought for a while.

'Loathing?' offered Joseph.

'*Yes*. Definitely that. *Definitely* loathing, yeah.'

The high street was dead and unfamiliar, although the new restaurants and the textile shops and the disappearance of Levinsky's Bakery were all tragedies of five years' standing. It was not quite Alex's suburb any more. Only the ground was unchanged, and he had not stopped finding these things inexplicably beautiful: the green shoots pushing up between paving stones, the names and footprints of past chancers who had dared wet cement. Also the irregular surfaces, back to back, testament to the contrariness of successive councils: black and stippled, red and yellow cobbles, solemn grey flagstones, getting old, cracking up. And Alex's favourite: knitted z's, in a rich burgundy patina, like a path leading to sleep. *Ug.* Was everyone asleep? Mountjoy's great flat-fronted houses could be seen a mile down the way, lights out. They seemed to sleep, but Alex knew there to be a spotlight in every driveway ready to go at the slightest intrusion by man or leaf. Inside, each house was pleached by those invisible lasers, criss-crossed through the landings and the stairs. A kind of trap for any fifteen-year-old trying to sneak –

'Remember that?' asked Alex, snorting, following the drunken delusion that his thoughts had been heard. 'When Rubinfine was seeing that Hindu girl – Bal-something . . .'

'Baljit,' said Adam, smiling. 'She was *gorgeous*.'

'*Baljit.* And he'd come through the window, Rube had – and he was gonner leave the same way – but they'd just done the deed . . . first time, wasn't it?'

'Think so, yeah.'

'And he was all loved up – so – *Ug* . . . Actually, I can't tell this, too pissed . . . Adam *tell* this –'

'All right, all right, so, he thought: *I'll just go to the loo, get rid of this* . . . the condom, but there're lasers all over the house – of course, he doesn't know this. Two minutes later: alarm, then police, fire-engine, father of Baljit holding a knife –'

'Holding a knife!' repeated Alex, in case Joseph had missed it.

'And there's Rubinfine in his kippah,' said Adam, laughing so loud it echoed through the street, 'with a handful of sperm and rubber . . .'

Alex gurgled with pleasure and gave up talking; it was a joy to hear the ancient story retold so well.

'And trying to assure Mr Baljit that despite this *rather embarrassing mishap*, there was no reason why he, the father, shouldn't keep doing his accounts with Rube Snr. *In his pants*, he was saying this. With a knife at his throat and the police coming up the stairs.'

'I have actually *heard* this one,' said Joseph, and lit a cigarette. Because he had not grown up in Mountjoy, and only moved there in his twenties, it was often assumed he did not know or did not remember the old Mountjoy legends. As a consequence he heard them more often and knew them better than anyone.

'Shush –' said Alex, putting his finger to his lips. 'Carry on, Ads, carry on, mate.'

'Well, you know what *that* was about . . . that was because of what his dad was *like*,' said Adam patiently, as they reached the monument, and paused underneath it. 'He was always *terrified* of his father, man. He was more scared of Jerry's tongue than Baljit's dad with a knife. Jerry was, I mean, he still *is*, an *incredible* bully. You just can't imagine.'

'Try my dad on for size, mate,' said Joseph, blowing smoke.

'Well, *yeah*. And Jerry's the same way. He bullied Rubinfine into rabbi-hood, knowing it wasn't for him – but he just wouldn't back down. And Mark would've spent all his time with *your* dad, Al, if he could've. He loved Li-Jin, that's what he *wanted*, that's what he needed, a father like that, you know? He wouldn't have been such a freak, maybe, if he'd just been given a little –'

'Yeah, well,' said Alex, and felt exhausted.

'I'm sorry that –' Joseph broke off, casting a wary look at Adam.

'No, go on, what?' said Alex, standing for the first time unaided.

'Nothing . . . just . . . I'm sorry I never knew him, your dad. I mean, I wish I'd had more of a chance to . . .'

'Well,' said Alex and sat on the lip of the monument, taking from his trench coat the materials necessary for a joint. 'You knew him the day he died. He was on good form that day.'

The world is made out of letters, words. Under every friendship there is a difficult sentence that must be said, in order that the friendship can be survived.

This was theirs.

2

A Mondō Joke

Q. What did the inflatable headmistress say to the inflatable boy who came into the inflatable school with a pin?

A. You've let *me* down, you've let *yourself* down – you've let the whole *school* down ...

This joke, told timidly and without expectation by Joseph, was now being hailed as the greatest joke of the century. Even taking into account the delirious effects of alcohol mixed with weed, Alex stood by this laugh – the one presently racking his chest – as quite unprecedented. He had been laughing for four minutes and every time he thought he was finished with it, it came burbling up again, like water in a blocked plughole. And then abruptly it was over. He breathed out, thoroughly. Realized he was cold. It was going to rain.

'You OK?' asked Adam, noting the shiver.

Alex nodded. He tried to stand. Nothing doing. He took the hand that Adam offered.

'I'm sorry about Kitty,' said Adam, sensing it was safe to say this now. 'I'm sorry to hear about it. I know you met her ... I know what she meant to you. I tried to call this morning when I heard – I thought you might do something stupid. Just wish I'd caught you earlier. I really think ... you should've *kept* those things, Alex, man ... You shouldn't have sold them. They were precious. You'll miss them.'

'Huh?'

'We saw the paper,' said Joseph. He stood and stretched and yawned. 'Look – ignore Adam, he thinks you collect religious relics or something – they're just autographs. It's all right. That's your job. You don't have to feel bad – that's what you do. You just pulled off one of the great autograph coups of the *decade*. Bloody *enjoy* it, I say.'

'Nnng?'

Adam hooked an arm around Alex's shoulders and squeezed.

'You made the evening edition, friend, page eight. Can I ask – I mean ... what're you going to do with the money? It's a hell of a lot, man. Because the shul ... I mean, no pressure, but, well – we'll talk about it tomorrow. Even *you* couldn't drink it all – though you gave it a fair old –'

Alex had started running down the street. At least, he had instructed his legs to run, but the message was poorly transmitted. It did not contain the idea of balance, of poise, of staying upright. He came to grief at the corner and tried to gather himself in a doorway. Joseph and Adam were upon him in a second, holding their knees and looking up, for the rain had started.

'We in a hurry?' asked Adam, getting his breath.

'You – follow –' said Alex, starting to run again. 'She's in the house. *She's in the house.*'

Now they were jogging the three of them and the rain was preparing to get serious.

'*Who's* in the house? Why are we running?'

'*She*. Kitty,' said Alex, and accelerated, his trench coat billowing cape-like behind him.

'The video?' called Adam, as Alex took a healthy lead. 'Just return it to me tomorrow. It's no big *deal*.'

'NO. SHE. *KITTY*. IN THE *HOUSE*.'

'*Alex*,' cried Adam, as they passed the video store and Alex vanished behind the curved wall of the bank that began his street. '*Alex*. Don't be *mad*.'

At this hour, Alex's street was sepulchral, residential, and Adam and Joseph turned its corner in silence, fearful of waking the parents of people they knew, not to mention the people they knew who were now parents, for these boys were getting old.

'Alex, *please*,' said Joseph, flinging himself finally at the gate, and addressing the Rasputin presently conducting a furious search for his keys. 'Slow down. Take it easy.'

With a yell of victory Alex retrieved his keys from deep within the broken seams of his coat.

'What's this *about*, Tandem?' asked Adam, dripping up the path.

'She. In there. Kitty. She's in my house. Right now.'

He opened the door and made the International Gesture of requested silence.

'She's in the living room,' he said in a loud, artless whisper. 'With Esther. They're chatting, they like to chat.'

He tiptoed through the hallway, opening the lounge door with ceremony and, as it swung on its hinge, bowing low. In this position he gagged. Joseph got him by the elbows and led him to the nearest place, the kitchen sink, where he was ponderously sick, in wave after wave. It was a long ten minutes before the expulsions slowed down, dwindling into a painful reflex cough from which nothing came, not even air. When he was completely done, Joseph lovingly washed his face for him with damp kitchen roll, and tried to give him a sleeping pill from his own prodigious collection of home-use pharmaceuticals. He drew a little aluminium pillbox from the inside of his suit jacket and opened it – sweets in a safe. But Alex refused. He had sleep. If there was one thing he had it was reserves of sleep.

Adam came in, sighed, held his friend's shoulders and walked him back to the lounge.

'I made up the sofa-bed. Esther must be upstairs – her bag's in here – she won't want you up there, though, you smell terrible. Sleep it off down here.'

'Mmm.'

'There's no obit,' he said, pointing to the evening paper on the coffee table. 'It'll be in tomorrow, I'm sure. You have to try and sleep now, not think about it.'

'Hnng . . . ug.'

'Now look, you've got a ten o'clock appointment with Rabbi Burston tomorrow, just to go over things. And then it's six o'clock for the service. OK?'

'Adam . . .'

'Go to sleep, Al. We'll see you tomorrow. Tomorrow. Later, man.'

And they left. They left. He passed out. The men didn't believe him. And the women, the women had closed ranks against him.

3

He had a dream. In real-time, in real-life, it lasted only a minute or two. But it went deep, as the short ones often do. It went like a knife-dive into a swimming pool. He was in a fabulous garden. The garden was in the old French style, that is, it was a pastiche of many things. It had beds for English roses, it had a pseudo-Indian scene, a circle of cypresses, tamarinds. It had formal European hedgerows moulded in soulless imitation of animals and trees, and a Japanese corner where stones made patterns on stones. Bamboo trellises framed the wide pathways, and, as Alex walked through an intricate arrangement of flowers, he realized that this would all be best viewed from the top windows of a great house – and then there it was, the great house, a trice after the thought, white and stately behind him. But now he was elsewhere. A maze had been waiting for Alex to discover the secret at its centre: naked Diana, pulling back her bow. Over there an artificial lake sat between two artificial hills, in imitation of a Tuscan valley. The final touch was the ha-ha, that cunning trench dug to give the impression that the garden went on as far as one could see, or, rather, that the garden did not exist at all. That it was simply at one with the surrounding country. That all of this was the work of accidental design, of streams following their course and flowers blooming wherever they wished to . . .

Alex was in this garden. Nobody else was. The windows of the great house were alive with sunlight, and somewhere in that direction he could hear a string quartet, the tinkle of glass and laughter, the usual counterpoint of a pleasant lunch party. But the garden itself was completely empty and this troubled him. He was earnestly looking for the gardeners. He wanted to speak to the men who had dug the lake, and planted the trees and trimmed the hedges. He knew, somehow, that they weren't at the party. Where were they? He became frustrated, treading the same paths again and again, knowing this was a dream, wanting to wake up. Then between two sentry-like fir trees the scene changed. It was the garden still, but some new, secret section of it, a water paradise, with pool after pool laid out in a line, and monuments – monoliths of white stone – placed here and there between them. In every pool and in synchronization, naked men were leaping from the water like seals, performing disciplined, improbable turns, showy flips and poses, before going under again. It was beautiful. Alex, crying, approached the nearest pool. He could see Esther at the other end of it, sitting nude in a hybrid of a lifeguard's chair and a director's, her name across the back. She did not move or speak. Alex turned his attention back to the men. Men? Half of them were young, seventeen, eighteen, and Adonises, but for one feature. A film of skin, like a closed pouch, covered their genitals. The rest were very old, with this same area unintelligible beneath sagging stomachs. But they were jumping! They were all jumping! Higher than before, an additional spin, an impressive extension of an arm or leg. Sometimes even a whoop; a clear note sung and then abruptly sunk as they broke the water's skin. Joyous Alex took off his clothes, and walked to the end. Here Esther (without speaking, without moving) let it be known that no man entered this pool without reading the inscription. Inscription? Naturally, Alex was now nose to stone with a monument, trying to understand a few lines of verse carved upon it. What *was* this script? The Hebrew, Latin, Coptic, Russian, Japanese, gobbledygook script ... the lines of it going one way, then another, looping, curling, dashing, dotting ... The men laughed when he said he couldn't read it. Esther would not speak or help. The men didn't believe him. And the women, the women had closed ranks against him . . .

He awoke with a single breathy phoneme and the feeling he was going to die. He tried to throw the cover off, but instead became involved in a protracted entanglement, kicking at the blanket until it agreed the best thing was for the two of them to go their separate ways. He could smell himself. He reeked. Though we are all of us attached to our own stench, this was turning *chemical*. Hydrogen sulphide was involved. And mucus had become circular, working a trail through the three holes in his face, eased in its passage by mute tears. Why had the women closed ranks? What had he *done*? Alex and his fug left the room and began on the stairs. But the stairs were not as he recalled. The stairs, it turns out, don't help you get any higher up. It's not like an escalator. You have to do all the leg-work yourself, they just *sit* there. And there is no warning either of when they will come to the end (it is dark and the blanket has custody of the Tandem glasses); there is only Alex feeling his foot propel itself violently into space; for a long second he is toppling forward into a cloud, until the floor returns, unbending and unamused. The hallway's not too bad. It's straight and it has two walls and he had the good sense, years ago, not to put anything in it that might only be tripped over later. Most decoration is future obstacle.

The door. His heart is doing its scatter-shout routine, beating whenever, wherever: his toe, his thumb, his thigh, his chest. He doesn't want to wake anyone. He eases the door. A light tap with the foot and it's off, the slow swing. *There* they are. He can hardly see them. Just shapes, really. They lie next to each other – top-to-toe, is it called? Each set of toes poking free from the duvet at different ends, like two children at a sleepover. No. He's still too drunk to get away with that. Like two women on a beach? No, no. That won't do. His brain is absolutely resolute in its intention to mess with him. Like two bodies in a morgue. Almost. Like two bodies in a morgue in a *film*. All that's missing is the tag (name, birth and the other) tied to that most unpresuming digit during life – the big toe. Is that what it was? The toe detail?

You watch too many films is one of the great modern sentences. It has in it a hint of understanding regarding what we were before and what we have become. Of few people has it been more true than Alex-Li Tandem, Autograph Man extraordinaire. And therefore suitably, *rightfully*, his first thought was: *they're dead*. That's it. They're dead. That idea (though it passed through him quicker than the sentence can be said) hollowed him out. It wrestled him and won. And then in the next second: *No, no, of course they're not*. Parents will know this feeling, the before and the after. The horror, the climb-down from horror. But after this, at least for Alex, there is the extension. The extension is lethal. It understands that this is just a time lapse. Because there was nothing wrong with that diagnosis except time.

They were not.
But they would be.
All his people, all his loves.

The dead walk. He was with them on the train. He had drunk with them, this evening. They carried him home; he was looking at them now. On the walls in black and white, but also in this bed, in full Technicolor. A child knows this, and is told to get over it. A famous Irishman knew it and made peace with it and said all that needs to be said on the matter. But it was still really messing with Alex. He was having trouble with it, basic as it may be. Ten years ago Sarah's sister had visited with her young children, and his cousin Naomi refused to sleep in this room because she was scared of the 'dead ones on the walls'. Everybody laughed, over breakfast. He had laughed. Everybody had laughed. Because it is wrong, says everyone, to take it so personally – and so he hadn't, he was a *grown man* (this is probably what everybody means, he thought, by this stupid phrase; they mean *don't take it personally, don't take growing personally, being grown*). He hadn't taken it personally, not for years. He took it cinematically, or televisually – if he took it at all. But here it came – he tried to grab the top of the door-frame to keep himself up – here was the death-punch, the infinity-slap, and it was mighty. He wheeled away from the spot, clutching in his hand something he had accidentally ripped from the wall, his mouth was open like someone had kicked a hole in his face. But he made no noise. He didn't want to wake the dead. He had control, still. He found some spot where he could not be heard, hot and dry and full of towels, and said his Kaddish without gesture or formality – just a wet song into his hands.

TEN / *In the World*

I

The doorbell rang. Alex crawled down the stairs. *Literally* crawled down the stairs. Terrified by the heady forward momentum but unsure about standing, he crawled, and, when that grew weary on the knees, he flattened himself out and slid down. He opened the front door on all fours, one arm stretched out for the knob.

'Mornin',' said Marvin.

'Marvin,' said Alex, getting to his feet.

'How was New York, man?'

'Big. Tiring.'

'You *look* tired.'

'I slept on the landing.'

'Uh-huh,' said Marvin, and took out his pad.

Somewhere a bird sang the first four notes of 'Ain't Misbehavin''. The light was white, the street overexposed. Nobody likes to talk about the first day of spring any more, it is seen as a wilful sentimentality on the part of nature. But it seemed like spring to Alex today. You could feel Passover and Easter and a long, sluggish, sofa-bound weekend of bad films round the next corner, coming with the sun. The whole day was in bloom.

'Tandem?' said Marvin, lifting his head and following Alex's gaze, which went straight upwards to the bleached sky.

'Hmm?'

'You gonner order or what?'

'Hell of a day, no?'

'*Every* day is a hell of a day.'

'What do you want to *do*, Marvin?' croaked Alex, and then coughed the frog out.

'Excuse me?'

'Apart from being a milk operative. I mean, what do you want to do with your *life*?'

Marvin eloquently groaned, like a disappointed academic, and slapped his own forehead. 'I tell you something, yeah? Das an idiot's question, yeah? Life is going to do things to *me*. And that's all there is. And it's all good. Yogurts?'

'No, no . . . just milk.'

Marvin made that same sound of disappointment. He put his hands on his hips. 'Look. I saw you in the paper, yeah? I wasn't even gonner mention it, 'cos that stuff don't jangle with me, not at all. I got mine – I'm not after anyone else's. I'm not like these other bredrin, always envious. But at the same *time*, I have to say I was gently assumin' you might be a bit more adventurous in your dairy needs from now on. Now dat the situation has changed. Though we would like it otherwise,' said Marvin, sombrely, 'the world is a market-place to a degree, bro. Now I got to be all unsubtle 'cos you've got me forcing the issue somewhat, you get me?'

'I will have,' said Alex, looking over Marvin's shoulder to his float, 'one each of the milkshake things, some yogurts, the weird Italian cheese you tried to sell me that time, and whatever else you think I might like.'

'*Boo*-yah. Return of the prodigal son,' said Marvin with a whistle, and pimped down the path clicking his fingers.

A few minutes later, carrying a cardboard box containing various degrees of fermented milk, Alex stepped back into his house feeling something like renewed hope. He closed the door with a jaunty nudge of his backside. Esther was in the hallway. A black silk Chinese dressing gown of his hung from her, open. She brought the two sides protectively together and hugged them shut with folded arms.

'There you are,' he said, and walked towards her, but she stepped back from him. Her face knew no false economy: it always gave out only what had been put in. Right now it was a picture of pain.

'Let me put this down,' he said, nodding at the box. He walked into the kitchen and put it on the sideboard. When he turned back round, there were two women standing in the doorway.

'I'm tired,' said Esther. 'I'm pretty angry as well, very, actually, but mostly I'm just really . . . I'm *tired*. You need to listen. And you need to shut up while you're doing it.'

Alex began his favourite noise, the first person pronoun, but she reached out one arm to stop him.

'I think you need to listen to Kitty first Alex, OK?'

'Good morning, Alex,' said Kitty quietly. She was, of the three of them, the only one fully dressed.

Alex tried again with that noise, that insistent *I*, but Esther shook her head.

'You know what I do this morning?' said Kitty, unfolding a newspaper she had in her hand, 'I wake up very early, and I step over you. And I go downstairs and I pick up the newspaper from the mat. And I read my own obituary. Now,' she said, smiling half-heartedly, 'this I think is a very harsh way to start the day.'

'Kitty, I –'

'In which it says, among other things, that in the end my career was something of an insignificance, and that – here it is – "*her chief interest in cinematic history was for collectors, for whom her autograph held an almost mystical fascination*". This is very prettily put, no? This is my whole life, apparently, in a sentence.'

'Oh, Kitty, I'm sorry. I'm so sorry. I thought – it was just for a day – I thought it made sense . . .'

'It says here also,' said Kitty, wiping away a tear, 'that although a natural talent, I wasted my ability in frivolity . . . it goes on to outline various frivolities in the most *vulgar* manner possible – and then, where it is – yes, that I became *more noted in Hollywood for the men and women I had slept with than for the films I made.* Silly, to be upset by it,' said Kitty, bringing both hands now to her eyes, dropping the paper. 'I am too old for such vanity . . . but I don't know. It is not that I ever thought I was Joan Crawford, do you understand? But can you *imagine*? Reading *this*? *Can* you?'

Alex opened his mouth and shut it again.

'And the worst thing is, it is written by a supposed friend of mine, this filth, would you believe.' Kitty threw the paper on the sideboard with a little noise of disgust. 'One always hopes that other people . . . well, that they will think better of you than you do of yourself.'

'All I can do,' said Alex slowly, 'is apologize. That's all I can do.'

Kitty nodded. Esther put a protective arm round her, but Kitty, after a moment, moved from underneath it.

'It was dishonest, Alex,' she said, looking squarely at him, taking a step forward.

'I *told* him it was a terrible idea,' said Esther vehemently. 'The worst *possible* karma.'

'And rather unfair to me,' said Kitty more gently, as if talking to a boy.

'*Completely* unfair, that's what I said,' agreed Esther, with a fury (Alex realized now) clearly stretching to another matter. 'That money should be returned *immediately*.'

'Oh, one minute, please,' said Kitty, tutting delicately and placing a finger on Esther's raised hand. 'We do not have to be completely *crazy*, now.'

Now Alex stepped forward to meet Kitty and held her by her shoulders. 'It's *your* money,' he said, 'and it's pointless giving it back. Even when they find out you're not . . . then it'll just be worth more because you'll be the actress who everybody thought was dead and her autograph went for such and such on the day that everybody thought she was dead – and on and on. That's the way it works. It's all madness anyway. Take it, Kitty. Take it and bloody *run*.'

'This is an interesting argument,' she replied, licking her finger and taking some sleep from Alex's left eye. 'I could be convinced thereon. So . . . what to do? I keep the money, I see. Minus your 10 per cent, naturally.' Kitty was smiling. Alex was smiling back at her.

'I already took that out. About fifteen grand. Thanks.'

'You are a *good* boy,' said Kitty, patting his face. 'I am very glad we meet. You are a realist, like me. This is good. You kill me, but then you resurrect me. And so you are forgiven.'

Kitty made the gesture of the cross, kissed her fingertips and reached up to ruffle his hair.

'Are you staying? Going?' asked Alex.

'I *stay*,' said Kitty, seeming to make the decision as she spoke, 'for a week or two, maybe. Don't panic, don't worry – now I have the means I think I move out of your bedroom. The room service is not very impressive. And we must separate Lucia and Grace before they become *completely* obsessive about each other.'

Alex kissed Kitty's hand.

'Well,' said Esther, chewing her lip as a tear journeyed down the bridge of her nose, hanging for a while on the tip, 'someone's got to call whoever needs to be called to retract this story, and I need the keys for the car if I'm going to get to bloody college on –'

'I *leave* you,' said Kitty, with an actress's wink and sense of timing. At the doorway she said, 'I know you have another big event this evening, yes?'

Alex, who had locked eyes with Esther, nodded in silence.

'I cannot come, sadly – I think the Pope would kill me. But maybe we have dinner afterwards, hmm? Yes, we do this.'

They were left alone. Esther broke their eye contact and looked to the ceiling.

'Yeah, so . . . I'll need the keys for –'

'You think I did it for me? Is that the problem?'

'I don't *know*,' she said, bringing both hands quickly to her face and putting a halt to crying, putting crying in its place. 'It actually doesn't really matter right now.'

'You think I did it for some kind of glory, personal glory? Right?'

Esther closed her mouth and spoke through her teeth, a trapped, staccato yell. 'It's not what I *think you did*. It's like the girl on the sofa – it's not what you did or didn't do. It's how I *feel* about it. It's about how you make people *feel*. You know? I'm coming up for an operation and you're with some *girl*. How do you *expect* me to feel?'

He wanted, desperately, to touch her scalp, to draw her into him. To save them both from all this second-rate dialogue, the stuff that love engenders, the stuff of lovers. But he was in the middle of an argument and you're not allowed to touch during a row, even though nine times out of ten it's the thing you want to do most.

'Please,' he said, raising his game, gesticulating, 'we've been together ten years. You know? And *that's* what you think of me?'

Here she swore at him and accused him of gross manipulation, but he persisted. And nothing about this argument was news. They had been performing variations on it for the last six years. It ran and ran. This is what relationships *are*; stage shows that run and run until all life is drained from them and only the gestures remain.

'You think,' snapped Alex, 'it's like, you think I have, like, the morals of a sewer rat, or something.'

'Let's not talk about morals,' said Esther solidly. 'Let's not do that.'

She nodded to herself three times as if agreeing to somebody's unspoken question. She left the room. Something gave way in Alex's stomach, something like a trap-door. Love, the withdrawal of love. Was this it? Now? The changeover? That day when the two-soldier fight, the war against plastic armrests and hypocrites and pseuds and television and food shaped in towers and triple-layered plastic packaging and consumer surveys and love songs and all organized religions – when this fight becomes singular? When you have to do it all *solo*? It had been threatening to come these last few years. Sometimes he wanted it to. The rest of the time the thought scared him half to death. On this occasion he made it to the stairs on adrenalin only and put himself between her and another step. He asked her. Loudly. Repeatedly. Is this it? Is this it? The End?

'We're both still alive, still here,' she said wearily, and hugged herself ever more tightly. 'The end looks more . . . bloody. Dagger, vial of poison, all of that. You know the drill. We're all right for today, OK? Beyond that – I just don't know, Tandem. We'll have to see, really.'

She stepped round him and continued up the stairs.

'Look,' she said, burning, and seeing the appeal for clemency in his eyes, 'have a shower, baby. You stink. Go and see Ads. I'm going to deal with the papers. I'll be at the service. We'll meet Kitty afterwards. Get out of the house for a while, out of my face.'

No withdrawal, then. Suspension, only.

2

Without taking Esther's advice (he was interested to know how far he could go with this fug thing), Alex got on a bus to the Mulberry synagogue and sat on the front seats of the top deck enjoying that charming childhood illusion that he was flying down the street.

'Not withdrawn!' he called down to a shopping family. 'Just suspended!'

'Good morrow, good wight!' he yelled at a vicar.

Get a job, said an old man in the bus.

'HELLO, BEAUTIFUL,' he shouted, sticking his arm out of the thin window and waving at a schoolgirl.

'Piss off, Humbert,' she called back, hitching her rucksack up her back, the better to give the two-fingered salute.

At Mulberry Central he got off and asked two passing Hasidim for directions to the progressive synagogue, which the men gave, along with looks of pity. Singing 'Old Man River', a song he found useful for steeling oneself, Alex walked through the leafy avenues of Mulberry. At almost every corner there seemed to be a Hasid waiting to make him feel like a mould the planet had grown. Could they smell him? Or did they just *know* him? A sort of spiritual x-ray vision; sensing his paltry soul, his fermented faith. Alex decided to counter-attack by waving at them. This was good. Waving felt good. To get absolutely no response to a friendly wave, waved with an open heart, is morally emboldening.

At the synagogue, morning service had just ended. Alex could see a milling congregation and a plain, concrete building in which a Star of David window sat flush with the wall, a shul without decoration but not without charm. A corridor of greenery led down to it, accompanied by a depressing and necessary security system complete with cameras up on their poles like berthed periscopes. Alex rang the bell and waved at the video-phone. He was buzzed through.

Rabbi Burston was outside in the sun, chatting with a gaggle of women, or, at least, that was Alex's guess. There was definitely a gaggle of women, and they were in a circle, talking and looking downwards. As Alex approached, the circle broke up and, although extremely small, it was the unmistakable figure of a pushy rabbi that came striding towards him. Alex felt any residual nerves evaporate; this was a reassuring comfort, this was the one thing you could count on: a rabbi is never shy. Alex had met those cringing vicars who seemed mortified by their own existence – how can you get faith from a man ashamed of faith? In comparison, Alex had to admit to a grudging admiration for the rabbinical vocation. They always, always gave as good as they got.

'HI,' shouted Rabbi Burston. He was about forty and quixotically handsome for a man no bigger than a nine-year-old child. He was wearing jeans and a white shirt. Now he was up close, at Alex's waist, and Alex began what he expected to be a long struggle to try not to stare at Rabbi Burston any more than one would if he were of normal height. He failed at once, full of wonder for the incredible barrel chest and curly black beard, the strong-man physique, radically caricatured in this tiny man.

'Hi.'

'ALEX-LI, IS IT?' shouted the rabbi again. The circle of women were smiling at Alex indulgently, and a child was pointing.

'Yes.'

'YOU WANT TO TALK OUTSIDE OR INSIDE?'

'Outside's fine.'

'GOOD. OUTSIDE DOES IT FOR ME. HOW ABOUT THAT BENCH?'

'OK. Is there a reason . . . I mean, why you're shouting?'

'I TRY TO DO THIS SOMETIMES, TO DISTRACT FROM' – he took himself in from head to toe with a flick of his wrist – 'JUST FOR THE FIRST FEW MINUTES. I FIND IT HELPS SOMETIMES. IS IT HELPING?'

'Not really.'

'Oh,' said Rabbi Burston, scratching his beard and smiling. 'Well, it's not for everyone. Please, Alex, come into my office.'

The rabbi skipped past a tree and hoisted himself up on the bench, his swinging feet far from the floor.

'So. Alex. Let's get right to it. Kaddish. Do you get it? I mean, do you really *get* it?'

'Yes. I think so.'

'OK. Explain.'

'Well, when I say . . . I mean, I believe I've got the basic –'

'TO SANCTIFY GOD'S NAME PUBLICLY IS THE HIS-TORIC DUTY OF THE JEW!' screamed Rabbi Burston with both of his little hands shaking in the air. He brought them down

again and smiled placidly at Alex. 'That's what th[...]
right? And it's true. But I don't want you to think of this as a[...]
It's a *pleasure*. It's a *gift* you're giving to your father. You're walking into a shul and you're giving a gift. And sometimes, when you were small and incapable, if you were giving a gift to someone, your mother would buy it for you, do you remember that? And just get you to sign the card – or just dip your hand in red paint and squish it on there. Did you ever do that?'

To this, Alex offered a non-committal shrug.

'OK!' cried Rabbi Burston, and then fell silent. Still trying to avoid staring, Alex looked up to where the rabbi was looking, at the first cautious buds of a cherry tree, presently being fooled by the clement weather.

'You know what?' said the rabbi, after a minute of nothing, 'let's walk. Let's walk around the shul and back, till we're back at this tree. Deal?'

The rabbi put his arms up, and Alex, nonplussed for a moment, realized with some horror that he was waiting to be lifted down.

'What? Never picked up a rabbi before? Joke. It's a joke,' said Rabbi Burston, and slipped nimbly from the bench to the ground. 'OK, let's perambulate. Let's get Socratic.'

Alex had made an earlier pact with himself to walk very slowly if any simultaneous walking-with-midget-rabbi was called for, but in fact, the rabbi overtook him from the first and it was Alex who had to keep the pace.

'The thing is,' said the rabbi, as a crowd of children scattered from his path, 'Kaddish was never composed for shul. It's a study-hall prayer, it's informal. It's a prayer that came out of a *need*. Now, that's very rare. This is not being forced from above, from the rabbis. This is being *cried out for* by the people as a *need*, as a human need. I take it you believe in human needs – we're not that far gone with you?'

'No, no – I'll go with you as far as human needs. I have them. I see them around.'

'OK. *Good*, that's good. Now. Notice in the mourners' prayer, there's no *Adoshem*, there's no *Elohim*, there're no formal names for God. There's only in Kaddish the informal, the intimate – *Kudsha Brich Hu*, the Holy One, blessed be He, and then *Avihun di bizshmaya*, their Father in heaven. You've even got *HaShem*, The Name, turned into *Shemo*, His Name. The Kaddish is a conversation between Jew and God, son and absent father, are you with me so far? It's one-on-one, though the community is still essential – when I say Jew, I mean *Jews* – but it's still *quality time*.'

Then Rabbi Burston jumped up unexpectedly and gripped the edge of a low wall that went around the shul's small back lot. He swung his body round, put his feet flat on the brick and stood up. Now he was about five-seven to Alex's six-one.

'What else do you want to know?'

'Um . . . OK . . . practical stuff. Like, I speak first –'

'You speak first and then the minyan responds. By the way, I know you've only got eight so far but I have two volunteers – they'll be strangers to you and your father but not to Him, and that's what matters. So: you speak, you speak, you speak, you speak, and then we respond. You recite again, we respond, one more time, and then everybody speaks together. Do you know your lines?'

'Almost. Basically.'

'Then we're more than halfway there,' said the rabbi happily and clapped his hands.

'But how does that work? I don't *feel* anything,' blurted Alex, and was glad that he had said it.

'Lift, please. Seriously this time – to the next bit of wall.'

Alex grabbed the rabbi in his armpits and hoisted him over the gap. Safely on the other side, the rabbi put both hands behind his back and continued his elevated stroll.

'Good. So you don't feel anything. That's honest. So you want me to convince you, is that it? Do we have to go through the Akiva story? Really? The father and the wood-carrying and the fiery torment?'

'No, no. I get the bit about I can bring my father eternal rest, etc. – but that's not really relevant, because he wasn't a Jew.'

'Ah, but you *are*. But you're not an idiot, you know that – that's why you're here.'

Two children raced past them playing a noisy game of tag and then, seeing Rabbi Burston, fell silent and hit each other surreptitiously, passing the blame.

'Alex, no need to look so miserable,' said Rabbi Burston, tutting. He reached the end of his wall, sat on it and then launched himself at the ground. He landed rather awkwardly this time, sliding a little in the gravel, but still there was nothing comic about him, nothing ignoble. This was irritating to Alex, who wanted and expected deflation in people above all things. Without it, as with Adam or Esther, your attachment grew too strong. The possibility of future pain only multiplied.

'Rabbi, I still . . . I understand what you're saying, but I don't see the point of it. Not with regard to me.'

Rabbi Burston kicked some pebbles across the yard.

'Uh-huh,' he said, nodding keenly. 'It's depressing, not seeing the point of things, I know that. It's like being fifteen all the time. That's not a great age.'

'I had better years.'

They stepped together through a large indistinct Star of David, shadow of the window, moving slowly across the yard as the sun climbed.

'Alex. Your friend Adam told me you collect autographs for a living. You see the point in that?'

'No, not particularly. But –'

'But it gives you pleasure.'

'Some.'

'So you collect, you get things. Famous things from big-shot people. Anything in that business have the status of a gift?'

'How do you mean, gift?'

'I mean does anything in your daily life have the status of a gift?'

'Well, I aim towards it,' said Alex, thinking, with defiance, of Kitty. 'That's the secular dream, isn't it? Love, art, charity, maybe. All gifts.'

'Yes,' said Rabbi Burston, smiling. 'That's the secular dream.'

'I don't see what that has to do with anything. I'm talking about ritual.'

'OK, then,' said Rabbi Burston, shadow-boxing. 'Give it to me. Talk about ritual.'

'Well,' said Alex, sheepish, 'well, OK, so I said it yesterday, the Kaddish, as a sort of practice . . .' They stepped into a gloom cast by the roof of the shul, and without the superficial warmth of the light the temperature plummeted. He shivered and drew his coat around him. 'I said it and I didn't feel a thing. I mean, I was feeling something anyway, but the Kaddish didn't help.'

'You were by yourself?'

Alex nodded.

'Come *on*. Do you play football by yourself? Hockey? You watch a play by yourself? Do the tango by yourself? You make love by yourself? Actually, don't answer that.'

Alex laughed, glumly.

'In the end,' said the rabbi, as they closed in on the confused cherry tree, 'it's *Tsidduk Hadin*, an acceptance of divine judgement. Instead of cursing God for our loss, we rise and praise him. We accept the judgement. He gave, he took away. We accept.'

'But I don't. I don't accept it,' mumbled Alex, feeling a familiar depression envelop him. 'It doesn't work for me. To me, it's obscene. All the suffering. I can't sign on that line, I can't.'

A woman, who had been lingering near by this last minute shuffling some sheets of paper, now said Rabbi Burston's name quietly.

'Yes, Mrs Bregman, I'm coming, one moment, please.'

The rabbi turned back to Alex and angled his head all the way back, braving the bright sun to look Alex straight in the eye. 'Alex. I'm pretty busy, you know? Do me a favour. Turn up here at six and say what you've been asked to say and give the gift. Your friends and I have written the card, bought the present and painted your hand red. Just turn up with your red hand, OK?'

3

On Adam's outdoor walkway, in deference to the unlikely sun, brunch was being eaten. Chairs had been placed so plates could rest on the wall and the Brunchers were seated in a line with their beers like truck drivers in a diner. Joseph and Rubinfine had their napkins tucked facetiously into their collars, while Adam hovered over them with a griddle pan of scrambled eggs laced with pink flecks of smoked salmon. Without a word Alex hitched himself up on to the wall next to Rubinfine and sat, legs dangling.

'And before you ask,' said Joseph, looking straight ahead over the rooftops, 'this is the first sick day I've taken off work in six months.'

'He's thinking of quitting,' explained Adam. 'But he's still blowing his wages. He paid for the salmon. Want a plate, Al?' Without waiting for an answer, he went indoors to fetch one.

'I'm thinking of quitting,' confirmed Joseph languidly, picking a sinking fly from his egg. 'Sun did it. Sun gave me a weird epiphany.'

'That's the trouble with this bloody sun,' said Rubinfine, frowning and pointing to it with his fork.

'What was the epiphany?'

'Umm ... something like: can't spend rest of life in total misery.'

'Right. Good one.'

'I thought so.'

'What will you do instead?' asked Alex, accepting his plate and a generous portion of egg and toast.

'Be irretrievably unemployable. That's the plan so far.'

'I had that plan once,' said Rubinfine wistfully. 'Didn't come to anything, though.'

'That's because you're a quitter.' Joseph raised a beer to the sky. 'I'm in this for the long haul. Bloody *hell*,' he said, turning to look at Alex for the first time, 'you look *terrible*.'

'I think,' said Alex, looking over Joseph and Rubinfine to Adam, seeking him out, his understanding, 'Esther might be leaving me.'

Adam looked alarmed and then averted his eyes as from an intimacy between parents. Joseph opened a beer and passed it to him. Rubinfine said, 'Everyone leaves everyone in the end.'

Alex scowled. 'Yes, but this *isn't* the end, you gaylord. That's the point, isn't it? I think she might be leaving me *midway*.'

'Only God is constant,' affirmed Rubinfine, and snatched the pepper from Joseph's hand while the man was in mid sprinkle. 'The thing he gave us is endings. Things end, here. They don't end *there*.' He pointed to the sky. 'That was his gift to us, endings. Now, you might say to me: *Yeah, nice gift, but can I take it back to the shop and exchange it?* At which point, I would say to *you* –'

'Roob, please save it, will you?' groaned Joseph. 'Who's that speech for?'

'For my heder group. I'm giving it next week,' said Rubinfine, chewing a nail off and spitting it over the wall. 'Ten- to fourteen-year-olds. You don't like? I mean, there's a lot more to it than –'

'It's not that I don't *like* . . . Roob, if someone had spoken to you like that when you were fourteen . . . No, look, it's not that bad. It's just that you express everything so damn clumsily – look, do you have a pen? Let's go over it, let's tidy it up.'

'We need more egg,' said Adam ruminatively. 'Alex, come and help me make more egg.'

He walked straight past the kitchen, though, and Alex followed him into the lounge. In front of the alphabet Adam gripped him by the shoulders. His eyes were an essence of Adam: the look you always hoped he'd give you, the one that turned up now and then and that you waited for. Clear, agonizingly honest, puckish, joy-seeking and full of the determination to take your pains on as his own. Alex put his hands in his pockets like a schoolboy embarrassed by unexpected praise.

'Are you ready?' asked Adam.

'For?'

The Autograph Man

'Tonight!'

'Oh . . . sure, yeah, 'course.'

'Did you see Rabbi Burston? Wasn't he useful?'

Alex made a helpless face, and in turn Adam's own look faded to be replaced by the same injured disappointment his sister had laid on Alex a few hours ago.

'It doesn't mean the same to me,' said Alex, pulling his hands from his pockets, dropping into the sofa. 'To me it's a gesture, you know? Nothing more.'

Adam looked confused. 'What's more important than a gesture?' he asked.

Adam knelt down where he was, and for a second Alex feared he was going to ask him to meditate or pray and he now knew – with more certainty than ever before – that those two acts were beyond him, no, more than that: he didn't want them. He wanted to be in the world and take what came with it, endings local and universal, full stops, periods, looks of injured disappointment and the everyday war. He *liked* the everyday war. He was taking that with fries. To go.

'What's . . . ? You dropped – oh, it's your note,' said Adam, picking it up. He came over and sat down on the sofa. 'It's all scrunched,' he said, giving it to Alex. 'I was going to bring mine too, for tonight. Seemed right to me as well.'

Alex remembered now, vaguely, ripping it off the wall last night. He took it from Adam and straightened it out with his fist against the table.

'They're *similar*, aren't they?' said Adam earnestly. 'I mean, you really write alike.'

Alex frowned. Picked up a pen and neighbouring TV guide and wrote his own signature perfectly on the back of the magazine.

410

'Look how similar,' murmured Adam. 'His *T* is exactly the same as yours – and that funny *M*.'

'I used to copy his,' said Alex, touching the note, remembering. 'I'd make him write it out so I could copy it. I'd make him write it over and over again, so I could watch the way his hand moved. Small hands. They were weirdly small and . . .'

Alex could not stop that trap-door swinging again. He clutched at his own hair. 'I thought,' he said shakily, 'I thought you said all this was going to make me *feel* better. I don't feel better. Telling Esther about Boot, that didn't *help*. And this thing tonight, talking to Rabbi Burston, none of it, it's not resolving anything, it doesn't cure *anything*. I miss him. I still miss him. All the time. I miss him so much. I don't *feel better*.'

'I said it was going to *be* better, not feel better,' said Adam, and he was deadly serious. 'It *is* better, even if you can't feel it.'

Alex laughed sullenly and set about a cuticle with his teeth. 'There's no other good but *feeling* good,' he said, shaking his head. 'Ads, that's what good *is*. That's what you've never understood. It's not a symbol of something else. Good has to be felt. That's good *in the world*.'

Adam relinquished the argument with a parting of his hands, but, as ever, nothing changed in that quiet, definite, iridescent shell that covers the religious, that home they carry with them, everywhere.

Alex sighed and stood up to get Adam's weed box from its place on a shelf, where it obscured the bottom half of Adam's little autograph tree.

'I was thinking,' began Adam in a cautious voice, 'about making a Kitty autograph the final branch, if you'd like that, if you have any left. Like, as a mark of respect. Be a way to keep it safe – in case you got tempted to sell every precious thing you own. I mean, say if that's a bad idea, but –'

Alex laughed. Adam frowned and tilted his head, and that same second sunshine hit the blinds and divided the room into paragraphs of dusty light and sentences of shadow. If anything is going to make you religious, it's this stuff. Timing. Coincidence.

'I sold them all,' said Alex contentedly, and let the facts lie, for the moment, where they were. 'There's none left. Ads, you've got a halo.'

Alex opened the box and shuffled it around, looking for a little lump of brown. Adam stood up suddenly, closed the lid.

'Better not, mate. Be clear today. Be there. Be there completely, don't you think?'

'Hmm,' said Alex. His mind was now – as the teachers like to say – elsewhere. The sun had washed the wall and made things look different. Feel different. That's the problem with the sun.

'And for when you see Esther. She wants us to stop smoking, you know. She's scared to tell you, but I know that's what she wants. Of both of us. But I don't know about that, man. That's a tall order. That's where I found the understanding,' said Adam, making the International Gesture of transcendence (brief upwards nod, eyes set on the ceiling). 'That's how Shechinah opened up to me, how things became manifest. That's how I climb.'

He eased the box from Alex's hands and returned it to the shelf.

'But for today she's got a point. I think we need to be present today, fully present. Alex?'

Alex bent down slowly for the note, straightened up again, and inveigled a tiny pinch of Blu-Tack from behind the autograph of Jimmy Stewart. He put one dot at each of the four corners of the note and stuck Li-Jin in the empty sun-faded spot, midway between – and elevated above – the popular philosopher Ludwig Wittgenstein and the popular writer Virginia Woolf.

EPILOGUE

Kaddish

Suppose I weren't allowed the gestures people make when they don't know what else to do: clicking the buckle of my wristwatch strap, unbuttoning and rebuttoning my shirt, running my hands through my hair. In the end I'd have nothing to sustain me, I'd be lost.

– Peter Handke, *The Weight of the World*

Standing up was the Autograph Man, Alex-Li Tandem. From where he was, he could see all of them. He could see everything they did. Sitting down were his friends Adam Jacobs, Rabbi Mark Rubinfine and Joseph Klein, his girlfriend Esther Jacobs, Rabbi Green, Rabbi Darvick, Rabbi Burston and his mother Sarah Tandem. Also sitting were two people unknown to him, Eleanor Loescher and Jonathan Verne.

> *Magnified and sanctified* (said Alex-Li, but not in these words)
> *May His great name be*
> *In the world that He created.*
> *As He wills,*
> Rubinfine was stripping the skin from his right thumb with the nail
> Of his left-hand forefinger,
> *And may His Kingdom come*
> *In your lives and in your days*
> *And in the lives of all the house of Israel,*
> Joseph was worrying his nose with a knuckle
> And then trying not to, and then doing it again,
> *Swiftly and soon,*
> *And all say Amen!*

Esther smoothed her skirt down
With her hands and twisted the seam until
It rested correctly!

Amen! (said the sitting people, but not in these words)
May His great name be blessed
Always and for ever!

Blessed (said Alex-Li, but not in these words)
And Praised
And Glorified
Rabbi Burston was swinging his feet
To some internal beat,
And raised
And exalted
Rabbi Green sniffed,
And honoured
And uplifted
Rabbi Darvick closed his eyes
And then opened them twice as wide,
And lauded
Be the name of the Holy One
Adam smiled and performed
A discreet thumbs-up,
He is blessed!
Above all blessings
And hymns and praises and consolations
That are uttered in the world
And all say Amen!

May a great peace from heaven –
And Life! –

Be upon us and upon all Israel,
Sarah cried and made no attempt
To disguise it,
And all say Amen!

May He who makes peace in His High places
Eleanor Loescher held her small
Belly with both hands.
(And Alex wondered what this meant)
Make peace upon us and upon all Israel,
Jonathan Verne yawned shamelessly.
(And Alex wondered what this meant)
And all say Amen!

ACKNOWLEDGEMENTS

The publisher is grateful for permission to reproduce the following extracts: *The Essential Lenny Bruce*, copyright © 1967, Douglas Music Corp. All rights reserved. Used by permission; 'Howl' from Allen Ginsberg, *Selected Poems 1947–1995* (Penguin Books, 1997), copyright © Allen Ginsberg, 1996, reproduced by permission of Penguin Books Ltd; 'Can't Help Lovin' Dat Man', words by Oscar Hammerstein II, music by Jerome Kern, copyright 1927 T. B. Harms Company Inc., USA, Universal Music Publishing Limited, Elsinore House, 77 Fulham Palace Road, London W6 8JA, used by permission of Music Sales Ltd, all rights reserved, international copyright secured; 'Ash Wednesday' from *Collected Poems* by T. S. Eliot, reproduced by permission of Faber and Faber Ltd; extract from *Zohar: The Book of Enlightenment*, translated by Daniel Chanan Matt, reproduced by permission of Paulist Press, www.paulistpress.com; excerpt from 'Casablanca' granted courtesy of Warner Bros.; extract from *Kaddish* by Leon Wieseltier, reproduced by permission of Picador, an imprint of Pan Macmillan, London, UK; 'Fame', words by Dean Pitchford, music by Michael Gore, copyright © 1980 EMI Catalogue Partnership, EMI Variety Catalog Inc. and EMI United Partnership Ltd, USA, worldwide print rights controlled by Warner Bros. Publications Inc/IMP Ltd, reproduced by permission of International Music Publications Ltd, all rights reserved.

ZADIE SMITH

NW

Zadie Smith's brilliant tragi-comic *NW* follows four Londoners – Leah, Natalie, Felix and Nathan – after they've left their childhood council estate, grown up and moved on to different lives. From private houses to public parks, at work and at play, their city is brutal, beautiful and complicated. Yet after a chance encounter they each find that the choices they've made, the people they once were and are now, can suddenly, rapidly unravel. A portrait of modern urban life, *NW* is funny, sad and urgent – as brimming with vitality as the city itself.

'Astonishing, dazzling. Really – without exaggeration – not since Dickens has there been a better observer of London scenes. Zadie Smith is a genius. It's hard to imagine a better novel this year – or this decade' **A. N. Wilson**

'Intensely funny, richly varied, always unexpected. A joyous, optimistic, angry masterpiece. No better English novel will be published this year' **Philip Hensher**, *Daily Telegraph*

'Captivating. Funny, sexy, weird, full of acute social comedy. She's up there with the best around' *Evening Standard*

'Marvellous . . . crackles with reflections on race, music and migration. A lyrical fiction for our times' *Spectator*

'Undeniably brilliant . . . rush out and buy this book' *Observer*